THE STAN TURNER MYSTERIES
by William Manchee

Undaunted (1997)
Brash Endeavor (1998)
Second Chair (2000)
Cash Call (2002)
Deadly Distractions (2004)
Black Monday (2005)
Cactus Island (2006)
Act Normal (2007)

"*Undaunted* proves it to me; William Manchee is a master at story telling. He has a way of spinning a tale that will leave you breathless every time. . . . (Pam Stone, MyShelf.com)

Brash Endeavor ". . .fabulous-a real page turner-I didn't want it to end!" (Allison Robson, CBS Affiliate, *KLBK*)

Second Chair ". . .appealing characters and lively dialogue, especially in the courtroom. . ." (*Publisher's Weekly*)

"Cash Call. . .Richly textured with wonderful atmosphere, the novel shows Manchee as a smooth, polished master of the mystery form . . . " (*The Book Reader*)

Deadly Distractions ". . .each plot line, in and of itself, can be riveting . . . " (*Foreword Magazine*)

Deadly Distraction ". . .a courtroom climax that would make the venerable Perry Mason stand and applaud . . . " (Crescent Blue)

Black Monday ". . .Settle down to a good mystery from an excellent writer. I became a fan of William Manchee with his novel Plastic Gods. One of the tightest plots and best writing styles I had seen in quite a while . . . (Harold McFarland)

Cactus Island ". . .if you like shows like X-Files and books with paranormal or science fiction elements, read "Cactus Island," and you will be in heaven! I sure was. (Paige Lovitt, Readerviews)

Act Normal ". . .a fascinating science fiction legal thriller in which the government trades children for advanced technologies." Harriet Klausner, The worlds most prolific reviewer

Act Normal ". . .Readers who like to mix their legal thrillers with a bit of science fiction will enjoy Manchee's . . . latest Stan Turner mystery, in which the Dallas attorney, grief-stricken by the kidnapping of his son by aliens, is asked by the CIA to defend a woman accused of killing her husband and children." (Library Journal)

OTHER NOVELS BY WILLIAM MANCHEE
Twice Tempted
Death Pact
Plastic Gods
Trouble in Trinidad

Twice Tempted ". . .Manchee provides an awesome adventure for the thrill-seeking reader. . .." (Rapport Magazine)

"*Death Pact* ". . .one of the most exciting fiction novels of the year." Harold McFarland, Amazon Top 50 Reviewer (#39)

Plastic Gods ". . .Non-stop plotting action makes *Plastic Gods*; a book you can't put down." (Denise's Pieces Reviews)

Plastic Gods ". . .this stunning work as writer Manchee offers the reader a peek into a side of banking and credit most of us never realized might exist. (Molly Martin Reviews)

Trouble In Trinidad ". . .It's terrorist suspense at its best!" MyShelf.com

Tarizon: The Liberator

Acknowledgments

A special thanks to my son, Michael Manchee, who was invaluable in his input and critique of Book I. Also, much appreciated was the tireless editing and proofreading of Zoila Iglesias Finally, for his excellent performance during the audio production of the book, I will be forever grateful to William Timnick.

Tarizon: The Liberator

Book I

By

William Manchee

Top Publications, Ltd.
Dallas, Texas

Tarizon: The Liberator
Volume 1

© COPYRIGHT
William Manchee
2008

Cover Design by Dan Silverman

Printed in Canada

Top Publications, Ltd.
3100 Independence Parkway, Suite 311-349
Plano, Texas 75075

ISBN 978-1-929976-48-5
Library of Congress #2008921046

Also in Audio CD ISBN 978-1-929976-49-2
Read by William Timnick

Dedication

The Tarizon Trilogy is dedicated to my grandchildren, Joshua, Alex, and Isabella. They are too young to understand them now but, hopefully, will enjoy Peter's adventures when they get older.

1

Loyalists

A nervous Lorin Boskie knocked on the door to her father's office. This was the second urgent summons this week. The situation was getting desperate and she was worried about the toll it was taking on her father's health, not to mention the danger he'd be in when Vice chancellor Videl Lai seized power. She heard his voice say to come in, so she took a deep breath as the retinal scanner verified her identity and the door slid silently open. Her father, Councillor Robert Garcia, several advisors, and his military liaison, Colonel Tomo, were huddled over a pile of maps and intelligence reports. Their disheveled appearance told Lorin they hadn't slept for some time. Her father looked up and motioned for her to join them. She walked over and asked, "Where's Jake?"

Jake was her mate and currently served as a fighter pilot in the Tarizonian Global Army or TGA as it was called. Lorin was worried about his safety too, since Videl Lai obviously knew where his loyalties would lie when civil war broke out. She feared a preemptive strike against the two men she loved could come at any time. That was Videl's style to ruthlessly eliminate any opposition as soon as they were identified. Only her father's position as a councillor and his friendship with two TGA generals had protected him so far, but the time was drawing near when that wouldn't be enough.

"He should be here any moment," the Councillor replied.

Lorin loved her father and was proud that he was leading the movement to preserve the Supreme Mandate, but she didn't always agree with his policies and strategies. He was far too trusting and optimistic. She

1

feared this would be his downfall.

The door slid open again and a tall man in a flight suit strolled in. Lorin glanced over at him and smiled. He came over to her and put his hand on her shoulder. She grabbed it and gave it a squeeze.

Councillor Garcia nodded to Jake and said, "Let's get started." Everyone immediately stopped what they were doing and gave him their full attention. . . ."As you know the Super Eclipse is almost upon us—just ten days from now. If the Prophecy is true, the Liberator will come on the night of the eclipse."

Lorin shook her head. "You don't really believe the prophecy do you, father?" Lorin asked.

Councillor Garcia shrugged. "No, but it doesn't matter what I believe; it's what the people believe that is important. Our political analysts tell me that a large majority of our citizens believe in the Prophecy. Almost 90 percent of the mutants and Seafolken believe the Liberator will come to free them. Of course, we haven't been able to poll the Nanomites, but if we could I'm sure the result would be the same."

"Well, they're going to be sorely disappointed when he doesn't appear," Lorin said.

"Exactly. That's why I called this meeting," the Councillor said turning to Colonel Tomel. "I'll let Colonel Tomel explain."

"Yes, sir," Colonel Tomel said. "We all know of the ambitions of Vice-chancellor Videl Lai and what his rise to power would mean to all of us on Tarizon. The Prophecy promises that a Liberator from Earth will come to Tarizon and save the planet from a dictator, presumably Videl Lai. The sad reality is that if Videl Lai takes power he will be nearly invincible. Our Loyalists' movement, which we have all been working so hard to build for so many cycles, isn't nearly strong enough to defeat him. He's got the overwhelming support of the military because he's promised them much power and glory in his new regime."

Lorin frowned."So, you called us here to tell us the situation is hopeless?"

"No," Colonel Tomel replied. "We called you here because one of our spies informs us that Videl Lai is worried about the Prophecy and is devoting considerable resources to insure that it is not fulfilled."

"You're kidding?" Lorin said. "Videl believes in the Prophecy?"

"I don't know what he believes," Colonel Tomel said, "but he's not a man to ignore any threat against him. That's what makes him such a formidable adversary."

"So, do our spies know what he plans to do?" Jake asked.

"Yes. He's ordered the assassination of anyone coming from Earth who remotely fits the description set forth in the Prophecy."

"That's why we called this meeting," the Councillor said. "Because the people believe in the Prophecy and Videl Lai fears it so much, we have no choice but to do all we can to make the Prophecy a reality."

"How do you plan to do that?" Jake questioned.

"There happens to be an Earth shuttle docking on the day of the Super Eclipse," Colonel Tomel replied. "If there is a Liberator he would have to be on that shuttle. We know that Videl Lai will have his agents there when the shuttle lands. It's imperative that we find the Liberator before Videl does and protect him."

Lorin shook her head. "But even if there were a Liberator, how would you recognize him?"

"You're right. There would be no realistic way to do that, so what we propose is to select the most likely person and protect him."

"What good will that do?" Lorin asked. "So you protect this person. What if he is not the Liberator?"

Councillor Garcia stood up. "It doesn't matter. We'll say he is. Who could prove he isn't? Videl will no doubt kill the true Liberator, if we're wrong."

Lorin looked aghast. "We're going to stand by and let him kill innocent Earth children?"

The Councillor sighed. "Videl's supporters control the shuttle port. We'll be lucky to protect even *one* of the passengers."

"Even if we succeed, how long will we be able to keep up the charade? It will soon become apparent he's a fraud when he cannot fulfill the Prophecy," Lorin argued. "It's a dangerous idea and could easily backfire on us."

"Maybe. It's a gamble for sure, but it will give our citizens hope and buy us time to strengthen the Loyalist army. If the Liberator does not come, the people will lose heart and won't have the will to fight."

Lorin shook her head. She knew her father's mind was already made up, so there was no use continuing to argue. "So, who will you pick? Is there anyone on the shuttle who could possibly be the Liberator?"

Councillor Garcia nodded. "Yes, there is one possibility—a young American who was brought aboard the shuttle and placed in protective custody. His father was recruited by the American CIA to help with our Repopulation Project and inadvertently discovered our presence on Earth. Normally we would have simply erased his memory, but he found out from his father that erased memories can be restored through hypnosis. That left us no choice but to bring him back to Tarizon."

"How old is he?"

"He's seventeen—very smart, and I'm he told has a kind heart, which is mentioned in the Prophecy."

Lorin folded her arms and laughed. "This is so ridiculous. It will never work." Councillor Garcia gave her a frustrated look. She sighed. . . . "But I guess anything that will give us more time to strengthen our army is worth pursuing."

The Councillor smiled broadly. "Good. Then I can count on Jake's and your support?"

"Of course, Father. Jake and I will do whatever we can to make everyone believe this American teenager is the Liberator, no matter how pathetic he may turn out to be."

2
Encounter

   Peter Turner sat nervously in the living room of his home waiting for his father to come home. He'd heard on the news that the trial had been recessed early that afternoon. Stan Turner, a prominent defense attorney, usually came straight home after a trial was over. When he hadn't shown up by 4:00 o'clock, Peter began to worry. His mother, Rebekah, called his office but noone there had heard from Stan either. Next she called Paula Waters, Stan's partner, but there was no answer at her apartment. Peter had a hunch his father had gone to Possum Kingdom Lake, 125 miles west of Dallas, to look for his client Cheryl Windsor, who'd been abducted right in the middle of her murder trial. He figured his father must have come to the same conclusion he had. The aliens had taken her. Peter wasn't sure why they'd done it, but he guessed she must have known something they didn't want her to talk about on the stand in front of the press. As Peter was thinking, the telephone rang. It was Paula. His father was missing!

   His mother became frantic at the news and immediately called the police. The dispatcher put her through to a sergeant who said they'd already been contacted by his partner and had contacted the FBI. He told her to stay at home, remain calm, and they'd contact her if there was any news. She hung up and immediately began to cry. Peter felt his mother's pain and wanted to tell her about the aliens and what they'd seen at the lake, but he had promised his father he wouldn't tell anyone about it. Peter didn't know what to do. Finally he decided he had to go to Possum Kingdom Lake and look for his father. There was no other choice. Neither the police, the FBI, or his father's private investigators knew about the aliens. Peter was the only one who knew what was going on. He was his father's only hope.

Since Rebekah wouldn't have allowed Peter to take her station wagon to look for his father, he told his brother Reggie he was taking it to visit a friend and would be back in a few hours. Reggie warned him that he'd get in trouble for taking the car, but that didn't stop him. Ten minutes later he was on the road to Possum Kingdom Lake. During the three hours it took to get there, he thought about what he would do if he found his father. He had no weapons and even if he did, he doubted they'd be any match for what weapons the aliens might have. His only hope was to find his father and pray he'd have an opportunity to free him. If not, there was a cell phone in his mom's station wagon, so he'd at least be able to call the police.

It was dark when he arrived at the stable where he and his father thought the cave entrance was hidden; a cave that led under the lake to Cactus Island where the aliens landed and hid their ship underground. It was a huge metal building that his father believed was built over the mouth of the cave to hide it from neighbors and passer-byes. On the radio the announcer had warned of a line of thunderstorms moving through Palo Pinto County and, sure enough, it arrived just as Peter did.

When he drove up, billows of smoke were pouring out of the building. Panic stricken, Peter jumped out of his car and stopped a fireman working the blaze. "What happened here!" he screamed.

The fireman stopped and looked at him. "There's been an explosion. The place has been burning for half an hour."

"Oh, my God!"

"You can't be here," the fireman said. "You should go back to the main road."

"But I think my father was in there. I've got to go in and see."

"No. No. Nobody can go in there. What's your father's name?"

"Stan Turner."

"The attorney?"

"Yes."

"Oh, he's okay. He's on his way to the sheriff's office."

"Really? Where is it?"

"In the courthouse at Palo Pinto."

"You mean the courthouse off the main highway, the one that sticks up over the trees?"

"That's it," the fireman said smiling.

"Thanks."

For a moment Peter watched the firemen, police, and FBI agents who were swarming around the warehouse like bees tending to their hive. What had happened here? He couldn't wait to find out. The news that his father was okay comforted him, but he wanted to see him in person to make sure. He debated whether to go to the sheriff's office or just drive home. Then he remembered his father didn't have a car with him. The aliens had brought him here in a van. He would need a ride home, so it made sense to go to the sheriff's office. He got in the big station wagon and headed back toward Palo Pinto.

Halfway there he caught up with the line of thunderstorms that he'd encountered earlier and the rain became so intense he could hardly see. Not wanting to smash his mother's car, he decided to pull over and wait for the rain to let up. Twenty minutes later it was still raining just as hard and he was beginning to worry that he might miss his father. That would ruin his plan. He wanted to be the one to bring his father home, so his mother wouldn't be mad at him for taking her car.

He started the engine and continued cautiously back onto the highway. As he was pulling out the wind became so strong the car began to shake. Peter swallowed hard and looked around wondering if he was sitting in the path of a tornado. Memories of a Colorado encounter with a tornado years earlier came flooding through his mind. They'd been driving down the freeway one afternoon when his father told them a tornado was coming down the median straight at them. Just as Peter looked up a big Ryder truck was tossed in the air like a tin can and tumbled off the highway. The car if front of them stopped suddenly, so his father slammed on the brakes nearly throwing them to the floor. For several anxious moments they watched the tornado advance toward them. His father told them that if the tornado was going to hit them, they'd have to abandon their car or they'd surely die. Luckily the tornado had gone up in the clouds just in the nick of time.

Peter unbuckled his seatbelt. Warily, he accelerated down the highway. He couldn't see a thing it was so dark. Suddenly, the lights went out and the engine stalled. Fear shot through him like a hollow point shell. He looked around trying to get his eyes to penetrate the total darkness.

Intermittent flashes of lightning provided the only illumination.

What should I do? This is too dangerous. What if an eighteen wheeler comes barreling around the bend and crashes into me? I've got to get the car off the road. I'm a sitting duck out here.

He cranked the engine but nothing happened. He tried again but all he heard was a faint clicking sound like you hear when the battery is dead. After banging the steering wheel a few times, he resigned himself to the fact that he'd have to push the car off the road himself.

He climbed out into the torrential downpour and began pushing with his left hand while he steered with his right. Intermittent flashes of lightning provided just enough light to see where he was going. Fortunately, the road was downhill so as he pushed the car gained momentum. When it had picked enough up speed he jumped back in and shut the door. A hundred strides down the road a flash of lightning revealed a gravel road going off to the right, so he turned onto it and rolled to a stop.

Now that he was safe from any traffic all he had to worry about was the tornado. Peter looked around expectantly still seeing nothing but darkness. He knew the odds of getting hit by a tornado were slim, so the fear that had gripped him earlier began to wane. What concerned him now was how he'd get his car started once the storm had passed.

As Peter was contemplating his predicament, lightning struck a power pole nearby. An eerie blue glow permeated the sky around him. He wondered if his car had been hit. Another strike hit the ground nearby. He reeled from the barrage of sparks in panic. The car began to shake again, then was lifted off the ground only to be dropped rudely back down.

The eerie blue light hung in the air even after the lightning strike. The rain suddenly stopped. Peter looked around in shock and panic. As the minutes ticked off the blue light intensified. Peter suddenly realized it was coming from directly overhead. He opened the door, looked up warily, and gasped at the huge spaceship hovering overhead.

He knew in an instant he'd made a mistake not obeying his father. The aliens had discovered he knew of their existence. His father had told him to stay in the living room when he was being hypnotized by Dr. Gerhardt, but Peter hadn't listened. He'd suspected his father was working for the CIA and the aliens but he wanted to be sure. They'd have to eliminate him now. "Oh, God! What am I going to do?" he moaned. Peter slammed the door, frantically rolled down the window and stuck out his head. "I won't tell!" he screamed. But he knew that wouldn't matter. Why should they trust him? They couldn't afford to. He knew they existed, and for that they had to strike him dead!

Panic gripped Peter like a vice, but he told himself to remain calm. There had to be a way out of this. He knew he was a sitting duck in the car. If he stayed put, they'd hit him with a laser and he'd be incinerated in an instant. The car began to shake violently again. What were they doing? Were they going to take the car into the ship? "You're not taking this kid!" he screamed as he opened the door and made a run for it.

He ran along a fence line and then through a grove of trees. Suddenly he slammed into the drenching rain that had been deflected by the ship. He kept running, faster than he'd ever run before. He had to get away. Behind him he heard the big spaceship emit a deep whirring sound and he could tell it was coming after him. Somehow he ran even faster, but it wasn't enough. A beam of light shot out from the ship temporarily blinding him. His legs were lifted off the ground and he was sucked up in the beam like soda pop through a straw.

As he was pulled into the ship the sensation reminded him of body surfing when he was on vacation in California. When the big wave broke over you, there was nothing you could do but let it drag you along until it lost its momentum. If you fought it, you'd only injure yourself. This felt the same way so he instinctively relaxed and just waited. The beam sucked Peter into the ship and spat him out onto a slippery surface. He rolled over twice and slid hard against a spongy wall. It was cold, wet, and dark as midnight. Peter was petrified. He began to shake incessantly and could hardly breathe.

3
Earth Shuttle 21

After what seemed like an eternity to Peter a soft blue glow lit the room. A hatch opened and a man stepped inside. He was medium height and build, with short dark hair, and wore a blue and grey uniform. He didn't look much like an alien. In fact, in his uniform he looked a lot like a bellhop at the Sheraton Hotel. He approached Peter cautiously and said, "Mr. Turner?"

"Yes," he replied trembling.

He extended his hand. "I'm Lok Thorz. . . . Welcome aboard."

Peter shook his hand tentatively. "Where am I?" he asked looking around what appeared to be the inside of a large tank. It was a stupid question, really. He knew he was in a spaceship, but he still felt compelled to ask.

He smiled and said, "You're on Earth Shuttle 21 and this is the transport hold."

Peter looked back at Lok. He felt a little better since Lok seemed friendly and spoke English. Still, he knew evil people often pretended to be nice to get you to trust them. His father had warned him about that."Where are you taking me?"

"The shuttle goes back and forth between Earth and Tarizon."

"There must be some mistake. I don't want to go to Tarizon. I've never heard of the place."

Lok shrugged. "Well, I'm sure that's true, but—"

"How did you get me up here, anyway? I mean, nothing touched me. I was just sucked up like a dry leaf."

"We transported you into the ship through a compression tube."

"A compression tube? I didn't see any tube."

"It's an electron tube. You can't see it. It didn't hurt, did it?"

"No, it was like riding a wave."

"Yes, it was a wave of sorts. Don't ask me how it works, though. I'm a diplomat, not a scientist."

"A diplomat? For what country?"

"Ah . . . not a country . . . Tarizon. It's a planet in another solar system."

"Another solar system? But you look and talk just like an American."

"I have dual citizenship. I was born in Irving, Texas but my father is from Shisk, the capital city of Soni on the planet Tarizon."

Peter just stared at Lok in awe. *Dad was right. There are aliens living on Earth! My God!* "But I've never heard of people from other planets living on Earth," Peter protested. "It would be on the news if it were true."

"No. It's a top secret program between our governments."

"You mean the government knows about it?"

"Yes, but like I said, it's very low profile. Only a very few people are aware of it. Your CIA runs the program. That's why we had to bring you on board."

"What do you mean? What do I have to do with the CIA?"

"Well, your father works for them. Didn't he tell you?"

"No."

Peter's father hadn't told Peter about the CIA but Peter suspected his father was doing more than just practicing law. None of his friends' fathers got shot at or had their cars blown up. Peter couldn't remember how many times he'd sat with his dad in the hospital after he'd been mysteriously hurt. He wasn't stupid. He'd read the newspaper articles and his dad had hinted that he was involved in *other* things.

"Right. Well, I guess he couldn't tell you. Anyway, I'm sorry to have to break this news to you. This ship is on its way back to Tarizon. You're going to have to live there for awhile; maybe, well . . . for the rest of your life."

Lok's words stunned Peter. He turned pale. It suddenly hit him like a Mack truck. He was being taken to another planet! Panic engulfed

12

him. He looked around for a way out, but he couldn't even find the door Lok had entered.

He ran to the wall searching for it. "No! You can't do this! I've got to get home! My mother will be worried. I've got school. I've got to take my dad home. He's at he Sheriff's office in Palo Pinto. He may be hurt! There was an explosion!"

"Calm down!" Lok said. "Take a breath. None of that's important anymore."

"Not important to you maybe," he screamed, "but it's my life!"

Lok grabbed his shoulders trying to calm him.

Peter finally took a breath. He could scarcely believe what was happening to him. One minute he's driving along the highway and the next minute he's on a spaceship heading for Tarizon? "Oh, God! No," he moaned. "This has to be a dream." Tears began streaming down his cheeks. "It must be a dream. Please God, let it be a dream."

Lok walked over to the wall and pushed a button on a small control panel. A shield protecting a large window retracted. Peter's jaw dropped as he saw Earth in the distance. Utter despair came over him. He staggered to the window and ran his hands along its surface to make sure it was real. "No," he moaned as he began to feel weak and light headed. He felt his heart pounding in his chest and his knees suddenly gave way. Lok grabbed him from behind to keep him from collapsing.

"I know this is a lot to assimilate at one time," Lok said, "but the Treaty requires us to be honest with you and to keep you informed. We are a highly civilized society and live in accordance with the Supreme Mandate."

Peter blinked and looked at Lok who appeared fuzzy to him now. He rubbed his temples trying to clear his head. "What . . . I mean . . . ah . . .what's the Supreme Mandate?"

"It's like your Constitution and Bible all rolled up into one. It's the foundation of our civilization."

Peter shook his head and his vision began to clear. He was starting to recover a little from the shock of his abduction. He wondered if he'd heard Lok correctly. "Did you say you had to be honest with me?"

"Yes. Our treaty with the United States demands it."

"So, I can ask you anything?"

"Yes. Ask away."

Peter blinked a few times and then questions began flooding his mind. "So, you said my being here has something to do with the CIA?"

"Yes, it seems your father has been recruited by them to be a part of the Tarizon Repopulation Program—some sort of legal liaison or something. Regrettably, in the process of his recruitment I understand you became aware of the program's existence."

"No. I've never heard of it."

"You must have or they wouldn't have ordered your exile."

"Exile. Is that what they call this?"

"Yes. It's much more humane than killing you, don't you think?"

Peter couldn't argue with that so he didn't try. "Well, now that I think about it, I guess my father and I saw one of your ships take off, but I don't have any recollection of it myself. I only know about it because my father had himself hypnotized so he'd remember it."

"Precisely; so you admit you knew about us?"

Peter shrugged.

"So, they had to bring you aboard. They can't allow anyone to compromise their mission."

"The Tarizon Repopulation Project?"

"Yes," he sighed. "But I think we've probably talked enough for now. I have to get you ready for deep space transport."

"Deep space transport? Prepared? How?"

"I know this is a little scary, but I'm going to have to put you to sleep for awhile. It's a long ride to Tarizon. We have to conserve food and water to get you there safely."

A cold chill washed over Peter. "How long do I have to sleep?" he asked.

"A little over a year," he replied without emotion.

"A year!" he gasped. "You've got to be kidding me. No way!"

Peter looked around the room again frantically as if he was searching for something—an escape pod, perhaps.

"Don't worry," Lok said reassuringly. "It won't seem like more than a single night. You'll go to sleep and wake up just like it was the next morning. You won't age hardly at all. Time slows down as you approach light speed. I've done it several times now. Everyone who travels between

14

our two worlds has to do it."

Peter's eyes widened. "You said light speed? I didn't think that was possible."

"Actually the ship goes faster than light speed."

"I don't think so," Peter gasped.

Lok frowned. "You don't have a choice. It's either the sleeping chamber or death. Without the protection of the chamber, the moment we went FTL your body would disintegrate, not to mention the tremendous radiation your body would be exposed to."

"FTL?"

"Yes, faster than light—don't ask me how much faster—like I said, I'm no scientist. Somehow they create a huge magnetic field and the ship drops right into another dimension. It's pretty scary if you think about it, so I try not to."

Peter swallowed hard but couldn't think of a thing to say. Lok went over to a control panel on the wall and pushed a button. A door opened and he motioned for Peter to go in. He reluctantly followed Lok into the rectangular room approximately twenty feet deep. On either side were what looked like enclosed sleeping compartments with a myriad of wires, monitors, and tubes. Several of the compartments were already occupied. Peter's hands began to shake and he felt nauseous.

"I won't be able to sleep in there," he protested. "I'll go crazy."

"No, you won't. We have a drug that will put you into a deep coma-like sleep. You'll be out in a flash."

Peter folded his arms struggling to keep his composure. Tears welled in his eyes. Then he felt a sharp pain in his arm and the room faded.

4

Dreams

The drug put Peter into a deep sleep and dreams and memories began flooding through his subconscious mind. One memory that played over and over was of Peter in a car speeding down a two lane road in central Texas. He glanced over and saw his grandfather at the wheel. Ahead he could see the Palo Pinto courthouse sticking up above the trees. He'd unexpectedly been called as a witness in Stephen Caldwell's murder trial and his grandfather was driving him to meet his father who was representing Stephen in the trial. He couldn't imagine why the assistant district attorney prosecuting the case had called him. His grandfather had suggested it was just a ploy to anger his father and distract him at a critical time in the trial. Whatever the reason Peter was scared and afraid he'd mess up his father's case and hurt his friend's chances of acquittal.

The scene shifted to the courtroom where Peter was being called to testify. He got up and made his way to the witness stand. The courtroom was as quiet as a library on Christmas Day. Stan began. "Peter, how many years have you been going to Camp Comfort for camping trips?"

"This was my fourth trip," Peter replied.

"And were Steven Caldwell and Jimmy Falk with you each of these times?"

"Yes, they were."

"Now, what do you do at night on these camp outs?"

"At night there's always a campfire."

"What do you do at these campfires?"

"Well, we sing, have contests, tell jokes, give out awards and tell stories."

"What kind of stories are told?"

"Ghost stories, stories about cowboys and Indians, and stories

17

about Cactus Island."

"Who tells these stories?"

"Our scoutmaster and sometimes the scouts themselves."

"Have you ever told a story at one of these campfires?"

"Yes."

"Which one?"

"At the last camp out I told the story about the alien landings at Cactus Island."

"How do you know that story?"

"Someone tells it at every campfire. I heard it the first year I went to camp. It's kind of a tradition."

"Could you tell the story to the judge and the jury?"

"Objection!" Carla Simms, the Assistant DA yelled. "Your Honor. This is totally irrelevant, prejudicial, and a waste the court's valuable time."

Stan replied, "Your Honor. I beg to differ. Steven Caldwell's state of mind is an issue in this trial. If he heard this story four or five times, it could go a long way in explaining his behavior on the day of Jimmy's death."

The judge smiled. "Actually, I would like to hear the story, and I think everyone in the courtroom would like to hear it as well. Am I right?"

The gallery responded with screams of approval and applause. Peter started to laugh. Simms glared at the judge who finally picked up his gavel and banged it a few times. "All right. Let's get on with it."

"Go ahead, Peter," Stan said. "Tell us the story of the landings on Cactus Island."

Peter wiggled in his chair and with a deadly serious look on his face began. "Shortly after World War II, two veterans and their fishing guide were out on Possum Kingdom Lake fishing near Cactus Island. It was late afternoon and the men were about to call it a day when a terrible wind came up, creating monstrous waves that nearly capsized their boat. They held on for dear life as the small bass boat was tossed up and down by the waves and spun around by gale force winds. Then the sky got very dark and they saw blue lightning in the distance and heard a noise so shrill it nearly busted their eardrums.

"They held their ears trying to protect them from the noise, but it didn't help. Finally, the noise died down and they noticed the blue lightning coming closer and closer. They wondered what was causing it as they'd never seen anything like it before. They watched it until it was directly overhead.

"Then they realized the blue lightning was coming from a huge spaceship the size of a football field. Both of the men had seen some pretty strange things while fighting in the war, but nothing like this alien spacecraft that was hovering over Cactus Island. As they watched in sheer terror the spaceship began to drop lower and lower until it had landed on the island.

"Although they desperately wanted to stay and watch the spacecraft, they feared for their lives so they tried to start the outboard engine and get away as fast as they could. Unfortunately, the motor wouldn't start and they found themselves dead in the water. Lucky for them the aliens paid no attention to them and went on about their business.

"As the two fishermen watched, the spacecraft's huge side doors opened and out came what seemed like ten thousand huge frogmen. They looked like humans except for their pale green colored skin and webbed hands and feet. The frogmen, each over six feet tall, dived into the lake and began to feed.

"The fishermen were panicked now with swarms of frogmen all around them, swimming, diving, jumping, and churning the water like a beater in a mixing bowl. It was all the men could do just to keep the small boat afloat.

"Finally, the frogmen began to move away from the island as the schools of fish around it began to flee from their new predators. With the frogmen gone the fishermen decided to use their emergency oars and go ashore and take a closer look at the spacecraft. They didn't think anyone was on the ship, but before they reached the shore they saw people running around the spacecraft like mechanics or pilots checking out the condition of the ship. The men all wore blue uniforms with a yellow triangle on their chest. There was some kind of writing within the triangle but it was not a language the fishermen had ever seen.

"The fishermen hid behind some rocks and watched the aliens at work. When they appeared to be finished with their preparations, a giant drill dropped from the belly of the ship and began to turn and drill deep into the island. The men watched in wonder until they heard the frogmen returning. The fishermen jumped into their boat, and using their emergency oars, made a quiet escape. From a distance they watched the huge spacecraft take off, flashing its blue lights over the landscape as it glided toward them.

"When the big ship passed over them and they were engulfed by the blue light, a strange thing happened. The fishermen forgot what they'd seen and only had a vague recollection that something unusual had transpired that day. Within a few weeks it all just seemed like a bad dream, except one odd thing they remembered; not a single fish was caught in the lake for weeks after that fateful day.

"Even though the blue lightning made it difficult for people to remember what they'd seen, over the years the spaceship returned many times and people began to piece together what was happening at Cactus Island. When the fish quit biting for a week or more, they knew they had been visited by the alien spacecraft. The fishermen called it the Blue Tide.

"Many believe that the big drill that came from the belly of the spaceship created a shaft down to a cave that lies under the lake and surfaces on dry land. Some believe the aliens wander around at night looking for women and children to kidnap and take back to their dying planet. Some say the frogmen, if the fish don't satisfy them, will come on land at dusk and feed on dogs and small children."

"Objection, Your Honor!" Simms protested. "This is—"

"Okay, okay," Judge Applegate said. "I think that's enough. Objection sustained. Thank you, Peter. That was quite a story, but I think we get the picture."

Peter shrugged. "Yes, sir."

The dream shifted to a conversation Peter and his father had shortly after Stephen Caldwell had been acquitted by the jury. Although he was glad Stephen had been found innocent there were still a lot of unanswered questions. The most troubling being whether aliens had indeed landed at Possum Kingdom Lake. The evidence his father had been gathering pointed to that distinct possibility and he had to find out if it was true.

"I'm intrigued by your Cactus Island story," Stan said. "Oh, and by the way, you did a great job telling the story to the jury. Thank you for doing that."

Peter smiled proudly. "No problem. It was cool. All my friends said they heard about it on the TV. Even Michelle talked to me and before I testified she didn't know I was alive."

"Wow. Your popularity rating went up, huh?"

He grinned and replied. "I guess."

"Anyway. I'd like to find out if there really is a cave that leads from the shore to Cactus Island. It seems that some oil operator a few years back claimed one showed up on a geological survey he commissioned."

"Really? But I thought you didn't believe in the alien landings," Peter asked.

"I don't know. Like I said, I'm intrigued now, so I thought maybe you and I could check into it."

"What do you want me to do?"

"I'm trying to locate a copy of the geological report showing the caves. If I get it, we'll have to go out to Possum Kingdom Lake and try to find it."

"But what if there *are* aliens landing at Cactus Island and they don't like us messing around in their caves?"

Stan laughed. "I thought *you* didn't believe in aliens."

"I don't, but . . . well . . . what if I'm wrong? What if there are aliens and they attack us?"

"Don't worry. If we find the caves I don't plan to do any exploring right away."

The dream faded and Peter found he and his father at Possum Kingdom Lake. It was a beautiful night and the stars were very bright. They were starting to walk along the shore when they heard something out in the lake. They looked over and saw a strange creature surface not fifty feet away. It was like nothing they'd ever seen before standing up like a man but having webbed hands, pale green skin and being over six feet tall."

The greyish green creature watched them with its orange penetrating eyes. It had what must have been a three-pound striper in its mouth struggling to get free. Its arms seemed as functional as any human and it looked to be incredibly strong. Peter was scared and started to scream. Stan put his hand over his mouth and told him to shut up.

They slowly retreated from the beast, Peter trembling and

breathing hard. The creature watched them closely as it chewed but didn't seem to care that they'd seen him. Once they were out of his sight, they turned and ran as fast as they could back to their motel. With the door closed and the deadbolt latched, they both took a breath. Peter was pale and still trembling. Stan took him in his arms and held him tightly. They were both in shock and had little to say. As Stan held Peter, he thought back to his testimony in court about the frogmen who were supposedly the slaves of the aliens and provided the labor for operating the spaceship. As he recalled from the story, the spaceship landed at Cactus Island so the frogmen could feed off the fish in the lake. Stan wondered if the story was actually true.

Excited by the possibility that aliens might actually be visiting Cactus Island at that moment, Stan told Peter to stay in the motel room and he'd be right back. He rushed outside and looked out at the lake. There was a faint glow above the island. He ran toward the shore to get a better look, his heart pounding, not from running but from the thought that alien life might actually exist.

A strong wind suddenly whipped up making the trees sway and the leaves rustle. There was a thin layer of clouds in the sky and the moonlight created an eerie ambience over the lake. Suddenly there was a flash of blue lightning from the island that stopped him dead in his tracks. Something hit him from behind startling him—scaring the Hell out of him. He turned and was relieved to see it was only was Peter.

He put his arm around him and they both gazed out at the island in amazement. There was one heck of a light show going on out there. By now the wind was blowing fiercely and they could hardly keep their footing. The glow from the island kept getting brighter and brighter. Then a giant object shot out of the island. It fired bursts of blue lightning as it came right at them. There was a terrible piercing noise that forced them to grab their ears or lose their eardrums. It was like nothing they'd ever seen before—a flat grey object the size of a football field drifting across the sky.

5

A New Beginning

There was the sound of a pressure seal being broken as Peter's compartment opened. A man in white came over to him, released his restraints, and unhooked the tubes and wires connected to him. Peter sat up. He felt weak and very hungry. The man helped him out of the compartment and as he stood up precariously, the man said, "Welcome to Tarizon!"

Lok had said it would take more than a year to get to Shisk on the planet Tarizon, but it seemed to Peter just yesterday that he'd been transported aboard Earth Shuttle 21. As he waited in line for someone to escort him off the ship he thought of home. It made him sick to think so much time had passed and that his family probably thought he was dead. His father knew the truth, surely, but they'd forbid him from telling anyone. Tears began to well in his eyes as a desperate sadness came over him.

Oh, Dad. Such a secret you'll have to keep from Mom. How will you bear it? Will I ever see you and Mom again? . . . Why did this have to happen? Why did you let the CIA do this to us? It's not fair. I don't want to be here. I want to come home!

The line began to move and they filed into the large room where Peter had first met Lok. It was there he'd looked out the portal and seen Earth in the distance. Lok wasn't anywhere to be found this time, however. Instead a lady named Lurh gave them their disembarkation instructions. She was pleasant enough, but all business. Lurh pushed a button and a door appeared in front of them. A pale green humanoid creature about a foot taller than Peter stepped inside and motioned for them to exit through the door. Peter recoiled at the sight of the strange man who looked human but not of a race he'd ever seen before.

"Don't be alarmed," Lurh said. "This is Durisk. He's a Seafolken. He's human just like us, but his race has adapted to life in the sea. He won't hurt you if you do what you're told."

Whatever he was, the sight of this huge creature made Peter uneasy. He slipped by him quickly and was astonished to see Cheryl Windsor, his father's client who had disappeared during her trial, and her children in line ahead of him. They were complaining about being hungry. Lurh overheard their complaints and said not to worry—they'd be eating soon enough.

As they stepped out onto the tarmac, Peter looked up, anxious to see the Tarizonian sky, but it was overcast and there was nothing to see but a dim greyish mist with two moons side by side barely visible through it. The moons were almost touching and then Peter realized they were on a collision course and would soon be one behind the other.

"Look," Lurh said. "It's the Super Eclipse. Take a good look. It only happens every 434 cycles."

Everyone stopped and gazed upward as the two moons became one black circle with a thin halo. A few moments later they began to separate again and the sky lightened.

"I can't believe we were able to see it. The air pollution usually hides our moons," Lurh noted.

Peter looked up again and the moons were gone. An eerie sensation came over him. He took a deep breath. The air was thick and stifling and he wondered if it was always so polluted. Lurh led them across the tarmac to a large building. Peter thought it was some kind of space terminal. He looked back at Earth Shuttle 21 and saw the entire ship for the first time. It was gigantic. There were at least a hundred of the little hatches like the one from which they'd just disembarked. He made a mental calculation and estimated the ship could carry at least twenty-five hundred passengers. Most of the hatches were open now and people were leaving. He wondered if they were all involuntary guests or willing passengers. It gave Peter hope to know there was a ship going back to Earth on a regular basis. He told himself that some day he'd be on it.

Lurh led them into the terminal to a decontamination chamber where they were segregated by sex, disrobed, and given a chemical shower. It reminded Peter of gym class back at Hillcrest High School except the water there wasn't florescent green. When they were cleansed to the satisfaction the inspectors on duty, they were issued new clothing—loose fitting white slacks and matching pullover shirts like the kids wore who were taking karate lessons. They were comfortable at least, so nobody was complaining.

Once they were all dressed, Lurh took them to a cafeteria the size of a Tom Thumb Supermarket. Peter was glad as he was so hungry he would have eaten a mutated rat, had he seen one. The spread of different types of food was impressive—assorted fruits and vegetables, meats, cheeses, and desserts of every description. They didn't look familiar to Peter, but they all looked and smelled quite appetizing. As he was selecting his dinner, Peter saw Jimmy Falk, his friend from back home who Peter thought had died, setting his tray on a table. He headed his way and sat down beside him. Jimmy had a vacant look in his eyes.

"Jimmy? Is that you?"

Jimmy looked at Peter for a moment and said, "Peter?"

"In the flesh," he said. "I thought you were dead?"

"Dead?"

"Yeah, the Jeep accident. They said you died on impact."

Jimmy frowned and said, "Is that it? We're all dead? Is this heaven?"

"No, I don't think so. They said something about Tarizon—it's got to be another planet somewhere. I've never heard of it."

"I don't understand."

"You and me both. I think we were abducted by aliens. What I gather is they do this a lot. They have shuttles going back and forth to Earth."

"Shuttles?"

"I know its mind boggling. What's the last thing you remember back on Earth?"

Jimmy thought a moment and replied, "Driving with Steven back to camp."

"Right. Do you remember the accident?"

He shook his head. "No."

"Did you see the spaceship?"

"No. I don't remember a spaceship."

"Man, this is so weird. They had a funeral for you. I saw them bury you. Steven was tried for your murder. Luckily my Dad got him off or he'd have gone to Huntsville."

"Why would Steven murder me?"

"He didn't. It was all BS. They claimed he was pissed off because you took his girl away from him—what's her name?"

"You mean Susan?"

"Right. Susan Weber."

"So, Susan thinks I'm dead?"

Peter took a deep breath and replied, "Yeah, I'm afraid so."

Jimmy stood up abruptly. "Oh, God. I've got to contact her—tell her I'm alive!"

"It's too late. We're too far away from Earth. I'm sure my family thinks I'm dead, too."

"Why did they bring us here?"

"Well, I think *I'm* here because of my Dad," Peter replied. "They want him to do something for them back on Earth. I don't know why you are here unless it has to do with your father. He may be a Tarizonian."

"What?"

"I'm not sure, but my Dad suspected your father was an alien—and not the kind from Mexico. Now it seems even more likely. I bet he'll be here soon to pick you up. I saw his wife and kids here earlier. I don't see them now, so I imagine they've been picked up already."

"Cheryl?"

"Right. She was on trial for your father's murder, except he wasn't murdered. I think he was on the ship with us. It's all very confusing, but I think he'll be picking you up soon. Then maybe you'll get some answers."

"I don't know. Dad doesn't confide in me much. Just about everything he tells me is a lie."

"It may be different now that you're back here on Tarizon."

Jimmy knew what Peter had deduced was true. He'd suspected it for years but tried hard to ignore it. Having an alien for a father wasn't something you wanted to tell your friends about. A week before he'd gone to boy scout camp his father let it slip that he might be transferred. When Jimmy pressed him for more information, he told him the details hadn't been worked out yet, so not to tell anyone about it—particularly his stepmother. That got him to thinking. If he was being transferred, why wouldn't he tell his wife? She'd be the first one to give the news to.

Jimmy sighed. "Maybe so, but I'll still never see my mother again."

Peter nodded. "At least you have your father and your brothers and sisters."

"Half brothers and sisters," Jimmy corrected him.

After awhile their hunger became more important than solving the mystery of their abductions—at least for the moment. They began to nibble at the strange fare they'd gathered on their trays. After awhile they decided the food was actually good, so they cleaned their plates and went back for seconds, and thirds. By the time they were summoned to leave the cafeteria, they were so stuffed their stomachs ached.

Their next stop was some sort of waiting room. There were sofas, chairs, tables, lamps, magazines, and photographs on the walls. They were told to take a seat until each was called. Peter sat down and picked up a magazine. It was printed in a language he couldn't read but there were a lot of interesting pictures. He assumed the photographs were of Tarizon.

The first article was about a volcano. There was a picture of it spewing lava out over the countryside. Smoke billowed up from its cone. Although he couldn't read the article the pictures told the story of the tremendous devastation that the volcano had caused for many miles around it. Peter remembered his dad telling him about the eruption of Mt. St. Helens in Washington state. He had been flying to San Francisco the day it erupted and he said there was so much smoke and volcanic ash coming from the volcano that it left over a foot of soot on the ground for a hundred miles in every direction. While Peter was grappling with the magnitude of this, he heard his name called.

Peter looked up and saw an open door and a man standing in it. He motioned for Peter to come. Peter got up and walked over to him. He was an average looking man—black hair, medium build, mustache, and was holding a file in one hand. He pointed to a chair and Peter took a seat.

"Welcome to Tarizon, Mr. Turner. I'm Samilh, you can call me Sam. I trust your trip was uneventful."

"I guess so, I don't remember more than a minute of it."

"Well, it's the only practical way to transport large quantities of people between the planets. You can imagine what it would be like if you were awake for over an Earth year in that little compartment."

"True," Peter admitted. "You'd be sitting across from a lunatic right now."

"Well, actually your body would have been torn apart molecule by molecule. You wouldn't be a lunatic, you'd be dust," he said and then opened the file he had been holding. "I see your father is in service to the repopulation effort."

"I guess. I really don't know much about it."

"As you may have noticed it's quite dark outside although it is midday. This isn't the way it's always been on Tarizon. A hundred years ago Tarizon was a planet much like Earth—clear skies, clean rivers and lakes, majestic mountains full of game, and endless grasslands."

"What happened?"

"There were the worldwide wars that lasted for several decades but, shortly after unification, we had what you would call on Earth a super volcanic eruption. Unfortunately it was not just one volcano but thirteen. Millions of people were killed, but the worst tragedy was what it did to our atmosphere. It is so full of ash and toxic chemicals now that rarely do you see our sun. You can imagine what that did to agricultural production. For many cycles, which are similar to Earth years, we lacked sufficient food to feed our people and millions starved to death. Our population has been declining rapidly and even though we've come up with new ways to feed our people, the toxins in the atmosphere have made most of our men and women very weak and sickly. Infertility is a major problem.

"Fortunately, the worst is behind us and the atmosphere is gradually getting back to normal. The polar regions are already almost clear and, if weather conditions are favorable, we could see clear skies as far north as Lortec and the Beet Islands soon. Our scientists have also made great strides in cleaning up our water and filtering the air that we breathe. In ten or fifteen cycles we may see the sun again on a regular basis over all of Tarizon and our population will stabilize once again. That's why the Repopulation project is so important."

"Why couldn't you have just left me alone? I wouldn't have told anyone about what you were doing."

"You say that, but is it really true? Could you have kept such a secret from your family and friends?"

Peter shrugged. He knew deep down the man was right, of course. He didn't know for sure he'd have kept the secret. He would have tried for his father's sake, but who knows what he'd have done if push come to shove. "Still, you don't have the right to kidnap people and haul them off to another world. We have rights, you know."

"It certainly was regrettable that we had to bring you here, Mr. Turner. We don't like having to do this. We are a civilized people, but there was simply no choice. Let me assure you that while you are our guest on Tarizon we will do everything in our power to make your life here pleasant and fulfilling."

Peter glared at Sam wondering if it would be wise to show his anger. His father had always advised against it. His advice when someone made you angry was to count to ten before speaking, or better yet, say nothing. Peter had too many questions he needed answered, so he counted to ten and then asked evenly, "So, are you saying at some point I may be able to go home?"

"Perhaps. That depends on you and your father."

"What do you mean?"

"Well, it's complicated and probably a bit premature to discuss that now. The purpose of our visit is to welcome you to Tarizon and assign you temporary quarters pending permanent assignment."

"Do I have any say so in my permanent assignment?"

"Probably not," Sam said and shrugged. "Tarizon is in crisis, Mr. Turner. You will go where you are assigned and do what you're asked to do. If that is not acceptable . . . well . . . lets just say, you won't like the alternative."

There was a glint of a smile on Sam's face that Peter didn't like much. It seemed he was to be a prisoner and forced to work as his captors willed. He wondered what that work would be and what his temporary quarters would be like. In his mind's eye he saw a prison cell and bars. He just prayed he was wrong.

After the interview Peter and Jimmy were instructed to go with a group of thirty other passengers for transport to their temporary quarters. Peter scanned the group to see if there was anyone else he knew. Most of the group were young like he and Jimmy and seemed just as scared and disoriented as they were. He didn't see any faces that looked familiar. Ahead he saw two maintenance workers working on an escalator. The men stopped and looked up as the group approached. Peter felt the men's eyes on him almost immediately.

Suddenly, there were bright flashes of light. Peter jerked around to see where they were coming from. Two soldiers were trotting toward them with guns shooting out pulsating beams of light. One of beams hit Jimmy knocking him off his feet. He screamed and writhed as he held his smoldering stomach.   Peter fell to the ground beside him and tried to calm him. Others around him were also being hit and were falling left and right. The two workers rushed toward them, tore Peter away from Jimmy, and pushed him through an emergency exit.

"Where are we going? Who are you?" Peter protested.

"We're here to protect you," one of the workman replied. "We need to get you away from here immediately."

"What about Jimmy?" Peter screamed trying to break free of the two men. "Why are they trying to kill us?"

"There's nothing you can do for them," the workman said pointing what looked like a slim flashlight at him. There was a blue flash and Peter collapsed like a rag doll. The two men picked him up and carried him outside to an awaiting vehicle that rushed him away.

6
Shisk

Peter opened his eyes and realized he was in some sort of car or train moving quickly along the ground. The ride was quiet and smooth like an airplane. There were several others with him, but he couldn't remember getting on the vehicle. The last thing he could remember was meeting with Sam at his orientation meeting. Turning to the boy next to him, he asked. "Where are we going?"

"To Shisk," he replied. "Weren't you paying attention?"

"Ah. I must have fallen asleep. What kind of vehicle are we on?"

"It's a subtram, a supersonic subway. Isn't it cool?"

Peter nodded and then felt the subtram slowing down. A few minutes later they were at their destination. The subtram door opened on a street corner in downtown Shisk. Peter was awestruck by the strange city that stood before him. His group were escorted by a Seafolken to a tall building that looked like a giant crystal stalagmite. Peter gasped at the beautiful structure that towered above him. He wondered how something so magnificent had been built. Its surface was so irregular and design so complex that Peter thought it must have been molded into its shape. He couldn't imagine it having been transported, so he wondered if a giant mold had been built on site and filled with the hot crystal. He marveled at the incredible sight.

Inside was even more amazing. The lobby was carved right out of the crystal. There were no beams, sheet rock, ceiling tile, or flooring. The crystal had been perfectly formed to create each room in the building. He ran his hand across the surface of the crystal. It was very hard and perfectly

31

smooth. The furniture in the lobby was white and of a simple and functional design. The temperature of the room seemed quite comfortable. A tall, slender lady wearing a silver skirt, white blouse, and grey sandals met the group in the lobby. She was accompanied by many similarly dressed assistants. In fact, there seemed to be as many women as there were guests, as they called them. She said her name was Lucinda Dimitri.

Lucinda called out each name and one by one each guest was led into an elevator. Peter was the last to go and there were no other women left, so Lucinda escorted him to the elevator. While they were waiting for it, he asked, "How did they build this place? It's amazing."

She gave him an amused look and replied, "It wasn't built in the traditional sense, Mr. Turner. It was sort of grown."

"Grown? You grew a building?"

"Well, the Nanomites built it, but if you were watching the construction it would appear to grow a little each day."

"What? I don't understand. Who are the Nanomites?"

"They are a life form here on Tarizon. They live in swarms. Each swarm is controlled by a swarmmaster who communicates and controls all of the individual Nanomites. They are very small by themselves but together in a swarm they can be quite large. Still, you couldn't see them with the naked eye as they usually live inside a solid object. The building was designed by our architects and then their design was communicated to the swarm through the swarmmaster who controls them."

"Wow. That's bizarre. . . . How does the swarmmaster communicate with them?"

"I don't know. It's kind of similar to the way our human brain controls the cells of our body, except the Nanomites don't have to be connected. The only have to be in the swarm field to be under the control of the swarmmaster. This gives them the ability to avoid barriers and slip through cracks and voids in an object they are penetrating."

"Amazing. So you don't need construction workers, building materials, nothing?"

"Sure. It takes many people to culture and nourish the Nanomites swarms and care for them between building projects."

"I see."

Peter looked around again in wonder. How could a microscopic life form build something so immense and complex? The elevator door opened and they stepped in.

"So it takes months for the building to grow into fruition?" Peter continued.

Before Lucinda could reply the door opened again. They got out of the elevator and stepped into a long corridor with many doors. It was almost like a futuristic Hampton Inn.

"Yes, sometimes more than a cycle."

Lucinda led Peter down the hallway and stopped near the end. She said something in her native tongue and the door clicked open. She stepped inside and Peter followed her in. The room was identical to every other part of the building—cold crystal walls with white and grey furniture. There was what looked like a flat screen TV on one wall, a sofa, coffee table of sorts, and a built-in bar. A door led into a kitchen area complete with table, four chairs and a built-in hutch.

"Do you think this will do, Mr. Turner?" Lucinda asked.

Peter nodded enthusiastically, "Yes, quite nicely. Is there a bedroom?"

She nodded and pointed to another door. Peter walked over and opened it. It was a spacious room with a king size bed, crystal headboard and a large window overlooking the city. Peter went to the window, looked out over the city and his breath was taken away. Lucinda came up behind him and put her hand on his shoulder, and said, "Do you like our city?"

Peter turned and looked at her surprised that she'd touched him. She was older than he—maybe in her early 20s. She had black hair, brown eyes, and her skin was white as a dove. His pulse quickened. "Yes, I've never seen anything like it."

"They say it's even more beautiful when the sun shines. Of course, I've never seen the sun. I've seen stills and flashbacks, of course."

"Stills? Flashbacks?"

"What do you call them—pictures?"

"Oh, photographs and movies—got it."

"Yes, I hope one day to get a suntan."

Peter laughed. He suddenly realized why her skin was so fair. "Yeah, well they're overrated. If you're not careful you can end up with a sunburn that will hurt like crazy. Besides, your skin is so perfect, you wouldn't want to take a chance on damaging it."

"No. I suppose not," Lucinda admitted. "So, if you need anything I will be in the next room. Just call out and I will hear you."

"You'll be in the next room?" Peter repeated incredulously.

"Yes, I will be your guide while you are in Shisk," Lucinda replied.

"You mean you're going to stay with me?"

"Well, I'm going to be assigned to you; to be with you wherever they send you. I'm to make sure you are happy here on Tarizon."

"Wow, my own personal guide."

She nodded and walked over to a control panel near the door and pushed some buttons. Peter admired her svelte physique as she worked. A smile crept over his face. When he left Earth, he was a junior at Hillcrest High School. He'd dated a little, but had never actually been with a woman. He'd thought about it a lot and, like most teenagers, was somewhat obsessed with sex, but this was unreal. To live with a woman like this was unimaginable.

In his mind's eye, Lucinda gave him a seductive smile, and moved toward him. As he looked in her eyes she slipped her arms around him, drew him to her bosom, and kissed him gently. Her lips felt soft and sweet and the scent of her body was dangerously intoxicating. Then he heard the door close to Lucinda's room. He blinked, looked around, and realized he'd been daydreaming. He was alone. Alone for the first time since he'd landed on Tarizon millions of miles from Earth.

He looked around at the strange room. It was deadly quiet. Panic came over him suddenly. He curled up on his bed and began to quiver. *I'm on another planet! Oh, God! How can that be! How could you have done this to me, God? What did I do wrong?* Then he remembered she'd said he could summon her at any time. That possibility gave him comfort even though he knew he'd never take her up on it. She'd think he was weak if he did and he couldn't have that. He wanted her to like him, to be attracted to him, so someday she might be more than his guide. He rolled onto his back, stretched out, and yawned. He was soon asleep and erotic dreams of Lucinda got him through his first night on Tarizon.

7

Orientation

Soft and melodious chimes awoke Peter the next morning. He opened his eyes, looked around, and for a moment, wondered where he was. Then he saw Lucinda standing over him. "It's time to get up," she said smiling down at him.

He rolled over. "Not yet. It can't be morning."

"I'm afraid it is," she said sympathetically.

There was an instrument near the bed with a digital readout. Peter assumed it was a clock but he couldn't read it. "How do you keep track of time here on Tarizon?" he asked.

"It's similar to Earth except we have a 27 hour/kyloon clock and a 408 day calendar year/cycle. Months are phases, weeks are called segments, loons are similar to minutes and kyloons are more or less equivalent to your Earth hours."

"What time is it now?" Peter asked.

"0900. Which means we need to get you up so I can give you a shower. You've got a long day ahead."

Peter noted that Lucinda had said *she* was going to give him a shower. He wondered what that meant exactly. He imagined her in the shower with him. It was a very erotic image, but somehow he doubted that would actually happen. Maybe she'd at least wash his back, he thought. Either way having Lucinda staying with him would totally take his mind off of the fact he'd been abducted and was a prisoner. He wondered if this was some sort of psychological technique to make him cooperate and give his captors exactly what they wanted, whatever that was. If that was the case it was working and he didn't feel like rocking the boat.

35

"Are you hungry?" Lucinda asked.

"Yes, I'm famished."

"Good. Let's have breakfast. Do you like eggs?"

"Yes."

"Well, we don't have chickens on Tarizon but there is bird called a squit that lays a pretty tasty egg. I think you'll like it."

Peter shrugged. "How do you know about American food?" he asked.

"Oh, I was born in Waxahachie, Texas. I lived there with my father until I was seven. That's where I learned English and came to love bacon and eggs with biscuits and gravy."

"Waxahachie? Why were you living on Earth?"

"At the time of my birth the air on Tarizon was toxic and food was scarce. It wasn't a very good environment for conceiving and raising children. Infertility was a problem and many children born back then were mutants. My father was sent to Earth to propagate. Fortunately it didn't take our people long to regain their health once they got to Earth. So, once he was declared fit by our doctors, he found my mother, married her, and got her pregnant. Experience has taught us that you can't separate a child from its mother too early or the child will develop psychological problems. It was also difficult to raise small children with the planet in such distress, so he waited until I was older and stronger."

"How did you feel about leaving your mother back on Earth?" Peter asked. Lucinda gave him a hard look, then turned away. It was obvious to Peter that this was a touchy subject for her. "I'm sorry. I didn't mean to bring up unpleasant memories."

"It's okay. It was a sacrifice that was made for the survival of our planet. I have two mothers actually—a biological mother on Earth and my true mother here on Tarizon. I honor my biological mother for giving me life, but I love and cherish my true mother who loved and cared for me everyday when I was a child.

"But, don't you miss your biological mother? If you left her at seven you must have been pretty attached to her. I've just been away from my mother for a little while and there isn't an hour that goes by that I don't yearn to see her. It kills me that she thinks I'm dead."

She shrugged. "The extrication took place a long time ago for me.

. . . Anyway, it will do neither of us any good to dwell on the past. You should try to focus on the future."

Peter raised his eyebrows but didn't immediately respond. It was obvious she'd been expecting that question and was ready for it. He wondered if he should be candid or keep his true feelings to himself. Although he had no way of knowing for sure, Lucinda seemed to be talking to him openly and truthfully. It didn't seem like she was just giving him government propaganda. He decided to be candid.

"Extrication? Is that what you call it?"

"Yes."

"No offense, but isn't it actually kidnaping?"

"That's what your government calls it, but nobody is kidnaped. We asked your government for help and they agreed to give it to us in exchange for certain technological assistance. It was their decision to keep the Tarizon Repopulation Project secret not ours."

"I understand. I'm not angry at you. It's just if the people on Earth knew what was happening they'd be outraged."

"Then your government has done them a disservice by signing the treaty."

"Yes, that's an understatement. . . . It's the mothers on Earth who lose their children that concern me the most. It's their rights that have been most violated."

"I agree. But it's beyond our control. You should focus on your future here on Tarizon, not on events you had nothing to do with."

Peter shrugged. "It's just hard to focus on the future when I know so little about your planet and what your government expects of me."

"Be patient. I know what you're going through. I went through it too."

"But you had your father and a family to go to. . . . I have no one."

She smiled sweetly, took his left hand, and squeezed it firmly. "You'll have friends and family here soon enough. In the meantime, I'm your guide. I'll be with you."

He turned away and asked, "For how long?"

She shrugged. "I don't know. As long as you need me."

"But what if I always need you?"

She gave him a hard look, then laughed. "Don't be silly. Eventually you'll tire of me and move on, then I'll be reassigned."

After they'd showered separately and gotten dressed, Lucinda took Peter to a restaurant on the first floor of the guest house. They had scrambled squit and some green melon called *togen*. There was even a drink called *sankee* that was similar to coffee except it was very strong and thick like a milkshake. Peter ate everything like a trooper but his stomach was soon rebelling from this strange fare. He wondered if they had a drugstore that sold Tums.

After breakfast Lucinda took him to a government warehouse where he was issued some clothing. The clothing was basic casual attire, loose fitting, mainly white or light pastel colors. The shoes were light with soft sides—a cross between a tennis shoe and a moccasin. When they were finished, they went back to the compartment to unpack everything.

Later that morning Lucinda said she had to go home for a few hours to take care of some personal business. In the meantime she said Peter had been invited to have lunch with Robert Garcia, one of the Members of the Council of Interpreters. Lucinda explained that the Council of Interpreters was the judicial arm of the Tarizonian government. They were the guardians of the Supreme Mandate and could veto any law or administrative decree that they felt was contrary to its dictates. She explained that the Supreme Mandate had been ratified by the general population over a hundred cycles earlier after a bloody world war that nearly destroyed the planet. Since then Tarizon had enjoyed peace and prosperity until the cataclysmic volcanic eruptions.

According to Lucinda, Tarizon had been divided into thirty-one separate nations prior to the Supreme Mandate. These nations had been fighting amongst themselves for thousands of cycles. In the twenty cycles before the adoption of the Supreme Mandate millions of soldiers and civilians had lost their lives and much of the infrastructure of the planet had been destroyed. From out of the rubble a peace movement was born led by a charismatic holy man named Sandee Branh. Sandee had been elected Chief Minister of Lyon, the largest nation of Tarizon. Sandee claimed as a child that God had chosen him to save Tarizon from self destruction. From the day He first appeared to him, Sandee devoted his life to spreading God's message of peace and unity. Sandee told his followers that the petty national governments should be scrapped in favor one worldwide authority. Since so many were weary of war and feared the destruction of civilization on the planet if something wasn't done, Sandee's movement gathered momentum until there was enough support to call a World Council.

At the World Council, representatives from all of the thirty-one nations hammered out the Supreme Mandate and then called for a worldwide referendum to ratify it. All of the nations agreed to abide by the decision of the people. If the Supreme Mandate was ratified by a majority of its citizens, each nation agreed to subject itself to the World Council and abide by the Supreme Mandate. The World Council set the referendum date off six cycles to allow plenty of time for debate. On the day of the referendum nearly seventy percent of the population voted and the Supreme Mandate was ratified by sixty-one percent of the popular vote.

Meeting with what amounted to a Supreme Court justice was pretty exciting and a little scary for Peter. Lucinda had told him he'd be picked up at midday, so he got ready to go way early and sat by the door of his compartment anxiously. He didn't have a feel for Tarizonian time yet, so he kept a close eye on the clock on the console next to the door. Each room had one of these control consoles on the right side of the door at eye level. He assumed they were a combination clock, intercom, radio, telephone, camera, and thermostat.

Right on time a member of Robert Garcia's staff arrived to escort Peter to the restaurant where Councilman Garcia was having lunch. He led him down to the lobby and out to the subtram station. They entered a car and just a few seconds later the door opened in front of a restaurant called Scuggi's. It had a kind of Mediterranean look but Peter didn't know if that was intentional or just a coincidence. He led him inside to where the councilman was sitting with a young blond woman. The councilman stood up and bowed slightly. Peter did the same.

"Mr. Turner," Garcia said. "Thank you for coming." He pointed to the young lady sitting next to him. "This is my daughter Lorin. She's been anxious to meet you, so I invited her along. I hope you don't mind."

Peter smiled. "No, I don't mind at all. It's a pleasure to meet you, Lorin."

"Sit," Garcia said. "What would you like to drink?"

Peter shrugged. He had no clue what people drank on Tarizon. He finally replied, "What are you drinking?"

"Tekari. It's a bit like your beer back in America."

"Oh. I'm only seventeen. I guess I better get something non-alcoholic."

"There's no age limit for drinking Tekari here. Since nobody drives, we don't have to worry about drunk drivers."

Peter nodded and smiled. He was liking this place more and more each minute, "Okay, Tekari it is then."

Garcia smiled and motioned to the waiter. "Get Mr. Turner a Tekari and I'll need another one too." The waiter nodded and Garcia continued. "You're probably wondering why I have a Spanish name. I was actually born in El Paso, Texas. My father was Manuel Santiago Garcia. We were extricated in 1959 when I was five years old. I barely remember those years on Earth and have little memory of my natural mother."

Peter shook his head and took a deep breath. He couldn't believe so many aliens had lived on Earth without anybody knowing about it. He thought of his own mother, Rebekah Turner of Dallas, Texas, USA, planet Earth, at home sick because she lost her youngest son, except he wasn't dead . . . or was he? And there was his grandmother and grandfather of Richardson, Texas, USA, planet Earth whom he'd never see again either. He knew that all these children from Earth must live with an empty feeling inside knowing that even though their real mother is alive, they will never be able to see her. He knew it because he was feeling that same horrible feeling of emptiness and despair.

Lorin smiled and said, "So, Mr. Turner. How do you like Tarizon?"

Peter's eyes shifted to Lorin. He couldn't believe how everyone was treating him like he was a tourist. They seemed oblivious to the fact that he'd been abducted from his family and taken to another planet. The urge to grab Lorin and shake her violently came over him, but he thought better of it. The fact that he was here wasn't her fault, he kept telling himself. "Well, what I've seen so far is quite amazing."

"Isn't it? I hope you'll let me show you around later . . . when you have time."

He shrugged, still amazed at how everyone was being so nice to him. It seemed very odd, indeed, but there wasn't much else to do but go along with them.

40

"That would be great," he replied appreciatively.

The waiter came with the Tekari and then asked what they wanted for lunch. Peter looked at the menu and then closed it and smiled. Lorin said, "The back page is in English."

Taken aback, Peter turned the menu over and was shocked and delighted to see that Lorin was right, it was in English. "Wow. That's a relief."

"There are so many Earth children living in Shisk a lot of the merchants have English menus," Lorin said.

Councilman Garcia replied, "It's probably not a good idea. The Earth children need to learn Tari, the native language of Tarizon, when they come home so they will feel comfortable and be accepted into the community. If we allow them to continue to speak English it only impairs their ability to assimilate."

"I know you're right, father, but American English is the rage nowadays and the day is coming when Shisk will be a bilingual city."

"Well, I'm not so sure about that. Anyway, we better not bore Mr. Turner with such a trivial debate. I want to make him a proposition."

Peter looked at Councilman Garcia with interest. "Oh, really. What's that?"

"First, let's order."

Although the menu indeed was in English Peter didn't see anything familiar on it. Lorin recommended the *pollib* which she said was like lamb. He took her advice and prayed he'd like it. It would be embarrassing if he got something so grotesque he couldn't stand to eat it. Or worse yet, he vomited it all over the table.

"Tomorrow, Central Authority will be giving you a temporary assignment," Garcia advised. "I did a little checking around and found out they intend to assign you to a chemical factory."

"A chemical factory?" Peter groaned.

"Yes, I'm afraid the people at Central Authority don't trust Earth exiles very much so they tend to assign them to rather menial jobs in obscure locations."

A sick feeling came over Peter. A chemical factory would be so boring. "But, I didn't even take chemistry in high school," he protested.

"Don't worry. I've studied your file and I know you've done very well in school and were a championship debater."

"Well . . . yeah, I guess. We did go to the state finals."

"So, I suspect if you were back on Earth you'd follow in your father's footsteps and become a crackerjack advocate."

Peter nodded. "If you mean an attorney, that was a distinct possibility. I hadn't made up my mind entirely, but it was either that or some kind of business."

"So, I guess you know what I do?"

"Well, my guide told me you were a member of the Council of Interpreters, the highest court on Tarizon."

"Yes, and I was thinking that you might enjoy being an intern in my office."

Peter nodded enthusiastically, "Definitely. That would be cool . . . I mean . . . . excellent—much better than working in a chemical factory."

"Good. Then I'll contact Central Authority and request you as an intern, but there will be a couple of conditions."

Peter hated *buts*. They always complicated matters. He held his breath as he waited to hear what they were. "First of all you'll have to be our guest at my home for awhile until they find you a permanent place to live."

"We live on a hill overlooking the city," Lorin added. "Our house is quite nice. I'm sure you'll love it."

"I would love to stay with you, but won't that be an inconvenience?"

"Nonsense," Lorin said. "We have plenty of room and we would love having you."

"Okay. What's the second condition?" he asked.

"You'll have to give me your word that you will be on your best behavior at all times," Garcia said. "I will be responsible for you and if you cause any trouble, I will be held accountable."

"I would never intentionally do something wrong," Peter replied assuredly. "I assume someone will give me instructions on what to do and what not to do on the job?"

"Yes, of course, but let's be perfectly candid here Mr. Turner."

"Okay."

"You're what we call an Earth exile. You're not here voluntarily so you may harbor some animosity toward our government for taking you away from your family and friends. Many exiles have difficulty accepting their situation and become hateful and belligerent. Worse yet, some get the idea that they can somehow get back to Earth and they waste much time and energy trying to figure out how to do that."

The Councillor's words jolted Peter. He had already vowed to do that very thing. Could he promise to give up his quest to return to Earth? But if he didn't he'd end up doing manual labor in a chemical factory. The idea of that horrified him. Finally, he shrugged and said philosophically, "My father always told me to go with the flow—you know, don't try to swim upstream because you'll probably drown."

"Your father is a wise man and I can see much of his wisdom has rubbed off on you. I'm looking forward to having you on my staff."

"Me too. When will I start?"

Garcia thought a moment and replied, "It will probably take seven to ten days for the bureaucrats to do the paperwork. That will give us time to ready you a place at our home. I trust your current accommodations are satisfactory?"

"Oh, yes. Quite. Thank you."

"Your guide is taking good care of you?"

Peter nodded enthusiastically. "Yes, she's been quite helpful."

The councilman gave Peter a wry smile. Lorin frowned. Their food came and Peter was pleased that it did indeed taste like lamb. They ate and continued to talk for quite awhile. Peter liked Councilman Garcia and enjoyed Lorin's witty sarcasm although she seemed to him to be preoccupied at times. He was excited about his new job and the prospect of living in a mansion. Despite his good fortune, his enthusiasm was dampened a bit by the thought of losing his guide, Lucinda. He hadn't known her long but there was something about her that was intoxicating. She was one of those women who took your breath away when you first saw her. Besides being beautiful, she made him feel so comfortable and safe in this strange world and, most of all, she seemed to like him. He wondered if there was any chance she could come with him to the Councilman's mansion.

8
Central Authority

When Peter got back to his compartment he was glad to discover that Lucinda was back from her errands. He told her about the counselor's offer to make him an intern and she seemed genuinely excited for him even though that would mean they'd only be together a little while longer. This disappointed Peter because it meant she didn't have the same feelings for him as he was quickly developing for her. He was confused about that since she'd been so open and intimate with him. They hadn't had sex, but they talked like they'd been together for years. *There must be some chemistry between us. She must be feeling something when we are together. I can tell it when she smiles at me. She wants me, I know it.*

That night Lucinda said she was tired and suggested they order pizza in rather than going to the restaurant downstairs. "You can get pizza here?" Peter asked in shock.

"Yes, so many of Earth children were used to eating pizza as kids that one of the local merchants figured out how to make it and put in on their menu. It was such a hit, pizza parlors sprung up everywhere."

"So do they have pepperoni?"

"A close replica. There are no cows or pigs on Tarizon so it's made from the range deer and durk birds."

'Durk birds?"

"Un huh, they're kind of like a big turkey—very tasty."

"Get us a large, I'm starving."

Lucinda smiled and went to the control pad on the door. She punched in a number and placed the order. Peter chuckled at the thought of eating pizza. He wondered what other kinds of American junk food they'd have here. As they were waiting for the pizza, Peter looked over at the TV screen on the wall.

"Do you all have television?" he asked.

Lucinda smiled and replied, "Sure, but there aren't any English stations yet. There's been talk about it, but Central Authority is against it as you might expect."

"Right. It will hurt assimilation," he said, recalling Councilman

Garcia's comments.

"Exactly."

"What are your schools like here?" Peter asked. "I hadn't graduated from high school yet when I left Earth. Will I have to finish school?"

"No. Most children complete school at age twelve. Many cycles ago a teaching method called *rapid absorption* was discovered. Scientists found that with the use of certain mind relaxing drugs and audio visual stimulation, knowledge and information could be injected into the mind at a dramatically faster rate than using conventional teaching skills. This was a tremendous discovery which has made it much easier and less expensive to educate the workforce. It's also been a boon to commerce too, as labor is now more abundant and cheaper than it's ever been."

"Wow! No school."

"Well, I wouldn't say that, but whatever Central Authority thinks you need to learn shouldn't take long to inject into your brain."

"They don't actually stick anything into my head, do they?"

"No. Like I said, they give you this drug and then they sit you in front of a VC monitor with some electrodes attached to key points on your body."

"VC?"

"Video communicator."

"Oh, I guess that's what we call a TV on Earth." Peter shivered. "Hmm. I don't know about that."

"It's painless, trust me. Anyway, the information is absorbed by your mind quickly and painlessly."

Peter recalled that his dad had told him to watch out for people who asked you to *trust them*. He was contemplating that alarm when the door chime rang and Lucinda got up to meet the pizza delivery man at the door. Once he'd handed her the pizza she immediately shut the door without paying, which surprised him.

"Do you have an account with the pizza parlor?"

"No, he just scanned my credit strip."

"Credit strip?"

"Right. We don't use money here. Everyone has a credit strip which is credited with production points and debited for expense points."

"No checks, huh?"

"No."

"What if you lose your strip?"

She laughed. "You can get it replaced, but I wouldn't recommend having to do that. Cental Authority doesn't like carelessness."

"What if it gets stolen?"

She shook her head. "No one would steal it. Only the person who owns it can use it. It has a chip censor."

"A chip sensor? What's that?"

"It's a sensor that communicates with the chip implanted in your shoulder."

"What! I'm not letting them put a chip in my shoulder."

She laughed again. "Peter, it's already there. Everyone gets one implanted on the ship when they are brought here."

"You've got to be kidding me?"

"No. It's standard procedure. Everyone on Tarizon has a chip sensor. It's very useful to Central Authority in managing the planet. They have an up-to-date census at all times and know exactly where everyone is at any moment. No one has to worry about getting lost. If you get sick Central Authority will know about it immediately and dispatch medical help."

"What about privacy? Don't people have the right to do as they please in private as long as no one else is affected?"

Lucinda gave Peter a queer look. "Privacy? No. The Supreme Mandate does not guarantee personal privacy. What is best for the people as a whole is our guiding principle."

Anger welled in Peter. He squirmed uncomfortably in his chair. What had he fallen into? A communist state in full force and glory? He couldn't believe what he was hearing. He recalled that the Berlin Wall had fallen in 1989 marking the beginning of the end of Communism on Earth. But had Communism prevailed on Tarizon? Was he now a member of a pure socialistic state similar to the one Karl Marx conceived and Lenin had done his best to force on the Russian populace? His arms and legs erupted in gooseflesh.

"Can they hear us talk?" He asked.

"No. They haven't developed that technology yet, but they are working on it. They can monitor your vital signs and can tell pretty much what you're are doing at any moment by analyzing that data."

"So, when you're . . . ah . . . having sex, they know it?"

"Probably," Lucinda laughed. "That reminds me. You've got to make a sperm donation tomorrow. It's on the schedule for 1400."

"Whoa! Nobody talked to me about donating sperm."

"You have to. Everyone has to contribute to the repopulation effort, particularly Earth children who have clean sperm and healthy eggs. It's your duty as a citizen of Tarizon."

Peter wondered if Lucinda was going to start singing the Tarizon national anthem, if they had one. The look on her face was so stern and sincere.

He forced a smile."Okay. So, what are we going to do with no TV?"

Lucinda's eyes lit up. "We can talk. I'd love to hear about your life on Earth."

He nodded. "Okay, and you can tell me more about yourself. That sounds good."

"Fabulous. I'll make us some sankee and have them bring up the blueberry pie."

"Blueberry pie?"

"Yes, the agricultural ministry has a developmental station that experiments with Earth crops. I checked with them and they had blueberries available. I had a pie especially made for you."

"Wow! You're amazing. I can't believe you went to all that trouble. What am I going to do without you?"

"Don't be silly. You'll do fine without me. I'm just a guide. I'm nothing special. Let's just enjoy the evening. I can't wait to hear more about Earth. I was so young when I left there, it almost seems like a dream."

As she got up to go to the kitchen, Peter tried to shift his thoughts to other things, but he couldn't. He was falling for Lucinda and helpless to do anything about it. The thought of losing her was unbearable. If he could just convince her to stay with him. His pulse quickened at the thought of it. Somehow he had to do it, he just had to keep her from leaving him. But what if the Central Authority didn't want that? What if they had other plans for her? His anger returned with a vengeance. He'd only been on Tarizon a few days and he already hated the commie jerks that ran the place.

9
The Prophecy

In their evening conversations Peter learned that Lucinda was the daughter of a middle aged banker named Shrie Eckvall. When he was extricated from Earth fourteen cycles earlier he brought Lucinda and her younger brother Roben back with him. Their Tarizon mother Doren Eckvall welcomed them with a thankful heart as she could never have children on her own.

Shrie Eckvall started at the bottom and worked his way up to the position of Vice President of the Central Urban Finance Office within five cycles of his return to Tarizon. This meteoric rise, however, was accomplished at a high personal cost in terms of Eckvall's family. He worked long hours and had little time for his mate and children. As a result Doren Eckvall ended up raising Lucinda and Roben almost exclusively. Although Lucinda recalled her childhood with little emotion, Peter could feel the resentment toward her father and a yearning to know more about her natural mother. He tried to flush out those feelings.

"Would you like to go back to earth and visit your mother?"

She frowned. "No, that wouldn't be possible. She thinks I'm dead. It would be very traumatic."

"I know, but aside from that, wouldn't you like to see her again?"

She thought about that for a moment and replied, "There's no use even thinking about it. It can never happen."

"I know, but don't you ever fantasize about impossible things?"

"No, there is no purpose in that."

"Sure there is," he replied. "Thinking about something or visualizing it is the first step to making it reality."

"But some things can never be reality no matter how hard you think about them."

Peter smiled at her stubbornness and replied, "True, but many things that seem impossible are not. I'm just saying you should keep an open mind about visiting your mother someday. I'm certainly not giving up hope that one day I'll return to Earth and see my family again."

Lucinda shook her head, "You need to face reality, Peter. Tarizon is your home now and you need to accept that. The Central Authority will never let you go back to Earth. How do you think they kept the Tarizon Repopulation Project secret for all these cycles? They don't take chances like sending an Earth alien back home."

As much as Lucinda and others tried to convey that message to him, Peter couldn't accept it. Deep down he knew somehow he'd get back to Earth. He had no clue how or when that would happen, but somehow he knew it would. Perhaps he was only in denial, he admitted to himself, and Lucinda was right, but for now he needed hope to keep his sanity. He needed to hold on to his belief that one day he'd be reunited with his family and friends back on Earth.

The following morning Peter did his patriotic duty and made a sperm donation. It was quick and painless and the nurses who processed him were very courteous and professional. When he was done, they advised him he was to return once each week to repeat the process. As he left the clinic, he wondered how many women his sperm would impregnate and how many children would eventually bear his resemblance.

Lucinda had accompanied him to the clinic and was waiting for him in the reception area when he got out. She had promised that she'd take him to lunch and then for some sightseeing. Peter hadn't seen much of the city up close and was curious as to how the general population lived. The restaurant she chose was the Satellite Café. It had many American dishes on the menu which made him feel right at home. They both ordered chile dogs, french fries, and cherry cokes. While they were eating he asked her if the toxins in the atmosphere had affected her in any way. She said they had.

"Fortunately, Shisk is a domed city."

"Domed?"

"Yes, there is a huge air dome over the city that keeps out the toxic air. Filtered air is constantly pumped into the city and the air pressure keeps the air dome inflated."

"Really. I couldn't tell there was a dome over the city."

"It's transparent and with the grey sky above, it's nearly invisible."

"Does anyone live outside the city?"

"Yes, but they have to stay indoors or wear breathers."

"Breathers?"

"It's a mask with a filter attachment that removes the toxins in the air."

"So, are all the cities of Tarizon domed?"

"No, just a few cities in each province."

"How many provinces are there?"

"There are seven on the continent of Turvin where Shisk is located and twenty-four more on all five continents, so I would estimate maybe a hundred domed cities on the planet."

He nodded.

Lucinda continued,"Domes are difficult to build and expensive to maintain. You can't imagine how much air is inside a dome and how difficult it is to keep it filtered."

"Right."

They continued to talk during lunch, and when they were done eating they headed for the subtram. Lucinda said she wanted to take Peter to the Shisk Museum of Political History. She told him it housed the original copy of the Supreme Mandate and the World Proclamation. When they reached the subtram station, Lucinda punched in some numbers and swiped her ledger card. After a minute the door opened and they stepped inside. There was a slight sensation of movement but it was barely noticeable.

"We could really use a subtram system like this in Dallas. I wonder why your government hasn't shared this technology?"

Lucinda shrugged. "I don't know. You don't have a good public transportation system?"

Peter shook his head. "No, it takes us much longer to get around in our big—"

The subtram suddenly bucked, lurched, and started vibrating violently. There was a jerk, then it came to a screeching halt slamming them hard against the side panel. Lucinda screamed as they first hit the wall and then fell backward on top of each other.

"What the—" Peter said, rubbing the back of his head where it had struck the hard surface. It was swelling and pain was shooting into his neck and shoulders. Lucinda was moaning.

"Are you okay?" she asked as she struggled to her feet.   "Nothing a half a bottle of aspirin won't fix," Peter replied. "What happened?"

"I don't know. I've never known a subtram to malfunction."

Lucinda opened the control panel on the right side of the door and punched some numbers on a keypad. She waited but nothing happened. She tried again and then looked at Peter and shrugged. "We'll have to wait for help to arrive. It shouldn't be long."

Looking around the interior of the subtram Peter noticed an escape hatch near the top. He pointed to it. Lucinda glanced at it and shook her head. "No, it wouldn't be wise to go outside. We don't know where we are."

Peter smiled and said, "You mean we might be in a bad neighborhood?"

Lucinda nodded. "That and parts of the city have been quarantined due to a virus."

"A virus. You have viruses here too?"

"Yes, the toxins in the air weaken the immune system. Viruses spread like bad news."

Peter took a deep breath and shook his head. "Wonderful. So, how long do you think it will take them to find us?"

"Not long. I'm sure they were monitoring us."

They waited for awhile in silence but no one showed up. Lucinda looked worried, so Peter took her hand in his and squeezed it in a reassuring gesture. She smiled and said, "I don't understand this. They must know the subtram has stopped. An alarm must be blinking somewhere."

"Maybe whoever is running the system today is sleeping on the job."

"No. That's not possible."

After it seemed they'd been trapped in the subtram for over a kyloon, Peter pointed to the trap door again. Lucinda shrugged and said,

"Okay, can you boost me up there."

Peter nodded and cupped his hands making a foothold. Lucinda put her hands on Peter's shoulders and he lifted her up to the ceiling. The trap door opened easily and she pushed it aside. He gave her a heave and she pulled herself up through the trap door and disappeared. A few moments later she reappeared at the trap door and said, "I'm going to throw down a rail. I think if you wedge it against the wall you can climb up high enough to reach the ceiling. Then I can help pull you through."

Peter nodded and stood to the side while she tossed down the rail. It made a loud clanging noise when it hit the floor of the subtram. After wedging it between the wall and the floor, Peter tried to climb it rapidly and grab the edge of the trap door, but it gave way and he fell hard to the floor. Lucinda cringed at Peter's plight. Luckily he wasn't seriously hurt, so he scrambled to his feet and tried again. This time he took more time to be sure the rail was wedged securely and he was able to climb high enough to grab onto the edge of the trap door. Lucinda immediately grabbed his wrists and helped pull him up and through the small opening.

Once outside the subtram, Peter realized they were on an elevated trestle high above the city. A pungent odor hung in the air. Lucinda pointed to a metal ladder that was built into the column supporting the beam. It led to the city far below. They looked in every direction searching for rescuers but saw nothing. After awhile they decided they had no choice but to climb down to the city, so they began to descend the ladder welded to the side of the column. As they got close to the ground sounds began to filter up to them—voices, music, traffic, sirens, and a dog barking.

"You have dogs here on Tarizon?" Peter asked.

"No. We have an animal that looks like a dog. It's called a *rhutz*."

"Ruts?"

"Rhutzzz."

"Do you have one?"

"No. They don't usually like people. They're only tolerated because they control the rodent population and the holy man Sandee used to have one as a pet."

"Really. So, if they are so dangerous, why did he have one?"

"It's a long story. I'll tell it to you later. Right now we better concentrate on getting home."

53

"Is that American music I'm hearing?" Peter asked.

"Yes, the Earth children are addicted to it. The Central Authority doesn't like it but they tolerate it since it makes the Earth children happy."

When they reached the ground they found themselves on a busy street. Lucinda started walking and Peter followed close behind her. As Peter began to focus on the people that were walking by, he noticed they were dirty, poorly dressed, and looked sickly. He cringed as a man walked by with a limp extra arm coming out of his stomach. Many of the men and women had huge warts and giant pimples on their faces. Lucinda looked back at Peter with a worried look on her face.

"Do you know where we are?" Peter asked.

"No. She said. I'm looking for a communication post so I can call for help."

"What do they look like?"

"Like one of your telephone booths but silver colored with a VC monitor."

We walked on but saw nothing resembling a communication post. After awhile Peter felt eyes on them. They must have stuck out like tall mushrooms in green grass with their clean white clothing and black sandals. Peter looked around and made eye contact with a rough looking group of men across the street. Then he noticed what looked like a very large German Shepard following them. It was salmon colored with yellowish brown eyes.

"Has this ever happened to you before?" Peter asked in a low voice.

"No. This is very strange. Central Authority should have picked us up by now."

"Is that a rhutz?" Peter asked.

Lucinda turned and stared at the wild-eyed creature following them. "Yes."

"It looks a lot like a dog," Peter said. "I can't believe it doesn't like people."

Lucinda frowned. "Don't mess with it. If it thinks you are a threat it will attack you. I've heard of people being killed when they encountered a stray rhutz."

"I just want to pet it. I had a dog like that once, until someone poisoned her."

"Poisoned her?"

"Why?"

"One of my father's enemies trying to scare him, I guess."

Lucinda shook her head. "Evil is just part of human nature, I guess. Most of us are strong enough to resist it but some are weak and inevitably will succumb to it," she said, hesitating as they approached a noisy tavern. It was called the Mighty Jolly and they could hear much laughter inside. She looked back at Peter and said, "Maybe in here someone can call Central Authority."

Peter put his arm on her shoulder. "I don't think going in a bar in this part of town would be wise. Let's find a restaurant or a public building."

Lucinda nodded and started to move on down the street. Peter looked into the bar as he walked by. A small man sitting on a bar stool saw him and motioned to Peter to come in. Peter stopped and stared at the little man. Lucinda turned and said, "What's wrong? Why are you stopping?"

Peter shrugged. "Some dude wants me to come inside."

"What?" Lucinda said as she hurried back to the door of the bar. She looked at the man who was now waving frantically for them to come inside. Lucinda looked at Peter.

"Well, I guess it won't hurt to talk to him," she said and then stepped inside the tavern. Peter looked back and saw the rhutz just a few feet behind him. It looked so much like his old dog, he knelt down, extended his hand, and said, "Here boy."

Lucinda gasped when she turned back and saw Peter kneeling before the rhutz. The rhutz bared his teeth and growled at him. Peter withdrew his hand, stood up, and looked at Lucinda. She shook her head, turned, and started to go toward the little man, but he had disappeared. She looked around and not seeing him went straight to the lady bartender who was dressed in tight leather-looking pants and a gold blouse. Her bright yellow hair had purple highlights that clashed with her pale green eyes. Peter joined them unconsciously staring at the woman's odd appearance. He couldn't understand a word they were saying so he just smiled at her.

When the conversation ended, Lucinda said, "She doesn't want to call Central Authority because if they came here they'd bust up the joint and cause her a lot of grief. She said there was a communication port three blocks east of here.

Peter looked around at the room full of strange people most of whom were now staring at them. He nodded and said, "Let's go, then."

When they turned to leave a large muscular man stepped in front of them. He was flanked by the midget who had lured them into the tavern. For a moment Peter thought his eyes were out of focus. The man seemed to have three heads and six eyes. Peter blinked several times but the image didn't change. He glanced over at Lucinda and noticed her mouth had dropped open. The three-headed mutant gave Peter a once over and said, "Hi there, laddie. You must be Peter Turner."

Lucinda gasped and looked at Peter. Peter shrugged. "Yeah, but how—"

The man extended his hand. "I'm Threebeard. I hope your little subtram mishap didn't cause you any alarm."

It was clear where the name Threebeard had come from. The man had three chins each with a little clump of hair at the end. His three heads were not separate and distinct but three heads joined together below the ears. His three pairs of bright blue-green eyes had red pupils that moved in different directions. The sight gave Peter the creeps and caused him to break out in gooseflesh. Threebeard had just one wide nose and a single long mouth covering not less than forty pearl white teeth. Peter reluctantly shook the mutant's hand and asked, "So, you stopped the subtram?"

"Yes, I'm sorry to intrude on your evening, but there was no other way for us to meet."

Lucinda frowned and said, "Central Authority is going to be quite distressed that someone sabotaged a subtram. I hope you're prepared to spend the next twenty days in a labor camp."

Threebeard laughed and replied, "I don't think so. After you got out, I sent it on its way and rewrote the history file so that this stop will never show up in any record."

"How did you manage that?" Lucinda asked.

"Well as they say on Earth, three heads are better than one, right?" Everyone in the bar had crowded around them now and laughed heartily at Threebeard's joke. "I'm what you call on Earth, a genius."

Peter swallowed hard. "So, what do you want with us? And how did you know we would be out on the subtram today?" he asked.

Threebeard dug into his coat pocket and pulled out a small laptop computer. He held it out and said, "I make it my regular business to tap into Central Authority's computer and monitor traffic in and out of the capital city. I had noticed your name on the roster for Earth Shuttle 21 and was surprised to see an Earth alien aboard."

"Not as surprised as I was." Peter noted. "So, what do you want from me?"

Peter looked around at Threebeard's entourage who seemed to be listening intently to the conversation. He wondered if any of them spoke English and knew what they were talking about. They seemed to laugh at the right times, so some of them must have spoken English, he thought. Threebeard seemed to pull the question out of Peter's mind and replied, "No, they don't understand a word we are saying, but some of them can read your mind."

Peter winced and looked around at the faces that were staring intently at him. "Ah. . . Where did you learn to speak English?" he asked.

"Watching American movies for cycles on end. It's so generous of your cable companies to broadcast them into the airwaves so we can download them into our video converters."

"The signal makes it all the way to Tarizon? There's no way."

"True enough, but our shuttles record everything that is transmitted while they are on Earth. All I have to do is tap into their systems and the information is mine."

Peter nodded. "Don't the shuttle computers have security against unauthorized entry?"

"Sure, but nothing that I can't penetrate."

There was general laughter again. Peter looked around amused. He was starting to like Threebeard. Lucinda, on the other hand was getting more nervous by the minute.

"That's pretty impressive," Peter said.

"Yes, and I speak all thirty-one of the languages and dialects spoken on Tarizon. As you say on Earth, I'm a quick learner." There was laughter again.

"That's really amazing. But you still haven't told me what you want?"

"Videl Lai tried to kill you just as soon as you got off the shuttle. That piqued my curiosity."

"What? What are you talking about?"

"They erased your memory so you wouldn't know it happened."

"Who erased my memory?" Peter said irritably. "You're not making any sense."

"Remember your friend, Jimmy Falk?" Threebeard asked.

"Yeah. I had lunch with him when we got off the shuttle."

"He's dead. Videl Lai had him murdered along with thirty-two other passengers from Earth Shuttle 21."

"Jimmy is dead?"

"Yes, I'm sorry to say he is and the only reason you aren't is that someone is protecting you."

"Who is protecting me and why does Videl Lai want me dead? Who the hell is he anyway?"

Threebeard ignored his questions still sizing him up. Peter was visibly shaken by all that Threebeard had thrown at him. Lucinda put her arm around him and held him tightly. "I've been with Peter since he arrived on the subtram," she protested. "Nobody has tried to kill him."

"It happened right after he got off the ship. Peter didn't come with the others, did he? He was personally escorted to the subtram. I believe you were expressly told to watch out for Peter, weren't you?"

"Well, yes," Lucinda admitted. "That's true, but—"

"You're the head guide, aren't you? Don't you usually make your own assignments?"

Lucinda thought about it for a minute and then realized what Threebeard was saying was true. She wasn't usually told who to pair up with. That was left to her discretion.

"Everyone seems to think you're *the one*," Threebeard continued looking Peter directly in the eyes. "You must be. You were the only Earth alien on Shuttle 21 that could possibly be him. I think you are surely him, but I must be absolutely sure."

"The one? What one?" Peter asked, feeling very confused.

Threebeard looked at his entourage expectantly. They all gave him a blank look in return. He said, "There is an old Prophecy:

When the sun and the moons align,
amongst the Earth children will come
one wise and pure in heart.
A man of humble birth,
who'll tame the savage rhutz,
unite those who'd have liberty
and justice restored to Tarizon,
and rid it of its evil tyrant.
Known as The Liberator,
he'll restore the Supreme Mandate
and free from bondage
The Mutants, Seafolken, and Nanomites.

Peter started to laugh but then realized Threebeard was dead serious. Lucinda looked at Peter with a look of wonder in her eyes. Peter felt uncomfortable and replied, "Ah. . . . I hate to disappoint you, but you've got the wrong guy. I'm no Liberator or whatever, I promise you. I'm just a poor high school kid who got on the wrong bus."

Threebeard gave Peter one of his long smiles and replied, "You are modest like the Prophecy says. I detect too that you do indeed have a pure heart. It is said that like Sandee Brahn, the Liberator will tame the savage rhutz and they will walk together in triumph. I noticed there was a rhutz outside following you."

Peter looked toward the door. The rhutz was peering into the tavern. "Yeah, well he's not exactly tame," he said. "In fact, he almost bit my hand off."

"Well, only time will tell, but I do believe I have met the Liberator. Yes, I'm sure of it."

Lucinda gave Peter another look but Peter could only think about the fact that someone was trying to kill him and that Jimmy was already dead! He looked around the bar at all the strange faces. He felt sick. All he wanted to do was get the hell out of there. He forced a smile and said, "It was a pleasure to meet you Threebeard. I suppose we'd better get back on the subtram before we are missed. I'd hate for anyone to get hurt on account of our disappearance."

Threebeard bowed and then stepped aside. Lucinda walked past him and Peter turned to leave. "When you accept your destiny—the fact that you *are* the Liberator—I am your loyal servant," Threebeard said. "Come to me to summon your army. We will be waiting to follow you to victory."

Threebeard's words sent icy shivers through Peter. He stumbled out of the Tavern and walked briskly in the direction of the communication station. Lucinda had to run to keep up. He looked back at the tavern and shook his head in utter disbelief over his encounter with Threebeard. He noticed the rhutz again following him, studying him, sizing him up like Threebeard had done. He continued to walk nervously, wondering if his life was really in danger or if Threebeard was back in the tavern having a good laugh at how he had terrorized an Earth alien.

As they walked, Peter couldn't help but notice the poverty, disease, and desperation of the neighborhood they were in. Lucinda saw the repulsion on his face. "It wasn't always this way," she said. "Before the great eruptions there were no slums in Shisk, few mutants, and the Nanomites and Seafolken were free."

"Really? The volcanoes really did screw up your world."

"Indeed. It was Videl and his followers who used the calamity to subvert the Supreme Mandate."

"Who is he, anyway? Threebeard never said."

"He's the Vice-Chancellor—a very powerful man that you don't want as an enemy. Some say he is plotting to take over the government."

"So, what about this Prophecy? Did you know about it?"

"Yes, everyone knows about it, but not everyone believes it."

"That's good news. Not everyone on this planet is insane."

When they got to the communication station, Lucinda punched some numbers on the console and said something into the receiver. When she was done she took a deep breath and said, "It won't be long now. They've sent someone to pick us up."

As they were waiting Peter noticed a gang of menacing looking thugs coming out of the shadows. They had clubs and knives and didn't look the least bit friendly. He nudged Lucinda and she looked up and gasped at the sight of them. Before they could react they were surrounded and the menacing mob was closing in on them. As the noose tightened the mob started chanting something which upset Lucinda greatly. She began screaming at them. A man in a shabby dark cloak pulled a knife and stuck it in front of Peter's face narrowly missing his cheek.

Suddenly a growling sound came from behind them. The man turned around but it was too late. The rhutz came at him so fast he didn't have time to defend himself. The teeth of the rhutz sank deep into the thug's groin. He let out a scream of intense pain and struggled to free himself of the vicious animal but with no success.

The other thugs watched with their mouths open as dark red blood squirted in every direction around them. Finally the rhutz let go and the man fell to the ground, rocking back and fourth, holding himself, and moaning in great agony. When the rhutz beared his teeth at the rest of the mob, they all turned and scattered in every direction. When Peter and Lucinda were alone again, Peter made eye contact with the rhutz. In his mind he thanked him silently for saving their lives. The rhutz lowered his head almost like a nod and then laid down. In the corner of his eye, Peter saw Threebeard looking at him from across the street. When their eyes met, Threebeard gave Peter a toothy grin, turned, and walked away.

In the distance there was the sound of an approaching aircraft. It was sort of like the sound of a helicopter but steadier—like a harsh wind. The sound intensified and suddenly a black object appeared with blue and red flashing lights. It hovered overhead for a moment and then dropped down to the street. Two soldiers jumped out of a side door and motioned for them to come aboard. They followed them and climbed inside. As they were about to leave, Peter looked at the rhutz. It was standing now watching them. Peter put two fingers in his mouth and whistled.

"Come on boy! Let's go," he said.

The rhutz hesitated and the soldiers started to close the hatch. Peter put his hand on the door to give the rhutz one last chance to jump in. This time the rhutz sprang to its feet and ran toward them. It jumped through the door, narrowly making it before it closed. One of the soldiers pointed his gun at the rhutz, but Peter put his hand on the muzzle and shook his head.

The rhutz backed away into a corner. Everyone stared at it. Peter knew having a rhutz as a pet on Tarizon would be the equivalent of running around with a pet wolf in Dallas. Most people would feel uneasy with such a beast lurking about and they'd wonder about the pet's master as well. It was the Prophecy that was on his mind, though. Would this rhutz befriend him? He'd already saved his life and jumped into a helicopter on his command. It seemed definitely within the realm of possibility.

Peter walked slowly over to where the rhutz was standing and sat down next to it. The rhutz looked at him warily and then inched itself closer. Peter extended his hand and the rhutz began to sniff it. A moment later the rhutz let him touch the back of its neck. Soon he was petting it gingerly.

"That a boy," He said smiling up at Lucinda. "We *are* going to be friends after all. You had me wondering there for minute."

Lucinda shook her head. "What are you going to feed it?"

Peter shrugged. "I don't think we'll have to worry about that. It's been taking care of itself for a long time, I suspect. There are probably plenty of rodents in our sector of the city. If not, he can live off of our table scraps."

It was late when they got back to their compartment. They were both hungry and exhausted from their ordeal. They ordered Chinese this time and then readied a place for Peter's new friend to sleep. By that time they'd determined the rhutz was female. When they'd finished, Lucinda asked, "What are you going to call her?"

That was a good question. She'd need a name."

"Remember Threebeard said the rhutz walked with Sandee Brahn? Maybe you should call her Sandee."

Peter nodded and replied, "I don't know, some may think it disrespectful to name an animal after a holy man. Let's see what else would be good? . . .Let me see. . . . Killer . . . Rambo?"

"Rambo?" Lucinda asked. "Where have I heard that name?"

"You know, Sylvester Stallone? Vietnam? You must have seen the movie when you lived on Earth."

"Right, I vaguely remember it."

"Nah. Rambo doesn't quite fit. How about Rin Tin Tin?"

"Rin Tin Tin?"

"He was a famous American dog that starred in the movies back in the 30s."

"Hmm. Rhin Tin means *iron jaw* in Tari."

"Rhin Tin. Hmm. That's cool," Peter replied. "We can call her Rhin for short?"

Lucinda nodded her approval. They both looked over at the rhutz to see if there was any reaction to her new name. She was sniffing and poking around the blankets that were to be her new bed. Finally she laid down and looked at them. She seemed satisfied with the choice. "What do you think, girl? Is Rhin okay?"

Suddenly he felt a strange sensation in his head. He rubbed his forehead. It wasn't a bad feeling, just different than anything he'd ever experienced. He looked at Rhin who was now asleep.

"I think she likes her new name," Lucinda said. "She'll be a good companion for the Liberator."

Peter rolled his eyes. "So, you were going to tell me how Sandee Brahn and rhutz became friends."

"Oh, yes. Well, when Sandee was a boy he lived with his parents in Lecton which is part of northern Azallo. They were poor farmers who barely survived in the barren land that is characteristic of that part of the world. Sandee was eleven years old and had no brothers and sisters. He had to hike many kylods every day to go to school and when he returned home in the afternoon there were many chores to be done before he could have dinner and go to bed.

"It was a time of near anarchy in Lecton. It was at war with its neighbor Serie. Soldiers from both sides often raided each other's territory and plundered and pillaged everything in their path. One day the Brahn farm was overrun and Sandee's parents were murdered. Sandee himself would have been killed except that he was on an errand for his father when the soldiers came. When he returned home, he'd lost everything that was precious to him.

"Unknown to Sandee the soldiers had left two men behind to be sure they'd taken everything of value. When these men saw Sandee they vowed to kill the last witness to their murderous venture, but God had other plans. Upon seeing the men Sandee fled along the river trying to outrun them, but they were stronger and faster and soon overtook him. This is when the rhutz appeared. He came out of the brush and nearly ripped off one of the soldier's legs. The other soldier tried to shoot the rhutz but couldn't get a clear shot. He finally decided to flee while he had the chance, but after the rhutz finished off the first soldier he went for the second. The second soldier never had a chance.

"This is when God appeared to Sandee who was lying on the bank of the river in great shock and sorrow over the death of his parents. God told Sandee that he'd been one of many victims of the evil that was choking Tarizon. He told him He wanted him to bring peace and justice to Tarizon and that He would give him the strength and power to do it. Of course, this eleven year old boy was shocked and confused at this and nobody believed him at first when he told them God had spoken to him, but the rhutz stayed with him and became a constant companion. This odd and wondrous sight of a small boy protected by the savage rhutz gave many pause. There were other miracles too and within a few years it was clear that God was indeed with this boy and he quickly became renowned for his intelligence and wisdom."

"Wow. That's quite a story," Peter said. "I wish God had talked to me. It would have made all of this a lot easier to accept."

"I don't know, you'd still wonder if it was really God who had spoken to you or just your imagination."

Peter nodded. "That's true."

"Whether God talked to you or not the fact that you walk with a rhutz will make many people believe you are the Liberator."

There was a long silence while Peter and Lucinda contemplated this. Eventually Lucinda got up to go to bed. She was dressed in a short white gown that exposed her perfect legs. Peter had been eying them all night barely able to keep his hands off them. Peter jumped up and followed her to the door to her bedroom. "Wait," he said breathlessly. She turned and looked at him expectantly. As he gazed into her alluring eyes he took her hand and pulled her next to him. They kissed passionately.

When he finally let her go, she gave him a wry smile. "It's about time, cowboy. You had me worried there for awhile."

Peter didn't understand exactly what Lucinda meant by her comment, but he didn't much care. All he knew was that his yearning for her was over. She had made it clear she wanted him. Tonight she would be his lover and he was going to make it a night neither would ever forget.

10
Embracing His Destiny

Two weeks went by before Peter got confirmation of his permanent assignment. He was to report the next morning to Robert Garcia's office in the Hall of the Interpreters. As Garcia had promised, he was to be an intern on his staff. Later that week his quarters would change as well to Garcia's home. It was all so unreal—particularly after his visit with Threebeard and being told he was supposedly some sort of Liberator.

Much to his delight Lucinda had stayed with him the entire time. They were very happy and getting closer each day. He dreaded the thought of having to leave her soon. It was his intention to ask Robert Garcia if Lucinda could come to stay with him at his home. His daughter Lorin had said they had plenty of room. He feared he was pushing his luck, but he didn't figure it could hurt to ask. Unfortunately, the issue became moot.

Rhin had been at his side every minute since she'd followed him out of Shisk's mutant sector, except for an occasional absence when Peter suspected she was hunting for food. At meals he'd always offer her some of his scraps, of course. Sometimes she'd snatch the offered snack and other times she'd sniff it and then walk away. Her health seemed good and, in fact, her pale salmon coat seemed to brighten each day. Peter certainly enjoyed the company and prayed it wouldn't be a problem having Rhin when he went to live with Councillor Garcia.

Lucinda had gone for a doctor's appointment that morning and when she returned she informed Peter she had good news. "I'm pregnant!" she said. "Isn't that fabulous?"

It was a good thing Peter was sitting down when she gave him the news. The thought of her getting pregnant hadn't crossed his mind. He assumed in this advanced society that they would have some kind of birth control. Then it dawned on him—it was probably illegal to use birth control.

"Wow! You're pregnant," he repeated, trying to show some enthusiasm.

"Yes, I'm so happy. I've wanted a child for so long and now you've given me one. Thank you, Peter," she said as she bent down to kiss him.

"This is great, but what about my new assignment? I won't be able to see you or the baby."

She smiled, "You're so sweet. Don't worry, you can come visit us when you come back."

Peter frowned. "That's not exactly the kind of relationship I want to have with my child and the woman I love."

Lucinda gave him a sympathetic smile and replied, "Peter, you knew I was only going to be with you a short time. I have to go back to my mate."

Her words hit Peter like a brick. "Your mate? You mean you're married?"

"No. We don't have marriage on Tarizon. I was assigned a mate and I must return to him. We'll raise the child you've given us."

"What do you mean assigned? Was your marriage arranged?"

"In a way, but not by my family. All the people of Tarizon are mated by Central Authority. At age fourteen all men and women go through extensive testing and the results are imputed into a mating data bank. The data is then analyzed and categorized so that people can be matched for both physical, genetic, and emotional compatibility. It has worked very well. My mate and I get along quite well. We like the same sports and entertainment, we have similar backgrounds, so it's all very comfortable. "

"What about love?"

"Love? That's the instinctive feeling a parent has for its child. It's not necessary for the purpose of mating. The Central Authority frowns on love between mates. It's illogical, unhealthy, and often causes conflict—even crime sometimes."

Peter sensed Lucinda was giving him a rehearsed speech. He thought it was sickening and was sure it had been programmed into her mind by one of those accelerated learning programs provided by Central Authority. He shook his head in dismay.

"So, your mate couldn't get you pregnant so you shacked up with me? Is that it?"

"I didn't think you'd mind. You seemed to enjoy my company and my body."

"Why didn't you just go to the sperm bank? Your mate couldn't have been happy about you spending time with me."

"He was glad I found someone who could make me pregnant. He felt badly that he couldn't do it himself. It's very expensive to go to the sperm bank since there are so few good donors on Tarizon. The waiting list is quite long. Only the very wealthy or politically connected are able to get prime sperm."

"So, you have no feelings for me? When I leave tomorrow, you'll forget all about me?"

"No," Lucinda said. "I do care about you. Our time together has been . . . dreamlike, but there is nothing I can do. I'm forbidden to leave my mate."

"Forbidden? You mean there's no divorce or separation on Tarizon?"

She nodded. "No, once you're mated, you are required to live with your mate until you die."

Lucinda's explanation of family law on Tarizon shocked and angered him. How could a society exist without love? It totally blew his mind and he dreaded the idea that one day he would be mated with a stranger as well. He wondered if Earth was headed in this same direction with the divorce rate skyrocketing and family values falling into the dumpster. He thought of the ever-strengthening United Nations and shrinkage of the world through technology. Is this where Earth was headed—a central all-knowing, all-powerful, tyrannical government? He shuddered to think of it.

Their little spat that night made leaving Lucinda a little easier. He gave her a kiss and a polite hug and then he was off with Rhin to the Hall of the Interpreters. When they got off the subtram he was met by a tall black man in a white uniform. It had a blue and green insignia on it which Peter had never seen before, but assumed had something to do with the Council of Interpreters. The man introduced himself as Brille Rama. The man reached for his weapon when he saw the rhutz behind Peter. Peter screamed, "No! She's with me. Don't hurt her."

The man frowned and said, "You can't bring a rhutz into the Hall of Interpreters!"

"She's tame. She won't hurt anybody."

Peter didn't know that for sure, but he felt like he could control Rhin. Since the first day they'd hooked up she had obeyed his every command, although Peter wasn't sure how she even understood him. She just seemed to know what Peter wanted her to do and would do it immediately.

Rhin sat and looked up at the man with her tongue hanging out and her tail wagging furiously. A grin came over the man's face and he said, "I'll have to check with the Councillor. It will be his decision."

Peter nodded and Brille led them down several blocks until they were in front of what looked like a thousand stairs leading up to an enormous round marble building with a huge statute in front of it. Lucinda had brought him there before, so he knew this was the Hall of the Interpreters and that the statute was that of Sandee Brahn.

Peter was about to start climbing the stairs when Brille pointed to a sunken staircase and began walking toward it. At the bottom of the stairs was an elevator door. Brille stuck his thumb on the control panel next to the door and it opened. They went inside and within seconds were exiting into a long corridor that led to a large rotunda full of people milling around, apparently waiting for something or somebody. Peter asked Brille what was going on and he told him interested parties were gathering to listen to oral arguments for the council's morning session. He said they needed to hurry because the Councillor wanted to talk to him before the session began.

Brille brought them to a door with a sentry posted out front. The sentry saluted and then let Brille and Peter pass through the door. He stepped in front of Rhin and shook his head. "Animals are not allowed in the building."

"She's okay," Peter protested. "She goes wherever I go."

The sentry shook his head again and showed no sign of changing his mind, so Peter said, "Well, can she wait here with you until we talk to the Councillor? If not, I'll have to take her home and then come back. The Councillor won't like that. He's expecting me right now."

The sentry took a deep breath and then nodded. "If she gives me

68

any trouble, I'll have to shoot her."

"Don't worry," Peter said confidently. "She'll be good."

Peter turned to Rhin and started to tell her to stay, but realized she already knew what he wanted her to do. In fact, she had already laid down next to the sentry like she was his best friend. Peter smiled, turned, and followed Brille into the offices of Councillor Robert Garcia. The offices were spacious and lavishly decorated. A receptionist told them to wait and pointed to a thickly cushioned bench of what looked like white satin. They sat and waited. It wasn't but a few moments before the receptionist showed them into Garcia's office. They exchanged greetings and took a seat at a small crystal conference table. Brille remained for the meeting.

"Peter. So good to see you again. I only have a few moments before our morning session, but I just wanted to greet you and tell you a little more about what I expect from you as an intern."

"Yes, that would be helpful."

"I understand you brought a rhutz with you?"

"Yes, sorry about that, but she won't let me go anywhere without her."

"That is quite amazing. I haven't heard of a rhutz bonding with a human. They usually stay clear of people. That's one of the reasons we tolerate them."

"Her name is Rhin, " Peter said. "She saved my life and seems to have become quite attached to me. I had a dog on Earth when I was younger. Rhin reminds me a lot of her. She died when I was quite young. I would really like to keep Rhin, if I could. She's been very obedient and no trouble since I've had her."

"Well, as long as she stays that way; but if she causes any trouble, you'll have to send her back to wherever she came from."

"She won't be, I promise," Peter assured him.

The Councillor nodded to Brille and said, "Bring in the rhutz, I'm anxious to see her." Brille left to get Rhin and the Councillor continued, "I understand they are telepathic."

"Telepathic? Really? I wondered about that. She seems to know what I want her to do immediately after the thought comes into my mind."

"Yes, our holy leader, Sandee Brahn, had a rhutz that followed him everywhere he traveled. Legend has it that the rhutz helped him greatly in his successful unification of the planet."

"Yes, so I heard." Peter replied.

"It is said that a great liberator will one day come to Tarizon and that he will be followed by a rhutz who will be instrumental in liberating the Mutants, Seafolken and Nanomites who are in bondage."

"Right. I heard about that too." Peter told him about his encounter with Threebeard.

"Yes. I know of him. It is said he has three brains and working together it's like having twenty-seven. Not only is he telepathic but telekinetic as well. They say he may be the smartest and wisest man on Tarizon. Unfortunately, I've never met him, but I certainly would like to some day."

"He said I was welcome to visit him anytime," Peter laughed. "I'm sure he'd be honored to meet you."

"Well, maybe one day I'll have you arrange a meeting."

"Yeah, I'd be happy to. He really likes me. He thinks I might be this Liberator you're talking about. That's a laugh, huh?"

The Councillor raised his eyebrows, "You, the Liberator? He told you that?"

"Yeah, on account of the fact that someone tried to kill me just after I arrived on Tarizon. I don't remember it, but apparently the people who saved my life erased my memory."

"Well, perhaps you *are* this Liberator. Only time will tell, I guess."

"No. It's not me. I know next to nothing about Tarizon."

"I don't believe that, Peter. You have already learned more about Tarizon in just the few days you've been here than many Tarizonians have learned in their lifetime. The Central Authority doesn't include history in its curriculum."

Peter frowned. "Why not?"

"These are difficult days on Tarizon and I believe the Central Authority would rather people not remember when times were good. Such memories could breed insurrection."

"Hmm. Well, I'm sure I'm not this Liberator. I'd know it if I were."

"Well, as I said. Only time will tell . . . but let me tell you why I have enlisted you into my service. As I said, all is not well on Tarizon. Even though the great volcanic eruptions were long ago, our world is still in turmoil. There are those who would like to use this turmoil as an excuse to seize complete control of Tarizon and rule it for their own advantage. Of course, that would be the end of the Supreme Mandate and all the protections it affords."

"You mean Videl Lai. Lucinda, my guide, told me about him. Threebeard thinks he's the one who tried to kill me. I guess a lot of people died at the space port the night I arrived. I was lucky someone was there to protect me. I wonder who it was and why they chose to save me?"

"Actually, Peter. It was me."

"You?"

"Yes. We had intelligence that Videl was going to kill anyone coming off Earth Shuttle 21 who could possibly be the Liberator. We couldn't protect everyone, so we had to pick one person to protect. That turned out to be you."

"Really?" Peter replied skeptically. "It was you?"

"Not just me. The Loyalists. An organization pledged to preserve the Supreme Mandate."

"Wow! I guess it was my lucky day. . . . Thank you. I'll forever be in your debt. I'm curious, though. Why did you erase my memory? And how do you do that, anyway?"

"You were already under so much stress having been abruptly taken from your family and brought to Tarizon. We were afraid seeing your friend murdered and other passengers gunned down right in front of you, might be more than your could handle. You were too important to our movement to take a chance on anything happening to you, mentally or physically. And as far as erasing your memory, its too complicated to explain so suffice it say we have developed a beam of blue light that can kill surface memory molecules so that anyone exposed to it will forget what has happened a short span of time. We have to be careful using the device as too big a dose can cause brain damage. "

"Huh. . . . I still don't understand why you'd pick someone from Earth to be the Liberator."

"Actually we didn't pick you. You were described in the Prophecy and those who want to control Tarizon also have plans for Earth. If they gain control here, they may want to conquer Earth as well."

71

Peter was taken aback. It hadn't occurred to him that Earth would be in danger, but what the Councillor said made sense. "Control Earth! Is that true?"

"Yes, I'm afraid so," the Councillor said and sighed. "I don't have much time, but I suppose I should briefly tell you how the Repopulation Project got started. It will help you understand how your father got involved in it and how you ended up on Tarizon. Then, perhaps, you'll understand why its not surprising to us that you would turn out to be the Liberator."

Peter swallowed hard. "Go on. I'm listening."

"It was my father who was selected to contact the authorities on Earth to seek their assistance in preserving human life as we knew it on Tarizon. The great eruptions had so poisoned the planet that human life could scarcely exist anymore. Fortunately, we were a very advanced society and were able to use our technology to survive. We built great domed cities and moved a good deal of the population into these safe havens. Of course, we couldn't fit everyone in the cities, so millions were left unprotected. Most died but some survived and over the cycles adapted to Tarizon's now toxic atmosphere. These were the Mutants—human in name only. They lived outside the cities in anarchy and chaos.

"Within the cities the Central Authority remained in control and the Supreme Mandate was still the law; however, there was a great division over how to deal with the Mutants and how to preserve human life as it existed prior to the cataclysmic eruptions. The Purists, the group that is now led by Videl Lai, wanted to exterminate the Mutants as the only practical way to keep them from overwhelming the cities and eventually overrunning them."

"Oh, my God!" Peter gasped. "You mean kill them? All of them?"

"Yes, they wanted to kill millions of innocent people."

Do they still think that's the answer. Is that what Videl Lai wants?"

"Oh, yes and if Videl obtains power, that will no doubt be one of his first priorities, so millions of lives are at stake."

Peter shook his head in dismay, feeling for the first time the weight of responsibility that was being placed on his shoulders. They expected him to somehow stop Videl Lai!

The Councillor continued. " This of course was only one of the problems they faced. The other was the rapidly declining population of healthy, non-mutated humans. The Purists believed that the answer to that problem was Earth. They demanded Earth's immediate conquest and colonization."

"Conquer Earth? Could they do that?"

"We have vastly superior technology. It might be possible. It would depend a lot on how it was done, but Videl Lai is very cunning; he just might be able to do it."

"Anyway, with Earth under Tarizon's control there would be millions of healthy humans to repopulate Tarizon as its ecology recovered.

"The Loyalists, the group that supports Chancellor Bassett Alls, argued it was illegal under the Supreme Mandate and immoral to kill human beings just because they were different and no longer pure by their definition. They proposed reentry into the mutant regions by TGA forces to restore order and organize a civilian government to rule the mutants. Of course, this was a massive undertaking and would take many days to accomplish.

"As far as the colonization of Earth the Loyalists opposed it as again, being illegal under the Supreme Mandate, and immoral in the eyes of God.

"There was a long bitter battle over these issues, but eventually the Loyalists prevailed. Troops were sent out of the domes to restore order and reestablish a viable government that could deal with the problems of the Mutants. In order to prevail on this issue, however, the Loyalists were forced to compromise on the issue of the colonization of Earth. They agreed, rather than to try to conquer Earth, to send diplomatic envoys to the nations of Earth to seek their help in preserving human life on Tarizon.

"My father, whose Tarizonian name was Rammel Garcia, was selected to be that first envoy to Earth. It was thought since the United States was one of the largest and most powerful nations on Earth that the first envoy should go there. This story that I'm about to tell you was first told to me when I was about your age, Peter. It was 1947 when the first Earth shuttle landed in a secluded location in southern New York, not too far from New York City."

11
Contact

Rammel Garcia marveled at the clear blue sky, the green grass and the yellow flowers that adorned the path he and his party was following, hopefully to a place where they could obtain transport. It had been many cycles since he'd seen such wonders and seeing Earth in such splendor gave him great determination to make his mission a success. There had been much debate on how to make contact with the government of the United States. There had never been contact between these two worlds and everyone knew the wrong approach could be catastrophic.

The Deep Space Authority or DSA, had been sending probes to Earth for many cycles to study the planet and its people. Though there had been no landings on Earth, much was learned from the vast amounts of radio and electronic communications intercepted by the probes. In fact, Rammel had learned English and was anxious to try it out on the first humans he encountered now that he had finally made it to Earth.

As they came to the crest of a hill they saw a small town in the distance. There were eight in the party and they had no weapons. This was a peaceful mission and they wanted to be sure there was no doubt about that, so they left their laser rifles and other personal armaments in their ship. They could have brought a hover vehicle for transportation, but that would have prematurely made it apparent that visitors had arrived from another world.

They had brought many things with them, though—gifts for the U.S. President, their credentials, a letter from the Chancellor, and things that would prove they came from another world. They knew that it might be difficult for the government to accept the fact that human life existed in other solar systems. If they weren't convincing they knew they could easily end up in a prison cell for the rest of their lives.

The initial approach was critical so they had decided to make their first contact with the U.S. Ambassador to the United Nations. They felt if anyone would listen to them and believe what they had to say, he would be the man. Their immediate problem, however, was to get into town unnoticed, obtain transportation, local currency, and get something to eat. None of them had eaten for over a year!

Although they'd been fed during their voyage from Tarizon it wasn't by mouth and they longed for some good solid food. On the outskirts of town they hid their luggage and walked into town like they'd been out on an afternoon stroll. Although many people looked at them in their unusual attire as they passed by, nobody seemed alarmed or distressed that they were in town. So far, their arrival had been perfect. They hadn't stuck out. Now they needed local currency and their plan was to find a pawn shop or jewelry store.

The got directions and found a jewelry store where they were able to sell an assortment of precious stones for pennies on the dollar. The proprietor must have thought he'd gotten the deal of a lifetime when he showed them out the door having parted with less than $5,000 for stones worth ten times that. But they'd gotten enough money to buy a used car, get new clothes, gasoline, food, and a hotel room when they got to New York City.

They arrived on a Sunday a few days before the next session of the United Nations General Assembly. Now the question was how to approach the Ambassador. It wouldn't be easy to get a meeting since he was always surrounded by an entourage of diplomats and support staff, not to mention his security team. They'd have to call and try to make an appointment, but they couldn't tell his staff the truth or they'd think it was a prank call or a lunatic had gotten hold of a telephone.

Rammel was nervous when he picked up the telephone to make the call. He was not used to the clumsy American telephones as all communications on Tarizon were hands free. The operator finally connected him to the Ambassador's Secretary.

"Hello," the voice said.

"Hello. Hi. This is Rammel Garcia."

"Who?"

"Rammel Garcia, an emissary from Turvin. I'd like to make an appointment with the Ambassador."

"What's the nature of your visit?" she asked.

"I've come all the way from Shisk. We'd like to obtain membership in the United Nations and wanted to see if the United States would support us."

"Well, I'll discuss the matter with the Ambassador but he's very busy. I can't promise you he'll be able to see you."

"Tell him our government has much to offer in return for his support."

"Well, okay. I'll do that. Give me your number and we'll get back with you."

Rammel gave the secretary their hotel telephone number and then took his small delegation to the library. He knew there wouldn't be a return call that day. In fact, he didn't really expect a return phone call at all since, when the Ambassador tried to find *Turvin* and *Shisk*, he obviously wouldn't have any luck. His intention was simply to get the Ambassador curious. In the meantime they had decided to learn as much about Earth and America as they could. The library was the obvious place to start, but the lure of the city soon got them out onto the streets amongst the hustle and bustle of New York City life.

The following day Rammel called the Ambassador's office again and was told the Ambassador had gotten his message but hadn't been able to fit him into his schedule yet. This went on each day for a week until the secretary finally asked. "Where is Turvin anyway? The Ambassador says he's never heard of it."

"It's a new nation very rich in oil and diamonds. If the Ambassador will see me, I'll show him where it is on the map and let him see some of the stones mined in our great nation. I have a gift for the President too, from our Chancellor."

"A gift?"

"Yes, something quite magnificent. We were hopeful the Ambassador would see that he got it."

"Well, he might do that. I'll tell him what you said and get back with you."

"Thank you. And tell him again that we can provide the United States much in return for its support."

"Alright. I'll remind him."

Two days later the secretary called back and said the Ambassador could see them for ten minutes during the noon recess of the General Assembly. They were instructed to meet him at one of the conference rooms in the United Nations building and told them where they could get credentials and directions to the room.

Rammel was ecstatic that he'd finally gotten his audience with the Ambassador. He knew the Ambassador would be very skeptical about this nation of Turvin that nobody on his staff could find on a map, but he was sure his curiosity would give him a few minutes to make an impression. He'd didn't think he'd need long.

The following day the delegation went to the United Nations Building as instructed, picked up their badges, went through a security check, and were escorted to the conference room where they were to meet the Ambassador. He hadn't arrived yet so they were asked to wait. While they were waiting a young staff member questioned them.

"Where is Turvin, anyway? We couldn't find it on any map. Is it in Africa?"

"No. It's a very small nation. It's not on the map."

"So why do you think there is any chance it could get a seat in the United Nations General Assembly? The ambassador doesn't have time to waste on hopeless causes."

"It's not a hopeless cause. Believe me, we will make it very worth while for the United States to support us."

The young staff member was about to ask another question, when the Ambassador walked in. Rammel stood, smiled and bowed to the Ambassador. The Ambassador nodded and motioned for them to come into the conference room. The young staff member shook his head and walked away. Rammel and his delegation followed him in the conference room where the Ambassador's staff was already seated. Security guards were posted at the door.

"Okay, tell me about this mysterious country called Turvin." the Ambassador said.

"Yes, actually Turvin is a continent like North America. Shisk is the capital city of Soni which was once an independent nation but now is a state on Tarizon."

"What? Tarizon? I'm afraid I don't understand."

"Tarizon is not of this world. It's a planet in another solar system. We have traveled for more than a year to get here."

The ambassador started to laugh. "Is this some kind of joke?" He looked at his assistant. "Who put you up to this?"

"I assure you, Mr. Ambassador this is not a joke," Rammel said strongly. "We have been sent by the Chancellor of the Tarizon World Council to establish diplomatic relations with the United States. I have a letter from the Chancellor himself if you'd like to see it."

The Ambassador laughed again and glanced over to his assistant again. The assistant shrugged. The Ambassador turned back to Rammel, took the letter from him, and opened it. It was in Tari so the Ambassador handed it back and said, "Would you read it for me. I speak eight languages but certainly not one from another world." He stifled another laugh and then forced himself to listen.

Rammel pulled out a small square metallic object from his pocket and placed it on the table. "Actually," he said. "The Chancellor will read the message himself." Rammel tapped the box and immediately a circular area on the top of the object lit up; a hologram of the Chancellor appeared above the box. He immediately began giving his message in English.

To the Most Honorable United States Ambassador to the United Nations:

Greetings from the people of Tarizon.

Forgive me for the manner in which we made first contact, but I think you can understand the need for the greatest discretion. Because our two worlds know nothing of each other and the greatest fear humans can face is fear of the unknown, we are making this first contact with you, America's greatest diplomat, and have sent our most esteemed emissary, Rammel Garcia to bring our message. We trust that the two of you can breach the great gulf that stands between our two worlds so that a great alliance can be forged.

My emissary will explain our predicament and what

assistance we will require. We pray that you will hear him out and help us in this time of great crisis. Your nation's aid will be remembered and rewarded tenfold. I look forward to a long and profitable relationship between our worlds.

Malnor Artiss
Chancellor of Tarizon
Protector of the Supreme Mandate

The image disappeared and the room was so quiet you could have heard a feather drop. The Ambassador looked at Rammel and then at one of his staff members. Finally he spoke. "Well, that is quite a little device, but that doesn't prove you are from another planet. Scientists have been working on holograms for years but, I'll admit I haven't seen one quite like that."

"We knew you would be skeptical so we brought a lot of proof to convince you," Rammel said. He took a stone out of his pocket and tossed it to the Ambassador. "Give this to your geologist. I think they will attest there is nothing like it on Earth." Before the Ambassador could respond Rammel snapped his fingers and one of his female staff members came forward, put her arm on the table and pulled out small knife. The security guards drew their weapons. The Ambassador gasped and came to his feet. Before anyone could stop her, the woman slashed the knife across her forearm. Blood immediately began to bubble out of the wound. The Ambassador looked at Rammel in horror.

"Don't be alarmed Ambassador," Rammel said. "This is just a simple demonstration of some of our medical technology that we hope to be able to share with your government." Everyone in the room gathered around the woman to watch Rammel, who had pulled out a small jar and unscrewed the lid. The woman wiped the blood away with a rag and Rammel began applying the white liquid contained in the bottle on the wound. The bleeding immediately stopped and before their eyes the skin began repairing itself. In just a minute the horrible gash was gone.

The Ambassador looked up in astonishment. "Very impressive." He laughed. "Your going to make a believer out of me yet."

"Yes, but I can see you're not a hundred percent certain quite yet.

I think what I'm about to show you will change that. I'll need a glass of water for this next demonstration."

The Ambassador motioned to one of his aides. The aide produced a glass of water and handed it to Rammel. The woman who was still standing amongst the eager onlookers began to disrobe. The Ambassador looked around nervously. Some of the male aides were unable to stifle their amusement until the Ambassador gave them a dirty look. When the woman was finished she was standing before them in a bikini. Beneath the bra there were gills that were slowly moving in and out as the woman breathed. Several of the onlookers gasped in amazement.

"Lucilia is one quarter Seafolken. The Seafolken are a race of humans on Tarizon that has adapted to life in the sea. A full blood Seafolken has a tough light green skin, feet and hands that become webbed while in water, and is amazingly strong. Quite interestingly the quarter breeds can look almost like you and I, except for the gills." Rammel took the glass of water and began pouring it on Lucilia's feet. Immediately they began to transform until they were much wider and webs began to form between her toes. Again their were gasps from the onlookers. Lucilia extended her hands and Rammel poured water on them as well. They began the same sort of transformation. "A quarter-breed can swim underwater for up to twenty minutes without surfacing. A full blood Seafolken can stay under water for hours."

The Ambassador shook his head. "All right. I'm a believer. Can I see your ship?" he said smiling broadly.

"Of course, " Rammel replied, "but only when we leave to go back to Tarizon. We can't disclose its location yet."

"I understand," the Ambassador said. "This is indeed a momentous occasion. I am honored that you chose to make first contact with me. I promise I will do everything in my power to persuade our government to assist you in any way it can."

Rammel bowed. "Thank you, Mr. Ambassador."

"Tony," the Ambassador said to one of his aids, "I want you to assign a full security detail to our guests and I want you to move them to the Hilton. No one is to talk to them. Put them on their own floor. Also, contact the director of the CIA and tell him I have to meet with him ASAP and I'll need to see the President!"

12

The Pledge

Peter wished he could have witnessed the historic meeting between Rammel Garcia and the United States Ambassador to the United Nations. He couldn't believe the government had been lying to the American people for over fifty years.

"The day after the meeting with the Ambassador," the Councillor continued, "Rammel met with the director of the CIA and a delegation sent by the President to commence negotiations. Rammel explained to them our plight here on Tarizon and how we thought they could help us. It was our intention to make the Repopulation Project voluntary. We had read of the great pioneering spirit of the American people and were sure many would volunteer to help conceive a new generation of Tarizonian citizens. We also were planning to go to many nations on Earth for help and share our technology with them as well in exchange for their assistance; however, the CIA had other ideas. They forbade us to go to any other nation. They wanted the technology for themselves and promised to give us the new generation of citizens that we needed."

"That sounds like our government," Peter said. "I guess that partly explains why the United States has been so powerful over the years. It's had the advantage of Tarizon's technology."

"Yes, they also insisted that the project remain top secret. They explained that there would be general panic if the American people found out that alien life actually existed and that a project like the one we were proposing would cause such a moral outrage that it would never be approved by Congress."

"They may have been right about that. The press would have gone

83

nuts over something like this," Peter agreed.

"Anyway, the CIA designed the Repopulation Project to allow Tarizonian men and women to travel to Earth, marry Americans, raise a family and travel back to Tarizon when all the children were old enough for deep space travel. Of course, the tragedy of the project was the innocent spouse being left behind not knowing what happened to his or her family. But this was the CIA's doing, not ours. They insisted that no American go to Tarizon except to prevent the project from being discovered. It is under that provision that you were brought to Tarizon."

"How did my father get involved in the project?" Peter asked.

"Over the years our numbers on Earth grew and it was inevitable that some of them would get into trouble. Most of the problems the CIA could deal with, but occasionally the legal entanglement they found themselves in required the CIA to recruit attorneys into the program to defend them. Attorneys who would be sure that the project would not be inadvertently revealed. Your father was one of those attorneys recruited for the project."

Peter drew in a deep breath. "I see. That explains a lot."

"Yes, I hope you will forgive us for all you and your family have been forced to endure."

Peter shrugged but didn't say anything.

"Anyway, as I was saying, we need your help. Since you are from Earth, have no allegiances here, and can now see that by helping us you can help your own world as well, I assume we can trust you."

"Of course, I'll do whatever I can to help."

The door opened and Brille walked in with Rhin. The Councillor stood up and smiled. Rhin strolled over to Peter and sat. The Councillor smiled and said, "Well, it is true. I never dreamed I'd see the day that a rhutz would walk into my office as an ally in the battle to protect the Supreme Mandate. This is truly extraordinary."

Rhin nodded, seeming to understand the Councillor's awe. Peter squatted and began petting Rhin. He motioned for the Councillor to join in. The Council stepped forward, bent down, and patted Rhin gently on the back.

"Good, boy," the Councillor said. "Good to have you aboard."

"Actually, Rhin's a girl," Peter said.

He laughed. "Sorry, girl."

"So, who are Videl Lai's supporters?"

"Three of the seven generals of the TGA for starters. We believe they are planning the assassination of Chancellor Bassett Alls and, if that happens, Vice-chancellor Videl Lai could legally step in and take control of the government with the help of the three generals in his pocket If we allow that to happen it will likely mean the end of the Supreme Mandate and the rule of law on Tarizon."

"Do you know any of Videl Lai's plans?"

"No, we have infiltrated his staff but our spies inside have been unable, so far, to get any detailed plans of the assassination. These types of plans are kept highly confidential until close to the time of implementation. We were just lucky we learned about the assassination attempt at the spaceport in time to do something about it."

"So, what do you want me to do now?" Peter asked.

"Well, I have let the word out that you are staying at my home in hopes that you will impregnate my daughter Lorin."

"Huh?"

"Don't worry. It's not true. Lorin has a mate whom she loves and would not betray."

"I thought love was frowned upon by Central Authority."

"It is, but love does still exist. It's a human emotion that can't be extinguished entirely. It's only discouraged because some people think it impairs the repopulation effort."

"Who is Lorin's mate? I'd like to meet him."

"His name is Jake Boskie. He's a fighter pilot for the TGA. He'd kill you if you laid a hand on Lorin, but he understands that you must spend some time with her for appearance sake. Will you do that?"

Peter shrugged. "If it's necessary, sure, but a cover should be believable. Who's going to believe a father would bring in a man to—you know, I mean a father would try to keep the men away. Besides you have the sperm bank. You could send your daughter there."

"Unfortunately, most of what is donated is poor quality and should be thrown away, but there's such a demand for sperm that the technicians sometimes will relax their standards. Because of that, nobody in the government would let their daughter near a sperm bank. You wouldn't want your grandchild to have gills or an extra finger. That's why this cover is so good."

The Councillor stood up. "Well, I must leave now for the morning session. Brille will show you to your office and brief you as to your duties as my intern. If you have any questions we can discuss them tonight at dinner. If I'm not home when you get there, Lorin will show you around."

Peter stood up and nodded. "Yes, sir. I'll see you tonight then."

After the Councillor had left, Brille showed Peter to his new office. It was small but adequate for what he'd be doing. Like any new job, he felt out of place. He had no clue what he was supposed to be doing, so he got bored and started crumpling up paper into balls and throwing them into a waste basket. After awhile Rhin got into the game and intercepted one of his shots. They started playing and were having a great time when Lorin walked in. Peter looked up and said, "Hello."

Lorin looked at Peter and wondered how this kid from Earth could possibly be mistaken for the Liberator. He knew nothing about Tarizon and didn't seem to care about anything except having sex with his guide and playing with his rhutz. It had been a mistake pretending he was the Liberator, she thought. But she'd been through Earth Shuttle 21's passenger list and there was nobody else who could possibly be the Liberator. She was sure the Prophecy must be a hoax or someone's wishful thinking. She frowned and asked impatiently, "What are you doing?"

Peter stood up and wiped off his pants. He felt very embarrassed and wondered if Lorin would tell her father that she'd caught him playing with Rhin when he should have been working. "I'm sorry. I haven't been given any assignments yet, so I . . . Rhin and I were just killing time."

She shook her head. "You're the Liberator? Sandee help us. . . . Has my father told you of the urgency of our situation?"

Peter nodded. "Briefly, Vice-chancellor Videl Lal and the three generals are plotting to overthrow the government."

"Yes. Well, I doubt any of *them* are playing games these days."

"Right. I'm sorry. It won't happen again. I just feel so out of place here. I want to help, but I don't know what I can do."

"Do you have any military training?"

"What?. . . No. I haven't even graduated from high school yet."

"Any special skills?"

"Like what?"

"Are you a pilot? A hunter?"

"No, but I'm a good writer and I'm on the debate team."

She frowned. "Well, the first thing you'll need to do is learn your way around the capital complex so you can make deliveries and do the normal chores of an intern. You'll also need to learn Tari, of course, so you can communicate with people and in case you overhear something important, you'll understand it."

"Tari? I don't know. I'm not so great at foreign languages."

She half smiled. "Don't worry, we have a system for teaching that is very effective, even for slubdubs."

"Slubdub? What's a slubdub?"

She stifled a laugh. "Moron, halfwit, idiot—."

"Thanks a lot. I may not be a nuclear physicist but I have other talents."

She raised her eyebrows. "You mean in the bedroom? I heard you've already got your guide pregnant."

"Yeah, well, I aim to please."

She shook her head. "Come on. I'm going to take you to see my mate. He's anxious to meet you, although I don't know why."

Lorin walked out the door and Peter wondered whether to follow her or stay put in protest. He couldn't believe her attitude. It was apparent she hated him already and he didn't know why. Reluctantly, he followed her out of the building with Rhin at his heels. Just outside a side entrance was a small aircraft. Lorin pushed a button on her belt. A hatch opened and a ladder descended to the ground. Without skipping a beat, Lorin climbed into the craft. Peter started to follow her and then thought about Rhin. She wouldn't be able to climb the ladder so he picked her up and put her aboard. Then he climbed up and stepped inside.

Lorin had already taken a seat in the solo cockpit. There were four passenger seats, so he strapped Rhin in one as best he could and sat in the one next to her. Rhin didn't seem the least bit nervous about being in the ship which kind of surprised Peter, but he guessed she trusted him not to put her in danger. He just prayed her trust was warranted.

The ship lifted into the air about twenty feet and then began moving forward in a smooth rapid motion. There was no engine noise which surprised him greatly. He wondered what kind of propulsion the ship utilized. Whatever it was it was amazing!

There were several portals in the body of the ship. He watched their flight out of the one to his right. After about twenty loons he saw they were approaching some sort of military base. There were thousands of aircraft parked on the runway, mostly fighters, it appeared, but also other types that he didn't recognize. A minute later they landed and stepped out onto the tarmac.

In the distance a vehicle that looked like a large floating golfcart approached. He assumed it was Lorin's mate. It came to a halt in front of them. A tall, dark-headed man, who looked to be in his mid-twenties, jumped out and embraced her. He kissed her and then looked over at Peter and smiled. "You must be Peter," he said.

Peter nodded. "Yes."

"Jake, meet our Liberator," Lorin said in a sarcastic tone.

Jake frowned. "What's wrong, Lorin? Did something happen?"

"Lorin doesn't seem to like me much," Peter said. "I guess I wasn't what she expected."

Jake raised his eyebrows. "Well, first impressions are often deceiving."

Lorin shook her head and said, "I'm just disappointed. Peter has no military training, no significant skills or knowledge, and absolutely no idea what's going on here on Tarizon. He couldn't possibly be the Liberator!"

As Lorin was ranting, Rhin jumped out of the aircraft and landed on the tarmac next to Peter. Jake's mouth dropped open as he studied the rhutz. Peter bent down and began petting her. Jake said, "So, it is true. The Liberator will tame the rhutz. Look at that!"

"He can't be the Liberator," Lorin objected. "When I came to get him he was playing a game with a trash can."

Jake smiled. "That's an earth game—basketball, isn't that what it's called?"

"Yes," Peter said, smiling gleefully at Lorin.

Her eyes narrowed and she turned away. Jake said, "So, the rhutz couldn't be wrong, I mean. Have you ever met a rhutz that would let you pet him?"

Lorin shrugged. "Are you going to gamble the future of our world on the judgment of a dumb animal?"

Rhin's ears perked up and she growled at Lorin. Peter said, "This dumb animal saved my life, so show her a little respect."

Lorin took a deep breath. "I'm sorry, Rhin. I didn't mean it. I'm sure you are very smart. I'm just not sure your master is who he says he is. I wish you could talk so we could find out why you are so sure he's the one."

"Listen. I don't claim to be the Liberator, okay?" Peter assured her. "It's your father and that mutant, Threebeard, who say it. I'm quite happy being Peter Turner. Just send me back home and I'll forget any of this ever happened."

"Nonsense," Jake said. "There is no doubt you are the Liberator. I've heard of Threebeard. He's one of the most intelligent persons in the galaxy and only one of a very few who can speak to the Nanomites. If he thinks you are the Liberator then you must be."

Peter raised his eyebrows. "So, if he's right, what should I be doing?"

Jake shrugged. "We've got a lot to do to prepare you for the task ahead. Videl Lai is making preparations to seize control of the government. We can't let him do that."

"How much time do we have?" Peter asked.

"One cycle at best, maybe less."

"Well, I'll do whatever it takes to stop him, but you all are going to have to give me some direction. I have no idea where to begin."

"I'll discuss it with father tonight," Lorin said. "We'll come up with a plan and pray to Sandee that you'll be up to the task."

Jake smiled, "In the meantime let me show you around the base."

That night when Peter got back to his compartment, depression set in with a vengeance. Lorin's contempt for him hurt, yet he could understand how she felt. He would have probably felt the same way had he been in her position. Who was responsible for this Prophecy anyway? How could anyone see into the future? To see into the future would mean that the future was predestined or time travel was possible. Neither seemed plausible to Peter, yet living on a planet millions of miles from Earth wouldn't have seemed that plausible either.

As Peter sat on edge of his bed, he felt so alone. He missed Lucinda. She was his only real connection to this world and now she had been stolen away from him. How was he going to live up to everyone's unrealistic expectations? It seemed ridiculous to think that somehow he would make a difference in the struggle for control of this strange planet, yet how could he defy the Prophecy?

Rhin jumped into his lap, distracting him momentarily from his troubled thoughts. He stroked her coarse coat and then rubbed her gently behind the ears like he used to do to his old collie, Sheila. She closed her eyes and wagged her tail briskly. This was the first time that Rhin had shown this much affection. Up until now she had only allowed Peter to pet her for brief periods. She must have sensed his depression and was trying to cheer him up. After a minute she jumped off his lap and looked up at him.

"Thanks, girl," he said. "I love you too. . . . It's getting late and we've got a big day ahead tomorrow. We better hit the hay."

Rhin just looked at Peter and when he started to take off his clothes, she walked over to her bed and settled in for the night. Sheila used to sleep at the foot of his bed, but Rhin so far had kept her distance at night. He wondered if that would change in time. "Lights!" Peter said in a commanding voice and the room became dark. If he said *lights* again the lights would come back on. That was one of the cool things about this world—everything was ultra hi tech. It had been a long day so it didn't take long for him to fall asleep.

Sometime during the night Peter woke up abruptly. A strange and eerie sensation had come over him. It was dark, darker than it should have been. The control panel by each door normally illuminated the room enough to safely navigate it if a trip to the bathroom was necessary. Some light would also filter into the bedroom from the big window in the living room that overlooked the city. Yet with eyes wide open Peter couldn't see a single ray of light anywhere. Fear began to creep through him. He yelled, "Lights!" but the room remained black. Swallowing hard he looked over where Rhin should have been sleeping, looking for those bright green eyes that glowed brilliantly in the dark. Still he saw nothing but bold blackness.

"Rhin, are you there?"

In the distance he could hear barking. It was Rhin but she seemed a kylod away. What was going on? Was he dreaming? He wished it were so, but he could feel the bed beneath him and when he rubbed his arms he felt his own touch. This was no dream. Slipping off the bed, he started to walk slowly toward where he thought the door ought to me but almost immediately ran into the wall. That seemed impossible as the bed should have been six feet from the door. Following the wall he circled the bed and, much to his dismay, realized the walls had moved in on him and the door had disappeared!

Panic quickly swept over him as he frantically searched for a way out. "Rhin! Where are you?" he yelled. She was barking but from behind the wall. Peter stood still trying to fathom what was happening. Suddenly he realized the wall was creeping toward him. It pressed against his legs until he was forced back onto the bed. A moment later he could hear the strain of the walls against the bed frame. Soon, he'd be crushed like a Chevy in a scrap yard, if he didn't figure a way out of the room. His pulse quickened fearing the end was near. Was his compartment, or what was left of it, to become his tomb? Was he to die here tonight—killed by four walls?

Suddenly, the lights came on and the walls became still. It took a moment for his eyes to adjust to the light, but when they did he saw words on the wall before him. Words that were not written but molded into the crystal walls. Words that were not in Tari, but English, and meant for him to read and understand.

A Liberator shall come from the amongst the Earth children and free the Mutants, Seafolken, and Nanomites from bondage. This is your destiny, Peter. Delay not, as the future of Tarizon is your hands!
Your servant,
Allo of the Nanomites

Suddenly the walls began a silent retreat, and before long the bedroom was almost back to normal. In time a door began to appear and, when it was completed, it popped open and Rhin came running into the bedroom barking. She quickly ran around the room sniffing and inspecting each corner and even crawled under the bed.

A rush of adrenalin surged through Peter. It was clear the

Nanomites could now be added to the list of those convinced he was the Liberator. Could they all be wrong? He didn't feel any different than he had back on Earth, yet the message was clear. He was the Liberator whether he liked it or not. As he gazed at the Nanomite's message engraved on his wall, a surge of confidence came over him. He finally could see himself leading the enslaved masses to victory. He knew then his life would be important. He had been given the opportunity to alter the history of Tarizon by stopping Videl Lai. For some reason great power had been thrust upon him—the power of the people's trust and allegiance. He could feel that power now. It was swelling within him. Yes, now he felt for the first time the Prophecy might be true. Perhaps he was the Liberator after all!

13

Colonel Tomel

Soon the day came for Peter to move into the Councillor's private residence. It was a spacious home up in the hills just a short ride by subtram. The view of the city was spectacular. Peter marveled at the exotic architecture—giant golden pyramids, massive crystal spike-shaped structures built by the Nanomite, flat green government buildings, and silver windowless skyscrapers all interconnected by the intricate spider-web-like subtram system.

Lorin led him upstairs and showed him to a small room where he was to stay for the indefinite future. She seemed to him to be a bit friendlier than their last meeting, but it was still bare tolerance that he saw on her face. Before she left him to unpack, she indicated a plan had been concocted for his training and that her father would outline it for him at dinner. Peter looked at her expectantly, hoping she'd give him some details.

"Can't you just tell me now? I'll play dumb at dinner," Peter asked.

She took a deep breath and then smiled wryly, "Okay, For starters there is a boot camp for new recruits going into the Tarizonian Army. Dad is going to arrange for you to join a unit. You'll learn tactics, weaponry, and get lots of PT. It will be good for you."

"How long is the camp?" Peter asked.

"That's all I can tell you. You'll have to wait for the rest," Lorin replied.

The thought of going through military boot camp scared Peter. His father had been drafted into the Marines and ended up going to officer candidate school. He had to go through boot camp and he had told him how horrible it had been. In fact, his drill sergeant beat him up one day and he'd ended up in the hospital. Of course, this was Tarizon and it would be totally different than the Marine Corps, he told himself.

"But I don't speak your language," Peter reminded her.

"Right. I think father has you scheduled to start a language school next week. If you have half a brain, it shouldn't take but a few weeks and you'll be speaking like you've lived here all your life."

Lorin's obvious contempt for him bothered Peter. He looked at her trying to figure out why she hated him so. "But what about my internship? How will your father explain my absence?"

She shrugged and replied, "I don't know. You'll have to ask him. Dinner is a 2100, don't be late."

When she was gone, Peter started unpacking his things and came across a picture of Lucinda and he having dinner. He'd never seen the photograph before but he remembered the street photographer who'd taken it. A rush of excitement flashed over him.. If Lucinda bought the picture from the photographer and left it in his suitcase, she must have wanted him to remember her. She must care for him. His heart was pounding. He picked up the picture and put it on the night stand next to his bed where he could see it from anywhere in the room. The picture of them together brought memories flooding through his mind. He could hear her cheerful voice, visualize her caring smile, and feel the warmth of her love. He wondered how his baby was doing inside her womb.

Peter arrived late for dinner. There were eight place settings in the elegant dining room. Along with Councillor Garcia and his mate, Rosa, there was Lorin and Jake, Colonel Tomel and his mate, Egga, Peter, and Rhin the rhutz. Of course, Rhin wasn't allowed at the table. Instead she curled up under Peter's feet, hoping he'd drop her a scrap or two. Two waiters served them with course after course of food. Peter thought each to be interesting and, for the most part, delicious, but several dishes looked so odd he discreetly avoided them.

When the meal was over, they were all served sankee and small dessert cakes. Rosa and Egga excused themselves as the rest of them began to discuss Peter's role in the imminent civil war. He hadn't told anyone about his encounter with the Nanomites the previous night, so he thought he should do that first as it could impact the evening's discussions.

"Before we begin," Peter said. "I want to apologize if I seemed to lack enthusiasm for the role of Liberator of Tarizon. I know I've disappointed some of you and for that I'm sorry."

The Councillor looked at his daughter and frowned. Lorin looked away and rolled her eyes. Peter continued,"You see, I've been a bit overwhelmed by all that's happened to me. Less than a month ago I didn't even know Tarizon existed. Now suddenly I'm here, not just as a visitor, but someone who is to play an important role in the history of the planet.

"The other night I felt very overwhelmed and depressed and then something happened to me. The Nanomites paid me a visit." Peter told them about waking up and finding the room had shrunk and thinking he would be crushed.

Colonel Tomel's eyes widened and Lorin looked Peter in the eyes for the first time that evening. He continued, "But as it turned out they meant me no harm. They had a message to deliver. They wanted to be sure I understood what it meant to be the Liberator. Like Lorin, they were concerned that I didn't fully comprehend my role here on Tarizon. And, I will confess, until last night I didn't. All this talk of being the Liberator seemed a bit fuzzy—like a dream. I heard everyone say it, but it didn't sink in.

"The Nanomites assured me again that I *was* the Liberator, that I had a job to do, and that God and Sandee were behind me. They made me realize that time was short and I must move quickly to fulfill the Prophecy. I want you all to know that I am now ready, all trepidation aside, and I am anxious to get started with the task at hand—the defeat of the Vice-chancellor and the preservation of the Supreme Mandate."

The Councillor replied, "Forgive my daughter, Peter. She's always been a bit impatient. I understand how strange all of this must be to you. I'm glad the Nanomites came to you. Now you will understand them better and be able to see how they can assist us in the war effort."

Lorin said, "I am glad as well. I hope the words you spoke are true for there is little time to waste. I look forward to seeing you fulfill the Prophecy."

Peter nodded and for the first time, Lorin smiled at him. "As do I," Peter said, smiling back at her. "As to the Nanomites, yes, they have shown me their extraordinary power, but I still know very little about them. I'd like to know more."

The Councillor replied, "I think I'll let Colonel Tomel do that. He served in the Nanomite war and I'm sure has some vivid memories of that campaign."

Colonel Tomel was a short, stout man with white hair. His complexion was dark and his face battle-worn. Peter suspected he was in his late fifties but he may have been younger. It was hard to tell. It seemed the bad air on Tarizon made people age quicker than they did on Earth.

Colonel Tomel nodded. "Up until the day the sun disappeared the Nanomites were a rather obscure life form living mainly in the desert regions of the southern hemisphere—"

14

The Nanomite War

"After the volcanos erupted and the sun was hidden by thick clouds of ash," Colonel Tomel continued, "everything changed dramatically on Tarizon. You could still tell the difference between day and night, but barely. Many plants and trees died for lack of light. Forests became dangerous tinder boxes ready to explode if ignited by lightning or careless soldier. Wildfires raged across the planet exacerbating the pollution in the atmosphere.

"The soot was the first big challenge. Everything was buried in it—up to your elbows in most places. The wind used to whip it up into great clouds and the rain swept it into the rivers turning them into cesspools. In this dim, polluted world, crime escalated, the economy soon crashed, transportation came to a standstill, and the health system became clogged with millions of people who were sick and dying.

"During this time building and construction almost came to a standstill. With so little sunlight filtering through the surface of the planet, Tarizon literally turned yellow within a few segments. There was still lumber that could be harvested even if the trees were dying, but there was nobody to harvest them. People in the rural areas were being evacuated to the domed cities and most of the planet's resources were being directed to restoring law and order, providing clean air, water and food, and expanding the health system to accommodate millions of people in need of medical care.

"Building maintenance and new construction was critical to all of these efforts. Millions of refugees needed housing and support facilities, which prompted the government to start searching for non-conventional

97

building techniques. One of the men assigned to this task was Berne Baldrich. Baldrich had been aware of the Nanomites for many cycles and was impressed with their ability to quickly construct rather complex crystal structures in their desert homeland. Now, with a staff and an unlimited budget, he started to study them in earnest.

"The Nanomites had never been considered an intelligent life form. Being extremely small, so small a human could only see them in a microscope, it was thought they were like plants with little or no intelligence or ability to communicate. Baldrige, however, believed the Nanomites had to be highly intelligent because of their building and engineering skills. He also was sure they had some means of rapid communication because to build these structures took considerable coordinated effort.

"When Baldrige went to the Nanomite's desert homeland, he estimated there were about five million swarms. In the course of his study he discovered that their numbers had remained fairly stable since scientists had begun studying them, shortly after unification under the Supreme Mandate. He wondered why their population hadn't grown and expanded. Was it that they needed certain chemicals and nutrients that only existed in their desert homeland, or did the desert climate have something to do with it? His finally realized it was both. The Nanomites needed a dry environment to build. Moisture slowed them down and made it impossible for them to work efficiently. They also needed a chemical called bacuum that was naturally produced in the desert where they lived.

"Baldridge conjectured that the number of swarms would multiply almost geometrically if they were put in an ideal environment and given all the chemical ingredients they needed. When Baldridge asked his scientists if they could reproduce bacuum in the laboratory, they assured him they could. This excited him since it meant he could take them anywhere on the planet to build, as long as he kept the construction site dry.

"Of course, increasing the Nanomite population would do Baldrige no good unless somehow he could communicate with them and get them to build structures that would be useful to the government in the recovery effort. So, his study turned to figuring out how to communicate with them.

"In researching previous pre-eruption studies of the Nanomites, he learned that the swarmmaster, a loosely connected array of super-nanomites, acted as the brain of the swarm and controlled its members within a swarm field. Nobody knew exactly how the swarmmaster communicated with each of the individual Nanomites in the swarm field, but it was presumed there was some kind of common will within the swarm. This led Baldwin to experiment with telepathic communication.

"To do this he enlisted the help of those most gifted with telepathic abilities. Although, none of these persons were able to establish reliable communication with the Nanomites, there was some reaction from the Nanomites to their efforts. This made Baldrige believe he was on the right track. What he needed was someone with stronger or more precise telepathic abilities. This is when he was told about Threebeard, the mutant Peter mentioned earlier.

"It was said Threebeard was the most intelligent person on the planet, and he proved it by quickly establishing telepathic communication with Nanomite swarmmasters. He confirmed that they were indeed intelligent, disciplined, and a vibrant life form that could be quite useful to the Central Authority. Even better was the fact that the Nanomites were a docile life form. Their primary concern was survival. They were natural builders, because they had to protect their population from the environment, specifically rain and moisture. That was why they had learned to build such strong and magnificent structures.

"Using his telepathic abilities, Threebeard could communicate with the swarmmasters almost instantaneously. In time Threebeard taught other humans with telepathic abilities to communicate with them too. This was fortunate for Central Authority, for Threebeard soon withdrew from the project when he realized that it cared little about the Nanomites as a life form and only sought to exploit them."

"Why would he have to teach others how to communicate with the Nanomites?" Peter asked. "You'd think anyone with telepathic abilities could do it."

"No. It doesn't work that way. Not everyone has the same level of skill. The level of a person's telepathic abilities depends on his intelligence, training, and experience. Many people who are telepathic never know it."

"So, anybody can be taught to be telepathic?"

"No. They must have the gift, but just having it by itself isn't enough. They must be trained to use it effectively. So, Threebeard taught others how to increase their abilities to the point where they could converse with the Nanomites."

"I see," Peter said feeling disappointed. Having felt first Threebeard and then the rhutz touch him with their minds made him wish he could do the same.

"So," Colonel Tomel continued, "through Rupra Bruda, a Purist and one of Threebeard's telepathic pupils, Central Authority immediately began to negotiate with the Nanomites to build a few small buildings on an experimental basis. To do this, of course, architects and engineers were brought in to draw the plans and specifications. These plans were communicated by Bruda to a high swarmmaster who coordinated the project with other swarms. In the end the experimental buildings turned out to be quite satisfactory and the first major construction projects were soon underway.

"What was perfect about utilizing the Nanomites to rekindle the building industry was that they asked for so little in return—just an adequate supply of the food and bacuum needed to sustain their optimal physical health, the right to live in the core of the buildings they built, and time to rest and pray to their God. They had no desire for wealth or power, just to reproduce in a safe environment. Since humans would be occupying only the interior rooms, halls and compartments, the two life forms could live together without even knowing the other was there."

"Why couldn't the Nanomites expand out of the desert on their own? Couldn't they bring the bacuum with them and transport it when they ran out?" Peter asked.

"They didn't have the ability to transport it over long distances or store it for later use. Remember they are a fairly fragile life form. Too much water or cold can kill them. Their entire existence was devoted to building structures that could protect their population from these natural enemies. When the Central Authority promised them a controlled environment, unlimited food and nutrients, they jumped at the opportunity because it meant their species would be freed from their desert confinement and would be able to live anywhere on Tarizon. Since they were so small and lived inside solid objects it didn't matter to them where Central Authority took them. Their environment was always the same.

"The partnership between the Central Authority and the

Nanomites worked well for many cycles and dozens of great buildings were constructed, including the Hall of the Councillors. Then the Purists, led by Videl Lai, began to worry about the Nanomites becoming too powerful. It seemed that their numbers had grown from five million swarms to over a hundred million and, of course, they were living within the walls of the government buildings they had constructed. The Purists feared that the Nanomites were spying on the government, and might use any information overheard to subvert it. This was ridiculous but many began to believe it.

"These fears led to Parliament passing an edict requiring all Nanomites to vacate each building after it had been constructed. This was a direct violation of the agreement with the Nanomite and didn't make a lot of sense because these buildings needed constant maintenance, and the Nanomites were happy to provide it since the buildings were their homes. Making the Nanomites leave after a construction project caused a enormous logistical problem as well. Nanomite farms had to be established all over the planet so that Nanomite workers who were not on a job could have a place to live.

"After a job was completed they would be transported to the closest farm where they would wait for their next assignment. It often took many days for the Nanomites to vacate a building, get settled in their temporary transport vehicles, and moved to the nearest farm. These farms were expensive to maintain and the controlled environment they needed often wasn't provided, causing many to die and others to live in agony. Being moved all the time, they never felt like they had a home either. In the farms they were far worse off than they had been in their desert homeland.

"Things came to a head about twenty cycles ago when a construction superintendent, who was in a hurry to go on holiday, decided he didn't have time to transport the workers back to their farm after the job was done. He decided it would be easier just to fumigate the building and kill all the Nanomites living within it. He had little respect for the Nanomites since there was a surplus of them at the time, and didn't figure he would have trouble finding new ones for the next project. What he forgot about was the Nanomites ability to communicate with each other even over long distances.

"Word spread quickly to the Nanomite farms about the

extermination of over fifty of their brother swarms. Of course, they were outraged and demanded that the humans responsible be brought to justice. Charges were brought against the superintendent and nine members of his crew for genocide, but many argued that killing a Nanomite was not illegal under the Supreme Mandate. After all, the Nanomites life form was unknown when the Supreme Mandate was written. After a long trial the superintendent and his crew were acquitted on the technicality that Nanomites were not a protected life form under the Supreme Mandate.

"The Nanomites had never organized politically before, but fearing their survival was at stake, elected a leader. His name was Allo; and he had promised retaliation if the humans weren't punished for their crimes and within hours of the verdict that retaliation began. At the time I was a member of a cleanup crew sent to recover the bodies of human workers who had been killed by the Nanomites. It was a chilling site seeing the dead human bodies, without a scratch or a wound of any kind, incased in clear crystal crypts. Survivors said the Nanomites would first build crystal restraints over the legs and arms of their sleeping victims. When they later woke up, they couldn't escape and were helpless as they watched the crypts forming around them. Eventually the victims would use up the oxygen within the crypt and they would die. The look of horror on the victim's faces haunt me to this very day.

"The incident eventually escalated into all out war and Purists, led by Videl Lai, called for the total annihilation of the Nanomite life form on Tarizon. But the war didn't turn out to be an easy one. The Nanomites waged an effective invisible war against the Central Authority for nearly two cycles. After the war began I was promoted and put in charge of an infantry unit. It was an impossible war because the Nanomites could hide themselves in almost any dry inanimate object. Fortunately, they couldn't invade living organisms because they contained so much water, but they found indirect ways to attack us. Many lands were scourged in a futile effort to kill the Nanomites, but they always managed to elude us.

"During those cycles they destroyed communication facilities, invaded computers and rendered them inoperable, caused power outages, and subverted key stress points in buildings until they collapsed—not to mention the fact that for two cycles construction on Tarizon once again came to a halt. Frustrated with their inept attempt at defeating the

Nanomites, they turned to Baldrige again for help. He reluctantly told them how to defeat the Nanomites. All they had to do was disrupt their supply of bacuum and they would be brought to their knees. Of course, this simple solution was easily accomplished by seizing control of all bacuum supply depots, all bacuum mines and natural deposits that could be found on the planet. Once the supply of bacuum was cut off the Nanomites were forced to surrender.

"Since that time the Nanomites have been treated as slaves and required to live on their farms unless they were on a construction project. The farms are encircled by deep moats filled with poisonous chemicals that radiate into the ground and prevent the Nanomites from escaping. If they refuse to work they are denied food and bacuum and threatened with death until they cooperate. Of course, the Vice-Chancellor has been the primary proponent of anti-Nanomite legislation and denies they have any rights as a legitimate life form.

"As you can imagine this issue is of great importance to all of us. The Supreme Mandate clearly protects all life forms and does not tolerate slavery. Videl Lai is deliberately trying to subvert the Supreme Mandate and the ideals and values that we all cherish. We must stop him or die trying."

15

Learning Tari

Colonel Tomel's tale of the Nanomite War fascinated Peter. He couldn't believe an advanced society like the one on Tarizon would tolerate slavery. For the first time he realized what it must have been like back in the day of Abraham Lincoln, knowing that millions of human beings were being treated worse than farm animals. Although the Nanomites were not human beings, they obviously were very intelligent, aware of the quality of their life, and enjoyed their freedom. It felt good to be fighting for the abolition of slavery. He felt like he was going to be doing God's work.

Language school turned out to be an amazing experience for Peter. It only lasted ten days or the equivalent of two school weeks on Earth, yet in that short period he had mastered the Tari language, which was vastly different than anything on Earth. When he thought of how little he'd learned in the three agonizing years he'd spent in high school Spanish class, he couldn't believe how archaic the education system was on Earth.

The first thing they were given before class began each day was a drug called parazene. It was a mind stimulant that made the students feel very awake and keenly focused. Then they were taken to classrooms similar to the language labs Peter had back in school, except in this classroom the teachers attached electrodes behind the student's ears and to their foreheads. There were big TV monitors where the teacher began the instruction at a very rapid pace, but Peter had no trouble following her and felt exhilarated when the session was over.

After each instructional session the students all met in small groups of six students and one teacher. They spoke only Tari and even after just the first half day session Peter felt he was communicating fairly well. In the evening they watched a film in Tari and even though Peter didn't understand it all, much of it he did. That night they gave earphones to each student and placed monitors on their heads again. There was music at first, to put them to sleep, and then the instruction began—or at least that's what they were told as most of the students only remembered the music.

The next day Peter's mind ached from the incredible stimulation it had been receiving. It wasn't exactly a headache, but more like extreme fatigue. He asked one of the teachers how the brain held up to this kind of intense concentration. She said that even at this level of brain activity only sixty percent of the brain's capacity was being expended, so there was nothing to worry about. Nevertheless, Peter continued to worry and wondered what impact a second day of this type of stimulation would have on him. The greatest danger he feared was a stroke, and he was keenly aware that a stroke could lead to permanent mental and physical disability. He just prayed the teachers knew what they were doing.

After the third day Peter's mind had adjusted to the intense teaching routine and each morning thereafter he looked forward to that day's session and all that he would learn. In the past he'd never had a thirst for knowledge, simply a desire to graduate and get into college. Now, he suddenly wanted to learn for the sake of gaining knowledge and understanding. It was a strange and wonderful feeling. When the two-week crash course was over, Peter felt a little disappointed. He didn't know if it was that he was getting addicted to the parazene, or if he was worried about starting boot camp.

Fortunately Peter had three days between language school and having to report to camp. When he returned to the Councillor's mansion from his break, Rhin was there to welcome him.

"She really missed you," Councillor Garcia said. "She roamed the grounds every day looking for you and would hardly eat."

Peter sat on the ground Indian style and gave Rhin a hug. She wagged her tail frantically and tried to lick his face. He laughed as he dodged her drooling tongue.

"So, is there anything you would like to do during your break before boot camp?" the Councillor asked.

"Yes, I would like to visit Lucinda," Peter said.

The Councillor frowned. "Do you think that is wise? You should try to forget her."

"But I'll never forget her. I think about her every day, if not every loon."

"If you need a woman's company, I can—"

"Not any woman. I want to see Lucinda. She's carrying my baby."

"Of course. I'll see what I can do, but I would recommend you focus on your task ahead. She can only be a distraction."

"If I know she and the baby are well, I'll be less distracted."

The Councillor shook his head, "Love is frowned upon by the Central Authority, as I'm sure you know."

Peter nodded. "So I've heard."

"But love is part of human nature and cannot be expunged by act of the legislature. So, I won't tell you who to love or not to love. My only interest is to lessen your pain, for I fear there is little hope for you and Lucinda."

"I appreciate your concern, but I would still like to see her."

"Like I said, I'll see what I can do."

"Thank you," Peter said as he stood up and began to walk toward the house. Rhin, in her excitement, ran as fast as the wind all the way to the front door and then dashed back and circled them as they walked. They laughed at her exuberance and exhibition of inexhaustible energy.

Inside Jake was waiting for them. "Sorri lanei," he said, which in Tari meant *good day*.

Peter smiled and said, "Ubba san tone," which means "same to you."

Jake led them to the study where a kitchen robot named Zippo had prepared them Sankee and sweet biscuits. This was the first time he'd seen a robot in the country mansion, so he asked about him. "I don't remember seeing this robot at the house before I left for language school."

The Councillor replied, "Oh, that's right. Zippo was sent back to the manufacturer for repairs. He was just returned to us last week."

"So, he just cooks?" he asked.

"That and any other tasks we have him do. He can fix just about anything."

"Are there a lot of robots on Tarizon?" Peter asked.

"At one time there were, but since the day the sun disappeared their production has been a low priority and they have become quite expensive to own and maintain. Only the wealthy can afford them now."

After they had downed a few sweet biscuits, Jake said, "So, are you ready for boot camp?"

"I guess," Peter replied. "Ready as I'll ever be, but how are you going to explain my absence from the Councilman's office? I'm supposed to be his intern and people will expect to see me from time to time."

"Well, I've got that all worked out. Your name from now on will be Leek Lanzia from Lower Azallo. Lower Azallo is the largest continent in the southern hemisphere. You're from the city of Luva in the province of Queenland. It is rather remote area with a very cold climate similar to your Alaska on Earth. Have you been to Alaska?"

"Yes, my dad took me and my brothers there on a fishing trip one summer."

"Good, if anyone asks you what your homeland is like, just describe what you saw in Alaska."

"Sure, that should be easy."

"Your mother's name is Gilva and your father's is Ruggi. You have two brothers and a sister who are Earthchildren so you can just use your Earth siblings names, Reggie, Mark, and Marcia. We thought that would be less confusing for you."

"Yes, that will make it easier."

"If they ask about your mate, you can describe Lucinda. That way your story will seem real."

This intricate cover that Jake had conceived for him started to make him worry. What would happen if his cover were blown? He hesitated to bring that up but finally decided it would be better to know the stakes up front. So he asked the question and Jake responded, "They will assume you are a spy trying to work yourself into a high military position where you can acquire critical information to pass on to the enemy or commit acts of sabotage."

"So, if I'm discovered, they'll kill me?"

Jake nodded. "Yes, I'm afraid so, but that's not likely to happen. We've had a lot of experience with creating fake identities and the ones we've got for you are nearly impossible to tell from the real thing. A greater danger is that you will say something wrong. That's one reason we have you coming from Queenland. The people down there are somewhat strange, so if you say something that's not right they'll probably just laugh at you and chalk it up to being from the Underland."

"The Underland?"

"Yes, Queenland is so far south it is often called the Underland, bottomland, or some even refer to it as the butt of the planet."

They all laughed. "Great, so I'm going to be the joke of the squad."

"I'm afraid so," Jake said smiling.

"Okay, but what about my internship? You still haven't told me how you're going to handle that."

Jake looked at Peter and then at the Councillor. The Councillor smiled and replied, "Only a handful of people have actually seen you and they are all at Earth Shuttle Intake. We thought about having a clone engineered to take your place while you're gone, but we didn't have time. It takes a full cycle to produce a viable clone. So, we have a young man that looks a lot like you who will act as your double while you're gone. I've managed to substitute his picture in your file for yours."

"What about my tracking device? Didn't they implant one when I arrived here?"

"Yes, you'll have to have a little minor surgery before you leave. We'll replace your implant to match your new identity. Don't worry about it. It's like having a mole removed."

Peter took a deep breath. Somehow he doubted it was all that simple. "What about Lucinda, Jimmy Falk, and Cheryl Winston and her children? They all know what I look like."

The Councillor shrugged. "There's little likelihood that any of them will show up at the Hall of Councillors. I wouldn't worry about them. Just worry about doing well at boot camp. When you get back, I fear the war will be eminent and we will need you to unite the Mutants, Seafolken, and Nanomites against Videl Lai."

After their discussion was over, Jake gave Peter a packet full of information on his fake identity. Information about his parents, the schools he attended, his medical history, family, friends, and relatives. He cringed at the thought of having to memorize everything in the packet. It was his hope that he could relax during his break and mentally prepare himself for the difficult weeks that lay ahead, but that obviously wasn't going to happen.

The next day the Councillor told Peter he had made arrangements for him to see Lucinda that evening. He said she had agreed to come visit him here at the country house as it would provide more privacy than a meeting in the city. He was ecstatic with the news and started watching the clock wishing the day would go by more quickly.

While he was waiting, he wondered if she had missed him the way he had missed her. He didn't figure she had since she had made it clear her main attraction to him was as a sperm donor. But still, while they were together, it seemed there was a spark, something more than just sex. At least he hoped that was the case.

Depression started to set in as the day progressed. It occurred to him that even if she wanted to be with him as a wife or a mate, it wouldn't be possible. She was already mated and he wasn't sure a person could be unmated. He wondered if the Councillor had been right. Was seeing Lucinda really a good idea?

The moment Lucinda stepped out of the subtram, Peter was glad he'd insisted on the meeting. She looked even more beautiful than he'd remembered. There was a glow about her that took his breath away. He figured it must be the pregnancy. Peter had heard pregnancy had that kind of an effect on women. She was dressed in a white pant suit with a red scarf. She smiled warmly when she saw him. He rushed over to her and they embraced.

"Lucinda. I'm so glad you came. You look great."

"Thank you. It was so nice of you to invite me. I couldn't believe it when I got a call from the Councillor's office."

"I couldn't bear not seeing you again. I'm going away in few days and I'll be gone for quite awhile."

"Where are you going?" Lucinda asked with a hint of concern in her voice.

"I don't know exactly. Some kind of training facility."

"What kind of training do you need to be an intern?"

I shrugged. "You got me. I just do what I'm told."

They walked over to the house and went inside. The Councillor and Lorin were out, so aside from the housekeeping staff and Zippo, they had the place to themselves. Peter asked Lucinda if she wanted some sankee. She said she did.

"Lucinda. I want you to meet Zippo," he said.

Zippo bowed slightly and said, "At your service, Lucinda Dimitri."

"Bring us some sankee, would you Zippo? And some of those sweet cakes too."

"Right away, Peter Turner," Zippo said and then turned and headed toward the kitchen.

"The Councillor has a robot," Lucinda said. "I haven't seen a robot in a long time."

"Yeah, I heard they were kind of rare these days. . . . So, how are you feeling?"

She smiled and rubbed her belly. "I'm feeling a little queasy in the mornings, but I'm not showing yet."

"Well, it hasn't been that long."

"It's going to be a boy," Lucinda said proudly.

"Oh, wow! A boy? You know already?"

"I had a test done. It turned out blue. I can't wait to hold him in my arms."

He was about to say he couldn't wait either, then he stopped himself. It was probably unlikely that he would be allowed to see or hold the baby. On Earth he would have rights, but on Tarizon he was just a sperm donor with no parental rights whatsoever. It made him angry to think he'd never know his own child. If he had consented to it that would be one thing, but he hadn't. His only hope was to somehow make Lucinda fall in love with him. Then they could live together as a family.

The kitchen door swung open and Zippo came out with a pot of sankee and a plate full of sweet cakes. He adroitly set everything on the sankeetable and then asked if they wanted anything else. They said no and he retreated back to the kitchen.

"So is your mate happy you're pregnant?" Peter asked.

Lucinda shrugged and replied, "Not as much as I would have thought. He's happy for me of course as it is a great honor to be pregnant, but I'm not sure he's ready for a child. There are a lot of things he wants to do before we get tied down with a family."

"Really? Like what?"

"He wants to travel. His father was a sea captain from the Isle of Muhl. I think he wishes he could be out sailing the ocean blue on a freighter like his father."

"Where is the Isle of Muhl?" Peter asked for the sake of conversation.

"It's in the southern hemisphere near Ock Mezan."

He didn't ask her where Ock Mezan was because he didn't feel like a geography lesson right then. There were more important topics to cover like: *Do you miss me? Would you leave your mate if I asked you to? Do you love me?*

Their eyes met and his pulse quickened. *God this was hard.* "I think a lot about the time we spent together."

"Really? I would think that with all that you are doing you wouldn't have time to daydream."

He smiled. "I'm afraid I haven't been all that busy up until language school here recently. That was pretty intense, but even so, I often thought of you."

She raised her eyebrows and looked away. Almost as an afterthought she said, "I thought of you as well. We had some fun times together."

Peter smiled broadly.

She looked back at him stifling a laugh. "So are you going to show me around?"

"Sure," Peter said and stood up. "This way."

Peter led her through the dining room to the study and then showed her the kitchen, game room, and the living room. She was obviously impressed. "So, where's your bedroom?" she asked.

"Upstairs. Would you like to see it?"

She gave him a wry smile and said, "Yes, of course."

After showing her the Councillor's huge bedroom Peter led her into his room. Just as soon as they were inside she shut the door and put her arms around him. They kissed each other frantically and began to undress, but before they made love, Peter said, "Are you sure you want to do this? You don't have to. You're already pregnant."

She laughed. "You don't think I enjoyed getting this way?"

He laughed. "Well, I wasn't sure."

She kissed him again and there were no more questions. While the made love Peter wondered if it meant that she did love him? He still wasn't

112

sure, but he thought for the first time it might be so. When they were spent, Lucinda fell asleep. As he watched her peaceful slumber, he dreaded the thought of letting her go once again. Soon she would be back with her mate and he'd be on his way to boot camp for six phases. How could he ever win her love if he couldn't be with her? Depression surged through him like water through a storm drain. There was little doubt in his heart that his love for Lucinda was doomed.

16
Boot Camp

The night before Peter left for boot camp he was in a melancholy mood over Lucinda's departure. He had hoped she would profess her love for him, but she hadn't. They'd had sex, but love seemed to be a scarce commodity on Tarizon. Peter wondered if Lucinda even understood the concept. Fear also lingered in his mind. Fear and dread of what lay ahead for him in boot camp.

In the morning he was to report to the air transport station to be flown to the Island of Pogo where his military training was to take place. Pogo was to the southwest, some 1800 kylods from Shisk. For hundreds of cycles it had been a strategic military installation between the two continents of Lamaine Shane and Ock Mezan. Before unification Lamaine Shane and Ock Mezan were bitter enemies and were constantly fighting over the two big Islands between them, Pogo and Muhl. Pogo and Muhl were two of the few places where the air was clean enough to breathe. The prevailing westerly winds in these regions were so strong there that they kept most of the bad air away, making it a logical place for the TGA Training Center.

The depression that gripped Peter ever since Lucinda had left, he decided, was due to the fact that for the first time since his arrival on Tarizon he would be completely on his own. There would be no one whom he could confide in or turn to for help if things went wrong. At dawn's first light he was up and ready to go. After eating a quick breakfast, Lorin, Jake and Rhin escorted him to the subtram and gave him some last minute advice and encouragement.

"Don't worry, Peter," Jake said, "you'll do fine. The key to success

115

in boot camp is to blend in and not to be conspicuous. Just pay attention and do what you are told. They don't expect you to know anything when you get there. They'll teach you everything you'll need to know to make it through."

Peter nodded appreciatively. "Right. Thanks."

Lorin said, "Keep your ears open while you're there too. Many of the officers at Pogo are friends of the Vice-Chancellor. You may overhear some things that could be useful to us later."

"And make friends," Jake advised. "The more friends you have the easier time you'll have getting through."

"Yes," Lorin said, "The friendships you develop on Pogo may also prove helpful when the war breaks out."

"Yeah, but won't that be a little difficult? How will I know who to trust? If I make it known I'm a Loyalist, Videl's spies will know it as well."

"True. You'll have to be very careful. Don't tell anyone your true colors until they've disclosed theirs."

It was obvious to Peter that Jake and Lorin were as worried about boot camp as he was. They both had great expectations about how much he'd learn there. Peter just prayed he wouldn't disappoint them. His gear was stashed in a small backpack that he carried with him. The orders he had received indicated he would need nothing on Pogo Island other than personal hygiene items and any medicines that had been prescribed for him.

Lorin gave him a hug and Jake shook his hand as the light above the subtram entrance indicated the subtram had arrived. Peter knelt down and hugged Rhin. She barked as he got up and climbed aboard the subtram.

"Take good care of my rhutz," Peter said to them as the door began to close.

"Don't worry. We will," Jake replied.

It wasn't long before the doors opened again and Peter stepped into the transport station. He recognized it as the place where he'd first landed on Tarizon on Earth Shuttle 21. He noticed one of the big Earth shuttles being unloaded and many disoriented Earthchildren wandering around probably wondering who slipped them the LSD. He looked at his papers and saw that he was to go to Gate 33b. As he walked toward the gate, he noticed many different types of aircraft. He wondered what kind would be taking him to Pogo. When he got to the gate he was surprised to see a large transport plane being loaded. At the rear of the plane there was a table, manned by two men in miliary attire. Several recruits were talking to the soldiers at the table. He took a long breath and then made his way over to them.

"Sorri lanei," Peter said. "I'm Leek Lanzia."

The soldier in charge looked him over and then said, "Where are your orders?"

Peter pulled them out of his pocket and handed them to the soldier. The big man took them and gave them a once over. "Welcome, soldier. I'm sergeant Xorn Baig. Get you gear and climb aboard."

Looking up the ramp that led into the transport plane, Peter saw a group of recruits milling around. He picked up his bag and started up the ramp. A sudden chill made him shudder as he realized his military career had just begun. He thought of his father and the day he had reported for duty with the United States Marine Corps. In less than 24 hours after reporting for duty, his father had already been singled out as being a troublemaker and beaten up by his drill sergeant. Peter wondered if his luck would be any different.

A tall blond boy about Peter's age was standing at the top of the ramp, looking as scared as Peter was feeling. Peter said, "Hey, how is it going?"

He nodded and replied, "Okay, I guess. At least for now."

"I'm Leek," Peter said. "Leek Lanzia from Lower Azallo— Luva to be exact—have you ever heard of it?"

"The Underland, huh?" he said with a smile.

"I'm afraid so. How about you?"

"Syril Johs from Tributon, Lamaine Shane," he replied, "a little town called Lurka. It's on the east coast along the straits. You can call me Sy."

Peter nodded pretending to know where that was. "So, have you always wanted to be a soldier?"

Sy nodded his head and said, "Yes, of course. I must do my duty for the sake of Sandee and the people of Tarizon."

Peter looked into Sy's eyes to see if he was serious or just trying to impress anyone who might be listening.

"Right. What would you be doing if you weren't joining the army?"

He thought for a moment and said, "When my service is complete, I plan to be a second tier teacher."

"Really? I don't think I'd have the patience to be a teacher."

"What then?"

Peter thought a moment and replied, "Well, I was thinking about becoming an advocate."

"Ah, very good. You must be smart then."

Peter frowned, "I don't know about that. I just like to debate. I got it from my father; he was an advocate as well."

Sy and Peter talked for quite awhile as recruit after recruit appeared and made their way aboard. Eventually Sergeant Baig stood up and started packing up his paperwork. When he had everything stowed into a briefcase, he started up the ramp. At the top of the ramp he said. "Find a seat and fasten your seat belts. Takeoff will be at 0830."

Everyone began scrambling to find a seat and get buckled in. Baig was a tall, intense-looking man with wide shoulders and a muscular physique—not a man you wanted to mess with, Peter reckoned. Sy found an empty seat and waved for Peter to take the one next to him. After everyone was buckled in, the big ramp began to close. Soon it snapped into place and Baig went forward out of view. A few loons later the big ship lurched and began to vibrate. Syril looked at Peter and he smiled. Then suddenly the ship thrust forward with a tremendous jolt. Had they not been buckled in, they'd of been flung into the bulkhead and severely injured. Peter's ears began to ache as they gained altitude. He yawned and felt his ears pop and then he settled back for the flight to the Pogo Island.

It seemed like a very long flight. There weren't any windows to look out, so he just closed his eyes and tried to sleep. He'd never been able to sleep very well sitting up but for some reason he had no trouble on this day. When he awoke, he could feel the plane descending. He looked over at Sy and raised his eyebrows.

"I think we're about to land," Sy said.

Peter leaned back, took a deep breath, and rotated his neck back and forth trying to relax. "I'm not looking forward to this," Peter said.

"Then why did you join?" Sy asked.

That was a good question, unfortunately Peter couldn't give Sy a straight answer. He started to say his father was in the Army but then realized he'd have to come up with a story about his father's military career. That wouldn't work, so he said, "I want to go into politics someday, so I figured a military background would be good."

Sy nodded, "That makes sense. . . . I joined because I've always loved guns and weaponry and wanted to make a career of it."

"Really? How did you get interested in that?"

"Oh, I don't know. My father used to take me hunting and he usually had one gun or another around the house. He taught me to love and respect them."

"Hmm. I've had virtually no experience with guns. My dad owned a gun but didn't really like having it around. It was a good thing he had it though. A man attacked him with a knife one time and he had to shoot the guy to stop him."

"Did he kill him?" Sy asked.

"No. Just wounded him. My dad wouldn't kill someone unless he had to."

There was a bump and a lurch as the big transport made its landing. Sergeant Baig came forward and told them to remain seated until the plane stopped. A few loons later the plane came to a halt and everyone got up and gathered their things together. After the rear ramp had descended, Sergeant Baig led them down and onto a transport tram that looked like a giant silver bullet. Once inside they were whisked to their barracks at the Argot Army Training Center.

It was late afternoon when they marched into a large processing center where their papers were checked and they were assigned to their barracks. Fortunately, Sy and Peter were assigned to the same barracks and managed to get bunks near each other. After everyone had put their gear away, Sergeant Baig advised them on dining protocol and then led them to the nutrition center.

The nutrition center wasn't anything like what Peter expected. He had envisioned a large cafeteria style dining hall, serving barely edible food and manned by soldiers assigned to KP duty. But that wasn't the case at all. The nutrition center was very modern, clean, and staffed by robots. Soldiers, it appeared, were afforded a high standing on Tarizon. Instead of the long picnic tables with bench seats as he'd expected, there were individual tables of four like in a typical restaurant back on Earth. Sy and Peter went through the line and loaded up their trays with food and drink. When they started looking for a table a candidate got up from his chair and approached them.

"We've got room over here," the green-eyed boy said.

Peter was a little surprised by the invitation but grateful nevertheless, as he didn't see many open chairs. "Oh, great. Thanks," he said and followed the boy to the table.

"I'm Tam and this is Red," Tam said, giving Peter a hard look that made him uncomfortable.

Peter turned to the red-headed boy at the table. "I'm Pe. . .ah. . .Leek Lanzia and this is Syril Johs."

They all shook hands. Peter looked back the candidate who'd invited him to the table hoping for an explanation for his goodwill.

"I'm glad we found you," Tam said.

Peter frowned. "You were looking for me?"

Tam didn't answer, his eyes seeming to be transfixed on Peter. Red laughed nervously. "My real name is Loonas Levitur from Merria. But, you can call me Red. Everybody does."

Peter looked away from Tam hoping he'd quit staring at him. Noticing this, Tam sighed and said, "Sorry about that but I'm a bit unnerved by all of this." He extended his hand. "I'm Tamurus Lavendar from Serie. My friends, what few I have, call me Tam."

Peter smiled and looked into Tam's green eyes. Tam stared back and Peter felt a strange sensation in his head. He blinked and looked away. It was a weird, disturbing sensation that scared him. It was the same feeling he'd had when he first encountered the rhutz and later Threebeard.

Dinner conversation centered around their fears and expectations for the upcoming weeks. When that topic had been worn out, they started to talk about their homes and families. Peter gave them his imaginary story of his childhood in Azallo trying to sound as convincing as possible. He had always been good at story telling, so he didn't think anyone doubted any of his words except Tam, whose eyes seemed to slice through him like a molten knife. Red was next.

"I live in a city called Gult on the coast of Merria which is on the western end of Turvin. It's a domed city and we have a nice compartment near the ocean. My father is a dentist and I have an older brother and two younger sisters. I someday want to be a dentist like my father, but first I want to serve Sandee and defend the Supreme Mandate."

Tam rolled his eyes and said, "You think joining the TGA is serving Sandee and defending the Supreme Mandate?"

Red winced and asked, "Isn't it?"

Tam leaned forward and whispered. "The rumor is that the Vice-chancellor will soon take power and not by election or legal succession."

Red squinted, "Where did you hear that?"

"I . . . well . . . let's just say I have it from good authority. And, I guarantee you Vice-Chancellor Lai cares little for Sandee or the Supreme Mandate."

"We shouldn't be talking about this." Sy said. "They listen to everything we say."

Tam shook his head. "Don't worry about it. I picked this table because it's in a blind spot. The camera can't see us."

"What about the audio receivers?" Sy protested.

"Relax. I've disabled them."

"What if one of us is a Purist?" Sy retorted.

Tam laughed. "There are no Purists at this table."

They all just looked at Tam in disbelief.

Tam shrugged. "Okay? I'll admit it. We're not all siting here by chance. I made sure we'd sit together and I know none of you have any love for Videl Lai."

"And how did you figure that out?" Sy asked.

He shrugged. "I could just tell."

Peter gave Tam a hard look and then laughed. "I wish I could see into a man's mind like that."

"You can," Tam replied and met Peter's eyes again. Peter's body suddenly became numb as Tam's gaze pierced through him. He realized Tam *could* read his mind and probably knew his secret. Peter looked away trying to break the connection. Red and Sy looked at them curiously.

Peter shook his head trying to get rid of the strange feeling. "Okay," Peter said forcing a laugh, "So, Mr. Omniscient One, why have you gathered us here together?"

Tam didn't hesitate. "When I gave my oath to defend the Supreme Mandate, I meant it. I was looking for others who felt the same way."

"I meant it," Red said.

"So did I," Sy added.

Peter said nothing. Tam continued, "After this day we'll all be too busy for socializing, so I had to find you today."

"Why? What do you want from us?" Peter asked.

"If Videl Lai becomes Chancellor and stomps on the Supreme Mandate, I say we cut his heart out and feed it to the rhutz."

Peter was taken aback by the reference to the rhutz. He gave Tam a hard look again, wondering who he was and if he could be trusted. He didn't want to step into a trap on his first day, but Tam's feelings seemed genuine. He decided to go with his gut feeling.

"My sentiments exactly," Peter said smiling. Red and Sy nodded in agreement.

Tam raised his glass and gave a toast to their new oath. Peter said, "But let's not feed his heart to the rhutz. I keep one back home and I wouldn't want to feed her something so vile."

Red's mouth dropped. Sy's eyes widened, "You keep a rhutz at your home?"

Peter nodded. "She sleeps next to my bed."

Red began to laugh. "Boy I heard about the people of the Underland, but that takes the cake. You have a rhutz for a pet. Sandee, bless me."

Tam looked at him and Peter could see tears welling in his eyes. "I was right," he said. "You are the one. Oh, praise Sandee! You're the—"

"Don't say it," Peter said forcefully. "Not here."

Red and Sy stared at them. Tam looked away with a smile so broad on his face that he looked like he'd just heard the joke of the century. Peter started to laugh as well, acting like he'd just got the joke. Red and Sy joined in but only out of sheer spontaneity. They were still clueless as to what was going on between their two new found friends.

After dinner they were assembled in their barracks and were being addressed by their commanding officer. He was a tall, lean man, with a thin somber face. He wore a combat uniform with a green cap. Only three

122

silver bars on his shoulder distinguished him from the other officers they'd had seen since they arrived at camp.

He was introduced by Sergeant Baig as Commandant Bak Lithrum. He began, "Welcome to Pogo Island. I trust you have found your accommodations satisfactory—perhaps better than you expected, yes?. . .Well, let me explain. When each of you signed up for service in Tarizon's Global Forces you gave us the right to utilize your services as we thought best. As you will recall after you enlisted, each of you were given extensive physical, psychological, and intellectual testing. Based on the results of those tests you were assigned to one of the thirteen TGA global training facilities. Twelve of these training facilities are for regular ground units and the thirteenth is for officers and special operations personnel. If you haven't guessed already, Pogo Island is the thirteenth training facility. That means you have been assessed either to be officers in the TGA or have special abilities that suit you for special operations.

"Don't let me lead you astray, however. Just because we will be taking great pains to make your stay at Pogo Island as pleasant and productive as possible doesn't mean you have it made. On the contrary, we know that testing is only an indication of the probability of your success as an officer or a member of a special operations unit. We will be watching your actual performance very carefully to make sure the tests were right.

"Most of you know little or nothing about military operations, so a large portion of your time here will be spent learning tactics, weaponry, intelligence, meteorology, geography, and navigation. We'll also be spending a lot of time getting you mentally and physically conditioned for combat. So your days here will be long and hard and we will expect no less than your full attention and dedication to achieving these objectives.

"Like I said, you will be watched at all times; and if we determine that you are either unfit to be at Pogo Island or unwilling to give the attention and devotion necessary to be successful, you will shipped off to the TGA training facility at Muhl where you will find your accommodations much less pleasant.

"So, take the rest of the evening off tonight. Rest and get to know one another, for tomorrow at 0630 your training will begin and it will be an experience you will never forget."

The Commandant saluted and made his exit. Sergeant Baig said,

"At ease. . . . Now do as the Commandant has asked. Get acquainted until the night bell sounds at 2200 and the lights go out at 2250. Then there will be absolute silence until the morning alarm sounds at 0430. At that time you will immediately get dressed, take care of your personal needs, make your beds, and be standing at your bunks at 0500 for transport to the nutrition center. After breakfast at 0600 you will be transported to the quartermaster for issuance of outerwear and basic essentials. From 0700to 0830 you'll attend your first class in personal armaments. Lunch is at 1300. I'll fill you in the remainder of the day then. Dismissed!"

Just as soon as Sergeant Baig left the barracks, the room erupted in excited chatter. Sergeant Baig's news had everyone feeling good. Peter shook Sy's hand and said, "Congratulations!"

Sy shook his head and replied, "I thought I did terrible on all those tests. I can't believe I'm going to be an officer. My parents will be so happy."

Peter thought about his parents. They wouldn't be very happy to find out he was in the army and preparing to go to war. He wondered if he'd ever see them again. Red interrupted his thoughts.

"My parents will have a durk bird," Red said. "They thought I'd be lucky to even get selected for the TGA."

Tam put his hand on Peter's shoulders and whispered, "We need to talk."

Peter nodded and began scanning the room for a safe place. There was a door at the end of the room that was slightly ajar. He pointed to the door and then started toward it with Tam close behind. When they got to the door they slipped outside.

There didn't appear to be anyone around but Tam put his finger in front of his lips indicating he didn't want him to speak. He whispered, "Everything we say can be heard."

Peter nodded. He pointed to his head and looked him in the eyes. He felt Tam's eyes penetrate his mind and he could hear him in his mind's eye.

"*Everything we do or say is observed so we must communicate with our thoughts.*"

Peter blinked and stepped back. He had felt their minds touch earlier, but hadn't realized they could actually communicate without speaking.

Tam's thoughts popped into his head again, "*I know you can understand me. I can see it in your eyes. Look me in the eye and concentrate. I will listen.*"

Peter shook his head in disbelief. This couldn't be happening. Tam frowned. Peter took a deep breath, looked him in the eyes and concentrated, "*Who do you think I am?*"

Tam smiled and replied, "*The Liberator. When you said you had a rhutz for a pet, I knew.*"

"*You mustn't ever mention this to anyone.*"

"*Obviously. If the Vice-chancellor knew you were here he'd send an assassin to kill you and all your friends.*"

The fact that Tam had so quickly identified him made Peter worry. How long would it take for others to learn his true identity? "*Then why be my friend?*"

"*It is my destiny. Since the first day I heard the Prophecy of the Liberator, I knew I would somehow be involved in his struggle. For awhile I thought I might be the Liberator myself, then one night I had a dream. I was at the Liberator's side in battle helping to destroy our enemies. The dream came often after that—almost every night for weeks. So then I knew I was not to be the Liberator, but to be his protector. In my dreams we both wore the uniform of the TGA, so I knew when my age was right I must join it and let destiny be done.*"

Peter shook his head and smiled enthusiastically. "*I first learned that I was the Liberator from a mutant named Threebeard. It was a total surprise and shock. Then a rhutz saved me from being killed by a street gang. I'm still not used to the idea of being the Liberator.*"

"*Threebeard. Yes. I know of him. He talks to me through his mind as we are doing now, but I have never met him. He told me that he had seen you and the time of the Liberator had come.*"

Before Peter could send another thought an alarm sounded and the lights flashed two times. He shrugged and said out loud, "I guess it's time to crash."

"Crash?" Tam said.

"Sleep. Go to bed. We should hurry too. If we're not in bed when the lights go out, we'll get in trouble, and you don't want to get in trouble your first day of boot camp. Trust me."

Tam frowned but didn't question Peter further. They went quickly to their bunks, undressed, and jumped under the covers. Peter's head felt heavy and was throbbing a bit from the telepathic exchange with Tam. He couldn't believe that he was telepathic. It was totally amazing. As he was basking in the delight of discovery of his newly discovered gift, Tam's words came back to him. *"If the Vice-chancellor knew your were here he'd send an assassin to kill you and all your friends."*

Peter's joy suddenly evaporated and a dull pain settled in the pit of his stomach. Did Videl Lai already know he was here? If he was telepathic he might have heard Threebeard just like Tam had heard him. Suddenly, he wasn't very sleepy.

17

Friends and Allies

Peter's eyes wouldn't close. He tossed and turned trying to get comfortable so he could get some desperately needed sleep, but to no avail. His insomnia was not just due to his fear that Videl Lai may know of his arrival on Pogo Island, but for many other reasons as well. He was excited about the discovery of his telepathic abilities. He couldn't get over the fact that he could communicate with someone without opening his mouth. Then there was the arrival of dawn and the commencement of basic training. There was a lot of pressure on him not just to do well, but to do exceedingly well. He wondered if that were possible. Then, of course, there was Lucinda. Not a day, or even an hour, went by without him thinking of her. If he could have just called her; but Sergeant Baig told them during orientation that they could not communicate with the outside world during boot camp—no letters, telephone calls, or electronic communications of any sort. They were expected to devote every waking hour to completing their training without any distractions.

At the first crack of daylight the morning alarm sounded. There were moans from many of the candidates around Peter dreading the new day. They were called *candidates* now rather than recruits—candidates for admission into the elite group of officers of the TGA. Since Peter hadn't slept, he was up instantly making his bunk. He noticed Tam was still asleep, so he grabbed his leg and shook him.

"Get up! Didn't you hear the alarm? You don't want to get into trouble on the first day."

Tam rolled over and tried to go back to sleep. Peter shook him again until he raised his head and gave him a dirty look.

"Wake up. If Sgt. Baig catches you asleep you'll be in serious trouble."

Tam rolled over, dropped one leg off the side of the bed and yawned. "Okay. Okay, I'm getting up."

At that instant, Sgt. Baig emerged from his quarters and yelled, "Aaattent. . .tion!" He strolled down the center of the barracks looking at each candidate. When he came across a candidate still asleep, he kicked the bunk hard nearly knocking him onto the floor. The startled candidate grabbed the side of the bed to keep from falling off. He looked up at Sgt. Baig, his mouth wide open. Sgt. Baig asked him his name. He replied, "Lattie Burrows."

"Do you have a hearing problem, Mr. Burrows?"

"No, Sergeant," Burrows replied.

"Then what were you doing sleeping when you're supposed to be standing by your bunk?"

"Ah . . . Well . . .Sorry—"

"Sorry means nothing when you're in combat," Sergeant screamed. "You'll do extra PT tonight after everyone else is finished."

Burrows lowered his head and nodded, "Yes, Sergeant."

Baig continued down the row of bunks until he came to Tam's. He looked at the unmade bunk and Tam's disheveled appearance. "What's your name candidate?" Sgt. Baig asked.

"Tamurus Lavendar, Sergeant," Tam replied.

"Well, it looks like you had a problem waking up as well," the Sergeant said, and then yanked Tam's mattress onto the floor nearly beheading Tam in the process. "Now, when I dismiss the squad here in a tik you better get this mess cleaned up, and you'll be keeping Mr. Burrows company tonight when he does his extra PT."

Tam rolled his eyes and frowned. Sergeant Baig's eyes widened. He moved in on Tam until their faces were nearly touching. "Do you have a problem with that Mr. Lavendar?"

"No, Sergeant! Not at all."

"Good, because candidates who have problems with my orders won't be in this squad very long."

Sergeant Baig finished his inspection and dismissed the squad for breakfast. Tam stayed in the barracks to clean up the mess Sergeant Baig had left him. After breakfast they were transported to the quartermaster where they were issued their uniforms and boots. When they had secured their gear in the barracks, they went to their first class. It was on weaponry and was held in a crowded room in the armory. Their instructor, a stout muscular man with a red complexion, was Lt. Kreig Londry. He talked in a deep deliberate voice that reminded Peter of Marlon Brando. First he showed them a standard issue pistol.

"This is the C34 pistol. It is a semiautomatic, magazine fed, recoil operated, double action pistol with a smart heat-seeking ball. It's magazine holds fifteen rounds and if your aim is a little off the ball will veer toward the heat of your target. It's also good when you don't have a straight shot. You simply shoot as close to your target as possible and if the ball detects a heat pattern it will veer towards it. Now this doesn't mean you don't have to be a good shot, the C34 will only veer up to 18%, but it will give you an edge over the enemy."

Next he picked up a rifle and said, "This is the R6, the standard issue rifle for the TGA. Lightweight, durable, and always dependable, the R6 can fire either semi-automatic (single-shot) or 6-round bursts. It also can fire heat-seeking balls. Become proficient with the R6. It is your most versatile weapon, able to engage targets at long range and in close-quarters. As a general rule, select single-shot mode when attacking at long range. However, when you are going to be up close, such as in urban operations, switch to burst mode."

Lt. Londry set the R6 down and picked up another rifle and held it up. "This is the T7. It's a modular light rifle weapon system that delivers a coherent, directed lethal laser beam over a range in excess of 300 strides against visible targets. The T7 provides a total integrated weapons system, including high energy density power source, laser medium resonator and focusing system. It weighs approximately the same as the R6 and is capable of delivering a maximum rate of fire of approximately five lethal laser bursts per tik. Differing from other individual small arms, the T7 does not employ ammunition in the conventional sense, relying upon the thermal energy provided by a D33 power source. The T7 may be fielded for continuous tactical use for a period of over 60 days which gives it an obvious advantage over the R6."

Lt. Londry put down the T7 and continued, "Now this afternoon each of you will be issued a C34 pistol and either a R6 rifle or T7 laser rifle. You will be instructed in the proper use, handling, and care of these weapons. Over the course of your training you will become proficient in their use. These three weapons are the ones you will be using most often in your combat operations, but there are many more weapons that you will be trained to use in the course of your time here at Pogo Island."

Lt. Londry dismissed them to go to Physical Training or PT as the sergeant called it. PT started in a huge aircraft hanger where they changed into workout clothes and waited for Sergeant Baig to direct their activities. When he arrived he took them through some warmup exercises and then led them out the door for a long run through the base. Not being in such great shape, Peter began to lag after only the first mile. Fortunately, there were a few in worse shape than he who got the brunt of the sergeant's wrath that afternoon. Sy and Red were in better shape than Peter. They stayed well in the pack ahead of him. Although Tam didn't seem to mind the running and probably could have stayed up at the front of the pack, he hung back with Peter partly to keep him company but also to watch out for him. He was taking his job as the Liberator's protector seriously. When the sergeant finally turned and headed back in the general direction of the hanger, Peter was glad because he was exhausted and couldn't have gone much farther.

After dinner they broke up into three groups and three instructors from the armory taught them how to take apart and reassemble the C34 pistol, the R6 rifle, and the T7 laser gun. Then they were issued manuals to study that night before lights went out. When their instruction period was over Tam and Lattie Burrows were told to report for extra PT. Peter felt badly for Tam and Lattie and thanked God it wasn't him. The day had been so grueling, he couldn't imagine doing anything other than collapsing into his bunk and going to sleep.

Just before the evening alarm, Tam and Lattie returned from their extra time with Sergeant Baig. Lattie looked pale and was limping. Tam looked angry. When Peter saw them he rushed over. "So, what did he make you do?"

"I don't want to talk about it," Tam said. "I just want to sleep."

Tam fell into his bunk and closed his eyes. Peter turned to Lottie and said, "Tell me what happened."

Lattie shrugged. "He just lectured us on the importance of following orders. You know—soldiers die when orders are ignored or disregarded. Then he made us do every exercise imaginable until we were so tired we could hardly move."

"I know. You've been gone for a long time. I can't believe he kept you so long."

Before Peter could get more details out of Lattie, the night alarm went off and everyone scrambled to get into bed.

The next morning Lattie and Tam were up before the alarm went off and they had their bunks made long before Sergeant Baig showed up for roll call. They had obviously learned an important lesson—not to cross Sergeant Baig.

The next day all the candidates were issued their weapons and began learning how to take them apart, clean, and reassemble them quickly. Within a few days they were out on the shooting range firing them at target robots. Each day PT got a little more vigorous as their endurance increased and Sergeant Baig pushed them a little harder. Although they were only getting half the sleep they'd been used to, Peter felt strong and fit—better than he could ever remember.

At the end of their third phase there were tests and field exams scheduled. These were important because anyone who didn't pass them would be kicked out of the program and sent to the Isle of Muhl. The commandant had mentioned Muhl as not being somewhere they wanted to end up, but he hadn't elaborated. Since that time there had been much speculation about what went on at the TGA Training Facility on the Isle of Muhl, but nobody knew for sure until the matter came up during a weapons class. Lt. Londry was explaining to them how they would be tested on the T7 laser gun.

"Remember, always keep the safety mechanism engaged when you are using the T7. This is a very powerful and lethal weapon. If it accidentally goes off it will probably kill someone—and there's a fifty-fifty chance that someone will be you. If you forget to engage the safety after your test is completed you'll be severely penalized. If your other tests scores are just average, this penalty could throw you below an acceptable level and mean you'd soon be on you way to the Isle of Muhl."

Tam raised his hand. "Lieutenant."

Lt. Londry nodded to Tam.

"The commandant also mentioned the Isle of Muhl. I was just wondering about it. How is it different than here?"

The Lieutenant's eyes narrowed. "You haven't heard about Pegaport on the Isle of Muhl?"

They all shook their heads.

"Hmm. Well, we don't have much time, but I'll give you the short version.

"My experience on Muhl came by accident. I was here at Pogo teaching my weapons class as usual. The candidates were just about to graduate and go to their permanent assignments and I was scheduled for a holiday. Unfortunately, about this time there was word of an accident at the Pegaport Training Center on the Isle of Muhl. One of the drill sergeants had been killed by a candidate who mishandled a T7 laser gun. The commandant was outraged and humiliated by the accident and in the course of an investigation it was determined the weapon's instructor was to blame.

"Just about that time I was set to be transported to Dalo where I was planning to lie on the beach next to my mate for 14 days, I got orders to report to Pegaport. The next morning I found myself in the most horrid hell hole you could imagine. The island had been ravaged a few phases earlier by a hurricane and most of the buildings and training facilities were in shambles. I soon learned that Pegaport was where they sent all of the misfits, troublemakers, derelicts, mutants, and washed out candidates."

A sigh of despair went through the ranks of candidates listening intently to Lt. Londry's words. He continued, "The drill sergeants at Pegaport are tough and mean. They have to be to keep their recruits in line. Most of recruits who graduate will be foot soldiers so they have to be in top physical condition. A special emphasis is put on PT. Long morning runs, rigorous weight training, and strict discipline is the norm. Those who can't maintain the pace or follow the rigid rules end up in Hell Squad.

The candidates squirmed in their chairs and exchanged glances. Lt.

Londry's eyes narrowed. "Hell Squad is where *the accident* took place. I say *accident* but many believe it was murder. You see in Hell Squad recruits have to be treated differently. They have to be given special motivation to break their independent spirit. There is no room for independent thinkers—second guessers—in the TGA. Orders must be carried out quickly and precisely as given—command thinks, soldiers obey.

"Motivation is dished out in a number of interesting ways in Hell Squad—stick therapy, food or sleep deprivation, buzz gun motivation, or, if all else fails, electric implants. Stick therapy is pretty simple. The drill sergeant carries around a long white stick made of a hard rubber. When he strikes you with it, it'll hurt as much as a 8 ft. whip, and has been known to cause permanent scaring. It's used across a candidate's arm or back if he's not cooperating.

Peter looked at Red who looked pale and ready to puke.

"Food or sleep deprivation is employed in cases where candidates have a high pain tolerance, or actually enjoy pain. It's pretty self-explanatory. Meals and hours of sleep are taken away for bad behavior. Recruits who need food and sleep tend to become much more cooperative. But even that is not enough for some.

"The buzz gun is harmless but very painful. Ten times the pain of the stick. Electric implants allow the drill sergeant to impose pain from a distance for substandard performance or disobedience.

Peter swallowed hard.

"It was in Hell Squad that the sergeant was killed, or murdered, if you want my opinion. His name was Sergeant Zolt Hovic. He'd just led his unit on a grueling march through the swamp lands on the north part of the island. One of his recruits was a mutant who had a short attention span and often wandered off from the rest of the squad. The sergeant had an implant put in his back so whenever he seemed distracted or wandered off, he could give him a little jolt. It was very effective; however, it upset the rest of the squad. One of recruits, a mutant from Shisk, named Threebeard, was particularly offended by the use of the electric implants and complained to the Commandant that use of the device was cruel and inhumane. The Commandant rejected the complaint and told Threebeard he'd have one put in his back if he bothered him again with his petty complaints.

"Some say Threebeard was behind the killing of Sergeant Hovic, but luckily for him he had an irrefutable alibi—he was some distance away when the accident occurred."

The reference to Threebeard got Peter's attention. He thought about Lt. Londry's story. He obviously didn't know about Threebeard's telekinetic abilities. Threebeard didn't have to be close to the T7 laser to make it discharge. Peter chuckled to himself. The Sergeant had gotten what he deserved and the Commandant totally underestimated Threebeard. Now Peter understood how Threebeard had come to be the leader of the mutants. He wondered if he could learn anything else from the Lieutenant. Peter hadn't tried to read someone's mind yet but he figured he had to start sometime. Not knowing exactly how the process worked, he closed his eyes and tried to clear his mind. Then he positioned himself so he had an unobstructed view of the Lieutenant.

While Lt. Londry was winding up his story, Peter gave him a hard look and when their eyes met, he tried to look through them. Nothing happened so he tried again, this time concentrating hard on what he wanted to know, but all he got was a headache. On the third attempt Peter tried to imagine waves flowing between his mind and the Lieutenant's. Peter felt a dull pain in his head and noticed Lt. Londry looking alarmed and rubbing his temples. A name popped into Peter's head. The name of the Commandant responsible for the abuse and torture of TGA recruits on the Isle of Muhl was none other than Videl Lai.

Peter knew then how the Vice-chancellor had acquired his military connections. He'd apparently served for some time in the military before he entered into politics. No doubt the generals, who were expected to support him in his efforts to wrest control of the government away from its elected officials, were old cronies from his military service. There was no telling what rewards he had promised them for their support.

At dinner that night the upcoming exams and Lt. Londry's story of his short stay at Pegaport on the Isle of Muhl were the hot topics. If Lt. Londry's intention was to put the fear of Sandee into the squad he had certainly done so. Although Peter didn't want to wash out, he felt fairly certain if he did, he himself wouldn't end up on the Isle of Muhl. Surely, he thought, the Councillor would pull him out of the TGA and bring him back to Shisk. At any rate, thoughts of washing out were ridiculous. He was the Liberator, for the sake of Sandee, and wouldn't be at the bottom of the class, but at the top, surely.

As was their routine, Tam, Sy, Red, and Peter sat at their usual table in the nutrition center. They had become good friends and had made an oath to watch each others backs during boot camp. Videl Lai was on Peter's mind when they sat down at their usual table out of view of the several video cameras that kept an eye on the candidates during their meals.

"Guess who was the commandant at Pegaport when Lt. Londry was there," he said.

"Who?" Red asked.

"The Vice-chancellor—Videl Lai himself."

Sy squinted and replied, "How do you know that?"

He shrugged. "I read Lt. Londry's mind. Not very well, I am afraid, but I did manage to get that information. . . . I also know who murdered Sergeant Hovic." He told them about his encounter with Threebeard and then continued, "He's telekinetic, so I'm sure he caused the laser to fire and kill Sergeant Hovic. Pretty slick, huh?"

"I'm surprised they let a three-headed mutant into the TGA," Red commented.

"There are a lot of Mutants in the TGA, but none are allowed to be officers. As long as your mutation doesn't affect your ability to fight, they don't care what it is."

"What if we get assigned to one of the Vice-Chancellor's divisions?" Red asked.

"Don't worry about that," Peter said. "I'll make sure you get assigned to one loyal to the Supreme Mandate."

"How will you do that?" Red asked.

Tam looked at Peter and said, "We should tell them."

Peter took a deep breath and then nodded.

Tam told them of the Prophecy and Peter filled them in on his connection to Councillor Garcia. It was a gamble, but he had gotten to know them pretty well over the past few weeks and was sure they would be on his side.

Red shook his head and said, "Wow. So, you're the Liberator?"

"Some people think so," Peter replied. "Although, I don't claim the title. I didn't get a vision or talk to God or anything like that. I don't even know the name of the prophet who is responsible for predicting my arrival. It could be just somebody's joke."

"He is the Liberator," Tam said enthusiastically, "Without a doubt. Threebeard thought so and announced his coming. . . and he walks with a rhutz. I tell you, Leek is the Liberator."

"So, are you asking for our help?" Red asked.

Peter replied, "Yes, I need all the help I can get. We must fulfill the Prophecy and save Tarizon and Earth."

"Earth?" Sy asked.

"Yes, my planet is at risk as well. Lai has always favored colonizing earth. If he is successful here, he will then make war on Earth and rule both worlds. With Tarizon's advanced technology and weaponry, the governments on Earth will be at a tremendous disadvantage."

"Count me in," Red said.

Sy nodded, "And me as well."

Tam smiled and added, "I was on board before we even met."

Peter laughed. "Good, then. Now all we have to do is get by our field tests and written exams. I don't want our first mission to be rescuing one of us from Pegaport."

18

Detection

Lorin rushed to her father's office as soon as she received the summons. The message had been marked urgent. She wondered what it could be. Had it happened? Had the Chancellor been assassinated? She hoped that wasn't the case. They were nowhere near being ready for civil war. A rush of dread suddenly hit her. Was it Leek? Had he been discovered?

When she stepped through the door her father's assistant told her to go right in. Her father was seated at his desk looking pale.

"Father, what is it?"

He looked up. "Lorin. Thank God you're here. We've got a serious problem. Videl has discovered that Leek is the Liberator."

"How do you know that?"

"I know," he said running a hand through his hair, "because my intern has been murdered!"

Lorin let out a gasp. "Oh, Sandee, no!"

"They found his body a little while ago. They stabbed him the hall outside the courtroom. There was a lot of blood."

Lorin gave her father a thoughtful look "So, they found out you were protecting the Liberator and now they think he's dead. That is good, right?" Lorin muttered. "Where is the body? We mustn't—"

"It's too late. Someone discovered it right away and summoned the bodytakers. By sunset they will know they killed the wrong man."

"Father! What if they try to kill you? Videl will know you're the one organizing the Loyalist movement to resist him."

"Don't worry. I've got plenty of security, and besides, if I were murdered everyone would know it was Videl and it would give the

Chancellor an excuse to arrest him. It would be a stupid move to try to kill me before he legally succeeds to the Chancellorship."

"All right," Lorin said tentatively. "Promise me you'll be careful and not stray away from your guards. I couldn't stand to lose you."

"Don't worry. I'll be fine. It's Leek who you should be worrying about."

"Yes. We should get him a message. Videl will soon figure out he went to Pogo and try to kill him there. It will be easy—just another training accident."

"You're right," the Councillor said. "It will be risky but we have no choice. Send him a message and warn him; we can't let them kill him."

"Maybe we should pull him out of there? Take him somewhere else for his training?"

"No. There isn't time. He must learn all he can about the TGA and there's no better place than at their top school and from their most knowledgeable instructors. I've got a friend at the base who I'll have keep an eye on him."

"Sgt. Baig?"

"Yes, it will be hard to kill Leek when he's under such close scrutiny by so many military officers. Sgt. Baig can make sure he's never alone."

"But what if one of those very officers tries to kill him?"

"Videl wouldn't take such a chance yet. He's not ready to seize power. He wouldn't chance getting involved in a murder investigation at such a critical time. If he tries to kill Leek it will be an outsider who he employs for the task—someone he can disavow."

"All right. I'll get a message to him at least, so he will know of the danger."

"Good. . . . Now tell me. How is your intelligence network coming?"

"Very well. I've had my staff discreetly inquiring as to who in the Council of Interpreters will stand behind the Supreme Mandate should Videl assume power. Of course, a lot depends on how he becomes Chancellor. If there is an assassination over fifty percent indicated they will support you in leading a loyalist movement. If the assassination attempt

138

can be connected in anyway to Videl then you'll have nearly unanimous support as every Councillor has given oath to the Supreme Mandate."

"So, how many have agreed to provide us intelligence when the war breaks out?"

"Two hundred and twenty-seven so far are on board. Many are already sending us data."

"Good. What about Jake? How is his communications project coming?"

"He thinks he's discovered an outdated satellite network that was abandoned by the TGA about ten cycles ago. He's put together a team of communications experts who should be able to get it on-line and functional again. It won't be as good as what the TGA has but it will be better than working in the dark."

"All right. Go write your letter to Leek. Tell him our prayers will be with him."

"Yes, Father," Lorin said hurrying off.

Lorin was sick with fear. If it was so easy to kill the Councillor's aide, how much more difficult would it be to kill the Councillor himself? She wished she hadn't supported the Liberator charade. Now her father's life was in danger. Videl knew that her father had been harboring the Liberator. He'd be angry. Why not kill your most potent rival when he is weak and it is unexpected? Her father would be an easy target despite his protests. Instead of going straight back to her office to write the letter to Leek, she went to see Colonel Tomel about her father's security. After all, Leek was a nobody, just a pawn in the war against Videl, but her father was blood and would some day be, Sandee willing, the Chancellor of Tarizon.

19

Assassination

The night before their day of reckoning, Peter was summoned to Sgt. Baig's quarters. When he got there the sergeant told him to take a seat at a small work table. He was a little scared being summoned to his quarters as that usually meant he was in trouble. Racking his brain, however, he couldn't imagine what it was that he had done wrong. Sgt. Baig sat across from him and dropped a yellow envelope on the table. It had an urgent look and a fancy seal. Sgt. Baig looked at Peter warily and then pushed it toward him.

"This came for you, although I can't imagine why Councillor Garcia would have any interest in you."

Peter shrugged, not knowing how to respond. Sgt. Baig motioned for Peter to open it, so he did.

"It says *confidential* so I won't ask you to read it aloud, but if you want to keep it confidential, I'd suggest you burn it once you've read it. Otherwise, it's content will soon be discovered. Several people know it has been delivered and I'm sure they are wondering about it. Councillor Garcia has many enemies here at Argot. Fortunately for you, I'm not one of them."

Peter swallowed hard and opened the envelope. There was a single handwritten page. He recognized Lorin's handwriting.

L.L.,

It was risky sending you this letter, but we felt it was necessary under the circumstances. Something terrible has happened. The Councillor's intern has been murdered. He was shot at close range by assassins. You can figure out the *significance of this malicious deed.*

Although we mourn the loss of our friend this may actually work in our favor if people think you are dead. But, in the interest of caution, you must be alert. There are those who are not so easily fooled.

The man who gave you this letter is a friend. If you get in trouble, you can turn to him for help.

Sandee be with you!

L.G.

The sergeant said, "So, take your letter and burn it. Speak to no one about it, if you know what's good for you."

"Yes, sergeant," Peter said getting up. He turned and left the office. On the way back to the barracks Peter slipped into the men's room, tore the letter into little pieces and flushed it down the toilet."

When he got back to his bunk his friends were waiting anxiously. "So, tell us. What did the sergeant want?" Tam asked.

"To wish me good luck tomorrow."

"Yeah, right," Tam said.

Peter motioned for them to lean in close so he could talk confidentially. Then he whispered, "My stand-in at the Councillor's office has been murdered."

Sy let out a gasp and put his hand to his mouth. Peter frowned at him, grabbed his arm and pulled him back down. "Don't make a scene. I don't want anyone to know about this."

"Sorry," Sy said. "What are you going to do?"

"Nothing," Tam whispered. "It's good news. Now Videl will think Leek is dead and quit looking for him."

"Maybe," Peter said. "But the letter said to take no chances. We should assume someone here might try to kill me."

"But how would they know who you really are?" Red asked.

"Sgt. Baig says the Councillor has many enemies here. If they are not looking for me, they may be looking for those most loyal to the

142

Supreme Mandate," Peter said.

"Great," Sy moaned. "We could all be targets."

"Exactly," Peter said. "So, no more talking politics. We must be wary of everyone we encounter—even other candidates. Any one of them could be one of Videl's spies."

The night alarm sounded and the lights blinked on and off. As everyone started scrambling into bed Peter noticed another candidate staring at him. When their eyes met he felt him probe his thoughts. Peter turned away quickly. Fear shot through him like a bullet through a sponge. There was another candidate amongst them who had telepathic abilities. What had he learned from that short glance? Who was this candidate who had invaded his mind and what were his intentions? The lights suddenly went out and he was helpless to find out the answers to any of these questions.

"Great! A sleepless night is all I need on the eve of field testing and final exams," he muttered to himself. For hours Peter feared he'd been discovered and that he and his friends were in mortal danger. If they were, when would their assailants attack? Tonight, while they slept? Tomorrow, during the field tests? Unable to sleep, Peter crept over to Tam's bunk and awakened him. Tam sat up and rubbed his eyes. Peter whispered, "Someone stole a thought from me. He may know who I am."

Tam sat up. "Are you sure?"

"Yes, I'll stand watch for two kyloons. Then I'll awake you and you can watch for two more. Pass the watch to Sy after your turn is over." Tam nodded and laid his head back down on his pillow. Peter crept back to his bunk and in the dim light saw Sgt. Baig at the end of the barracks watching them. When their eyes met, he turned and went back to his quarters.

Peter's heart was beating hard as he lay sleepless in his bunk. Tomorrow would be the most important day of his young life, so far at least. If he truly was the Liberator he had to survive the night and go on to do well in the morning. But what if an assassin came now while he slept in his bunk? Even if he saw the assassin approaching he'd be helpless to defend himself.

Looking around the dark room, all seemed peaceful, so he slipped down to his locker and pulled out his C34 pistol. After making sure it was loaded, he climbed back into bed and put it under his pillow. Sy stirred above him, but did not awaken. After two kyloons had passed, he woke up Tam. Tam groaned a little but then sat up and blinked his eyes. Peter handed him the pistol and went back to his bunk. He was so exhausted he quickly fell asleep.

During the night Peter dreamt of Lucinda. They were in the woods running hand in hand. It was a warm day and the sky was blue. It must have been earth because he felt the warmth of the sun on his back. Lucinda was in a light blue paisley dress with white shoes and Peter wore white pants and a loose grey shirt. Her long black hair waved provocatively in the wind as they ran. Suddenly they stopped behind a big oak tree. They embraced and kissed passionately. As they were about to fall to the ground to give in to their passions, Peter heard a shot, felt Lucinda jerk in his arms, and whimper in painful agony. He looked in the direction of the gunshot and saw a man running away.

Lucinda suddenly became dead weight in his arms. He squeezed her tightly to stop her from falling. Then he felt wetness on his hand. He pulled it from behind and saw that it was covered with blood. "Lucinda! No!," he screamed.

A hand covered his mouth. "Leek!" Red whispered. "It's okay. "You're dreaming."

Peter sat up and looked at Red's concerned face. Several of the candidates were stirring. "Sorry," Peter said. "What a nightmare."

"I guess so," Red said, now smiling.

"What time is it?" Peter asked.

"Ten loons to the morning alarm. You might as well get up and get a head start on the day."

"Good idea. Any problems last night?"

"No, and I can't say I was thrilled to get awakened a kyloon early."

"Sorry, but I thought it necessary under the circumstances."

Red nodded, handed Peter his pistol, and went back to his bunk. Peter quickly began making his bed and getting ready to go to breakfast. When the morning alarm finally rang, Peter looked over at where the candidate, who had probed his mind, was sleeping. Surprisingly, the bunk was made and the candidate was nowhere to be found. Peter assumed he was in the bathroom, so he put his pistol back in his locker and pulled on his boots.

Later, when Sgt. Baig began to take roll call, the missing candidate had still not returned to his bunk. Fear began to gnaw at Peter. *Could this candidate be Videl's spy? Had his identity been discovered?* Just as the sergeant was coming to the empty bunk, the candidate scampered around the corner and took up his proper position in front of his bunk. The sergeant looked at him unapprovingly.

"Where have you been, Mr. Cystrom?" he demanded.

"Personal business, sir," he replied. "I'm feeling a bit queasy with the tests and everything."

The sergeant narrowed his eyes and then went on. Relief came over Peter like a cool breeze. *Perhaps he meant me no harm.* Peter began to doubt that whether his mind had been probed at all. Maybe it was his imagination, he thought. He finally convinced himself that it was probably paranoia triggered by the letter from Lorin. Nonetheless, he vowed to keep an eye on Mr. Cystrom in the future. He couldn't be too careful when there was so much at stake.

After breakfast the candidates reported to the first part of the field test which was an obstacle course of sorts. It consisted of a five hundred stride run, crawling under three wires strung low against the ground, climbing over a ten foot wall, traversing a fifty stride swamp, climbing a rope to the top of a twenty stride observation deck, swinging with another rope across a ravine, and then running another five hundred strides to the finish line. The hardest part of the obstacle course for Peter was the rope climb. His upper arm strength hadn't been so great when he'd arrived there. Fortunately, he had worked hard on the free weights and lost about twenty pounds, so he'd made significant progress in this event. Still, his best time was nearly 400t. The time needed to pass was 420t. The best time performed since camp had begun was Tam's last run at 360t.

About half the squad were already done when the four of them arrived. Sy was called first and took off with a group of four candidates. He led the group to the barbed wire and then dropped to the ground. He began to crawl, keeping as low as he could. Unfortunately his shirt got hung up on a barb and in the time it took to get unsnarled, two of the candidates passed him.

"Go Sy, go!" Peter yelled. When they got to the swamp, muddy water splashed everywhere. Sy was running third now but not far behind the candidates in front of him. He struggled over the wall and when he got to the observation tower one of the candidates was scampering up the rope like a monkey on speed. The other one slipped off the rope and fell to the ground. Sy jumped over him and started climbing quickly. He was only half way up when the candidate in the lead reached the top. By the time Sy made it to the platform the other candidate was sailing across the ravine. Sy immediately grabbed on the rope, swung hard across the ravine, dropped, and came down hard on the ground. He wobbled a bit and then began running, but it was too late, the other candidate crossed the finish line well ahead of him. Despite the fact he hadn't won his heat, Peter was certain his time was good enough to pass.

When Peter's name was called, he hurried to the starting line. When Sergeant Baig gave the signal, he took off with great urgency and concentration. Fortunately, the weight and bulk he'd lost made it easier for him to go under the barbed wire. He stood up quickly and hit the swamp, in the lead. The water splashed everywhere and he felt mud and water penetrating his clothing. Suddenly his eye began to sting as swamp water seeped under an eyelid. He closed the eye, winching from pain, but didn't lose concentration as he timed his jump perfectly and caught the top of the wall. He quickly pulled himself up, threw one leg over, shifted his weight, and dropped down the other side. Peter didn't hesitate at the base of the wall. He immediately straightened up and began running toward the dangling rope beneath the observation deck and began to climb.

The pain in his eye was distracting him more now and slowing his climb to the platform. The candidate behind him was gaining ground quickly. Ignoring the pain, Peter imagined Lucinda waiting for him at the finish line. His pace quickened and he reached the top just before his opponent. Dashing for the second rope he swung over the ravine, dropped, and rolled three times before he was on his feet running to the finish line.

"Go, Leek!" Sy yelled from the finish line where they were waiting anxiously.

Peter dug deep with one last burst of speed and finished well ahead of his opponents. Tam and Sy ran over and greeted him excitedly.

"Nice job," Sy said. "You beat the hell out of my score."

"You may have even beat me," Tam noted.

Peter smiled and replied. "That, I doubt. I got some mud in my eye that screwed me up. I'm lucky I was able to finish."

As they were talking, Red came storming across the finish line just a stride behind another candidate. When the times were announced, Red's was 401t, Tam had set a course record of 353t, Sy had run a 414, and Peter's was 359t. They all breathed a sigh of relief that they had passed phase one of the field trials, but they still had two more to go and several written exams in the afternoon. It wasn't time to celebrate quite yet.

Phase two of the field trials involved proficiency with weaponry. Handling, marksmanship, and maintenance were to be tested in this phase. Lt. Londry explained the rules. "Step one is to take each of our three weapons, the C34 pistol, T7 laser gun, and the R6 rifle through handling routines to show your speed and dexterity in using the weapons. In this step combat simulations have been set up and each candidate is expected to demonstrate the proper techniques for handling the weapons under different circumstances. In step two you will be given stationary targets to shoot at for accuracy. In step three you will have to hit moving and spontaneous targets within the simulated combat environment. Finally, in step four you are required to take each weapon apart, clean it, and reassemble it within an acceptable time period.

"Each of these field tests will be very demanding and quite intense. It will take tremendous concentration and rhythm to make it through each step with the accuracy and speed required. Any distraction or lack of focus will likely lead to failure. All right. Let's get started."

Peter took a deep breath when Syril Johs' name was called along with three other candidates. Sy looked at Peter with anguish in his eyes.

"Don't worry," Peter said, forcing a smile. "You'll do fine. Just get in there and show 'em how it's done."

Sy took his position at the starting point of the simulated combat zone. Each of the three weapons to be used were in front of each candidate. When Lt. Londry said go, each candidate grabbed his pistol and started down the path demonstrating the techniques they had learned in training. No shots were fired in this step. When they had completed the course with each weapon, there was a short break before the moving targets appeared. In this step each candidate went through the same simulated

147

combat zone, however, from time to time targets appeared that they were expected to hit. This reminded Peter of FBI training clips he'd seen in movies back on Earth. When the shooting had stopped, the candidates were given a 120t break before the final phase began—disassembling, cleaning, and reassembling each weapon. Sy did well hitting 123 of 144 targets within acceptable parameters and cleaning his weapons under the 120t limit.

In the next round Tam and Peter were called forward. Each of them came up and took their positions. Step one was fairly simple. They had practiced proper techniques for many hours and doing the routine seemed pretty natural. When step one was completed, however, things got more interesting. Now they had to not only use proper technique, but be alert for objects suddenly appearing or flying by. They'd only been given one practice run for this test, so Peter wasn't nearly as confident as he'd been in step one. When Lt. Londry said *go* Peter started along the path, his pistol pointed straight ahead with a two-handed grip.

As he reached the first corner, he stopped briefly and then peered around it. Seeing the coast was clear, he spun around the corner keeping his weapon ahead of him. Suddenly from a window an enemy soldier appeared and pointed his weapon at Peter. Without giving it any thought, he pointed his pistol at the soldier and fired. The bulled hit him just above the nose and he went down. A second later in another window an old lady appeared. Peter gave her a good look and then moved on without firing. At the end of corridor there was a large room. He slipped in and moved right along the wall. Suddenly a door opened and two soldiers stepped out. They immediately began firing, so Peter hit the deck.

They had him pinned down behind a bench and it didn't look like Peter had much time before he was going to be mincemeat, if he didn't think of something. The bench was not attached to the ground, so he kicked it straight ahead and then dived right behind a large planter. The two soldiers took the bait and started firing at the bench rolling down the path. Peter rolled over two times and fired at the exposed soldiers, hitting them with multiple rounds. As he was admiring the kill he heard a high pitched whining sound to his right. Looking up he saw some sort of missile coming right at him. Again, without thinking, he raised the pistol and shot the missile out of the air. Then he ran down the final corridor and out of the combat zone.

Peter hadn't seen Tam perform since each simulated combat zone was shielded from the others, but Peter noticed he was already finished when he came running out. He smiled at Peter. "This is fun, huh?"

Peter nodded and then picked up the rifle and got into position to enter the zone. Before Lt. Londry could say *go*, a barrage of gunfire erupted around him. He felt the whir of a bullet pass by his head. He immediately fell to ground and rolled behind one of the tables for cover. Is this part of the drill, he wondered? He looked up and saw Tam firing his rifle toward the observation deck. While everyone looked on, a man swung off the observation deck, dropped to the ground beyond the ravine, and then ran off.

Tam started to run after him but was stopped by Lt. Londry. "Let him go. You'll never catch him."

"You want to bet," Tam said and took off toward the ravine. Red and Peter started to follow but Lt. Londry stepped in front of them and yelled, "I *said*, let him go!"

They both stopped and watched anxiously as Tam disappeared. Soon a security vehicle with three soldiers arrived. Lt. Londry talked to the driver and they took off toward the ravine. A few moments later there were shots heard in the distance and fear plunged through Peter like an ice pick through the heart. Had someone been hit? He prayed to God it wasn't Tam.

Despite the apparent attempt on Peter's life, Lt. Londry advised everyone that the field tests would resume.

"But Sargent, someone just tried to kill me," Peter said.

He looked at Peter and frowned, "Why would someone want to kill you? It was probably just a pissed off washout trying to get a little revenge before he gets shipped off to the Isle of Muhl. You just happened to be at the wrong place at the wrong time. You better get used to being shot at, because that's a pretty common occurrence for a soldier."

Peter raised his eyebrows, nodded and replied, "Yes, Sergeant."

It was still pretty obvious to Peter that he was the target, but he couldn't really debate the issue with the sergeant without compromising himself. He figured it didn't matter now anyway, as the assailant was probably dead—at least Peter hoped he was dead rather than Tam. In his heart he believed Tam was okay. If he had died he thought he would have felt something. They had established a strong physic connection since their first meeting and he was sure if that connection were severed, he'd know it.

It was difficult getting through the rest of the day not knowing what had happened to Tam nor what repercussions there might be for his disobedience of Lt. Londry's orders. After dinner the results of the field tests were posted and fortunately Red, Sy, and Peter had all passed. There was a blank by Tam's name, and he hadn't shown up yet. The three worried candidates loitered around the bulletin board wondering what had become of their friend and looking at their watches as it was nearly time for the night alarm. Finally, they decided to go see Sergeant Baig. His door was closed, so Peter knocked. A moment later Sgt. Baig opened the door and took a deep breath.

"I suppose you're wondering what happened to Candidate Lavender."

"Yes, Sergeant. Do you know when he'll be back?"

"I'm afraid I've got bad news."

"Was he hurt?" Peter asked.

"No. In fact, he wounded the sniper and we have him in custody."

"So, where is he then?" Peter pressed.

"He's being processed to go to the Isle of Muhl."

The three boys' mouths dropped.

"What! You've got to be kidding," Peter exclaimed.

"He disobeyed a direct order from an officer,"Sgt. Baig explained. "That kind of behavior cannot be tolerated. We have no room for soldiers who do whatever they feel like doing."

"But he was protecting me," Peter said. "My life was in danger."

"Perhaps, but Lt. Londry was in charge and he gave an order and whether Candidate Lavendar liked it or not he was duty bound to honor it without question."

"Okay, he made a mistake. Can't you punish him or something—he'll never do it again," Peter pleaded.

"I'm not going to debate this with you, candidate. If you can't understand the importance of obeying orders perhaps you should join your friend at Pegaport."

Peter took a deep breath and exhaled slowly. Finally he said, "No, Sergeant. I understand. Thank you for your patience."

Sergeant Baig nodded. They turned and walked dejectedly back to their bunks. When the lights went off Peter couldn't sleep. He was sick at the thought of Tam being at Pegaport and having to face Videl's sick friends who ran that hell hole. He would never make it there. He was much too independent and they'd kill him before they broke him. Somehow, they had to get him off the Isle of Muhl—but how?

20

Marlais Beach

Even though the assassin was in custody, Peter wasn't feeling very safe. Several questions kept lurking in his mind. How had his identity been discovered? Who on Pogo Island wanted him dead? What would be their next move? As to the first question, he thought of all the people who knew his true identity. Would any of them betray him? He didn't think anyone associated with the Councillor would. Nor would any of his newfound friends. That left Sgt. Baig, Lucinda, and Threebeard. Threebeard had already told all his people that the Liberator had come. He wondered if he'd identified the Liberator by name. He couldn't imagine he'd be that stupid. He didn't think Sgt. Baig was the culprit either as Lorin had said in her letter that they could trust him.

Lucinda was another story. She was an enigma. Peter wanted to think she wouldn't betray him, but he couldn't rule her out. She had been the chief guide and had personally selected him over all the others on Earth Shuttle 21. Was that a coincidence? Or, could she be an agent for Videl or one of his cronies assigned to keep an eye on him. He almost dismissed that idea because his stand-in as the Councillor's intern had been assassinated. *Why kill the intern if you know he isn't the Liberator? Unless you want to give the Loyalists a false sense of security.*

Then Peter remembered the candidate who had probed his thoughts. Could he possibly be the one? He thought back to the day of the field tests and tried to remember if he'd seen him there. Could he have been the sniper? Probably not, but he could have been the one who figured out who he was and reported to one of the Videl's cronies. That made sense as the assassination attempt came very shortly after that encounter.

153

If it was him and he was working in concert with Videl, then what would be their next move—another assassination attempt?

With field training out of the way, the candidates were now scheduled for flight training. Peter's stomach felt queasy and he had a throbbing headache. He took a deep breath, trying to relax. He wondered how he'd make it through flight training with someone out to kill him. He'd already lost Tam. Now he would have to rely on Red and Sy to watch his back. He wondered if he should contact the Councillor and tell him boot camp wasn't turning out to be such a great idea. But how would he get the military training he needed so desperately if he was going to fulfill his destiny as the Liberator? It wasn't a time to panic. He had to be courageous and trust God to protect him, but then he realized God may not have dominion over Tarizon. That thought scared him, but then he dismissed it. It couldn't be true. God had to be everywhere, including Tarizon.

Fortunately, they were given a few days off before flight training began. It was their first leave and they decided to go to the only big city on Pogo, Marlais Beach. It was a domed city of about a quarter million people and well known for its great beaches, beautiful women, and gambling casinos. It was one of the few covered beaches on Tarizon. Peter was amazed to see a dome extend out to sea and plunge into the ocean. Sy and Red were anxious to gamble and hook up with some good looking *troebs*, the equivalent slang for *chicks* in the USA. Gambling didn't interest Peter much because he didn't really need credits, as the called money on Tarizon. The TGA was providing his room and board for now and when he got back to Shisk, they'd be at war, so credits would be his last concern. Nor did he want to hook up with a beautiful woman. He still couldn't keep his mind off Lucinda and hoped somehow they'd get back together. He knew it was probably a ridiculous idea. He was pretty certain Lucinda had forgotten him, but she still had a hammerlock on his heart and there was little he could do about it.

They took a land glider to the outskirts of Marlais Beach and then caught the local subtram to the beach resorts. Sgt. Baig had recommended the Southern Lights Resort and Casino, so they caught a public transporter, usually referred to as a PT, at the subtram station and asked the driver to take them there. After they'd checked into the plush hotel, the greeter took them to their suite and they unpacked. When they were settled, they went downstairs to the bar for a drink and to plan their activities for the next few days.

A scantily clad barmaid showed them to a table. She looked human but Peter noticed she had a long slit beneath each breast. He looked away trying not to gawk at it.

"Are you guys TGA?" She asked.

Sy replied, "Yes. How did you know?"

"We get a lot of soldiers in here from the military base. You guys have a certain look about you. It's not hard to pick you out."

Peter said, "It's probably because we're so horny."

She frowned, "Horney? What's that?"

"Ah . . . well . . . that's a term we use in the Underland for when a man or woman hasn't had a mate for a long . . . long time."

She laughed. "Well, yes then. That is a common trait of all the soldiers that come through here."

"That's one reason we're here," Sy added, "if you catch my code."

The barmaid gave Sy a wry smile and asked them what they wanted to drink. Sy ordered a high seas cocktail and Red asked for a double magic. Red swore by the double magic, so Peter decided to give it a try. Red promised it would relax him and make him forget his troubles. Peter hoped he was right.

"What are those lines under the barmaids boobs?" Peter asked.

"Boobs?" Sy chuckled.

Peter grinned. "Ah.. . . yeah. . . . breasts, I mean."

Sy nodded. "Oh, those are gills. She must be part Seafolken."

"Do they work?" Peter asked looking over at her at the bar.

"Yes, of course. She can swim underwater probably for ten loons without any problem, I'd guess—got fins I'd suspect too."

"Fins? Where? I didn't see them."

"They only show up when she's in the water. Otherwise you'd never know they were there."

Peter shook his head.

"You'd better watch her tongue, though. It's got fangs," Sy warned.

Peter's eyes widened. "Really? Fangs?"

"Yes, and if she bites, the venom will put you out for half a day and you won't remember what she did to you while you were unconscious."

Everyone laughed except Peter. He didn't know if they were joking or telling him the truth. While Peter was trying to figure it out, there was giggling from a table nearby. They all looked over and saw three attractive young ladies having a party. Red and Sy immediately began flirting with them and before long the three girls came over to sit with them.

The girls said they were hospital technicians who'd stopped by for a drink after their shift. They were impressed that they'd run into candidates in training with the TGA. After they'd talked awhile, Red suggested they take the ladies to the casino. He said they'd surely bring them good luck. Although Peter's heart wanted to resist, three double magics had weakened his resolve. Before he knew it he was at a tintan table with a killer brunette name LoreLai.

He had no clue how to play tintan, so he let LoreLai do the betting. Luckily they'd been paid before they left camp, so Peter had a few credits to invest in the enterprise. LoreLai turned out to be a pretty good gambler and before long she had accumulated a nice stash of loot. When they were tired of gambling, Peter asked her if she was hungry.

"Yes, I'm famished."

"Let's go spend some of your winnings on dinner."

She nodded and replied, "Good idea. Then you can tell me about yourself."

Peter smiled at this idea, but knew that it wouldn't be possible. He'd tell her about his fictitious life in Queenland and then shift the questions to her. Women usually liked to talk about themselves. At least that was true on Earth. He assumed it would be the same here as well, so he wasn't too concerned about keeping the conversation going. They cashed in LoreLai's chips and then stepped out onto the boardwalk that ran along the beach. The soothing sound of the waves breaking on the shore was like sweet music to Peter's ears. LoreLai said she was cold, so he put his arm around her as they walked. The restaurant where they were going was several blocks away, so they had a little time to talk. He told her where he was from and a little about his childhood. Then he started asking her questions.

"How did you get into the medical field?"

"Oh, I've always been interested in medicine. For a long time I wanted to be a doctor, but my OAS didn't support it. The only thing I could qualify for in the medical field was medical technician."

"OAS? What's that?"

"You know. Occupational Assessment Score. You must have gone through that testing."

"Right. I just forgot what they called it."

"It's horrible to be told by a computer what you must do with your life."

"Right."

"But, I guess the computers are wiser than us mortals."

"I . . . guess. So, do you like your work?"

"Well, it's a little monotonous drawing blood and processing it all day. I've always liked more excitement, if you know what I mean."

They arrived at the restaurant. It claimed to serve the finest foods native to Serie and Lyon. That didn't mean anything to Peter, but LoreLai seemed impressed, so he acted like he was too. The hostess showed them to a quiet booth and gave them menus. LoreLai opened hers and began studying it.

Peter said, "Any recommendations?"

She looked up and replied, "I've always been fond of grilled seequille with samini sauce."

Peter nodded. "That sounds good. I'll think I'll get the same thing." Peter had no clue what it was, but he assumed if she liked it, so would he. "So, do you have a mate?"

She looked up from the menu and their eyes met. She hesitated a second and then replied, "Ah . . . no, he died last year and I haven't put in for a new one yet."

As she was glancing up at him, he saw an opportunity to peak into her mind. This skill was still new to him, so he didn't know exactly what he was doing. It seemed by focusing on her eyes, some of her thoughts just flew into his mind through some kind of cosmic beam. Suddenly he realized she was lying about her mate. She *did* have one and he was back at a their compartment waiting for her. She turned away and he lost the connection.

Peter wondered why she would lie about her mate. Was it something akin to infidelity? He knew with a mate there wasn't the same commitment as with husband and wife on Earth, but why make up a story about your mate's death? He decided to press the issue a bit.

"What was his name?"

"Ah . . . Lenord. But let's not talk about him. I'd like to hear more about you."

"Lenord. Hmm. How did he die?"

"Ah. . . . respiratory failure. He worked outside the dome on a construction crew and his breather malfunctioned. It was an accident."

"So, you live alone?"

She looked annoyed but replied, "Yes. They haven't assigned anyone to share my compartment yet. You have two cycles to apply for a mate if yours dies."

She looked at Peter straight on again and her thoughts started streaming into his mind. There was a glimpse of a soldier, a TGA officer, and she was listening intently to him. She turned again and he lost the image. Peter's head started to ache. This was hard work he decided, but he had to find out who this soldier was and why LoreLai was thinking about him. Was he the one waiting for her back at her place? An ominous feeling came over him. He wondered what kind of a reaction he'd get if he suggested going to her place. He was pretty sure she planned on having sex with him, so the question was: Your place or mine?

"Listen, after dinner I'd take you up to our room, but it might be a bit crowded with Sy and Red and your friends. Is your place close by?"

"Ah . . . no it's way on the other side of the city and, well . . . it's kind of a mess."

"That's okay. I promise I won't look."

"No. No. Can't we just book another room? I'd feel more comfortable—"

"Sure," Peter replied as she looked at him again. Peter felt her anxiety and tried once again to find out what was causing it. He caught a glimpse of a bottle of pills. She was pouring them out on a counter and counting out a half dozen. She put them in an envelope, opened her purse, and stuck them inside. As she slipped them in, he thought he saw a small gun. He stiffened. What was this lady up to?

Peter's appetite suddenly vanished. His mind went into overdrive trying to analyze the images he'd seen. It suddenly dawned on him that LoreLai may herself be another assassin. If she was, then the pills were meant for him. This realization made him worry about Sy and Red. They had picked up these girls pretty quickly and easily. It almost seemed they were waiting there for them. Peter's anxiety turned to panic. He had to go to Sy and Red and warn them. He put his hand on his forehead and moaned, "Shit, I'm getting a killer headache."

LoreLai frowned and replied, "Are you serious? What happened?"

"I don't know. I get these sometimes for no apparent reason. It'll go away in a few hours."

"A few hours? But, I was looking forward—"

"I'm really sorry, LoreLai. We'll have to get together another time."

LoreLai just looked at Peter in disbelief. Then her face lit up and she said, "Oh, I just happen to have some lisen tablets. They'll take care of your headache in short order. Would you like one?"

"Ah. . . . No, I've got some special medicine prescribed to me by my doctor back at the base. It works good. Like I said, by morning I'll be fine."

Peter could feel LoreLai's mind working hard. He assumed she was trying to come up with some other angle to get him alone. He wondered how long her lisen tablets would take to kill him. Would she wait around to make sure the pills worked and, if they didn't, finish the job with a bullet in the head? Then he wondered if he was being paranoid. It was a delicate situation. He couldn't afford to accuse her of anything. If the local authorities came, there would be questions and his identity would be scrutinized. If he killed her it could even get worse.

Peter got up and told her he was going back to their suite. She gave him a frustrated look. "I'll come with you. I'll take care of you."

"You're too kind, but all I need is a couple of my pills and some sleep." He feared he'd find Sy and Red with a bullet in their heads if he didn't hurry. He turned and started to walk away. She got up and followed him. At the restaurant's entrance there was a crowd of guests waiting to be seated. As he slowed to maneuver his way through them, she caught up with him. Peter saw her hand reach into her purse and pull out the gun.

Before she could fire he pulled a man in front of him as a shield and pointed, "Watch out she's got a gun!"

Everyone's eyes turned to LoreLai. A lady screamed and people began pushing and shoving to get out of her way. In the commotion, Peter slipped out of the restaurant and ran back to the hotel. At the front door to the casino he resumed a normal walk. As the door swung open, he looked back but LoreLai hadn't followed him. He hoped she'd been caught by security. Relieved, he stepped inside and looked around. Sy and his date were at the same tintan table where he'd left them. Red and his companion were nowhere to be seen. Peter strolled over to the table. "Hey, you're still here. You must be winning."

Sy smiled and replied, "No, We've lost all my paycheck. Rhona and I were just killing time watching the game while we waited for Red to get finished with the room."

"He's upstairs with—"

"Rulle," Sy said smiling. "They're getting better acquainted."

Rhona asked, "Where's LoreLai?"

"Ah . . . in the ladies' room . . . Ah . . . she'd said to tell you to join her. She had a problem with her dress or something."

Rhona grimaced and looked toward the ladies' room. When she gave him a skeptical look, he said, "You better hurry. She seemed upset."

Rhona turned and walked quickly toward the ladies' room. Peter grabbed Sy's arm and said, "Come with me. Red's in trouble."

On the way up the elevator he gave Sy the short version of what had just happened. When the elevator door opened they ran down the hall to their room. After slipping the key card in the door, Peter tried to push it open but it was locked from the inside. From his waistband in the small of his back he pulled out the C34 pistol and shot out the locking mechanism. The door flew opened and Rulle looked up startled by the intrusion. She was half naked and brandishing a pistol of some sort. Just a few feet away Red was lying on the ground face down. When she started to raise her gun, Peter kicked her wrist hard and sent the gun flying across the room. Sy tackled her and, after a spirited wrestling match, finally subdued her.

Peter knelt down over Red and felt his pulse. It was weak and his face was pale. "She must have poisoned him. Oh God! What are we going to do?"

"Make him vomit," Sy said struggling to tie Rulle's wrists with her bra. "It couldn't have been in his stomach long."

"Okay," Peter said, and lifted Red up into a sitting position against the bed. With one hand he opened his mouth and then stuck his hand down his throat. Red coughed, choked, and grabbed his hand trying to pull it out of his mouth. They struggled and finally vomit came out like an overflowing toilet. It was a green slime with a strong chemical smell. "We've got to get him to a hospital!"

Sy, who had finally successfully tied up Rulle, stood up and said, "We can't call security. We'll have to get a PT."

"Fine," Peter said. "Make the call. Have them meet us at the side exit. Fewer people are likely to see us."

Sy went to the communicator and ordered the transporter while Peter picked up Red and started out the door. As Peter turned to go down the hall, the elevator door opened and Rhona and LoreLai strolled out. They both had their guns drawn and began shooting. A bullet hit the door jam inches from Peter's head. He staggered back into the room, lost his balance, and fell on his butt. Sy dropped the communicator, pulled out his C34, and rushed to the door and peered out. Peter struggled to his feet, pulled out his pistol, and joined Sy at the door. He motioned for Sy to cover him. Sy nodded and stuck his pistol out just far enough to take a wild shot at the approaching assassins. It missed, but momentarily put them on the defensive while Peter rolled across the carpet sending a flurry of bullets in their direction. One of them hit LoreLai and she fell to one knee. When Rhona looked at her fallen comrade, Sy stepped out and dropped her with a single shot from his C34. LoreLai coughed, blood spurted from her mouth, and then she fainted.

"Come on," Peter said. "We've got to get out of here."

They rushed back into the room, got Red, and started to the elevators. A bell rang indicating someone was about to step out of it, so they made a quick about face. Just as they made it into the stairwell, security police swarmed into the hallway. Fortunately, they hadn't seen them go into the stairwell, so they made it down to the bottom floor without incident.

The PT was waiting outside the side entrance. Sy had told the dispatcher there'd be a big tip for whoever got there first, so the driver was eagerly awaiting.

They jumped in and told the driver to take them to the nearest hospital. About ten loons later he dropped them off. Peter gave him some casino chips and then offered him a few more if he'd forget he ever saw them. He took the chips and nodded eagerly. They carried Red inside to the casualty unit. A nurse asked them what had happened.

"Ah . . . I'm afraid our friend went to a party house and they must have given him some drugs or something. When he didn't come out, we went in and got him. He was cold and pale when we found him. We made him vomit, but—"

The nurse frowned. "Oh, Sandee. Men are so stupid."

Sy and Peter shrugged. The nurse shook her head and started writing some notes in the new file she had made on Red. She asked us his name. They had to be straight with her because they didn't have fake identifications and didn't want her to doubt their story. When she was done asking questions, they went to the waiting room. Luckily it was empty.

Sy said, "What are we going to do about the resort? They are going to know we were involved in the shooting. All our gear is back in our room and the door is shot to hell."

I thought for a moment and replied, "We better call Sgt. Baig. Maybe he can help us out."

Sy took a deep breath and replied, "Yeah, maybe, but what if he uses this incident as an excuse to wash us out. I'd love to see Tam again, but not on the Isle of Muhl."

"Don't worry. Sgt. Baig will help us. He has no choice. He's already chosen sides and has a big stake in our success. You stay here. I'll find a communicator and call him."

Moments later Peter was on the communicator with Sgt. Baig. He said he feared there would be another attempt on their lives, but didn't think it would happen this quickly. He said he'd call the local authorities and make up a story that would put them in the clear. Peter breathed a sigh of relief and went back to the waiting room. Sy was talking to the doctor when Peter walked in. He joined the conversation.

"He's going to be okay, but it was good you made him vomit. Whatever he ingested could have killed him. Where was this party house? I need to report it to the authorities."

I looked at Sy and he looked back at me. "Gee. This is the first time we've to Marlais Beach. I'm not sure I could find the place again. Do you remember where it was, Sy?"

Sy shook his head. "No, I was so busy with Red and didn't pay any attention to the name of the place. We can try to go back over there and if we find it again, write down the information and call you back."

The doctor nodded, "Do that. I need to have them shut down. They could have killed your friend."

The next morning they released Red and the three of them made arrangements to go back to the base. Their vacation hadn't turned out so well as vacations go, but they'd survived and knew this was just the first of many battles to come. The important thing was that they had learned a lot about each other, gained a little combat experience, and, most importantly, survived. From that standpoint it had been a very successful vacation. On the way back to the base Peter thought of Sy's comment that he didn't want to visit Tam on the Isle of Muhl.

"I wonder how Tam is doing?" Peter said.

Red shook his head, "I don't know. I'd hate to be in his shoes."

"If he keeps his mouth shut, he'll probably be okay," Sy said, "but knowing him he's probably already on the list to have a pain implant inserted in his head."

Peter nodded. "You're probably right. That's why were going to have to rescue him here pretty soon."

Red and Sy both looked at Peter liked he was crazy. Peter laughed. "Don't worry. We have to get through flight training first. We'll need a ride to Pegaport before we can pull him out of there."

21

Flight Training

Flying had always fascinated Peter and he had actually been considering enlisting in the United States Air Force after he graduated from high school. Sy and Red felt the same way about flying, so the three of them could hardly wait for their flight training to begin. Flight training was mandatory for any officer in the TGA. The Tarizonian Global Forces were a highly mobile military force that depended on a myriad of aircraft to operate effectively. Officers were expected to be familiar with each of them and have the ability to fly them if need be.

The first twenty days were spent in the classroom learning the physics, aerodynamics, engineering, meteorology, navigation, and becoming familiar with the many aircraft that the TGA utilized. Like at the language school Peter had attended earlier, they were given the drug parazene to stimulate their minds and help them quickly assimilate the vast amount of knowledge and technical skills needed to become a skilled pilot.

On the last day of class Lt. Kechok Lemura began familiarizing them with the stalwart of the TGA, the hypersonic T-47 Fighter. "It's powered by a combination pulse detonation engine and kerosene fueled ramjet," Lt. Lemura advised. "This gives it both atmospheric and limited space flight capabilities. Its skin is made of lemdinium with sirilic leading edges which allows it to withstand the extremely high temperatures experienced in reentry from outer space. In addition, it has the ability to change its skin color using electrical charges. By emitting light through a series of slits, the aircraft can match the luminosity of the surrounding sky making it nearly invisible to the naked eye. It's shape and absorption qualities make it impossible to track on radar as well. Since it flies at mach-8 it will outpace its own sound waves and thus arrive at its target without

165

warning."

There was a buzz of excitement in the room. Red smiled at Peter. "I can't wait to get up in one of those birds."

Peter nodded. "I know. It's going to be so cool."

Lt. Lemura looked over at them and frowned. Candidates weren't supposed to be talking in class so Peter immediately shut up. Lt. Lemura took a deep breath and continued. "Of course, this isn't the most sophisticated of our aircraft. In fact, its use was discontinued before the great eruptions, but it is so much cheaper, more reliable and quicker to build that the Central Authority brought it back to aid in the recovery effort.

"Now you will all spend time in the simulators in the next few days to acquaint yourselves with this aircraft. Once you have mastered the simulators then you'll be given actual flight time. Any questions?" Seeing no hands raised, Lt. Lemura closed his training manual and said, "All right then, dismissed."

That night after dinner Peter, Red, and Sy were advised they'd been assigned sentry duty at the east entrance to the base. This was bad news because it meant they'd only get only four kyloons sleep that night. It was also unusual for all three of them to be assigned sentry duty together. Normally, two sentries would be assigned to man a post and the odds against Sy, Red, and Peter being randomly assigned to the same post on the same night were astronomical. They figured it either meant someone wanted to meet with them, or they were being set up for an ambush.

Later that night they went to the sentry post and relieved the two soldiers on duty. After they'd been there several loons, they saw headlights approaching. They readied their weapons as no one should have been out that late at night. As it got closer they saw it was a private vehicle, usually referred to as a PV, and not a military vehicle. It slowed down and stopped a few strides from them. They watched it warily as the door opened slowly and a man stepped out. Peter shone his light on the man. It was Sgt. Baig. They all let out a collective sigh of relief and relaxed their weapons.

He walked over to them and said, "Sorry to drag you out tonight, but it's important that we talk. I'm pretty sure anything said in the barracks is monitored. That's why I assigned all of you to sentry duty tonight. As long as we stay outside, I don't think anyone will overhear us."

"What's going on?" Peter asked.

"There has been an assassination attempt on the life of Chancellor Bassett. He's still alive and getting the best medical attention available, but word is he isn't likely to make it."

"Oh, Jesus," Peter said. "It's starting already."

"Sandee protect us, "Sy said taking a deep breath.

Red shook his head and asked, "So, how long before the war breaks out?"

"Not long. A few phases at the most. The generals and politicians who haven't committed to one side or the other will have to make that choice soon. The commandant here will side with the Vice-chancellor. That is why I wanted to speak with you. It will soon be time for you to leave Argot. You will be in grave danger as long as you remain here."

"What about you? You'll be in danger too," Peter said.

"I haven't officially taken sides. No one here knows I stand with the Supreme Mandate. I'm safe for now and I'll be of more service to our cause here, where I can listen and observe the enemy."

"So how will we escape?" Peter asked.

"I've arranged for each of you to take a T-47 out for a training flight the day after tomorrow. Once you take off you'll not return. When air control realizes you're not coming back, they'll try to override your manual control, but they'll find out the onboard computers have locked them out."

"Won't they go looking for who reprogrammed the onboard computers?"

"Absolutely, but I'll make sure there is. no trail leading to me. Eventually, they may figure it out, but I plan to be far away from Pogo when that happens."

"Where will we go?" Red asked.

"There are a string of over 10,000 islands in the Southern Sea called the Beet Islands. On one of those islands there is a secret base where soldiers loyal to the Supreme Mandate are gathering and making preparations for war. You will go there."

"We'll have to make a stop along the way," Peter said.

Sgt. Baig frowned. "A stop?"

"Yes, we need to rescue Tam. He's part of our team."

"No. I am sorry, I know he is your friend, but it will be too dangerous. You must fly immediately to the base."

Peter shook his head, "Tam is important to the cause. He heard the call of Threebeard and immediately joined the TGA. He's got extraordinary abilities and I promised him we'd come get him."

"Pegaport is a high security training base. There is no way you could break him out by yourselves," Sgt. Baig said irritably.

"I promised him we'd come get him," Peter said sternly.

Sgt. Baig looked at Peter and sighed. "Well, I guess you better keep your promise. I'll try to find out exactly where he's been assigned and see if there is anyone at Pegaport we can trust to help you."

"Thank you, Sergeant. You'll be glad we did this."

"Just be sure you make it to the base. If the Liberator is killed before the war begins, all might be lost."

"Do you think we'll be ready to fly the fighters in two days?" Sy asked skeptically. "We haven't actually flown one yet."

"You've all done excellent in simulation. Actual flying is not much different. The computers do most of the work anyway."

Sgt. Baig was right. The onboard computers on the T-47 were capable of full flight control. They did need a little instruction, however, and close monitoring in case there were flaws in the programming or data corruption. A good pilot was always ready to assume control if things didn't seem right.

"What about our gear? How will we get it on the fighters?" Peter asked.

"You won't. You'll have to go without it. When you take off, it can't look like anything other than a routine training flight. Each fighter has a small storage hold and there will be a few day's ration of food and water, first aid supplies, firearms, and ammunition stored there."

They talked awhile longer and then Sgt. Baig left. A few hours later two sentries arrived and relieved them. It was just two hours before dawn when they finally made it back to their bunks. Peter was exhausted and immediately fell fast asleep. When Peter was overtired he had a propensity to dream and this night was no exception. He first found himself in Lucinda's bed. The dream was so real he could feel the heat from her body and her breath on his cheek as he gazed into her sleeping eyes. He stroked her back and felt aroused by the touch of her soft skin. Then abruptly her image faded and he was in the thunderstorm near Possum Kingdom Lake. His car was shaking violently, so violently he bailed out fearful it might explode or be hurled across the landscape. He ran as fast as he could from the menacing ship hovering above, but soon felt his body being swept skyward toward it but, instead of going aboard, he found himself floating above a crowd of people in dark clothing in a graveyard.

He squinted to ascertain who he was watching. A chill came over me him as he realized he was watching his own funeral. His mother and father were standing with grim faces over his casket. A priest was talking to the crowd of solemn mourners. He saw his sister Marcia. She was crying and Mark and Reggie were trying to comfort her. Peter tried to yell, *I'm alive! Don't cry Marcia. I'm alive! Mom! Dad! I'm–* A hand suddenly shook him.

"Wake up! Leek. Wake up," Red said. "You're dreaming again."

Peter opened his eyes and saw Red's smiling face. He took a deep breath and then tried to shake the cobwebs from his head. "Wow. What a dream."

"It must have been," Red whispered as he looked around to make sure nobody was listening. "You need to get up. Sergeant Baig has arranged a special assignment away from the squad so we can have some time to plan Tam's rescue. He's got us maps and intelligence reports."

Peter nodded and swung himself out of his bunk onto the floor. They got dressed, made their beds and headed for the nutrition center. After downing a quick breakfast they went to a classroom in the armory. There was a large map of Muhl on the wall and several files on the desk. The room was deserted. The three of them immediately got to work.

When Peter looked at the map of the Isle of Muhl, he wondered if someone on speed had tried to draw the island. Except for its jagged and jittery form it was almost a perfect square, 257 kylods in length and 258.1 kylods in width. The western third of the island was separated north to south by the Drogal Mountains towering to a modest 3,254 feet at its highest peak. The Pegaport Training Center at Muhl was located on the

169

southwest corner of the island, west of the Drogal Mountains. To the south lay the Southern Sea and to the northwest the Yulev River. The Yulev River looked to be very wide and formidable and there appeared to be but one bridge across the river into the facility. This would make it nearly impossible to approach the base except from the east. This would mean crossing the Drogal Mountains.

On a table they found a map of the training facility itself. It lay in the shape of a triangle with a large airstrip and athletic field to the north. Along the river were hangers, fuel tanks, and the enlisted men's barracks. At the foot of the Drogal mountains was the armory, the officers' quarters, and an endurance course. A road wound through the center of the base and then made a large circle, within which lay the base headquarters, the nutrition center, classrooms, a detention center, and parade ground. A wide beach separated the base from the Southern Sea. Eight guard towers were situated along the river and the beach, but there were no towers along the foothills of the Drogal Mountains. For some reason the military command at Pegaport wasn't worried about an assault from over the mountains. Peter wondered why.

"We should come in by sea,"Red argued. "If we come at night they won't see us."

"Of course they will," Peter said. "They must have night vision equipment. Plus, the beach is probably mined," he said.

"We can swim across the river,"Sy said, "or take a small raft."

"The river is wide and there are four guard towers. There's no way we could get across. Besides, where are we going to hide our fighters? If we land anywhere near the base they'll see us on radar and be all over us before we get on the ground."

Red shook his head. "This is impossible. There's no way to get in without being detected."

"There's one way," Peter said. "We'll fly in on the east side of the Drogal Mountains. The map indicates it's a desert. It will be uninhabited so no one will hear us land. Then we'll have to hike over the mountains and sneak in behind the armory. If we can get a message to Tam, we'll have him meet us there."

"Hike over the mountains? By the looks of this map that could be nearly 100 kylods," Red protested, "and there doesn't appear to be any roads."

"That's no big deal," I've hiked fifty kylods before at scout camp. It took three days, but we weren't in such great shape. I bet in the shape we're in now we could get there and back in three or four days."

"But you hiked on a road, right?"

"A trail, actually. It was in Colorado where the mountains are five times the size of the Drogals."

"Five times? Wow. I'd like to see those sometime," Sy said.

Peter shook his head. "Maybe you will. Who knows."

"But did they have Drogals in Colorado?" a voice in back of the room asked.

They all turned and saw Sgt. Baig standing there looking amused. He a medical bag in one hand.

"What's a Drogal?" Sy asked.

"It's bird twice the size of any human being. It's native to the Drogal Mountains, hence the name. Its natural prey are mountain rats, durk birds, and range deer but if it's hungry or feels threatened it will eat humans as well."

Sy's mouth dropped open. "So, we don't want to go across the Drogal Mountains."

Sgt. Baig shook his head, "No, it's a dangerous place and few men have ever made it across."

Peter asked, "But can't we just shoot them if they come close. I've never heard of an animal that wouldn't run at the sound of gunfire."

Sgt. Baig's eyes narrowed and he replied, "Well, don't you suppose someone on the base might hear you if you start firing at the Drogals? Not that a bullet would do them much damage. Ninety three percent of their body is fluff and they wouldn't even notice a bullet going through it. You'd have to get lucky and hit the seven percent that mattered."

"What about a laser? We'll take our T7s," Peter suggested.

Sgt. Baig shook his head and replied, "The laser would be a good choice except that it won't usually kill a Drogal. Whereas the T7 laser is lethal to a human being, it just makes a Drogal mad."

"Wonderful," Peter moaned. "How are we going to sneak into the base? If we can't go across the mountain, there's no way in."

"You're right," Sgt. Baig said. "You should abandon your plans to save Tam. It's impossible."

"No, there's got to be a way," Peter insisted.

"Then, you'll have to go over the mountains," Sgt. Baig replied. "It's the only way you'll ever get onto the base undetected."

"So how do we get by the Drogals?" Sy asked.

"Drogals don't feed at night. So you'll have to travel when it's dark and hide during the daylight."

"Where would we hide?" Sy asked.

"The Drogal Mountains are rich with minerals. Over the cycles there have been attempts at mining some of them. Lemdinium in particular as it is very valuable. There is an old mining tram that runs through the mountains. It has been abandoned since the day of the volcanoes, but if you follow it, it will lead you across the mountains. You can sleep in the mines during the daylight."

"Where do the Drogals sleep?" Sy asked.

Sgt. Baig smiled. "High up in the trees. Don't worry, they don't see well at night, so they won't be disturbing you then. Just don't leave the mines during the day. They have a keen sense of smell and if you venture out they'll be on you like flies on a carcass."

"Okay," Peter said. "Assuming we make it to the base, can you get a message to Tam to be expecting us? It would be great if he was waiting there when we came off the mountain."

"I can get a message to him that you're coming, but it wouldn't be wise to tell him where or when to meet you. If the message is intercepted, you'll be walking right into a trap."

"So, how do we find him once we get there?" Peter asked.

"You'll want to come in at night to avoid detection. One of you should sneak into the barracks and get him. There won't be a guard there and everyone should be asleep. Tam will be expecting you, so it shouldn't be hard to bring him out. Bring your T7s in case there's trouble. If you have to kill someone, you don't want to make any noise doing it."

"Right," Peter said, his stomach tightening as he contemplated the daunting task they were about to undertake. It would be so much easier to fly to the Beet Islands and forget about Tam, he thought. He'd be just one of many who'd died to preserve the Supreme Mandate. But they had pledged to watch out for and protect each other. If he didn't honor that pledge, what was the point of fighting at all? If all he thought about was expediency, he'd be just like Videl.

"Now take off your shirts, I need to perform a little surgery on you."

"What?" Red exclaimed.

"You probably don't want to be running around with a tracking implant once you've defected to the Loyalist cause."

"Oh, Lord no," Peter said. "We'd lead them right to the Loyalist base."

Sgt. Baig raised his eyebrows, opened his medical bag, and then proceeded to one by one remove their implants. "Okay, we need to get back to the squad," Sgt. Baig said. "Some of the candidates will be getting suspicious we're gone any longer."

They all nodded, took one last look at the maps, and then joined the other candidates in the squad who were assembled at the airfield to inspect their aircraft before the following day's training flights. As they looked at the twenty-one fighters lined up in front of their hanger, Peter felt overwhelmed. Tomorrow he would not only be flying for the first time, but embarking on a most perilous journey. Was he ready? He closed his eyes and prayed to God that he would be.

22

Martyr

Lorin picked up the communicator and saw that it was Sgt. Baig calling. She swallowed hard as it was the first time he'd broken radio silence to call her. Something very serious must have happened for him to risk the call. She pushed the receive button and spoke into the device.

"Shisk 2, here."

"This is the teacher with a report on the pupil."

"Go ahead teacher. How can we help you?"

"The pupil won't go directly to school. He wants to pick up a friend along the way."

"What friend?"

"The one who says he was called to class before the pupil."

"He can't do that," Lorin said angrily. "He must do what his teacher says."

"He thinks he has no choice. He won't be dissuaded."

Lorin stood up and began pacing. She was beside herself with anger. Peter was about to jeopardize the whole mission trying to rescue some worthless kid who couldn't even obey orders. She took a breath trying to calm herself.

"How will he do it?" she asked.

"I've given him a map and a compass. He's very resourceful. I think he'll find his friend and bring him to school."

"Understood," she said stifling her anger. "I'll confer with the principal and get back with you."

"I'll need instructions before school lets out," Sgt. Baig said urgently.

"You'll have them. S1, out," Lorin said and closed the connection.

She stood up, hurriedly put on her jacket, and walked out the door. She couldn't believe she was going to have to disturb the Councillor with this nonsense. Why couldn't Peter just follow orders like everybody else? She stepped outside and hurried to the subtram station. It was close by so it didn't take long. At the door to the subtram she punched in her destination, the door opened, and she stepped inside.

A few loons later she stepped out of the subtram station in front of the Hall of the Interpreters. She hurried inside and went to her father's office. Court was in session so she waited impatiently for it to end. Finally, he walked into his office and looked at her in surprise.

"Lorin. I didn't expect to see you today."

"I know, Father, but I have an urgent matter to discuss."

He nodded. "Come into my office. What's wrong?"

They went into the Councillor's office and made themselves comfortable. An aide brought in sankee. Lorin looked at her father and shook her head.

"We've got a problem with Peter. I just got a message from Sgt. Baig. Peter is refusing to go directly to the Loyalist base."

"What?" the Councillor said incredulously. "Why?"

"He wants to rescue his friend Tam who was sent to Pegaport for insubordination."

The Councillor chuckled. "Well, our Liberator has a mind of his own, doesn't he?"

"If he were any other soldier, he'd be shot for disobeying orders."

"True, but he is not a common soldier and he didn't ask for the role we've given him. He's loyal to his friends. I like that. It shows his word is worth something."

"But, he's going to jeopardize the entire movement," Lorin protested.

"Not necessarily. I think we can use this sidetrack to our advantage. If he is successful it will only enhance his credibility as the Liberator. If he fails, he will become a martyr. We win either way."

176

"But Father, we're not ready to face Videl's forces yet. Peter's intrusion at Pegaport could prematurely start the war. That could be disastrous."

"Many of our staunchest supporters are at Pegaport. Videl has been exiling them there for years to get them out of his way. We'll need them if we are to win the war. Perhaps Peter can rescue some of them while he's there."

Lorin just looked at her father exasperated. She couldn't believe he was letting Peter do whatever he wanted. It seemed Peter had some kind of spell over him. Did he really think the Prophecy was true? Did her father really believe Peter was the Liberator? For the first time she believed he did. If so, arguing with him would be futile.

"All right, but he plans on coming in from the mountains."

"The mountains?" the Councillor repeated in surprise. "Does he know about the Drogals?"

"I assume Sgt. Baig would have told him of the idiocy of going through the mountains."

"Well, then he's a brave man. I'll have to say that."

"A brave lunatic, if you ask me."

"Or a brave genius," the Councillor said thoughtfully.

Lorin shook her head in frustration. "What do you want me to tell Sgt. Baig?"

"Tell him to give Peter whatever help he can. You'll need to find a way to get word to our supporters at Pegaport that a rescue mission is being planned. Let's make sure Peter's mission is successful."

"Should I tell Peter that, if by some stroke of good fortune he gets through the mountains alive, he'll be rescuing others as well?"

"No, not until the last moment. I don't want to put him under any additional pressure. He'll have his hands full with the Drogals. That's my only concern about this mission. He'll catch Pegaport by surprise. I have no doubt of that. But can he get by the Drogals! Few men have ever managed it. I pray Sandee is with him."

23
Flight of the T47s

That night when they returned to their barracks from dinner, Peter felt a tension in the air that he hadn't felt before. He couldn't put a finger on what it was exactly, but it seemed like everyone's eyes were on him. He tried to shake it off, thinking he was just nervous due to the fact that they were about to hijack three T47 fighters from the TGA, but the feeling grew stronger and stronger as the night progressed.

Just moments before the night bell was due to sound, Peter felt a tap on his shoulder. He whirled around and found himself face to face with Evohn Cystrom, the candidate who he'd suspected of probing his mind and whom he feared was one of Videl's agents. His heart rate quickened. Was he looking into the eyes of another assassin?

"What?" Peter said trying to seem irritated rather than scared.

"I know who you are and what you're going to do tomorrow."

Peter swallowed hard. He *had* probed his mind as Peter had suspected, but how much did he actually know? Peter didn't think he could have learned all that much in the few seconds he'd been in Peter's mind. Was he bluffing? In one of their classes they'd learned a common interrogation technique—to act like you knew something in hopes the suspect would acknowledge it. Peter wasn't going to fall for that trap.

"So who am I?" Peter asked.

"You're the Liberator," Evohn said firmly.

Peter looked around to make sure nobody was listening. "What in the hell is the Liberator?"

"Amongst the Earthchildren will come a humble man, pure in heart, and steadfast in his belief in liberty and justice. He will rid Tarizon

179

of corruption, restore faith in the Supreme Mandate, and liberate the Mutants, Seafolken, and the Nanomites forever."

Peter's face became rigid. "I'm from Queenland—you know—the Underland," he said firmly.

Evohn ignored his protest and continued, "Once you and your friends take off tomorrow, you won't be returning to base. You'll be flying south."

"You're nuts. Who told you this garbage?" Peter protested.

"You must know I'm telepathic. I sensed you were too."

Peter nodded slightly. "A little, perhaps. I didn't realize it until recently."

"Don't worry. I mean you and your friends no harm. I just want to come with you. I know you're going to join the Loyalist forces against Videl. I want to go with you. Some of my friends want to come as well. I've been told the Loyalist base is in the Beet Islands."

Peter shrugged. "I wouldn't know," Peter said wondering if he could trust Evohn."How many people have you told about these alleged plans?"

"Seven including myself. We were careful only to tell those who were loyal to the Chancellor and believed in the Supreme Mandate."

"So, why come to me? Go ahead and fly to the Beet Islands on your own. It's none of my business."

"It's not that easy. You have connections. You know how to find the base. If we have to search for it, we may not find it before we run out of fuel. As you are aware, once we vary from our flight plan, there will be no turning back."

"How do I know you're not an agent of Videl? If I did know how to find the Loyalist base and told you, he'd send a force there to destroy it."

"I detest Videl. I'd piss on him if I found him dying in the street. He killed my father."

"He did? When?"

"When he was commandant at Pegaport. My father was a recruit and died during his first week of training. Videl claimed my father had an undiagnosed heart condition and died of a heart attack during a combat exercise, but I know my father was in perfect health. When they refused to ship the body to my mother, I knew they were hiding something."

Peter nodded. It could still be a ruse, but he felt Evohn was being sincere. "Perhaps they tortured him for not living up to their expectations. I've heard some pretty horrible stories about Pegaport."

"So, can we join you?"

"How well do you know your friends? Would you trust them with your life?"

"Yes, I know them well. They are all loyal to the Supreme Mandate and anxious to join the Loyalist forces. I will vouch for them."

"Well, I know of no Liberator or plans to steal T47s for the Loyalists, but it's been an interesting conversation that I will share with my friends. I'm sure they will have a good laugh."

Evohn raised his eyebrows. "I won't laugh until Videl is in his grave."

It was late in the game to be altering their plans, but Peter thought seven more planes for the loyalist cause was a good reason to consider it. After the final alarm sounded the lights were still on, so Peter managed to run the idea by Sy and Red. They were pleased that others wanted to join their cause, but were reluctant to let them in on their plans without checking them out thoroughly. Unfortunately, they didn't have time to even find out which candidates wanted to join them, let alone have time to get to know them. They finally agreed it would be a gamble, but since they already knew about their plans, what choice did they really have? They either agreed to let them come along or abort the escape. If they aborted their escape plan, they might never get another opportunity to join the Loyalist forces.

The next morning Peter asked Sgt. Baig if he knew anything about Evohn Cystrom. He indicated he had considered him a suspect in the attempt to assassinate Peter and had him checked out. It turned out he was clean and his story about his father checked out. That made Peter feel better, so when he bumped into Evohn at the nutrition center, he told him his friends and he were welcome to join the defection, but that he wouldn't tell him the coordinates for the loyalist base until they were in the air and on their way.

He also didn't plan to tell them about their extraction mission to Muhl. They didn't need to know about that. As a further precaution, Sgt.

Baig said he would be sure the planes the seven candidates flew would have minimal armaments in case their real objective was to find the loyalist base and destroy it. Despite all of these precautions, as the time of their departure drew closer, Peter grew fearful something would go wrong. If Evohn had so easily discovered their plans, one of Videl's agents might have done so too. Then Peter realized if they even had an inkling of what he and his friends were about to do, they would have arrested them by now. With this realization, his confidence returned and he was ready for the mission to begin.

After lunch all the candidates assembled in the hanger to prepare for flight training. Their instructor pointed to a life-sized manikin dressed in a flight suit and began to explain all of the equipment they would be wearing. "From top to bottom you have a helmet, mask, survival vest, flotation device, harness, gloves, g-suit, liner suit, and boots. Just above your boots you have a pocket for maps. This suit has been carefully engineered to protect you during flight or in the event of a forced ejection. As you've learned, during flight you will be subjected to temperature extremes, pressure variations, and g-forces that the naked body cannot withstand. It's critically important to suit up properly before every flight to avoid death or serious injury during flight. Everyone has been issued a flight suit, so lets put them on now."

It took them nearly thirty loons to suit up in their cumbersome flight gear. When they had finished, they were escorted out to their fighters. Seeing the big T47 for the first time, gave Peter goose bumps. It was a little scary climbing aboard but once he'd settled into the cockpit he felt at home. It was exactly like the simulator where all of them had spent many hours and become very proficient. Now it was time to put their training to the test.

Engines all around Peter began to roar. After checking all his gauges and imputing the required information into the onboard computer, he pushed the ignition button and his fighter came to life. Soon he was among a long line of fighters taxiing out to the runway.

Since their training flights were the only activity planned for the day, the tower gave them immediate clearance for takeoff. As Peter turned the T47 into position, he gave it full throttle and the big fighter roared down the runway and into the air. The surge of power was exhilarating beyond anything he'd ever experienced. Soon Peter was flying in formation high above the base along their predetermined flight plan. The instructors were communicating with them from the ground and monitoring every move. They had agreed to break the flight plan at the farthest point from the base. This was to occur about twelve loons into their flight. When the moment came Peter said, "Five tiks to course variation."

A voice came over his radio and asked, "What course variation? Explain yourself, candidate."

Ignoring this instructor, Peter said, "Change now to alternate communication channels. Four, three, two, mark."

"What course variation!" an angry voice said over the radio.

The voice went silent when Peter switched channels. They were headed north over Pogo Island flying back toward the base, when they suddenly banked sharp to the left, swung out over the Coral Sea, and did a complete one hundred and eighty degree turn. Since they had broken off communications and gone off their flight plan, the tower and their instructors would know something was wrong. There were eleven other candidates in the air that could have given them chase, but this was their first flight so it was unlikely they'd be sent to pursue them. As a precaution against any of them trying to be a hero, Sgt. Baig had made sure they had only enough fuel aboard to do their flight training.

It was possible the tower would scramble some fighters to go after them, but by the time they got in the air they'd be long gone. At mach-8 in a stealth aircraft it would be nearly impossible to find them after getting a ten minute head start. What Peter wasn't counting on, however, were the Muscan missiles that came screaming after them. They had learned about them in class. They were heat-seeking missiles that would relentless pursue a target until it was destroyed.

"Three missiles on the radar closing fast," Red barked. "Taking evasive action."

This scenario wasn't new to them. Peter had practiced it a hundred times in simulation. Unfortunately, all he could think about were the many times he'd been blown up by some careless misstep. Now if he wasn't perfect in his evasive maneuvers, his life would be over and the hopes and dreams of freedom for the Mutants, Seafolken, and the Nanomites would go down in a fiery ball of flames.

Peter pushed a green button on the T47's control panel and a dozen hot metal decoys were ejected from a discharge shoot at the rear of the fighter. Then he banked hard left distancing himself from the decoys. There was an explosion from behind that rocked the plane, then another and another. He pressed his com button and said, "Everyone in one piece?"

There was a tense moment of silence and then Red replied, "Renegade 2 alive and well."

A moment later Sy checked in, "Renegade 3 still in one piece."

"Renegade 8's been hit!" Evohn screamed. "His plane has exploded. Oh, Sandee. No!"

Peter banked right and could see a ball of fire plummeting toward the ground. He cringed at the sight. *The poor kid. Oh, God what a way to die.* "Anything else coming at us?"

"No, we're out of range," Sy replied.

After a few moments, Peter regained his composure and put the fighter back on course. Soon they were on their way toward Muhl and the Beet Islands. As they approached Muhl, Peter radioed Evohn and gave him the coordinates for the Loyalist base. Then he said, "You head on to the islands, we've got a little errand to run before we join you."

"Can't we help out?" Evohn asked.

"No, we don't want to look like an invasion force. Three of us are enough for this mission. You all head on to the base. They'll be expecting you."

"Confirmed. Good luck," Evohn said.

They banked right and watched the six other T47's quickly disappear. Twenty loons later they could see the Isle of Muhl rapidly approaching. They flew in from the north and flew over the Yondi Desert. It was a vast sandy wasteland with little vegetation and almost no inhabitants. They chose this route to avoid detection. Their plan was to land on the salt flats near the base of the Drogal Mountains. The color of their planes closely matched the color of the salt flats, so it was unlikely they'd be discovered by aircraft flying overhead.

As they approached their landing site, Peter gave Sy and Red last minute instructions and then began his descent. Soon he was touching down on the hard white surface. Right behind him were Sy and Red. After they had removed and stored their flight suits, they secured the fighters and camouflaged them with white netting that made them invisible from the air. Then they put on their back packs and started walking toward the Drogals. Their map showed that they were about two kylods from the railroad tracks that would take them through the mountains to the Pegaport Training Facility at Muhl. Unfortunately it was very hot and even traveling just two kylods proved to be exhausting.

Sgt. Baig had warned them about the heat of the Yondi Desert. Even though Muhl was a relatively small island, about sixty-six thousand square kylods, it had a variety of different climates. The lands west of the Drogals were very wet and hot. In fact, northwestern Muhl was dominated by a tropical rain forest. East of the Drogals lay the Yondi Desert and beyond the desert to the northeast lay the rich farmlands of the Yellow Plains. Their immediate task was to traverse the Drogal Mountains. The railroad tracks went through Yulken Pass which had an elevation of approximately 3,205 ft.

They were tired and hot late that afternoon when they reached the deserted tram station at the base of the mountains. They decided to rest until it got dark. Sgt. Baig had advised them to travel only at night or risk being attacked by the Drogals.

"I wonder if we'll see any," Sy said.

"If we travel after dark, we shouldn't," Peter said. "With our night vision goggles it shouldn't be a problem. It will be much cooler at night anyway."

"I wouldn't mind seeing one of them," Red said. "It would be a great story to tell my mate and children, if I ever have any."

"I'd like to see one too. . . . At a distance, of course," Peter said with a grin. "Unfortunately, I won't be able to tell my child about it." Peter had told Sy and Red about Lucinda and the child she carried. They shook their heads sympathetically, but said nothing. Peter continued, "Since we don't have a weapon that will kill them, we'd best follow Sgt. Baig's advice and stay in the mines during the day."

"Don't worry about me," Sy said. "I have no desire to be snatched up, carried to the top of a tree, and fed to hungry young Drogals."

"Nor do I," said Red.

"Good, then I won't have to worry about either of you straying. Let's go inside. I need to call Lorin and then we can get a little shut eye before it gets dark. We've got a long hike over the mountains, so we'll need all the energy we can muster."

They went inside and looked around. The station looked like it had been vacated in a hurry. Furniture and fixtures were still intact, tables in the nutrition center were still set with dust laden dishes, glasses, and silverware, and there was even money in the cash register. It was odd looking money—a pale pink bill with a silver image of a man in the center. The man appeared to be looking at them. As Peter turned the bill the man's eyes followed him like he was alive and watching his every move. It was an eerie sensation that gave him the creeps.

"Take the money," Sy said. "We may need it later since I'm sure our credit strips have been revoked."

"But it doesn't belong to us," Peter said.

Sy shrugged, "It's been abandoned. It belongs to whoever grabs it."

Red nodded in agreement and they both began looting the cash register. Peter watched them for a few moments and then spied a cot in an adjoining room. Sleep seemed more important than money to him at that moment, but before he could succumb to his weariness he needed to call headquarters and advise them of their whereabouts. Fortunately, Sgt. Baig had provided them with a global communicator or GC that would allow them to contact headquarters from anywhere on the planet. He opened the box containing the device and pulled it out.

"I wonder how this sucker works," Peter said.

Sy looked over at him and replied, "I can help you with that. My father used to have a GC. He showed me how to use it."

"Good. It looks complicated."

Sy came over and pushed a few buttons. The communicator lit up and beeped. Sy punched in the number Peter had written down on a piece of paper and then handed him the receiver. After a moment Lorin's voice came on, "This is S2."

"S2, this is Renegade 1," Peter said.

"Thank Sandee. You went off the grid for awhile."

"It took a while to pull a blanket over our ride and hike to our hotel."

"Understood. Can we assist in any way?"

"Yes, we need to spend a couple of days in the mountains. There are a lot of old mines along the way. We'll need to use two of them, shafts 11 and 22, as shelters, but we don't know if we'll be able to get access. If we can't, we'll have a serious problem."

"I should say so. The big birds will never let you pass."

"Just get us access and we'll be okay."

"I'll see what I can do."

"Thanks. . . . Anything new on the Chancellor?"

"His condition is stable, but he hasn't been able to perform his duties. The Vice Chancellor has stepped in and is in control of the government. The battle lines are being drawn and it's just a matter of days before war breaks out."

"Well, we'll get out of here just as fast as we can. Sorry for the delay, but I think you'll be pleased when you meet Tam."

"I hope so. You're taking a great risk going after him. Be careful and get out of there as quick as you can."

"Will do. Get back to me with those security codes and access numbers."

"I'll get right on it."

"Oh, have you heard from Lucinda?" Peter asked.

"No. But I'll check on her if you like."

"I would. Thanks."

"All right. Sandee be with you. S2 out."

After putting the GC away Peter laid down. He thought of Lorin and how so much he wanted to please her. She had no faith in him and he wanted to prove her wrong. He liked her for some reason even though she detested him. His muscles began to relax. It felt so good to finally be able to sleep without fear of assassination. He closed his eyes and quickly drifted off. Dreams came quickly. It was twilight and he was soaring through the sky. Below him were lush green forests, golden meadows, and deep blue rivers. The air was cool and crisp like the spring days he remembered in Estes Park, Colorado where his family used to vacation when he was young. The view was exhilarating and he felt a tremendous sense of wonder until he felt a sharp pain in his back. Looking up he saw the gigantic foot of the Drogal that was carry him to its nest. Fear shot through him like a gladiator's spear. He began to struggle. "No! Let me go! Help!" he said and felt the big bird's grasp slip. Suddenly he was falling toward the forest far below.

When he hit the ground he felt a surge of pain that woke him up. He looked around and soon realized he'd fallen off his cot. Sy, who was lying in a pile of linen he'd fashioned as a bed, looked at Peter and laughed. "That must have been some rascal you were sparing with in your dreams."

Peter took a deep breath and replied, "You got that right. Is it dark yet?"

"I believe so. I suspect we should be moving along."

They woke up Red, got their things together, and started hiking along the tram line. Red said, "Too bad the Tram doesn't work. We'd be over the mountains in just a few kyloons if it did."

"Yeah, wouldn't that be sweet," Peter replied. "Unfortunately, it hasn't been running since the great volcanoes blew their stacks."

The trail along the tram line was steep, rugged, and in poor condition due to cycles of neglect. With their night vision equipment they had no trouble seeing but, even so, it was still slow going. About half a kylod into their hike Peter felt someone or something watching them. He stopped several times and looked around but saw nothing. When he heard it again he shone his light in the direction of the rustling bush. Two green eyes stared back at him It was a rhutz.

"Hey, look! We've got company." Peter said excitedly. "It's a rhutz!"

"Oh, Sandee help us," Red said. "They usually run in packs."

"He means us no harm," Peter assured him.

"What do you mean? Most rhutz are vicious and will rip a person apart if they're hungry or in a bad mood."

"No. He's just curious. I'm going to try to communicate with it. I'll tell him about Rhin."

"If we stop to play games we'll end up being breakfast for the Drogals," Sy reminded them.

"Right," Peter said. "I guess I'll make friends on the way back."

188

They started moving again and quickened their pace as morning approached. A kyloon later they were stopped in their tracks by a deafening screeching noise, "Screeeekchaa. Screeeekchaa!"

"What the heck was that?" Red asked.

Peter shrugged. "I don't know, but it doesn't sound friendly."

"Could that be a Drogal?" Sy asked.

"They don't feed at night, " Red reminded them.

"No, but that doesn't necessarily mean they are quiet," Peter noted.

"Screeeekchaa! Screeeekchaa!" the bird screamed.

"Let's get the hell out of here," Red said. "I don't want to be anywhere near one of those monsters daylight or night."

Nobody argued with Red. They walked double time the next few kylods until the noise of the screeching bird became a dull whisper in the wind. As they continued on Peter noticed the night sky lightening slightly. "We better find a mine to hide out in soon. It's almost daylight."

"There should be one up another kylod or two," Sy said. "Lets get moving."

They started hiking with considerable urgency but didn't reach the mine as quickly as they expected. The sky was getting brighter by the minute and Peter was getting worried that the Drogals would be out soon. He didn't voice that concern as he felt certain Sy and Red were thinking the same thing.

Sy yelled, "Up ahead. Look. It's the mine."

"You two go on ahead. I'm going to call Lorin and see if she has been able to get us access."

Peter squatted down and took out the communicator. After turning it on and punching in the correct sequence of numbers, he said, "S2, this is R1."

After a moment Lorin's voice came on. "S2 here."

"We're at the first mine after the tram station and it's starting to get light. Have you been able to get us access?"

"Not yet, R1, but I'm expecting that information momentarily. Stand by."

Peter looked up and saw Red and Sy walking briskly toward the mine. Suddenly he heard the wail of a Drogal, "Screeeekchaa! Screeeekchaa!" He looked up and saw a monstrosity of a bird swooping toward Red and Sy. Instinctively, he raised his laser and fired. The electronic pulses hit the bird dead on but seemed to be diffused by the bird's thick feathers. The bird squawked angrily and flew away. This gave Sy and Red time to move closer to the mine, but a moment later the huge bird came at them again. This time they split up, forcing the bird to choose just one of them to pursue. This tactic momentarily confused the Drogal and he hesitated before he finally went after Red. Peter took another shot at him with his laser, hoping to divert him away but it didn't work this time. He squawked at Peter angrily but didn't deviate from his course.

Just as the Drogal was about to sink his claws into Red's back, Peter remembered his C34 pistol with its heat seeking bullets. Even if he couldn't see the thin limbs of the big buzzard, if his shot was close enough the bullets would be drawn to the warmth of its limbs. Peter pulled the C34 out and opened fire. The first two bullets sailed straight through the mass of feathers scattering them about in a flurry but did no harm. The third bullet, however, hit something that made the Drogal screech. "Screeeekchaa!. Screeeekchaa!" the Drogal wailed, and wobbled in agony, trying to stay airborne. This second diversion gave Red time to make it safely to the mine's entrance. When the Drogal saw he'd lost his prey, he turned and flew directly at Peter screaming, "Screeeekchaa! Screeeekchaa!"

Peter unloaded his C34 into the monstrosity as it swooped down upon him, but every bullet passed through him like he was a ghost. Choked with fear, Peter prayed for God's forgiveness, and prepared himself to die. But just as the Drogal's claws were about to impale him, he heard a growl from an overhanging rock and saw the rhutz spring through the air and clamp his jaws around the Drogal's ankle. There was a loud crunching sound as the Drogal's claws were crushed. "Screeeekchaa! Screeeekchaa!" The Drogal screamed, shaking his leg violently to free himself from the rhutz. While the two strange animals were battling to their deaths, the Drogal came into close range where Peter could feel his brain waves like heat from a furnace. He had one shot left in the C34, so he aimed it toward the source of its being and fired. It went true and the bird let out its last cry, "Screeeekchaa! Screeeekchaa!" and fell to the ground.

The rhutz let loose of the Drogals claws and jumped out of the way of the bird as it came crashing to the ground. After eying the carcass warily for a moment, the rhutz shook himself violently trying to rid himself of the bird's feathers still clinging to him. As the rhutz circled his kill, Peter made eye contact and tried to thank him for saving his life. He couldn't tell if the rhutz understood him, but he thought he must have made a connection as he shook his head, howled to the morning sky, and ran off.

Sy ran over to Peter and said, "Where did that rhutz come from? I thought you were going to die."

"Me too," Peter said, his heart still pounding. "That's the second time a rhutz has saved my life."

"Well, for some reason they want to keep you alive."

"Thank God and Sandee," Peter said. "How do you suppose he knew I would be here?"

"You said they were telepathic. He either got the message from one of his kind, or when he saw you he connected to you somehow. Did you know he was still following us?"

"Yes, I saw him following behind. We did make eye contact. I suppose he could have read my mind."

Sy shook his head, "That's my guess."

From the mine Red yelled, "Did you get the access codes? We need to get inside. There may be more Drogals about."

"Hang on, " Peter said, as he picked up the GC.

"S2. Come in. Situation critical. Do yo have the codes?"

There was a moment of static and then Lorin's voice came on, "Yes, they should be on your screen."

Looking down at the screen he saw a series of numbers appear. He said, "Okay. I got them. Let's get into the mine."

They both ran as fast as they could to where Red was anxiously awaiting. "I've never been so scared in my life," Red admitted. "I thought that drogal was going to get me. Thanks for getting him off my back."

"No problem," Peter said. "I can't believe a laser didn't phase him."

"Sgt. Baig warned us. All those feathers act as insulation," Red replied.

From outside the mine there were screams, "Screeeekchaa!. . . Screeeekchaa! . . . Screeeekchaa!"

They turned, looked outside, and saw at least a dozen drogals circling in front of them. They screeched and wailed in apparent mourning

191

of the death of a fallen comrade. Peter feared it would not be long before they sought revenge against the one responsible for his death.

"Screeeekchaa! Screeeekchaa!" they squawked.

"Here are the numbers," Peter said. "Let's get inside quick."

Red punched in the code on the security panel mounted on the big iron gate at the mouth of the mine. It flashed green and Red turned the handle and pushed it open. The metal gate groaned as it gave way. They rushed inside and shut it behind them.

"I hope they go back to their nests when night falls," Peter said. "If not, we've got a serious problem."

"Sgt. Baig said they didn't fly at night," Sy replied. "So we should be okay."

"I hope so," Peter replied.

After retreating fifty strides into the mine, they set up camp, started a fire, and put on some sankee. Although they were all exhausted, none of them felt much like sleeping with the Drogals screeching just outside the gate. They prayed they would eventually tire and go away. If they didn't they were in serious trouble.

24
Good News

Since they couldn't sleep with the Drogals wailing outside, they ate some of their rations, drank sankee, and talked. It was the first time since they'd met that they actually had some privacy and could talk freely. On base there were bugs and cameras everywhere, not to mention Videl's spies. It felt good sitting in front of a camp fire, spilling their guts without fear of discovery.

Peter looked at Sy. "So, what was it like growing up in Tributon?"

"It was hard due to the volcanoes. When my father was young, two of them erupted in Rigimol just to our northwest. My grandfather had been a very successful farmer before then and my dad inherited the farm. After the eruptions there was very little sun and the ground was so polluted nothing would grow. For a long time it was impossible to work outdoors due to the bad air. Dad had to take a job in the city just to keep food on the table. Since it was too far to commute, he stayed in a compartment during the week and came home at break."

"How often did he get a break?"

"Normally every eight days entitles a worker to a two day break."

"We call them weekends on Earth," Peter said.

"Weekends? Huh. . . . It was hard for my mother to have him away so much. She had to do everything herself pretty much—cooking, cleaning, laundry, plowing the pastures, entertaining us kids. My two sisters and I helped as much as we could. We'd go to school during the day and just as soon as we came home in the afternoon, we'd have chores to do. We didn't have much time to relax or play with our friends."

"Why would you plow the fields if they were contaminated and the air was so bad?" Peter asked.

"The Central Authority required it. They gave us chemicals that were supposed to cleanse the soil. They had to be applied to the surface and then plowed in. The tractor my mother drove had a sealed cab with a filtration device so she'd have clean air. She still got sick, though, because she often had to leave the cab to remove obstructions or make repairs. They call it velvet lung. The pollution causes a velvet-like substance to form on the surface of the lungs. Over time the substance begins to inhibit the lung's function causing breathing difficulties and making the lung susceptible to infection."

"I can't believe your mother had to plow the fields. Couldn't you hire someone to do it?"

"No. We couldn't afford help since we had no income other than minimal subsidies from the government for fuel and equipment upkeep. Sometimes she'd take me with her if she was sick or just wanted the company, but she'd never let me leave the cab."

"So, has the soil restoration worked?"

Sy shrugged. "We don't know yet. Until the air clears and the sun shines again, it doesn't really matter. Plants won't grow without sunshine even if the soil is fertile."

"Hmm. When do you think the air will clear?" Peter asked.

"It was promised to us long ago, but as you can see it hasn't happened. Some say in five or ten cycles, others say twenty-five to fifty."

"That stinks."

"*Stinks?*"

"Ah. You know, a rotten turn of events."

"Hmm. Yes, it definitely *stinks*. Hopefully during our lifetime we'll see the sky back to normal."

"What did you do for fun when you were growing up?" Peter asked.

"My father and I used to go dickel hunting," Sy replied. "That was fun."

"What's a dickel?"

"It's a very tasty bird that crosses Tributon each fall during their annual migration to Ock Mezan. It's one of the few birds that were hearty enough to thrive in the post volcanic era. Thousands would fly overhead and we'd pick them off with a birdblaster."

194

"A birdblaster. Huh. We have a gun on Earth that does the same thing. It's called a shotgun."

Sy nodded. "Of course, we played a lot of screen games and simulations too."

"What about sports?"

"Sports?"

"Games between people."

"You mean like close combat?"

"I guess. What's that?"

"It a game of fighting skills—boxing, wrestling, and kick boxing. I was on our school team. We went to the Tributon Nationals."

"It sounds a lot like the sports we had on Earth. My favorite sport was baseball."

"Baseball? What's that?"

"It's a game where a pitcher throws a hard ball in front of you and you try to hit it with a wooden stick. It's hard to explain. I'll show you how to play it someday."

"Great. It sounds like fun," Sy said.

"Unfortunately, I doubt we'll have much time for games anytime soon," Peter noted.

Sy nodded dejectedly. They were all exhausted and were relieved when the squawking finally stopped outside, so they could get some sleep. When Peter woke up six kyloons later it was dark outside. His companions were still sleeping, so he rekindled the fire and then woke them up. After they had eaten some rations, they gathered their gear together and began their trek up the mountain. Luckily the Drogals were nowhere to be seen. Nevertheless, the three hikers kept a close eye out for them just in case.

By Peter's calculations it would take them two nights to get over the mountains and to Shaft 22, the mine closest to Pegaport. They would stay in the mine during the daylight and go in to extract Tam during the night. Once they found him they'd have to make it all the way back to Shaft 22 before the sun came up to avoid another encounter with the Drogals. That made it imperative that they get in and out of the training center without delay.

"They'll have no idea someone is coming for Tam. I bet we could just walk right in there and nobody would pay us any notice," Red said.

"I'm not so sure about that," Peter said. "The recruits will be segregated and closely watched. If we try to approach them, we'll be stopped."

"I wonder if Sgt. Baig has been able to get word to Tam that we're coming," Sy said. "If he could break away from his squad for a minute we could grab him and run."

"What if they come after us?" Red asked.

"We can't let that happen," Peter said. "We won't stand a chance unless we have a good head start. I'll call Lorin and see if she can get hold of Sgt. Baig. Hopefully, he'll have a contact lined up for us."

When they stopped to rest Peter got on the GC and tried to raise Lorin. "S2, do you read? . . . S2, this is R1, do you read?" . . . "Shisk—"

Blip . . .blip . . . "This is S2. Sorry, I was asleep."

"Right," Peter said. "Sorry to wake you, but we need you to check on something for us."

"All right. What is it?"

"Sgt. Baig was going to try to line us up a contact at Pegaport to make contact with Tam. We need you to see if he was successful. We'll be ready for the extraction at sunset and need to finalize our plans."

"I'll get right on it and get back to you,"Lorin assured them.

"Thanks."

"Oh, by the way. I had a long talk with Lucinda. She's fine . . . and so is the baby."

Relief rushed through Peter like a cool summer breeze but it didn't last. Although he was glad to hear all was well, the news of Lucinda also saddened him. The thought that she'd considered him little more than a friend was still hard for him to accept.

"Oh, thank God. . . . Did she—"

"She said she missed you. She'd like to see you."

"Really? She said that?"

"Yes. Her mate's not so excited about the pregnancy."

"Why not?"

"He's used to getting Lucinda's full attention, but now she's very much distracted by the baby. He doesn't like that."

"What a selfish pig," Peter said.

Lorin laughed. "He also doesn't like the fact that Lucinda is always talking about you."

"About me? She talks about me? . . . You think she misses me?"

"Obviously. I've taken the liberty of arranging for her to come visit you at our base in the Beet Islands. I'm going to personally escort her there. We should be at the base when you arrive."

"What! You've got to be kidding? I can't believe it. Lorin, you're an angel. Thank you so much."

"Now you have some real incentive to get your butt off Muhl and down to the Beet Islands."

"You're right about that. I can't wait to get there."

"I'll call you back as soon as I get word from Sgt. Baig. Be careful."

"Will do. Check you later. R1 out."

Peter was so excited he could scarcely contain his joy. In just a few days he'd be seeing Lucinda. It was so unexpected. He closed his eyes and thanked God—not just that he'd be seeing her, but that she was missing him. That was even better news. Perhaps there was hope after all that they might someday be together. As he was daydreaming about Lucinda, a loud *Screeeekchaa. Screeeekchaa* jolted him back to the present. He stood up and looked around warily.

"It's time to get going," Peter said. "We've got to make Shaft 22 before dawn."

Sy and Red got up and they began the last leg of their trek. It was a cool, cloudless night and the faint glow of Tarizon's two moons could be seen through the hazy sky. This was only the second time Peter had seen the two moons and he marveled at the oddity of it. As they walked, Peter looked out and wondered if he'd ever see Earth's moon again. He missed his family so much he started to choke up. Tears ran down his cheek. Fortunately it was dark and his friends couldn't see his pain. As he wiped the tears from his eyes, he wondered if his family thought of him as often as he thought of them. Suddenly he felt a strange sensation in his head. It was a faint voice that he couldn't quite understand, but knew very well. It was the voice of his father. Was it just his imagination or was his father trying to make contact with him? Surely it couldn't be—thoughts traveling millions of miles through space. But he did feel his father's presence and it was very comforting.

25
Preparations

When Peter, Sy and Red finally made it to Shaft 22, Lorin reported that Sgt. Baig had indeed found them a contact at Pegaport. He was a cook at the base nutrition center named Luga Vincete. Vincete had already alerted Tam that he was to be extracted. Lorin also told them they had some additional orders from the Loyalist command. They were to assist Vincete and some other soldiers to escape from Pegaport and destroy some key targets before they left the island. The only thing left to do now was to get word to Vincete as to the timing of the operation.

"One of us is going to have to walk into the nutrition center and talk to Vincete," Red noted.

"I'll do it," Sy said.

"It will be dangerous," Peter replied. "If you're confronted you won't have the proper identification. They'll take you straight to the brig."

"I'll slip into one of the barracks and borrow some clothes so I'll blend in. No one will suspect anything."

"I don't know. It's a small base, I'm sure all of the officers know each other."

"Not necessarily," Red interjected. "Back on Pogo Island personnel were coming and going everyday. I saw a lot of new faces, especially in admin and the armory."

"That's true," Peter said. "With civil war on the horizon I'm sure there will be a lot of new personnel on base. All right. I guess that's as good a plan as any. . . . But how do we get Tam away from his squad without anyone suspecting anything?"

"He could fake an injury or illness," Red said. "On the way to the infirmary we'll grab him. It'll probably be a kyloon or so before someone

199

misses him."

"That's a good idea," Peter said. "That should give us time to get well into the mountains. By the time they come looking for us, it will be too late. We should be able to make it back here to Shaft 22 before daylight. If they try to pursue us in the daylight they'll have the Drogals to contend with."

"What about Vincete and the other soldiers?" Red asked.

"Vincete, I'm sure, will have a plan for that. We'll help anyway we can."

They slept for awhile. At midday they proceeded to Pegaport's eastern perimeter. The mountains were densely forested with a variety of evergreens which provided good cover. Sy left them and made his way to one of the officers' quarters that looked deserted. He wore a personal communicator on his lapel so they would be in constant communication.

"I'm going inside," he said.

"Okay, good luck," Peter replied.

While Sy was out of view they carefully observed the layout of the base and the traffic patterns. They were directly behind the athletic fields and armory. To the north was an airstrip and to the south the officers quarters. Beyond the armory was the base headquarters, classrooms, the nutrition center, parade ground, and a brig. On the opposite side of the base, bounded by the river and the sea, were the base commissary, recruit barracks, and a large hanger. Fortunately most of the base activity was in the central part around the headquarters building, classrooms, and nutrition center. The athletic field was deserted, except for a handful of joggers, and there was but one guard at the armory.

"How about I go jogging?" Sy said over his communicator. "There's a complete jogging outfit spread out on one of the bunks."

"That's a good idea. You can do a few laps to enhance your cover before you go to the nutrition center."

"All right. Give me a minute—crap, someone is coming." There was silence for a few loons. Then they could hear a scuffling sound through the communicator. Peter's pulse quickened as he feared Sy had been discovered. He knew it would be a disaster if he got caught. What would they do? Suddenly someone emerged from the officers quarters dressed in a jogging suit. "That was close," Sy whispered.

"What happened?" Peter asked, feeling a flood of relief come over him. "We lost you there for a moment."

"A couple of officers walked in so I had to grab the suit and take it to the showers. I don't think they saw me."

"Thank God and Sandee."

They watched Sy walk briskly north to the athletic field where he started jogging around the track. There were several other joggers and he was about to pass them when he asked, "Should I salute these guys when they go by?"

"Jeez, I don't know. I don't think so," Peter said. "Not when you're in jogging gear. That would be stupid."

The joggers passed and Sy nodded but didn't salute. They didn't seem to notice. When he had completed two laps he slowed to a walk and started toward the base headquarters. He stopped a moment to read a message board in front of the main building. When he turned to leave a group of officers confronted him.

"Soldier," One of them said. "What's your name?"

"Lt. . ..ah, Tenyon, sir," Sy stuttered.

"Tenyon? Haven't seen you around before."

"Yeah, well I just shipped in from Pogo Island."

"Oh, really? I didn't hear about anyone checking in this week . . . That jogging suit, doesn't it belong to Colonel Armijo?"

"Ah. . .yeah, right. He let me borrow it. My gear got lost."

The man frowned, then shook his head and said, "That figures. . . . All right, carry on."

Sy nodded, turned, and resumed his trek to the nutrition center. The officer who had questioned him continued to watch him for a moment and then turned to another officer and said something. The other officer looked toward Sy and then disappeared into the headquarters building.

"Sy, we may have some trouble brewing," Peter said. "You better get inside quickly and find our man. I don't know how much time you have."

"Yeah, sorry. I guess that sounded pretty phony. It was the best I could do."

"No. I doubt I could have done any better. Just get in and out of there in a hurry."

"Will do."

Sy walked inside the nutrition center and for some reason the moment he stepped through the door the communicator went dead. "Sy? Can you hear me? Sy?"

There was no answer. Peter looked at Red. "We lost him. Crap! How did that happen? The communicator is supposed to have 99.9% coverage."

"I don't know," Red said. "I've heard there is one material that can block it—giddium, I think."

"But giddium is expensive," Peter replied. "I can't believe they'd line the nutrition center walls with it. More likely somebody grabbed him. I can't believe this."

"Should we get over there and see if he's in trouble?"

"No," Peter said. "Maybe his battery went dead. That's happened to me before."

The batteries they used were heat rejuvenated, so it wasn't likely there had been a battery failure. It was just an excuse to avoid thinking the unthinkable. It would have been extremely dangerous for all of them to walk into the nutrition center. That would have been too many unfamiliar faces all at one time. So, they nervously waited for what seemed like a kyloon. At one point Peter almost decided to risk it and go in after him, but he somehow restrained himself knowing that eventually he'd have to come out, one way or another. Finally, Sy emerged from the nutrition center and began to jog back toward the athletic field.

"Sy, you all right?" Peter asked.

There was no answer, so he assumed his communicator was still on the blink. They watched him silently as he ran another two laps and then walked quickly back to where they were hiding.

"Sandee. I thought you were a goner when those officers went in," Peter said.

"Me too. Fortunately, they didn't see me."

"Were you scared?" Red asked.

"Nah. I'd of thought of something had they confronted me."

"Thank God and Sandee that wasn't necessary," Peter said. "So, did you make contact with our man?"

"Yes, I took him aside and told him our plan. He said he'd get the message to Tam when he came in for dinner."

"Good. Did you tell him timing was critical? We need to do this just before sunset so it will be dark when we go back through the mountains. We want to make it hard for them to follow us and we don't want to have any more encounters with the Drogals."

"Yes, I explained that. He said there is a warehouse for the nutrition center just south of the infirmary where one of us could hide until Tam came by. He said he'd leave it unlocked."

"Good. What about him and the other soldiers?"

"They have a transport plane they plan to heist. They want us to fly over when we leave the island and hit a few strategic targets. During the confusion they think they'll be able to get their plane off the ground and escape. Amongst the targets you'll be hitting are the Muscan Missile Launchers. You've got to knock them out or none of us will make it off the island."

"Did he tell you where they are?"

"Yes, he said they are underground, just north of the airstrip," Sy replied. "He said to aim for the yellow lights at the end of the runway and you'll hit them dead on."

"Good. Should be a piece of cake."

"A piece of cake?" Red asked.

"Ah. . . . that's an expression back on Earth . . . you know . . . it means, it should be easy."

"Right. A piece of cake, but what is cake?"

Peter smiled. "It's a fluffy, sweet food that is served on special occasions—like birthdays. It's really good."

"Hmm. I should like to taste it sometime."

Peter nodded. "I actually saw it on the menu at a restaurant in Shisk. Maybe I'll take you there someday. It won't be as good as what my mother baked back in Dallas, but it will probably still be good."

Tears began to well in Peter's eyes as he thought of his home and family. He suddenly felt congested and choked up. The thought that he'd never see his mother again was unbearable. He loved her so. Sy gave him a queer look.

"You okay?" Sy asked.

Peter wiped a tear from the corner of his eye. "Yeah, I'm fine."

Sy smiled sympathetically and said, "I miss my mother too."

"Yeah, but at least you can call her and talk to her, and when the war is over you'll be able to see her again. I'll never have that opportunity. . . . My mother thinks I'm dead and she'll never know otherwise." Sy and Red just looked at Peter in silence. Peter swallowed hard. "Anyway, we should get some shut eye. We'll most likely be up all night. You guys sleep now and I'll keep watch. We'll each do two kyloon shifts."

Sy and Red nodded and started looking around for a place to sleep. While they were sleeping Peter played Tam's extraction in his head. Then he thought about the targets they'd have to hit as they left the island. There was the armory with a large supply of weapons, the big hanger housing two dozen or so assorted aircraft, base headquarters, and the officers' barracks where, with luck, they might take out the base commander or even a visiting general, and, most importantly, the Muscan Missile launchers. If they didn't knock that out, well, the war might well be over for all of them.

26

Extraction

Late that afternoon Red woke Peter up and said it was time to go. Sy had volunteered to wait in the storage room for Tam. Red agreed to back him up in case there was trouble. Peter would stay back and watch the base from a higher vantage point where he could quickly spot any potential threats to the mission. They'd all be in constant communication. Sy and Red left and Peter looked out over the base looking for anything unusual. All was seemed quiet.

After a few loons Peter noticed some commotion over at the officer's barracks. Two miliary police vehicles were parked outside and a group of officers and miliary police were having an animated conversation. Unfortunately, Peter didn't have long distance listening equipment, so he couldn't hear what they were saying. He figured they must have finally realized there was a stranger on the base.

"R2, there are three MPs at officers' quarters—may be looking for you. I'll keep a close eye on them."

"Confirmed," replied Sy. "I'm in place. They won't be able to spot me."

Red replied, "I can see the storage unit and have a good few of the surrounding terrain. No activity."

"Good," Peter said taking a deep breath and slowly exhaling.

It was near dusk and there was a steady flow of soldiers going in and out of the nutrition center. Peter searched for any other signs of activity but saw nothing. Then the discussion at the officer's barracks broke up and two ATVs began moving toward the infirmary. As he watched them, he noticed two men come out of Barracks C. One of the men shook his head and motioned back toward the barracks. The second man lingered, but finally went back inside. The first man looked around and then began walking briskly toward the infirmary. Peter was pretty sure it was Tam.

"Tam's on his way," he said into his communicator. "Two jeeps with MPs are heading your way as well."

"Great timing," Sy said with a sigh of despair.

"Confirmed," Red said. "No sign of them so far."

"What do we do if they spot Tam?" Sy asked.

"Just pray they don't," Peter replied. "I'd hate to have to engage them. That could jeopardize the entire mission."

"Just give the word and I'll neutralize them with my laser," Red said. "They'll never know what hit them."

"Only if there is no other option," Peter replied. "Maybe we'll get lucky and Tam will—."

"There he is. . . . Tam! Over here," Sy whispered. For a few moments sounds of running and heavy breathing came through the communicator. Then Sy said, "Okay, I've got him. Heading back."

"Wait," Red warned. "The ATVs are coming. Stay out of sight."

"Confirmed. Advise when clear."

There were several moments of silence and then Red said, "Crap! They must have seen you. They've stopped."

"All right. If they become a threat, take them out," Peter said. "Use your laser. We can't afford for anyone to hear gunfire."

"Confirmed. . . . Two of them are on foot and heading for the storage unit. I'm going to have to neutralize them."

The idea of killing someone hadn't ever even crossed Peter's mind prior to coming to Pogo Island. Then in boot camp, killing became the main focus of his life. Still, up until now it all seemed theoretical, like training on the simulators or playing a video game. Now suddenly reality was smacking him right in the face. His stomach turned. One word and two human lives would be destroyed. Their most precious treasure, life itself would be obliterated forever. These were living human beings, like himself, with families and friends who would be devastated at the loss of husband, father, or friend. How could he order such a horrible thing to be done?"

"Ten seconds and they'll be out of range," Red advised.

Peter swallowed hard.. He had no other choice. "There's no other option. Do it now!"

There was a flash of light in the distance. Peter closed his eyes and it felt like his heart had stopped for an instant. He began to tremble and tears welled in his eyes but he quickly wiped them away. *It was just a video game. Just a video game. None of this is real. You'll wake up soon.* Peter listened for any kind of reaction to the flash.

"Threat neutralized," Red advised, breaking the eerie silence. "We'll hide the bodies in the shed."

Peter took several deep breaths trying to calm his nerves. Then he replied, "Come back in the ATVs. It will save time and get them away from the bodies. That should buy us more time."

"Confirmed."

There was a scuffling noise through the communicator and then the sound of bodies being dragged through the dirt. A door creaked, . . . more dragging, . . . silence, and finally the hum of the ATV's engine. All seemed to have gone well. Peter watched the ATVs wind there way back toward him. They were driving slowly, trying not to attract attention. All was quiet on Muhl now, but that would be changing quickly. When the convoy arrived the passenger side door opened and Tam stepped out. Peter ran over to him and embraced him.

"Tam. It's great so see you. Are you okay?"

Tam shook his head and said, "What are you doing here? We're going to be in a world of trouble. When Luga told me you were coming to rescue me, I almost refused to meet you. This is treason."

"No, it's not. We're joining the Loyalists. We're pledged to defend the Supreme Mandate. It's Videl Lai who is the traitor. He's assumed power and is already making plans to scrap the Supreme Mandate and rule Tarizon as a dictator."

"How do you plan to get us off the Island?" Tam asked skeptically. .

"We've got a few fighters across the mountains. We don't have time to waste. We've come a long way to get you but I'll understand if you don't want to come. . . . If they catch us we *will* be put on trial for treason. But, if you go back now to the infirmary, they'll never know you were missing. We just killed two MPs so you don't have a lot of time to make a decision."

Tam smiled, "Go back? Are you kidding me? The only reason I'd ever go back to Pegaport would be to blow the place up. Do you know what they did to me?"

Peter smiled. "No, but I'm anxious to hear about it, and we *are* going back to blow it up, but not on foot."

Tam returned Peter's smile and got back in the ATV. Peter climbed in the other ATV with Sy and they began to lumber up the narrow road back into the Drogal Mountains. Just as they traversed the first foothill and were out of view of Pegaport sirens began to blare. Peter looked back and said to Sy, "Step on it."

Peter told himself that the sirens didn't necessarily mean that they would be pursued. It could be that the bodies had been found or Tam had been discovered missing and the base was being searched. There was no reason to think base command could know or suspect that their security had been breached and they were there to extract Tam. That idea was quickly dispelled when they heard the sound of choppers in the distance and saw fighters scrambling from the distant airfield.

"These ATVs are going to be sitting ducks for those T47s," Peter said. "As much as I hate hiking over the mountains, I think if we value our lives, we should go it on foot."

Sy nodded and put his foot on the brake. "Let's get the hell out of here," he said as he cut the engine and engaged the brake.

Peter jumped out of the ATV and advised Red that they'd best go on foot. He frowned but didn't argue. They gathered their gear and hustled off the main road. After they'd hiked for about fifteen loons there was a tremendous explosion behind them and they could see smoke rising from the trees in the distance.

"That would be the ATVs," Peter said. "We better get a move on. We're not very far ahead of them."

"How did they discover the bodies so quickly?" Sy asked.

"Oh, crap!" Tam said. "I didn't think about it, but the ATVs have tracking devices on them. Command knows exactly where they are at all times. The moment we left the base they knew something was wrong." Tam kicked at the dirt in disgust. Then he looked up in horror. "Oh, Sandee! I've got an implant as well. As long as I am with you, they'll know exactly where we are."

Peter swallowed hard. "I can't believe this! A man's got no privacy on this planet. They don't keep track of every single human being on Earth. Crap! What are we going to do now?"

"Surgery is the only answer," Sy said. "We'll need to remove the implant."

"But do you even know where it is located?" Peter asked.

Sy nodded, "More or less. I've seen the procedure done on the VC."

Peter rolled his eyes and replied, "Wonderful."

The sound of choppers could be heard in the distance. They all looked back anxiously. Tam said, "Do it. We don't have any choice."

Sy shook his head and grabbed his back pack. From it he pulled out a first aid kit and began rifling through it. He found a small knife and said, "Lie down on you stomach. I'll put some Painfree over the spot where I'll be making the incision. Hopefully it will ease the pain a bit."

"Hopefully?" Peter asked.

"Painfree is good stuff, but I'm not sure it was meant for surgery."

Tam closed his eyes and began to quiver slightly in anticipation of the pain. "We better hold him down, Red," Peter said. "We don't want anybody getting accidentally stabbed."

"Okay, I'm ready," Sy advised them.

Peter took a deep breath and held Tam's right shoulder while Red held his left. Peter closed his eyes when Sy plunged the knife into Tam's neck. Tam lurched about from the pain but didn't scream. Peter and Red struggled but managed to keep him still. Sy worked for a moment and then pulled out a small device that looked like an ordinary computer chip.

"Got it," he said. "Okay, I'll sew him up and then we can get out of here."

"You okay, Tam?" Peter asked.

Tam frowned. "Yeah. That wasn't any worse than being flogged by a drill sergeant."

"They flogged you?" Peter asked.

Tam nodded. "Pretty regularly, but like you said, we can talk about that later. Right now we better put as much distance between ourselves and this tracking device as we can."

Tam's words made Peter think. He'd seen it done in the movies many times—a tracking device or cell phone is used to lead a foe off in the wrong direction. "Too bad we can't put this implant on something moving in the opposite direction. That might take the heat off of us."

There was a explosion in the distance and the sound of the choppers getting closer.

"I don't know," Peter said and then noticed the rhutz sitting in the meadow watching them.

Red saw him too and said, "You think your friend could help us?"

Peter shrugged and replied, "I don't know. If I can make him understand, he might. Give me the implant."

Sy handed it to Peter and he walked slowly over toward the Rhutz. As he got closer the rhutz beared his teeth and growled. Peter took a long breath and closed his eyes. In his mind's eye he saw the rhutz standing before him. *Take this far away from us quickly. Drop it and then return. It's a matter of life or death.* Peter opened his eyes and wondered if there was any chance the rhutz had understood, or, if he did, would he do as asked. Suddenly, the rhutz stepped forward and opened his mouth. Peter dropped the implant on his tongue and he ran off in the opposite direction.

"All right!" Red said.

Tam shook his head and added, "That's incredible. I was almost killed by a rhutz one time."

"Really. You'll have to tell me about that later. Right now, let's get the hell up to Shaft 22. We'll be lucky to get there by daybreak."

The sound of choppers in the distance waned and the rest of their night's trek through the Drogal Mountains was peaceful and without incident. As they made their way in the darkness, Tam filled them in on his duty at Pegaport.

"After the assassination attempt I saw the sniper jump down from the observation deck,"Tam said. "I knew if I didn't go after him immediately he'd get away. I didn't have time to argue with Lt. Londry about it."

"He was really pissed off," Peter replied.

"Yeah, he gave me an earful when the MPs brought me back to

them. I thought he'd be happy that I'd caught the guy, but he couldn't care less about the fact that somebody had tried to kill one of his candidates. All he could think about was the fact that I disobeyed his order, even if it was a stupid one."

"So what did he do after he chewed you out?" Peter asked.

"He told me I couldn't be an officer in the TGA if I couldn't take orders. Officers had to take orders without question, even if they didn't like them. He said I had been a troublemaker since the first day I stepped foot on Pogo Island and if it hadn't been for Sgt. Baig's intervention, he'd of washed me out long before then."

"I can't believe he wouldn't give you another chance after all you had been through," Sy said. "I bet he's one of Videl's cronies."

"I wouldn't be surprised if he was in on the assassination attempt," Peter suggested. "That would explain why he wasn't concerned about the security of the squad. He knew there was just one target."

Tam nodded and Red asked, "So, what happened when you got to Pegaport?"

Tam sighed and replied, "I was in trouble almost immediately. They dumped me into the Hell Squad even though I hadn't had time to get in trouble. It was non-stop PT—long morning runs, forced marches through swamps and up steep hills, weight training, martial arts, and, in our spare time, latrine duty and trash pickup."

Red cringed. "Oh, Sandee. How horrible that must have been."

"I could handle that. It was the verbal abuse and the floggings that took their toll."

Tam stopped, turned around, and lifted his shirt. They all stared in disbelief at his mangled back. It was red and swollen with long deep scars from the lashings he'd taken. Peter shivered at the sight of it and thanked God that he hadn't had to go through that kind of an ordeal himself.

As the night slowly passed, they realized it was taking them longer to get to Shaft 22 than they'd planned. Peter didn't know if they'd slowed down while they listened to Tam's tale or they'd just underestimated the length of the journey, but as daylight broke Shaft 22 was not yet in sight. Now they not only had Pegaport Command to contend with, but the Drogals as well.

27

The Drogal's Last Stand

The sound of choppers in the distance sent a chill down Peter's spine. He looked behind and saw them coming in the distance. There were five of them flying in formation—five Model 28 Bosch Technology or BT 28s as they were more commonly called. Each of them were equipped with laser canons, rockets, and machine guns. Red looked back and then looked at Peter nervously.

"The mine should be right over that ridge up ahead," Sy said. Let's make a run for it."

There was no argument to Sy's suggestion. They all began running as fast as they could up the hill. The sound of the BT28s was growing louder as they scrambled toward the crest of the hill. Peter prayed that Sy was right and when they reached the top they'd see Shaft 22 just ahead. Suddenly there was a high pitched sound that meant only one thing—rockets were on their way.

"Take cover!" Tam screamed as he dived behind a fallen tree. Peter looked back and then scrambled in behind him. Sy and Red found a large boulder and flung themselves behind it. There was a thunderous explosion ahead of them. Debris flew through the air and fell everywhere. A tik later there was another explosion and then another.

"Come on," Peter said. "We can't stay here. We have to get to the mine. He peered up over the fallen tree and saw the BT28s bearing down on them. "Come on! There's no time to lose."

Staying low he began to run again, closer to the trees this time, toward the crest of the hill. Tam was at his back and Sy and Red were running up the other side of the path. Finally Peter reached the top and as he looked out expectantly, praying Shaft 22 would be just ahead, his heart nearly exploded in despair. Ahead, circling like vultures, were more than a hundred Drogals, waiting to devour them before they could reach the mine. "Screeeekchaa . . . Screeeekchaa . . . Screeeekchaa!" they shrieked.

"Oh, Sandee! No!" Red cried as he reached the ridge.

Tam looked at the circling beasts and then back at the choppers rapidly approaching. Sy sunk to his knees and began to pray.

"Sy. You and Red make a run for the mine," Peter ordered. "Tam will cover you with his laser and I'll use my rifle. Use your pistols if any of them get too close."

"But it's hopeless," Red moaned in despair. "There's no way we'll get through."

"There's no time to lose. Go! Now!" Peter yelled.

Sy nodded and gave Red a shove, "Come on. Get going. It's the only chance we have."

Sy took off and Red reluctantly began running behind him. Peter knelt down and put his rifle to his shoulder. One of the Drogals swooped down and headed straight at Red. Tam hit the big bird with his laser and feathers flew, but the bird was only momentarily distracted. "Screeeekchaa," it screamed and resumed its course. Peter knew there was little chance he could kill the bird, but he thought if he even grazed its skin, that would be enough to drive it off. He aimed his rifle at its foot and squeezed the trigger. The heat seeking bullet hissed as it rushed toward its target. Peter held his breath until he heard "Screeeekchaa . . . Screeeekchaa" and saw yellow blood spraying from the Drogal's severed claw. The bird dropped to the ground and hobbled around in pain.

For one brief moment Sy and Red stopped to watch the mangled Drogal, then they began to run once again. Peter looked back and saw troops being dropped from the choppers. A dozen were already on the ground and moving toward them. Bullets began to shoot past them. Looking at Sy and Red again, he saw they were nearly at the mine, but another Drogal was swooping down on them. Tam shot his laser again but with no measurable effect and Peter realized he was too far away to get off an effective round.

As the Drogal was about to snatch Red and carry him away, Sy aimed his pistol at the bird's jagged head and fired. "Screeeekchaa," the bird

214

wailed. "Screeeekchaa . . . Screeeekchaa." Dazed by the shot the bird flew around in circles. The distraction was just long enough to allow Sy and Red to make it to the mine. They both knelt down and motioned they were ready for Peter and Tam to come.

Tam didn't hesitate. He started running toward the mine. Peter looked back and saw the soldiers were but a hundred yards away. A bullet hit the ground beside him spraying him with dirt and pebbles. Peter lifted his rifle and shot twenty rounds at his pursuers. One of them fell and then another. As he watched, a bullet grazed his arm sending a surge of pain through him. He grabbed where he felt the pain and fell to the ground.

His arm was bleeding, but he didn't think it was serious, just painful. He had to move but his body felt like it weighed five hundred pounds. Another bullet passed by his head triggering a shot of adrenalin that got him to his feet. He stumbled forward toward the mine. "Screeeekchaa," a feathery monster screamed overhead. "Screeeekchaa. . . Screeeekchaa," another one echoed. Sy's laser hit one of the birds catching its feathers on fire. The bird flapped its wings frantically but the effort only made the fire become more intense. The other birds looked on in horror as their fellow Drogal burned and finally fell to the ground. Peter hoped the bird's plight would scare the other Drogals away, but just the opposite happened. They seemed only to be angrier and more determined to kill them all.

Peter started to run again but only took a few steps when he felt the vice grip of a Drogal on his shoulder. He pulled him forward and then lifted him off the ground. Peter struggled and tried to shoot the Drogal with his pistol, but in the struggle he lost his grip and the pistol fell to the ground below. Just as he was about to accept his doom, he heard the sound of a chopper. Looking up he saw a B28 Attack Chopper blocking the Drogal's escape. The bird darted to the left nearly pulling his arm out of its socket. Then the bird flew straight at the chopper. There was a tremendous collision which knocked Peter out of Drogal's grasp and onto the ground. The fall knocked the wind out of Peter and left him momentarily helpless. He looked up and saw the chopper swing around wildly, out of control. The bird and craft collided a second time and then there was a tremendous explosion. The blast caused the other Drogals to scatter giving Peter the time he needed to join the others at the mouth of the mine.

"Now what?" Tam asked. "The mine won't provide any protection from infantry."

Peter knew Tam was right. They could go into the mine but the soldiers would come after them. They could hide for a short time, hold them off with their rifles if they found them, but eventually they'd all die. There had to be another option. As Peter was frantically trying to come up with it, he heard "Screeeekchaa . . . Screeeekchaa . . . Screeeekchaa." The birds were back and they were livid! Fortunately they seemed to have forgotten about Peter and his friends and were swooping down on the soldiers from Pegaport pursuing them. One by one Peter saw soldiers grabbed by the big birds and taken away over the treetops. The other soldiers fired at them, but might as well been shooting paint pellets. Seeing their perilous predicament the other soldiers began to turn and flee back toward Pegaport.

Sy raised his fist and yelled, "Yes! Thank you Sandee!"

Peter smiled but before he could add his congratulations he heard the hissing sound of an oncoming missile. "Quick!" he screamed. "Back in the mine!"

They scrambled back from the mine's entrance and hit the dirt. There was a tremendous explosion as the missile hit its intended target. Debris flew in every direction. Dust filled the air and made it difficult to see or breathe. Red began to cough as the ground shook spewing up clouds of dust. Rocks started to fall and the ceiling seemed poised to collapse. "Quick!" Peter screamed. "Move farther back into the mine. The ceiling's about to go!"

They all scrambled again, this time back well inside the mine. The ground grumbled and shook one last time before the entire entrance to the cave collapsed. Dust engulfed them although they could not see it in the pitch blackness. Peter coughed and wheezed violently as did the others. Finally the ground stopped shaking and silence engulfed Shaft 22.

Peter pulled his night vision mask from his back pack and put it on. Looking around he saw that Red and Sy were lying on the ground seemingly dazed. Tam was standing, his night vision mask already in place. They looked at each other's eerie heat signatures through their goggles. They didn't need to talk. Their minds quickly connected. They were trapped beneath fifty tons of rock. How would they ever get out? Fear griped them like a Drogal's claw. Was this to be their final resting place? Was this to be their common grave where they would spend eternity? Peter dropped to one knee, trembling violently, then collapsed into unconsciousness.

28
Hope Dashed

"Father, Peter keeps asking about Lucinda. He seems very much distracted by her, particularly since she's carrying his baby. I'm worried his obsession with her will prevent him from fulfilling his full potential as a soldier."

The Councillor smiled up at Lorin. "Well, the relationship between a man and woman on Earth is much different than it is here. The Christian God demands that each man shall take one woman as his wife and they shall be together exclusive of all others. They know they've found their partner when they fall in love. Peter thinks he's in love with Lucinda, so it is just natural for him to want her as his wife. The baby makes it imperative since a Christian man, theoretically, can only have a child with his wife."

"But that's so illogical and inefficient. With so many people in the world, how could they possibly find the right mate?"

"They believe God will bring them together."

"Hmm. That's why God gave us computers."

"Maybe, but that begs the issue. As long as Peter believes the way he does, he's going to be distracted by Lucinda and the baby."

"So, what should we do?"

"You should go visit Lucinda and see if she might consider leaving her mate."

"What? Leave her mate! But that's not legal."

"No, but in extraordinary circumstances mates can be reassigned—computer error, serious injury or disease, criminal behavior, and in the interest of justice. Fortunately, one of my powers as a Councillor is making such determinations. I think this reassignment would be in the best interest of the people."

"I'm not sure Videl would think so," Lorin joked.

"Yes, well he's not Chancellor yet, so he won't be able to complain, will he?"

"Hopefully, he doesn't know that Peter exists."

"Oh, he knows he exists. He just doesn't know his identity yet. But he'll figure it out sooner or later."

The next day Lorin summoned Lucinda to the country home. She had someone meet her at the subtram station and drive her to the estate. Lorin went out to meet her when she saw the PV pull up. Lucinda opened the door and stepped out with a bit of a struggle.

"Lucinda, hi," Lorin said. "Thank you so much for coming."

"Oh, it's my pleasure. It was nice of you to invite me."

They went inside and Zippo took Lucinda's coat and offered them sankee. They accepted and Zippo went off to prepare it. Lorin led Lucinda to the patio where they sat in two plush chairs next to a crystal coffee table.

"How are you feeling?" Lorin asked.

"As big as a Zodilla," Lucinda replied.

Lorin smiled. "And how's the baby?"

"The doctors say he's strong and growing quickly."

"That's wonderful. I bet your mate is excited about becoming a father."

"He is, I think, but you know men; they don't like to admit it."

"Oh, he doesn't share your joy for the baby?"

"I'm sure he does, but he's worried that I won't have time for him *and* the baby."

"What? He thinks you are his slave?"

"No. He's just a typical immature male. A baby will be good for him. It will make him grow up."

"Listen, Lucinda. Peter has been asking about you and the baby."

Her eyes lit up. "Has he? How's he doing? I was hoping he'd be here."

"No, no. He's been deployed by the army. I'm not sure when he'll be back."

"Oh. I would have liked to see him."

"Well, that's why I invited you here this day. I've got a request from my father, Councillor Garcia."

"A request. What sort of request?"

"I'm sure when you were with Peter he told you how on Earth men and women get married and then have children."

She nodded. "Yes, he told me about that. He said he wanted me to be his mate but I told him that wasn't possible."

"What if it were possible? How would you feel about that?"

"I have a mate, so why speculate about something that can't possibly happen?"

"Let's say it was possible. Would you be willing to leave your mate and go to Peter and be his mate? The Councillor has the power to make that happen, if you consent to it."

Lucinda frowned. "I like Peter. We get along well together, but I like my mate too. What would become of him?"

"He'd be reassigned a new mate. The computer would find him someone suitable."

"Where would we live?"

"A good question that brings up some other issues I should, in fairness, disclose to you."

"What, the fact that Peter is the Liberator?"

"How do you know that?"

"I was with him when he met Threebeard."

"So, you know his life will be difficult and dangerous and if you're his mate, you'll have to endure much inconvenience and you won't always be together."

"Why does the Councillor want me to do this?"

"Because Peter is distracted by his love for you. He wants to be with you and has trouble thinking of anything else. You know, since Peter is from Earth he has no natural love for Tarizon or its people. He has no stake in the coming civil war. But, if you were his mate, he'd be fighting to keep you safe and for his future with you and his child. That motivation could make him a much more effective soldier and it could even be the difference between our victory or defeat."

"Then I have no choice. I must do as the Councillor wishes."

"I appreciate your loyalty, but unless you feel in your heart that you will be happy with Peter and grow to love him, I don't think you should do it. Peter is very perceptive and will know if you are unhappy."

Lucinda smiled. "Peter loves my, . . . our baby. That in itself will give me joy without measure."

Lorin nodded. "Good, then I'll arrange it. You'll leave tomorrow."

Lucinda smiled. "I must go then. I have to tell my mate. I hope he will understand."

"Do you want me to go with you to explain?" Lorin asked.

"No, that won't be necessary. This is something I must do myself. When will you come for me?"

"At midday. I'll be accompanying you to the Loyalist base where you'll be meeting Peter. You'll be with him in just a few days."

Lorin had mixed feelings about Lucinda being mated to Peter. She understood her father's thinking, but feared it would be even a greater distraction to have her close by Peter where her life might be in danger. If she were injured or killed Peter could very well be so emotionally distraught that he couldn't fight anymore. But Lorin didn't think it was her place to prevent Lucinda and Peter from being together. If it were her and Jake, she reasoned, she wouldn't want someone meddling her their affairs.

A few days later Lorin was going through TGA communiques that had been recently intercepted. She gasped when she read one from Pegaport Command.

"Three unidentified men and a TGA soldier have been killed in the Drogal Mountains on the Isle of Muhl while fleeing from base security. It's unclear if the soldier went voluntarily with the men or had been kidnaped. The security met up with the intruders in the Drogal Mountains near Shaft 22 and they were killed while trying to escape. Two security force personnel were also killed and seven are missing having been carried away by drogals who got caught in the crossfire. The abducted soldier was identified as Tamuras Lavendar a recent washout from officer training school at Pogo Island. We will update once the bodies are found and identified. . . . Col. Ruhl."

Lorin printed out the communique and took it to her father, who read it grimly.

"I can't believe this," Lorin said. "I just talked to Jake yesterday by GC. They were all fine."

"This could be the end of us. Just when Peter was really coming along and people were starting to believe in him. Had he come out of the Drogal Mountains having rescued his friend, no one would have doubted that he was truly the Liberator."

Lorin nodded. "I know. I was just starting to believe in him myself. I feel badly the way I treated him when he first came to Tarizon. It was just that he was such a disappointment compared to my conception of what the Liberator would be like."

"It wasn't your fault. It was my foolish plan to make people believe he was the Liberator. In my desperation to save Tarizon I forgot about Peter's rights as a human being."

Tears welled in Lorin's eyes. "So, now we've killed him," she whispered.

"Technically, he died trying to save a friend. I shouldn't have let him go to Muhl. It was an unnecessary risk, but I thought—." The Councillor ran his fingers through his hair. . ."I thought for sure he'd make it back." He laughed. "I was beginning to fall for my own deception."

"Are you going to tell Threebeard?"

He shook his head. "Nobody knows Peter is dead. They don't even know he went to Muhl. It could be many days before the truth comes out. We needn't dash the hopes of our citizens quite yet. Peter may yet fulfill the Prophecy."

"What about Lucinda?"

The Councillor sighed. "Don't tell her yet. Let's wait until we have some bodies. Pegaport command obviously hasn't recovered them yet, or they'd have already identified Peter and his friends. There's still a slim chance that the report was wrong. Go ahead and take Lucinda to the base and by the time you get there we should have more reliable information."

29

A Persistent Friend

While Peter was unconscious he had a vivid dream about the rhutz who had twice appeared during their journey across the Drogal Mountains. First, appearing out of nowhere to save his life from a Drogal about to carry him off to his nest. Then, appearing again just in time to draw away the soldiers from Pegaport. It was if Peter was looking through the eyes of the rhutz and his thoughts were in his head.

He was in the forest running, carrying the tracking device between his teeth. Two choppers were following him overhead, but he was deep in the forest and couldn't be easily seen. Ahead he was approaching a stream and for twenty strides there would be no cover overhead. He slowed down, looking up warily, but didn't stop. As he broke into the open, the choppers swooped down on him flying so close that the turbulence in the air nearly blew him over. The choppers circled several times and then disappeared back the way they had come.

"False alarm," the pilot in the chopper said to his co-pilot, "It was just a rhutz chasing a rabbit. Our tracking unit must be malfunctioning. We'll have to have it checked when we get back to base."

The rhutz felt relieved as he watched them fly away, content that he had done all that he could do. He had drawn the soldiers away from the Liberator and given his companions and he time to get to safety; at least he hoped that was the case. He wasn't sure where they were going, but he assumed they were going to hide in one of the mine shafts during the daylight while the Drogals were on the prowl. Who was this Liberator and why was he in these mountains? When their eyes first met he had learned much. They called him Leek but that was not his real name and he was not

225

from Tarizon, but the planet Earth. He was the one the prophets had often spoken of the Liberator—here to help free the Nanomites, the Seafolken, and the Mutants who had been enslaved by the Central Authority and soon would be slaughtered, if Videl were able to stay in power. Soon Peter, as they called him on Earth, would be fighting with the loyalists to regain control of the planet. Success was imperative for his species. Although the rhutz on Tarizon were not enslaved, as they would sooner die than do another's bidding, Videl had targeted them for eradication as a worthless species to the planet. After all, he told his cronies, if he couldn't control them, what use were they to him?

The rhutz started to go back to the cave where his pack lived. Then he began to worry. What if the boy—for his companions and he seemed so young—what if they didn't make it back to their hiding place before first light? As the rhutz considered that for a moment he realized it was a real possibility. At their slow rate of their travel they might indeed face daylight before they got to safety. The rhutz trotted over to the stream and dropped the tracking device into the water. He watched it for a moment float away and then turned and began running back through the forest.

He had found the spot where he had first seen the four humans and taken the tracking device from them. He sniffed around until he was able to pick up their scent and then began following their trail. Late that morning he trotted up a hill and ran across several dead soldiers. The strong reek of death almost made him lose the trail. He sniffed around for a long time until he caught it again and continued on his way. As he reached the crest of the next hill he looked down at the field of battle. There were no bodies here, as they had surely been taken away by the Drogals, but there was plenty of evidence of what had happened. Abandoned weapons, remnants of uniforms, and military gear of every sort scattered about. The Drogals would be dining royally this day, he thought.

The rhutz trotted on until he spotted a giant pile of boulders where once the opening of a mine shaft had been. He remembered it. A busy place cycles ago before the great volcano erupted. He hadn't been there himself, but the memory had been passed down to him by his mother. He sniffed around again as he had lost the scent he'd been following. Frantically he paced back and forth trying to pick it up again, but to no avail. He lied down to think. What had happened here? Then he knew. The Liberator and his companions somehow had been buried below the rubble. Fear and worry overcame him. The Liberator was dead. He hadn't done enough to protect him. All was lost.

There was only darkness in the cave when Peter finally regained consciousness, even though it was midday. Tam was sitting beside him holding a light stick. The strong green glow illuminated the cave quite well. Red and Sy were still lying still on the ground as he had remembered seeing them earlier. Tam said, "Finally, you're awake. Are you okay?"

He shook his head trying to clear it a bit and replied, "I think so. How long have I been out?"

"Less than an kyloon I think."

"Are Red and Sy alive?"

"Yes. They're both breathing. Hopefully they'll wake up soon. I tried to wake them a little while ago, but didn't have any luck."

"Did you try the communicator?"

"Yeah, we're too deep down here to get a signal out."

"Great. Do we have a map of the mine?"

"No, I looked around. There's nothing down here. All the mine records must have been kept topside."

"We've got to get out of here before nightfall or our timetable is going to be all screwed up."

"Screw the timetable. I just want to see daylight before we run out of air."

"What do you mean? Isn't there an air shaft?"

"Yes, but it collapsed during the rocket attack."

"Wonderful!" Peter exclaimed. . . ."Have you done any exploring? Is there another way out of here, you think?"

"No, I didn't want to leave you alone. Plus, it would be pretty easy to get lost down here. There are dozens of shafts going every which way."

"Ahhhh," Red moaned, struggling to sit up. "What happened?"

"Thank God," Peter said. "The chopper nailed the entrance to the mine with a half dozen missiles. We're buried under tons of rock."

"Oh, Sandee! Now what are we going to do?"

"There may be another entrance to the cave. That's what were hoping for. We still have some air, so there must be an open shaft somewhere."

"Is Sy okay?" Red asked.

"I don't know. He's been out for over a kyloon," Peter replied.

"I've got some conscious scents in my first aid kit," Red said and then started fumbling in his backpack. A moment later he pulled out a small box and opened it. "Here they are."

Red opened a small packet, took out a small tube and broke it apart. He stuck one end in front of Sy's nose. Sy's head jerked away and his eyes opened. He sneezed and said, "What the—"

"Sy, you okay?" Red asked.

"Huh?" he replied.

"Do you know where you are?" Peter asked.

Sy looked around and said, "Well, it's not hot enough to be Hell, so I guess it must be Shaft 22?"

"Good. You still have a sense of humor. You must be okay. . . . Do you remember the explosion?"

"Vaguely. How long have we been in here?"

"I'm not sure. I'd guess it's about noon outside," Peter replied.

"Only noon. Then we have a little time to find our way out of here," Sy said optimistically.

"Right," Peter said. "But first, do you have some of that Painfree. My arm is killing me."

"Let me look at it," Red said and scrawled around to get a good look at the wound. "Hmm. You'll need more than Painfree. I'll need to clean this and then I can rub on some mending cream. It will take away the pain and heal the wound. You'll be good as new in 27 kyloons."

"Good. It really hurts."

In the dim green light Red cleaned the wound, applied the mending cream, and then bandaged the arm. "Okay, all done. Let's get going."

"Right," Peter replied. "The only question is: which way do we go?"

Tam replied, "Follow the air."

"How the heck do we do that?" Red asked.

Tam pulled out another light stick and cracked it against the rock wall to his left. The stick instantly began to glow. He knelt down and picked up a handful of fine dust from the floor of the shaft. He held his hand up and then let the dust drop. The fine dust fell but not straight down. A slight breeze was blowing it away from them. "There must be a opening up ahead where air is entering. Let's go."

Tam led the way and they all followed; Tam in the lead, Sy right behind him, then Red, and Peter bringing up the rear. They walked in the darkness for what seemed kyloons with no sign of an exit from the mine. At each junction, Tam dropped to his knees and tested the wind. Each time the direction they should take seemed clear, but as they walked on endlessly there was still nothing but eerie darkness.

As time wore on, Peter reminded his companions that they hadn't slept since the sun had set the previous day. They had to stop and rest or they'd eventually collapse from fatigue or lose their ability to think clearly. Reluctantly, all agreed and they stopped to rest. Peter immediately fell asleep and as his head hit his makeshift pillow, the rhutz appeared once more in his dreams.

He was pacing frantically, wondering what he could do to get Leek and his companions out of the mine. He had no hands with which to dig or lift rocks like the humankind. He only had a keen sense of smell and a sharp and powerful mind. He was telekinetic but lifting large boulders was beyond his capability. He kept sniffing, as smells, more often then not, would provide the answers he was looking for. Then he inhaled a familiar smell—water—the scent of life. That was the answer. He lunged forward, following the scent. A few hundred strides away he saw the small stream crossing directly over the mine. He followed along the bank until the stream disappeared beneath a large boulder. This was not unusual. Many streams through the mountains ran above and below the ground depending on the terrain.

The rhutz sniffed around the boulder. He was sure the stream flowed through the mine as, in the past, he had seen the mine workers using large quantities of water. Why they needed so much he didn't know, but he supposed this stream was their source. There must be another entrance for the humans nearby, he thought, to control the water's flow. He just had to find it. He walked in circles around the place the water disappeared and finally he saw it, hidden between two boulders—a hatch that must lead down into the mine. He tried to open it with his mind, but it wouldn't budge.

A tapping noise in the distance awakened Peter. It was soft but distinct—a metallic noise—someone tapping in a definite rhythm. Peter awakened his comrades, hopeful that the noise meant something. Did somebody know they were trapped below? "Listen," he said. "I think someone is trying to communicate with us."

Tam sat up and replied, "Why do you say that? It sounds like a ventilator door flapping in the breeze."

"True, but either way it could be our way out of here."

Sy stood up and said, "As much as I'd love to debate the topic, why don't we just go check it out?"

Peter nodded and struggled to his feet. Sy kicked Red gently and said, "Come on. Wake up. We're leaving."

Red lifted himself up on one arm and moaned, "It's probably nothing. I'm gonna just stay here and sleep."

"No," Peter said. "We're staying together. Come on, Red. When we get to the Beet Islands you can sleep for a week if you need to."

"But I'm so tired *now*."

"It's the uthonic gas," Tam said. "With the main entrance blocked it's getting to dangerous levels. I'm feeling a little groggy too."

"Yeah, well. Let's be careful not to cause any sparks," Peter said. On Earth it's called *methane* and if it's the same stuff it's highly flammable. "I don't feel like being cremated today."

Red shivered and then exhaled sharply. "I can't believe this is happening. We're never going to get out of here alive."

Peter put his hand on his shoulder and said, "We're going to get out of here. There's someone out there trying to communicate with us. I can feel it."

"I feel it too," Tam said. "Someone is trying to help us find a way out of here."

"Then let's go," Sy said. "We're wasting time chattering."

They helped Red up and then started to walk slowly toward the persistent ping . . . ping . . . ping . . . in the distance. When they reached a fork in the shaft they went left but the sound faded, so they turned around and went the opposite way. Soon the ping . . . ping . . . ping sounded louder and louder.

"Whatever it is it must be just ahead," Tam advised.

"Be careful," Peter said. "Whatever is causing that noise could also throw off a spark and blow us halfway to Earth."

"If that were true," Tam said, "it would have already happened. No, I think the noise is coming from the surface, but somehow it's radiating down here."

As they walked around a bend in the tunnel, the faint green glow of their light sticks shone on several large pipes protruding upwards. Peter felt a flutter of hope at the sight. They kept walking and as they got closer they saw something that brought joy to their hearts. A ladder!

"Thank Sandee. Look at that," Tam said.

"And Lord Jesus," Peter said as he gave the sign of the cross.

"I'll go first," Sy said.

"Wait," Red replied. "This person topside. We don't know if he is friend or foe. It could be soldiers from Pegaport."

Peter took a deep breath and said, "I don't think so. I'll go first. I'm pretty sure I know who's up there."

Red squinted and asked, "Who?"

"You'll see," he said as he started to slowly climb the ladder. It was pitch dark as Peter climbed higher and higher. He kept expecting to see a glow—daylight in the distance—but there was nothing above but more and more darkness.

"I didn't think we were so deep," Red said. "I'm starting to feel faint again. The gas must be getting stronger."

"All the shafts we've been following today have been taking us down deeper and deeper," Sy said from below him.

"I don't know if I can hang onto the ladder any longer," Red moaned softly.

Sy looked up at him just as one of his hands slipped from the rung and he lost his footing. He swung outward holding on by just one hand. Sy grabbed his leg and tried to help him regain his footing but in the process Red's other hand let go and his whole body fell down on top of Sy, nearly knocking him off the ladder. Sy managed to hang onto Red's leg with one hand and to hold on to the ladder with the other . As Red fell hard back against the ladder his metal canteen was dislodged from his belt and fell down into the darkness.

It fell out of view and then there was a large bang as it hit the pipes at the bottom of the shaft. The glow Peter had been looking for previously came from below rather than above. It was a flicker and then a blast as the gas was ignited by a spark from the falling object. Flames began to engulf the lower part of the shaft.

"Get going!" Peter yelled. "Move!"

Red grabbed the ladder and, with Sy's help, managed to right himself.

Peter began to climb as fast as he could upward. His comrades scrambled up behind him. A blast of heat swallowed them as they climbed. Flames danced at their heels. The shaft was now as light as day from the flames and for the first time Peter saw where the ladder led. . . . Nowhere. It seemed to end abruptly at the shaft's ceiling. Utter despair came over him. They were doomed!

Then he saw it. A dark circular shape in the flickering light. "Wait! There's a hatch. Keep climbing."

By this time the heat was becoming unbearable and the steel ladder was getting hotter and hotter. Blisters began to swell on Peter's hands so he stopped, ripped off his shirt, and wrapped it around his hands for protection. Finally, he reached the hatch. The hatch made a metallic groaning sound as he opened the locking mechanism. Holding his breath, he pushed upward and felt it give way. "It's open!"

As he crawled out of the mine, the light nearly blinded him. When his eyes began to adjust he beheld the rhutz with his mouth open and his tail wagging excitedly. Their eyes met and their minds merged for a second time. It was like a gale force wind blowing through Peter's head. He struggled to close his eyes and stop the invasion. When he opened them, the rhutz was trotting away looking quite content that he'd saved the Liberator one more time. He had done well and perhaps helped ensure the survival of his species, Peter thought. The rhutz turned back and looked at Peter. Peter nodded, *I'll see you in my dreams, my friend.*

30
The Battle of Muhl

Exhausted, but relieved they'd survived the mines, they continued their journey over the Drogal Mountains. Darkness had just fallen and it was a long hard march to Shaft 11 where they would rest and spend one more day before they made it back to their fighters. They felt safe under the cover of darkness and with their new found friend, the rhutz, trailing them at a safe distance. During their first rest stop, Peter called Lorin to check in and see what word she had of Luga Vincete. He was afraid that Pegaport Command might have discovered that he'd been contacted and put two and two together. That would have been a disaster. Peter took out the GC and punched in Lorin's number.

"R1 calling S2?" Peter said.

"R1, is that you?" Lorin replied excitedly.

"Yes," R1 here."

"Oh, thank Sandee!" Lorin gasped. "You're alive! I never thought I'd hear your voice again. Pegaport command is claiming they killed all of you."

"Really? Well, they almost did. We barely made it out of Shaft 22 alive."

"Oh, I can't believe it. The Councillor will be so pleased. He was—we were all devastated by the report of your deaths. Are you hurt at all?"

"No, other than a few blisters and bruises. We're going to need a little shut eye here soon, though. We're pretty well spent."

"I can imagine. You've been through quite an ordeal."

"You've got that right. . . . So, how's our cook? We've been worried about him since we had to take out those two MPs."

"So far no one is on to him," Lorin said. "Apparently nobody noticed them talking. The rescue is on schedule."

"You don't think they suspect anything?" Peter asked.

"Well, I'm sure they did, but now that you all are dead the base is off high alert."

"Wonderful. Is my girl going to be waiting for me after the fireworks tomorrow?"

"You bet. We came down here yesterday."

"You didn't tell her I was dead, did you?"

"No. Fortunately we hadn't told anyone yet."

"Good."

"I've got Lucinda settled in a special house the Nanomites built for you."

"The Nanomites? They built me a house?"

"Yes. They've built most of the buildings on the base too. It's really quite amazing what they can do when they are treated with a little dignity and respect."

"Wow. I can't wait to see it. I loved the compartment in Shisk that I stayed in. I can't imagine having an entire house."

"A house with a pregnant woman living in it. She's showing pretty good. Are you prepared for that?"

"Oh, yes. That's my baby, remember?"

"Yes, I remember."

"Well, I've got to go. It's hard to keep up with the guys when I'm talking to you on the GC. Tell Lucinda I'll see her soon."

"I will. Be careful"

"Affirmative. Out."

Peter's mind whirled in anticipation of seeing Lucinda. Her sudden change of heart had lifted his spirits immensely. Was she falling in love with him? He prayed if only it were true. But even if she did love him, she still had a mate and her visit would soon have to end. He could see only disappointment and shattered dreams on the horizon. Yet, he couldn't make himself despair knowing he'd soon be in her arms.

They finally reached Shaft 11 as the eastern horizon was beginning to lighten. Once safely inside the mine they made a fire and ate the some of their dwindling rations. They'd eat what was left at the mine headquarters at the base of the mountains the following morning. Their next meal, if God and Sandee were with them, would be at the nutrition center on the Beet Islands.

Peter thought back on their adventure. It had only been a few days, but it seemed like several phases since they'd been candidates on Pogo Island. He wondered if time was the same on Tarizon as it was on Earth. It seemed like it moved slower here. It had only been a few phases since he'd been abducted, yet it seemed like a decade. He wondered what his parents were doing. He thought about Marcia and his brothers. Did they miss him as much as he missed them? Red reminded him of Reggie a little and Sy was a lot like Mark. Sometimes when he looked at them he would actually see his brothers. It was his mind playing tricks on him he knew, of course, but it made him feel good to see them, real or imaginary. Fortunately, sleep soon put his troubled mind to rest.

When they awoke that evening they were excited and relieved to be near the end their journey. They quickly ate, packed their gear, and moved out. They were traveling downhill now so the pace was much faster than it had been the day before. Their spirits were high so they were more talkative than usual. Peter thought it would be a good time to get to know Tam better. He knew quite a bit about Sy and Red but not so much about Tamurus Lavendar of Serie since he'd been sent off to Muhl soon after they'd met.

"So, what's it like in Serie?" Peter asked.

"It's nice in the spring and summer, but we're pretty far north so it's very cold in the winter."

"Really? Do you ski?"

"No, it's a very flat country. We use snow gliders to get around during the winter. They travel on a thin stream of air just above the snow."

"What does your father do?"

"He's a bureaucrat."

"A bureaucrat? Then you must have spent a lot of time with him growing up."

"No. Bureaucrats on Tarizon work long hours and must travel where they are needed. I didn't see much of him at all. My mother and older brother raised us."

"What kind of bureaucrat?"

"He was in charge of the subtram system in Serie."

"Oh, really? I love subtrams. I can't believe how fast they are. Our public transportation on Earth is very slow. I wish the Central Authority would share some subtram technology with Earth."

"Eighty percent of the subtram system in Serie hasn't worked since the great eruptions."

"How come?"

"Environmental quality and health services have taken ninety percent of the government's resources."

"So, you have great technology but you don't have the resources to mass produce it."

"Exactly. It's very frustrating. My father had a very difficult and stressful job."

"Hmm. So, when did you discover you had telepathic abilities?" Peter asked.

"At a very young age. I first started using it on my older brother and sister to beat them at Slabdab."

"Slabdab?"

"Yes. It's a memory game young children play on Tarizon. There are thirty-six slabs made of cardboard. On each slab is a distinct design. The object of the game is acquire six slabs of the same design. The first person to do that wins and yells out Slabdab. I used to always win because I could look into Sisel and Merkee's eyes and see what slabs they had."

Peter laughed. "They must have hated you."

"Yes, having a little brother who could beat you at any game they played was very irritating. Eventually they refused to play with me. I had the same problem with my friends."

"Hmm. Why didn't you just pretend you were normal—let everyone else win a game or two?"

He shrugged. "I can't stand to lose. It goes against my nature. I know that seems crazy, but I've always felt I was given this gift for a reason—some higher purpose. For as long as I can remember I've been trying to figure out what that was. When I heard Threebeard's call, I finally got my answer. It was a great relief to finally know why I had been born."

"That's the exact opposite of my experience," Peter said. " I never had a clue that I was telepathic, nor did I ever consider that God might have a higher purpose for me—particularly on Tarizon."

"God and Sandee work in mysterious ways," Tam said. "I wonder if they are one and the same."

"That could be. Jesus was the Savior on Earth as was Sandee on Tarizon. Perhaps their Father was the Creator of the Universe."

"Probably so."

"Do you know anything about the origin of life on Tarizon?" Peter asked.

"The historical manuscripts claim that there is a much larger and greater human civilization far away in another galaxy. It is said that these humans occupied a planet call Pharidon and were a very highly advanced people. In fact, they were so advanced that people there sometimes lived nearly a thousand cycles. Consequently, Pharidon became overcrowded and natural resources could not support the growing population on the planet. When the situation became critical explorers began searching for other inhabitable planets for Pharidonians to move. One of these groups of explorers came to Tarizon and another to Earth."

"Wow. I wonder if that's true."

"I don't know. It supposedly happened so long ago that nobody can prove it now. I wouldn't be surprised if it were true, though. It makes a lot of sense."

"Yes, that would explain a lot," Peter said. "There are many things in Earth history that our historians can't adequately explain. But if humans from Pharidon settled Earth millions of cycles ago, then a lot of our history starts to make sense."

"Mine HQ dead ahead!" Sy yelled.

They looked up and were glad to see their journey was about at its end. The small mining camp where they had stayed their first night on Muhl was less than thirty loons away. It was still dark so they knew they were right on schedule. They'd just have time to eat and then board their fighters for a sunrise assault on Pegaport.

Peter got on the GC and called Lorin. He told her they had made it back and were just about ready to take off.

"Everything is quiet at Pegaport. We've been monitoring their incoming and outgoing communications and nothing out of the ordinary has shown up. I don't think they will be expecting your visit."

"How can you monitor their communications? Don't they have it encrypted or scrambled?"

"We're all still on the same communications system. The war hasn't officially started yet. That will change soon after you wake them this morning."

"Understood. We'll check in after our wake up call."

"We'll be praying Sandee is with you."

After breakfast they uncovered their fighters and gave them a thorough inspection. Finding no problems they checked the weather reports and calculated their fuel levels. The weather was currently calm but a tropical depression was moving from Lortec toward the Beet Islands. Hopefully they'd beat it there, but if they didn't it could mean they'd hit some rough weather. As for fuel, there was enough to get them the Loyalist base, but with little to spare. This would mean they could have but one run on Pegaport and then they'd have to set their course straight for the Loyalist base. Any delay or deviation from their course could spell disaster.

Thirty loons before sunrise they were in their planes and ready to take off. Since their fighters were only built for one pilot, Tam had to ride in Peter's supply hold, which was a bit cramped and uncomfortable. He let it be known how much he hated the accommodations.

"You expect me to ride in there?"

"Yeah. I'm sorry, but it's the only space available. Sgt. Baig said you'd be okay in there. The cargo hold is part of the cockpit assembly and fully pressurized. He rigged you an oxygen mask for you to wear while we're in flight."

"How long will it take to get to the Beet Islands?"

"Just long enough for a good nap."

Tam sighed, shook his head, and climbed in the hold. Peter closed the door and then started his pre-flight instrument check. Once it was completed, he started the engines and pushed the throttle forward. The tires kicked up a trail of dust as they quickly gained speed. Soon they were airborne and heading toward Pegaport. Below them were the Drogal Mountains and Peter thanked God they were flying *over* it this time. Peter thought back to when he'd felt the claw of a Drogal grab his shoulder and yank him away. The thought of it gave him the shivers. He still couldn't believe he'd escaped. A loud thud from the hold brought Peter back to the present.

"You alright in there, Tam?" Peter asked.

"Not really, I can't get comfortable."

"Sorry, buddy." Peter chuckled. "Just hang in there. We'll be at Pegaport momentarily."

Their plan was to fly low to the ground to avoid the Pegaport Air Detection System. Together with their stealth capability it was unlikely they'd be spotted. As they flew low over Shaft 22, Peter thought of the rhutz who'd saved their lives. It was amazing to him how they had come to know of his presence on Tarizon and had become his protector without ever a word being spoken between them. Their speed brought them quickly to the foothills of the Drogals where their ATV had been blown up.

"Okay. In one minute we'll be dropping over the foothills and into Pegaport. Brace yourself, this could be a rough ride."

They had agreed that Sy would go in first and take out the hanger. Then he'd veer off to the right and try to knock out the Muscan missile launchers. Red would go in right behind Sy and take out the officers' quarters and then base headquarters. He'd then go left and do as much damage to the ships in port as he could. Peter would come in last and knock out the armory and then take another run at the Muscan missile launchers, just in case Sy hadn't been successful in putting them out of commission.

Peter watched as Sy dived down over Pegaport and headed straight for the main hanger. Sirens almost immediately began to wail as Pegaport's airspace was breached. Two missiles shot out of the nose of Sy's fighter. They ran true to their target and the hanger exploded into a fiery inferno. As smoke and flames were billowing up into the sky the officer's barracks suddenly exploded as did base headquarters. Red flew by and veered left. It was Peter's turn now. Blowing up the armory was a bit tricky. If he wasn't careful, when the armory was hit, the explosion could knock him out of the sky.

Peter came in straight at it, fired his missiles and then veered sharply to the right to avoid the concussion. The armory exploded when the missile hit and then a second later a series of explosions rocked

Pegaport. Peter's big fighter rocked from the concussion, but he didn't have time to worry about it. He was coming up fast on the Muscan missile launchers. They were on fire from Sy's assault but one silo looked intact. He locked onto it and fired. The last silo exploded and debris was shot high in the air. A large piece of it came at him and almost ended his short career as a fighter pilot. Peter ducked reflexively as the debris narrowly missed him.

Looking down at the base Peter saw a big transport plane starting to take off. It had to be Luga Vincete and the soldiers wanting to join the Loyalists. There were a couple of fighters being readied for take off as well. These would not be friendly. Although Peter had been advised that he should hit his targets and then immediately set a course for the Beet Islands, he couldn't let those two fighters get off the ground. If they did, they might take out the transport or try to engage them in battle which would waste precious fuel. After knocking out the last Muscan Missile silo, Peter swung around and took a run at the airstrip. There was one runway but two lanes on each side for aircraft waiting to take off. The transport was at the end of the west holding lane, just beginning to turn onto the runway. One of the fighters was on the move and halfway to the end of the east holding lane.

The fighter was much faster than the transport and Peter knew it wouldn't take it long to catch up with it. Once it swung around and started up the runway it could easily lock onto the transport and fire a missile. Peter had to nail it before it got on the runway. The problem was the fighter and the transport were directly in front of him. There was a danger his missile might lock onto the larger transport even though it was farther away. To avoid that possibility Peter banked hard left and then circled back so he was coming at the fighter from the side. The fighter was picking up speed, so his window of opportunity would come and go quickly. When the two lines on his targeting screen were aligned, he fired. The missile sped towards its target. For a second the missile appeared to be heading straight at the transport, but the transport moved off the screen and the missile went right past it. The fighter exploded, flipped over on it's back and slid a hundred strides before it hit a metal storage building and finally came to rest.

As Peter was flying overhead, he noticed the second fighter take a short cut across a grassy area to avoid the wreckage from the first fighter. His pulse quickened as he realized he wouldn't have time to swing around and take out the second fighter before he made it to the runway. He pushed the button on his communicator hoping Red was close by.

"R3. Where are you?"

"Coming at you."

"I'm not going to be able to take care of that second fighter in time. Do you have any missiles left?"

"No. I sunk the last one in the belly of a battleship."

"Crap!" Peter replied.

"Don't worry. I've got my laser. If I can get close enough I'll take him out."

As Peter swung around to head back across Pegaport, Peter saw Red come in low and when he got in range there was a quick flash; the fighter immediately began to smoke and veer to the left. It ran off the runway and smashed into a tanker truck exploding on impact.

"Nice job! R3. Now let's get the hell out of here."

"Acknowledged, R1. Setting course to the Beet Islands."

"R2. What's your position?"

"I'm halfway there," Sy said. "What's taking you so long?"

"We had a couple more targets to neutralize. We've got to check out our transport and then we'll catch up with you."

"Acknowledged. I 'll take it easy until you catch up," Sy said.

"Renegade 4. Come in," Peter said.

"Renegade 4 here," Vincete said.

"Congratulations! You're now officially Loyalists."

"Thank you. We're proud to be aboard."

"What's your condition?"

"Twenty-three soldiers strong, Sir."

"Excellent. How's your fuel? Got enough to get to base?"

"Should have. How about you?"

Peter glanced at his fuel gage and winced. "I don't know. I used a lot of fuel taking out that fly that was on your tail. I hope this baby gets good gas mileage."

"Don't count on it," Sy said. "They didn't build these things for

241

fuel economy."

"How's your fuel supply looking, R2?"

"I should be fine."

"R3, how about you?"

"I'm gonna go swimming, I'm afraid, if I try to go all the way."

"That's my feeling too," Peter replied. "Anybody got any bright ideas?"

Vincete replied, "There's a private airport on Lortec you could land there and possibly refuel. I'm not sure who owns that real estate right now, but it used to be a flight testing center for an aerospace company."

"Good. Red and I'll detour to Lortec then. If we don't show up at the base by tomorrow, you better come looking for us . . . and bring fuel."

"Acknowledged, R1. May Sandee be with you."

Red and Peter broke formation and set their course for Lortec. Peter was sick inside as he had been so looking forward to seeing Lucinda. Now they'd be delayed in Lortec for God knows how long.

31
Zodillas

They weren't sure exactly how to get to the airbase on Lortec. Vincete had only given them a rough idea where it was. As they approached Lortec, Peter tried to make radio contract, but then he thought better of it. By now news of their raid on Muhl would have spread around the globe. If Central Command had a military presence on Lortec, which was a sure bet, they didn't want a welcoming party ready to blow them out of the sky.

"Full stealth mode, R3," Peter said. "We don't know much about this island."

"Acknowledged. Full stealth initiated. I'll follow you in."

As they approached the island, Peter brought them in low just two hundred feet above the sea. At their speed no one would know they'd been there until they were long gone. Peter decided to take one pass over the island and hopefully spot the airfield, or at least, a place to land. As they headed over land Peter observed low rolling hills with lush green fields and many farm houses. The sky was almost clear here—not like Turvin or Lamaine where, on the clearest day, you couldn't even see the sun. For some reason the air over Tarizon was beginning to clear in the extreme lower and higher latitudes. The landscape below was what he had imagined England or Scotland to be like.

Ahead they were rapidly approaching a small mountain range. From what Vincete had told them, the private airfield was just beyond it. As they flew over the summit of the tallest peak, Peter looked out in anticipation of seeing the base, but instead of a small private airstrip there was a large military installation complete with runways, hangers, hundreds of military aircraft, dozens of barracks, training grounds, tanks, ATVs and hundreds of other buildings of every sort.

"Holy, Jesus," Peter said. "They've got a whole battalion on this island."

"I thought Lortec was mainly an agricultural community with no military importance," Red said.

"That's what I was led to believe."

"Now what, R1?"

"Standby while I let this sink in. . . .We can't land at the airbase, obviously. We'll have to find a soft spot somewhere nearby but where we aren't likely to be spotted. I'm going to bank right and swing around the western side of the island. You go east and survey that side. When we meet on the other side, we'll discuss what our best options might be."

"Acknowledged," Red said. "Banking left."

Peter peeled off to the right and when he hit the shoreline, he followed it completely around the Island. The shoreline below was spotted with small towns, marinas, and beach front resorts. When he circled around the lower part of Lortec he saw something that he thought might have possibilities. It looked like a golf course, but he doubted they had such things on Tarizon. Whatever it was it would provide a place to land and near the end of the grassy area there was a forest which would be perfect for hiding the fighters. When Red and he met up, a few loons later, Peter told him about the spot. He was relieved Peter had discovered it since he hadn't found anything suitable on the other side of the island.

They used their onboard scanners to see if anyone was located in the grassy area where they intended to land. The scan came up negative so they prepared to make a landing. They'd have to come out of stealth mode to land. This would be dangerous as one call to the Central Authority and they'd have a hundred soldiers after them.

As Peter eased up on the throttle and set the T-47 down on the soft turf, Peter thought he saw a man riding on a motorcycle of some sort. He was looking in their direction and looked startled to see them. After they landed the T47s Peter looked around for the motorcyclist, but didn't see him. Then he heard a pounding noise coming from the cargo hold. He unlocked it and the door flew open. Tam looked a little green as he crawled out.

"Whew! That was worse than Hell Hole back at Pegaport. I'm not usually claustrophobic, but that was like being buried alive in a coffin."

"Sorry, friend. I'm afraid it wasn't built for passengers."

"So, did we make it? Is this the Loyalist base?"

"No. Bad news. We were low on fuel so we had to stop here on Lortec."

"What! You gotta be kidding me. I'm not getting back in there for all the gold in Dalo."

Dalo, Peter had learned in geography, was an island between Turvin and Azallo in the Emerald Ocean. It was known for its rich deposits of gold and precious gems. The mines there were owned by Videl Lai and were worked mainly by mutant slaves who lived in abominable conditions. Videl's wealth and rise to power was financed largely from the profits of the Dalo mines.

"Well, you may have to, but I wouldn't worry about it quite yet."

Peter described to him what they'd seen. Spotting a large military presence on Lortec was a major stroke of luck. Loyalist command had to be made aware of the situation immediately. Peter got out the GC and called Lorin. He figured Sy and Vincete should be near the Loyalist base on the Beet Islands by then.

"R1 calling Base. Come in."

"R1. So glad to hear from you. Your friends just arrived. Are you all right?" Lorin asked.

"Yes, for now. We may have been spotted, however, during our landing."

"Acknowledged. We'll send out a refueling drone immediately. It should be there before sunset."

"Negative. On the ride in we spotted a huge military base brimming with activity. Don't you think that is rather odd for this corner of the planet?"

"Not necessarily. Lortec is one of the few places on Tarizon where the air and water have cleared. It could be Videl just wanted to train his troops under optimal conditions."

"Or Videl has found out that the Loyalist base of operations is in the Beet Islands and is getting ready for an all out assault. If he hit you

245

now it would be devastating, wouldn't it?"

"Yes. It would."

"On Earth we have a game called football. It's a game of strength and endurance as well as strategy. One rule of football is that you always train your players under the same conditions as they will have to play on game day. If you don't, your players may be overwhelmed by the environment and unable to fully concentrate on the game. I would think that would be especially true here on Tarizon. If Videl is here on Lortec it's because of its proximity to the Beet Islands."

"Did you learn all this in basic training?"

"No. I learned that watching Tom Landry and the Dallas Cowboys."

"Who?"

"Never mind. I just wonder how Videl figured out that the Loyalist base was in the Beet Islands?"

"If he does know, I suspect he learned from a spy here at the base or from satellite reconnaissance."

"Right. So, don't you think we ought to snoop around a bit so we can give you a full assessment of their armaments and troop strength?"

"Possibly. I'm still going to put the fueling drone in the air, though, just in case the base commander wants you to come straight on home."

"Acknowledged. We're going to strip the planes and move our gear down the road a bit just in case someone comes looking for them. We'll blow them up, rather than let them be captured."

"Understood. Check back with me in an hour."

"Copy," Peter replied.

"Sandee be with you," Lorin whispered.

While they were waiting to hear back from Lorin, they surveyed their stock of weapons, ammunition, and supplies. They'd used up most of their food going over the Drogal Mountains and fired all of their missiles at Pegaport. They still had plenty of ammunition for their rifles and pistols and their lasers were fully charged. If they had to stay on Lortec for any length of time they'd have to live off the land. Given the lush forests and grasslands they'd flown over, that appeared to be the least of their worries. After they'd moved their gear and set up a camp a kylod or so from the planes, Peter said, "Let's check this place out. It looks like a golf course."

"What's a golf course?" asked Tam.

"It's where you play golf. . . . Golf is a sport where you hit a little white ball with a stick and try to get it in a small hole. The object is to get it there with as few strokes as possible."

Tam nodded and looked out over what looked like a long fairway. Then he said, "To me this looks like a Zodilla track."

"What's a Zodilla?" Peter asked.

Just then the ground began to shake and there was a thunderous sound from behind them. Peter turned and saw a herd of gigantic monsters running toward them. They were four legged creatures, twice the size of a buffalo, and black as the ace of spades.

"Those are Zodilla and they feed on humans," Tam said glaring at Peter. "I can't believe you landed us on a Zodilla track! Sandee save us!"

All three began to run across the track away from the fighters. They didn't want the Zodillas crushing their ride home. The Zodillas had long legs and were faster than any thoroughbred Peter had ever seen. As they got closer to the edge of the grass, Peter understood why it was called a track. There was what must have been a fifty foot fence on each side. When they reached the fence it was obvious there was no way out.

"Don't stop," Tam yelled. "Run along the fence. They'll be an escape ladder up ahead."

Tam and Peter ran like they'd never run before and sure enough, up ahead, they saw a ladder running up the side of the fence. When they reached it Tam began climbing furiously. Red waited impatiently for Tam's feet to clear and then followed him up the ladder. Peter looked back at the Zodillas who had broken ranks and seemed to have one thing on their mind—having him for lunch. The lead Zodilla, anticipating his imminent feast, let out a snort, "Heeshi! Heeshi!"

Peter scrambled three rungs up the ladder just before the Zodilla crashed into it. The fence swayed back and forth nearly causing Red to fall off. Peter held on for dear life and then began climbing again as a second and third Zodilla rammed the fence. By now Tam had reached the top and was laughing at them. Peter glared at him and continued to climb. Finally they all made it over the fence, climbed down the other side, and breathed a sigh of relief.

"You know what a Zodilla is now, Leek?"

Peter smiled and said, "Yeah, I know what they look like now, but why are they in captivity and why do they keep them on tracks?"

Tam nodded and said, "Come with me and I'll show you."

Tam took off toward where the Zodillas had come. After they'd run about a kylod and a half they saw what looked like a giant stadium. Suddenly Peter understood. This was a Zodilla racetrack and they'd landed right in the middle of it.

"Wanna place a bet?" Tam asked.

"Jesus," Peter said. "How do they get them to race? I didn't see any jockeys."

"Jockeys?"

"Yeah. Little men who ride them and kick 'em if they slow down."

"Oh. They have electric collars that accomplish the same thing. If they slow down or go off course they're jolted with a surge of electricity. That's why they hate humans so much and it takes such a tall fence to keep them in."

"Okay, very interesting," Peter said. "Now for the big question."

"What's that?" Tam asked.

"How do we get back to the fighters?"

Tam looked at them. Finally, he said, "Where there's a Zodilla track, there's got to be Zodilla pacers."

"What?"

"A convertible PV of sorts that they use to teach the Zodilla how to run—a very fast one. Come with me."

They followed Tam toward the stadium. Behind the stadium there was a large barn. Tam went straight to the barn and went inside. Just as they were about to go in the front gate, Tam came roaring out of the barn in what looked like a giant dune buggy. He took a couple of turns around the barn and then came to a halt in front of them. He said, "Go inside. There's two more just like this one. We'll be back at the fighters in a flash."

Red and Peter ran inside and borrowed the other two buggies. Peter turned the ignition on his and the Zodilla pacer lurched forward, taking off like a race horse coming out of the gate. They followed Tam along the fence for at least five kylods before they reached its end. Tam hung left and followed the northern perimeter of the fence until they reached a gate. It was locked, so Tam backed up his buggy, came to a stop, put it in drive, and then accelerated. He busted through the fence like it was made of toothpicks and raced toward where they'd left the fighters. Red and Peter followed him and as he approached the spot, Tam slammed on his brakes. There was a military vehicle parked near their T47s and two soldiers were inspecting them. They'd been discovered!

32
Firefight

There was no way they could let them take their fighters. Fortunately they'd set up their camp away from the planes just in case they were discovered. Tam turned his buggy and made a bee-line for camp. Everything there was as they'd left it, so they put on their combat gear and headed back to the fighters. There was another ATV and a total of five soldiers milling around the fighters now. They had to move quickly as the place would be swarming with soldiers soon and they'd have no chance of escape.

Tam circled around behind and Red and Peter prepared for a frontal assault. When Tam advised he was ready, Red and Peter took out two of the soldiers with their lasers. A third soldier heard his comrades fall and looked over at them. Peter couldn't fire at him without taking a chance that he'd hit the fighter. The soldier raised his rifle to fire at Peter when Tam came up from behind and slit his throat.

The other two soldiers, who by now were trying to get into the cockpit of Peter's fighter, hadn't realized they were under assault. Peter ran toward them while Red got into his fighter. One of them saw Peter coming and screamed to his partner. They turned and fired at him. Peter fell to the ground and took shelter behind a log. They jumped down from the plane and advanced toward him. Red started his engine, rolled the fighter around, and started taxiing down the fairway. One of the soldiers began firing at the plane as it sped away, and the other one kept advancing toward Peter.

Suddenly, from their flank, Tam arose and fired at the soldier shooting at Red's plane. The soldier dropped his rifle and fell to one knee.

251

Tam fired again and the soldier fell over and didn't move. When the second soldier turned to aid his fallen comrade, Peter got up and fired at him with his laser. The laser blast knocked him backward onto the ground. In the distance there was the sound of vehicles approaching. Tam and Peter ran to the fighter and scrambled to get inside while they still had a chance. Tam frowned as he climbed into the small supply hold again. Peter shrugged sympathetically, and then closed the cover behind him. Bullets ricocheted off the cockpit window as he started the fighter's engines.

Red was already in the air when Peter started rolling down the grassy runway. Glancing behind them, Peter saw an ATV roll up with four more soldiers. One of them had a portable missile launcher. Peter pushed the throttle forward and prayed he'd be able to take off before being blown to bits. His only hope was a misfire as there was no way to take evasive measures on takeoff. He feared it was all over for he and Tam. Then the ground began to rumble, the plane jerked and listed to the right. There was a deafening noise behind them that didn't sound much like a missile.

Peter glanced back and saw a herd of Zodillas coming straight at them. The soldier who had been preparing to launch the missile was trampled before he could get off a shot. Then the Zodillas ran over the others and knocked the ATV aside like it was a plastic toy. They were coming at Peter fast and he prayed he'd be able to lift off before they overtook him. Suddenly the jostling stopped and the plane leveled off. Peter looked down and his heart leaped as he realized they were airborne. Then suddenly they were jolted. The fighter listed to the left. Peters helmet hit the side of the cockpit window hard. He winced in pain and the last thing he remembered was pushing the autopilot button.

He didn't know how long he'd been out, but he eventually awoke to Red's panicked voice.

"R1, do you read? . . . R1, do you read?" Red screamed.

"What? What happened?" Peter said as he began to regain consciousness. As he looked around and saw he was in the air he jerked himself upright. "Jeez, I must have blacked out. One of the Zodillas must have hit my landing gear."

"You okay?" Red asked.

"Yeah. . . . Yeah. . . . Give me a minute to get the cobwebs out of my head. . . . Man o' man my head hurts. . . . Where are we?"

Red laughed. "On our way to base, I hope."

"Oh. . . . Right. . . . Okay, did you check in with Lorin?"

"I'm here," Lorin said. "There's a refueling drone two loons away. Command wants you to refuel and go straight to base."

"Confirmed. I'll keep a lookout."

A few loons later Peter said, "Locking on drone now. Over."

"Acknowledged," Lorin said. "See you soon."

They came up quickly on the two refueling drones. Peter took the right line and Red took the left. In less than five loons they were off the drone and screaming toward the Loyalist base. Anticipation of seeing Lucinda began to swell in Peter's heart. Before the day was done, he'd be in her arms, he thought. He closed his eyes and in his mind's eye could see her smiling face and her hands stretched out to embrace him. He couldn't believe it, finally they'd be together—Lucinda and her baby, his baby. He was so happy and excited, he could hardly sit still in the cockpit. He banged the storage compartment with his fist.

"What?" Tam groaned.

"Almost there, my friend. Hang in there. I can't wait to see Lucinda."

"I can't wait to see daylight and stretch my arms," Tam moaned.

Smiling, Peter looked ahead at the open sea expecting to see the first of the Beet Islands approaching. Instead he saw enemy fighters up and to his right. His smile faded and his heart sank. "Rats!" he moaned. He gave them a hard look and estimated there were at least fifty of them.

"Rats? What does that mean?" Red asked.

"A rat is a rodent back on Earth that everyone hates."

"Oh, like our skutz?"

"I guess. So, when things go wrong kids often say *rats*. Anyway, things are going very wrong. We've got a flock of enemy fighters coming at us," Peter said nervously.

"Skutz! I see them," Red replied. "We don't have any missiles! What should we do?"

"Don't have a clue," Peter replied. "Base, are you there?"

"Here," Lorin said. "Drop to minimum altitude and go to stealth. You're only a fifty kylods from base."

Peter initiated stealth mode as they dropped and leveled off just above the Southern Sea. At this level they'd be nearly invisible as their planes changed colors to blend in with the sea. Lorin gave them their final coordinates and, before they knew it, they were getting landing instructions from Loyalist Command. Ahead an island suddenly appeared, the first of over 10,000 in the Beet Island chain. Soon there were islands everywhere, lush tropical ones with white sandy beaches and dark green jungles and other desolate ones with sparse vegetation and weirdly shaped rock formations. A moment later a larger island protruded up form the Southern Sea. It was a highlighted by an active volcano puffing out a steady plume of steam. As they skirted the edge of the volcano, they dropped into a valley, looking for the entrance to the Loyalist base.

The jungle was thick and there was no sign of civilization. Then he saw it, a crystal city built into the side of a cliff. Peter flew past it and then dropped, as instructed, into a narrow canyon barely wide enough for his plane. He glided between the rocks and there saw an open chamber ahead. Flying through the narrow entrance, he shivered, praying he wouldn't nick one of the sides and spin out of control. Somehow he made it, and once inside a spacious cavern emerged and he saw a landing strip ahead.

His heart leaped for joy at the sight until he remembered his landing gear had been hit by one of the Zodillas on takeoff. He wondered if it had been damaged. Since he had been knocked unconscious he didn't remember if it had retracted after takeoff. Would his autopilot know to do that? Fear wrenched his gut. His shoulders tightened and his head began to throb. Could he land safely? He pushed the button to lower the landing gear, but nothing happened. Had he been flying with it down all along? The instrument light was out which meant the landing gear was still up.

"R1 to base," he barked.

"Base here, R1. You're clear to land,"

"I'm going to have to do a flyover. My landing gear was hit on takeoff and may have been compromised. Take a look when I fly by and advise."

"Copy, R1. Will do," Lorin said.

As he flew over the base he looked down at the intricate conglomeration of white crystal buildings. It was a spectacular sight like nothing he'd ever seen before. As he circled the base, he saw hundreds of fighters all parked in a row ready for a quick takeoff. He wondered if they'd be enough to defeat Videl's forces.

"R1. Your landing gear appears to be down. Can't tell how well it will hold, though. We'll prepare for an emergency net landing, just in case."

"Acknowledged," Peter said. "Hold on, Tam. This may be a rough landing."

"I don't care! Just get me out of here," Tam spat.

"Hang in there, buddy. We're almost home."

He swung the fighter around for a final approach and then brought her in. Ahead of him he saw a huge net stretched across the runway. He held his breath as the T47's wheels touched ground. The landing gear groaned, then gave way. The nose of the jet dropped, but before it hit the hard surface they were enveloped in the emergency net and quickly came to rest.

An emergency reception team got to them quickly and removed the nets. The team leader asked if they were okay and Peter assured them they were. There were two sharp thuds from the hold. Peter switched the latch and let a much relieved Tam out. When they'd deplaned, the emergency team drove over to where Red's plane was sitting. Red was climbing down its side looking a little shaky. As they came to a stop, Peter saw a crowd of smiling people near the door of the hanger. In the crowd Peter saw Lorin, Jake, a few other faces from the Councillor's staff, and, looking a little out of place in her white gown, Lucinda.

A shuttle transport picked them up and drove them to where the reception party was waiting, They climbed out and quickly made their way to an anxious group of soldiers, officers, and politicians. The base commander, General Zitor, shook their hands and offered his congratulations for their accomplishments and expressed his happiness to see them in one piece. Lorin embraced Peter and Jake patted him on the shoulder. Peter's smile widened when he saw Lucinda with her round little tummy walking toward him. He rushed over to her, picked her up and swung her around in delight. She laughed, then they embraced and kissed passionately.

When they finally let each other go, Peter looked her in the eyes and said, "Now that we're finally together, I'll never let you leave me again."

She smiled and replied, "You better not, we've been mated."

"What?"

"We've been mated," she repeated cheerily.

"We have?" Peter said. "How could that be? You already have a mate."

"The Councillor arranged a revocation."

"A what?"

"I guess they call it a divorce on Earth. It almost never happens here on Tarizon, but in extraordinary circumstances it can be done. You have powerful friends."

"Wow! They didn't tell me they were going to arrange that. . . . Jeez. That's wonderful," Peter said smiling broadly. "So, are you happy about it, I hope?"

She shook her head, took his hands in hers and replied, "A little happy, a little sad."

"Sad?"

"To leave my mate so suddenly. He was shocked and badly shaken when I told him of the revocation."

"Oh, Jesus. I'm sorry. I didn't want to hurt anybody."

"No. It was for the best. When you left me in Shisk, I didn't expect to miss you all that much but—"

"You couldn't stop thinking about me?" Peter said gleefully.

She nodded, "Yes. I don't know why, but your memory was very distracting. It was hard to function on my job when my thoughts were always on you. When Lorin called and asked if I'd come to see you, I was . . . well . . . I guess, relieved."

"Relieved?"

"Yes, if I couldn't get you out of my mind, I was glad that I didn't have to try any longer."

"I'm sorry about your mate," Peter said.

She shook her head. "I'm not."

"You sure? I don't want you to have any regrets."

"I won't if we can be together."

"We will be. Do they have a mating ceremony when you get mated on Tarizon?"

"Yes, but it was waived in our case due to the war."

"Hmm. I guess it doesn't matter since my family couldn't come anyway. I wish my mother could meet you, though. She'd love you so much."

Lucinda smiled. "Maybe someday. You never know what fate has in store for you. I certainly never expected to find you."

"Leek!" Tam yelled. "Come on. They want us for a debriefing."

Peter nodded and said to Lucinda. "I'll see you soon, okay?"

"Yes, very soon. We have much to talk about."

"Yes, and other things I've been aching to do," Peter said with a wry smile.

She raised her eyebrows and smiled coyly. Peter squeezed her hand one last time, then turned, and followed the crowd heading for a nearby building. She waved and then went off in the opposite direction. Inside the building Tam, Red, and Peter joined Sy, Jake, Lorin, Lute Vincete, General Zitor, and several staff members in a conference room. On the wall was a map of Tarizon. Peter noted the five continents of Lamaine Shane, Turvin, Azallo, Lower Azallo and Oct Mezan. The Beet Islands, with a big star designating their base, was in the lower left corner of the map just southeast of Lortec. General Zitor stood up. "Welcome to Loyalist Base 1 or LB1 as we call it."

Peter smiled and the general continued. "As you know Videl Lai has advanced to the post of Supreme Chancellor of Tarizon's Global Assembly. Since his inauguration, seven Chancellors of the 31 Tarizon provinces have been assassinated. Under the laws in each of these provinces the Vice-chancellor immediately replaces any chancellor who is unable to perform his duty until the next regular election. The assassinations were carefully calculated to insure Videl Lai supporters would gain control of the Tarizon Global Assembly. Yesterday, in the first conclave of the Assembly, they did just that and passed several shocking mandates.

General Zitor looked down at his notes. First they declared a state of emergency which has the effect of suspending three fundamental rights of the Tarizonian people: the right to speak freely, the right to fair accusation and legal counsel, and the right to assemble. Secondly, they ordered the conscription of 1.2 million men and women to bolster the TGA which has been severely strained by recent defections to the Loyalist cause. Thirdly, they ordered the immediate summary execution of anyone deserting the TGA or joining the Loyalist movement. Finally, they ordered the immediate eradication of the Nanomites, Rhutz, Seafolken, and any others who refuse to serve the will of the Central Authority.

"What this means is the TGA is in turmoil at this moment. It will take them many phases to get their forces back to full strength and many more to get them trained and effectively deployed. We must therefore strike quickly and cripple the TGA before it again becomes strong.

"Recently it has been confirmed that the enemy knows of LB1. Lt. Lanzia and his companions have discovered a huge TGA base on Lortec obviously built for the purposes of waging an attack on this base. How did they find out? Well, we fear there is a traitor amongst us. Who that might be, we don't know at this time, but the traitor will be discovered and dealt with swiftly and severely. We don't think the enemy knows our precise location yet, but in time they will no doubt discover it. So far we've been lucky. LB1 is on an island chartered as uninhabitable and cannot be seen by satellite due to general atmospheric conditions and its own volcano, Mt. Javiyan, which provides a continuous cloud of smoke and steam over the island. But if the skies clear, which I'm told is a possibility in the next few days, they will surely find us by tracking air traffic in this area."

"In the meantime we must make plans to launch a preemptive strike against the TGA on Lortec. We must cripple them before they have the strength to destroy us. . . . Are there any questions?"

"Peter raised his hand. "Did you say Lt. *Lanzia?*"

"Yes, we've decided to consider you and your companions as graduates of officer training school given the contribution you've already made to the Loyalist movement. Accordingly, you have all been promoted to Lieutenant."

"Thank you, Sir. We appreciate your confidence in us."

"You're welcome. . . . Now are there any more questions?"

"We saw some blue sky on the way here from Muhl. Has the sky over LB1 ever cleared? If so, it could be that the base *has* been seen by satellite."

"It is true that when certain wind currents prevail the clouds thin in this area, but we have not seen any clear blue sky in many cycles. If the skies did clear and our base was detected we'd be obliterated in a matter of kyloons, as the TGA would launch a missile attack that would destroy the entire island."

"So," Red said. "Even if we destroy the TGA forces on Lortec, they could still destroy LB1 if they could find its precise location."

"Yes, that is why we are watching a new weather pattern that is currently developing. The weather stream that controls our local weather has been sinking in a southerly direction farther than we've ever seen it. We don't know what's causing it, but, if it continues, strong upper winds could actually clear the skies over the Beet Islands. If that happens, we'd have no other choice than to evacuate LB 1 and we'd only have a few kyloons to do it." The general sighed. "This couldn't have come at a worse time with our imminent attack on Lortec."

The room went silent with this chilling news. Finally, Peter broke the silence.

"Assuming the sky doesn't clear, we prevail at Lortec, and the war continues; what is our overall strength compared to the TGA."

"We control only nine of 31 Tarizon provinces. We have 21 secondary installations in these nine provinces with total troop strength at 197,000."

"So, its 197,000 versus how many million?" Peter asked.

"There are 2.1 million TGA troops by last count so to anticipate your question, yes, we are out numbered more than 10 to 1. In addition, as time goes on we expect significant human defections to our side, particularly if we can win a few early battles."

"A couple of rhutz have already come to our rescue on Muhl and I can see how the Nanomites have helped in building this base, but how will the Seafolken and the Mutants help us defeat Videl?"

"Most of the Seafolken and the Mutants are under Videl's control at this time, however, one of our strategies will be to liberate as many of them as we can. Once they are liberated, we expect they'll join our forces in the war against Videl."

"What kind of numbers are we looking at?"

"There are approximately 1 million mutants in Videl's service and 200,000 Seafolken."

Peter nodded. He didn't know much about the Mutants or the Seafolken but he didn't think the general would want to educate him on those subjects right then, so he kept his mouth shut. He figured Lorin or Jake could fill him in later. As they were wrapping up the meeting, General Zitor told them to take the rest of the day off, but to report for a planning and strategy session early the next morning.

After the meeting Lorin showed them to their quarters. Peter went inside and found Lucinda waiting impatiently for him. When she saw him, she rushed into his arms. With less than twelve hours before Peter had to report for duty, they had little time to waste. They kissed passionately, almost frantically, as they edged their way to the bedroom leaving a trail of clothing in their wake. They hoped it would be the first of many glorious nights together, but down deep they both knew that was unlikely, so they vowed to make every moment they had together memorable—and on this night they were true to their vows.

33

Eve of Battle

At the next morning's briefing General Zitor told the officers assembled that it was imperative that they destroy the TGA base on Lortec. If they did that they could probably take Muhl and then set their sights on the small continent of Ock Mezan which was strategically placed between Turvin and the Beet Islands. This then would set the stage for an assault on Pogo and another continent, Lamaine Shane. They already had a base in Rigimol, the northern most province of Lamaine Shane, and several guerilla strongholds in the mountains of Tributon to the west. With a little luck by year's end they would control the entire continent.

"But first things first," the general said. "Our immediate plan is a preemptive strike against the TGA base on Lortec to eliminate any threat to this base. We know there is huge army being assembled there. There's no telling how long it will be before they are ready to launch an all out attack against us, but probably sooner than later. Time is critical. If they attack us now, we'd be doomed. The only chance we have is to launch a preemptive strike and catch them off guard."

It was agreed a simple air assault wouldn't be sufficient since the TGA command now knew they'd been discovered. General Zitor asked for any ideas on how to handle the assault. Several of the staff presented ideas. The one that seemed most likely to succeed was a surprise air attack just as the sun was rising in the east. If the assault force came in from the east in stealth mode they wouldn't be detected by radar until they were over the island. The harsh glare of the sun would also impair visual sighting. If their fighters could knock out the runway and hit the TGA aircraft on the ground most of them could be destroyed. It would take them many phases to rebuild them and get in replacement aircraft. By the time they were back up at full strength the Loyalist army would be much stronger and on the offensive.

The General, however, didn't seem impressed. "They'll have several patrols in the air at all times and they could get off twenty or thirty fighters before we could knock out the airstrip."

Peter thought about that for a moment and then raised his hand. The General nodded. Peter told him what he was thinking. The general raised his eyebrows, "That's brilliant. Thank you, Leek. They've trained you well at Pogo. Since you and your squad have already been to Lortec, I think you should lead the ground unit."

"Yes, sir. That makes sense," Peter replied eagerly.

"Good. I'll have my staff put together a detailed plan this afternoon. We'll launch early tomorrow morning so we'll hit them at daybreak."

"Very well, sir," Peter said.

After the briefing, Tam, Sy, Red, and Peter went to the nutrition center for lunch. It was their first opportunity to really talk since they'd arrived at LB1. There was a lot to reminiscence about and much to consider before they left that night for Lortec.

"Are you going to be able to leave Lucinda after just one day with her?" Tam asked.

Peter looked at him and sighed. "I don't want to, but I guess I don't have much choice. Besides, if all goes well I'll be back tomorrow night."

"Yeah, but if your brilliant plan doesn't work we could all end up dead," Red noted. "There's only going to be twelve of us and 50,000 of them."

"That's true," Peter said, "so we'd better come up with a good strategy for getting in and out of there quickly and without anyone noticing us."

"Why not just go in with our fighters like we did last time?" Sy asked. "It worked once, it will probably work again."

"I don't know," Peter replied. They're going to be on high alert. They may detect us coming in and that would be a disaster."

"What about a parachute drop?" Tam said.

"That's possible, but the plane that dropped us might be spotted or someone might see us coming down," Peter replied. "No, I think there is just one way to get in and out. A small boat could come in nearly undetected. There were a lot of fishing boats in the harbor near the Zodilla range. If we came in there and borrowed some of the Zodilla pacers we could get in position without anyone noticing us. Being so early in the morning there isn't likely to be anyone at the range."

"Except the Zodillas," Red reminded them.

"Well, we'll just have to avoid them," Peter said. "We can stay outside the run."

"Good. Those monsters move faster than leaprohds on ice," Red replied. "I don't want to get in their path again."

"Leaprohds? What are they?"

"A Leaprohd is a type of bird commonly found on Glacier Dome. They travel very fast on snow, but on ice they are unbelievably fast."

Glacier Dome was the equivalent of the South Pole on Earth. Peter hoped some day he'd get to see a Leaprohd. They sounded fascinating and it would be fun to see them run at full speed. Red's fear of the Zodilla made him wonder, though. Would they have to go across their run to get into position for the assault on Lortec? Tam had said they wouldn't, but honestly he didn't know. Red was a worrier so he didn't want him losing any sleep over the Zodillas. If they had to cross their run, they'd do it very carefully. Worrying about it now wouldn't help.

After their strategy session Peter talked to the general and suggested that their ground unit go in disguised as fishermen. The general agreed and said he would round up a boat to use and have it fitted. He gave Peter the rest of the afternoon off to be with Lucinda. She was glad to see him but by the look on her face something was bothering her.

"I can't believe you have to leave already. You just got here."

"I know. It's unfortunate that we have to attack Lortec so soon, but if we don't, I fear all will be lost in short order. This is our only hope."

Lucinda sighed and looked away. "When you get back, how long will we have together before you must leave again?"

"I don't know. Not long I fear."

"So, why am I here if you don't have time for me?"

"Because I love you and I need you. I can't stop thinking about you. I know it's selfish and I had no right to break up you and your mate, but I can't help my feelings."

"I just want us to be together," Lucinda said frustrated. "I hate being alone."

"You sound like my mother. My father was a big trial attorney and we didn't see much of him. My mother hated it, but she loved him so she put up with it."

"How long do you think the war will last?"

"Jeez. I have no idea. On Earth wars usually take many cycles to be resolved unless one side is weak and then they are over quickly. If we don't destroy the TGA forces on Lortec tomorrow I fear the war will be very short."

"I almost hope you lose," Lucinda said. "Then we could be together."

"No you don't," Peter replied. "If we lose we'll all be shot as traitors."

"Why does it have to be this way? Why can't Videl live with the Supreme Mandate? It so unfair to drag everyone into this war because of one man."

"It's not just him. He has many followers who believe as he does, that humans are a superior life form and all others should be enslaved or eradicated. We had a man on Earth much like him many years ago when my grandfather was alive. His name was Hitler."

"Did your grandfather fight Hitler?"

"Yes, he served in the army during both World War I and World War II."

"So, was your father a soldier as well?"

"Not really, he came of age right after the Vietnam war. He served in the Marines briefly but was never in a war."

"It's been peaceful on Tarizon for a long time. It's a shame it's about to end."

"I'm going to have to leave soon. We shouldn't waste one minute of our time together."

"We haven't been wasting time, have we? I've learned a lot about you and your family."

"Right, but—"

"Is sex all you Earth Aliens think about?"

Peter laughed and replied, "No, but when you're a teenager it's something that is always on your mind. It's certainly been on my mind a lot since I met you."

"Hmm. I'm just so worried that something will happen and you won't come back to me."

"Yeah. Well, that's a possibility, but the Prophecy says I'm going to liberate the planet, remember. I can't die then, right? At least not until that's been accomplished."

Later that night Peter left Lucinda once again. His unit was taken to a small cove where a fishing boat lay waiting for them. It looked old and dilapidated, so it wouldn't likely attract any attention. However, below deck it was a state-of-the-art gunboat ready to do combat at a moment's notice. It was well stocked with all the missiles, guns, and ammunition that they'd need to complete their mission. They were told they'd have to leave immediately to get to Lortec and set up before dawn. That gave them seven kyloons to sleep before they had to disembark. The crew quarters had six bunks. They weren't very comfortable but Peter was so tired it didn't take him long to fall asleep and begin to dream. In his dream he was on the seashore.

In the distance he saw Threebeard approaching flanked by three Seafolken. They were armed with a few rifles but mainly swords and knives. When they met, Threebeard smiled. "These are the three generals of your army of Seafolken, Talhk, Rusht, and Quirken. They await your command."

Peter looked over at them warily. "Do you think the Seafolken will have a chance against the well-trained soldiers of the TGA?"

Threebeard straightened up and replied, "Don't ever underestimate a Seafolken. There is more to them than meets the eye."

Threebeard nodded to his three generals. Talhk bent down and picked up a large rock. He took two steps and threw it, what must have been two hundred strides out to sea.

"Wow! He'd have made a hell of a quarterback," Peter remarked.

Rusht dropped into a starting position. Threebeard said "Heed!" and Rusht took off down the beach at an incredible clip. A few seconds later Threebeard yelled "Yonga!" and Rusht put on the brakes, changed directions, and came right back at them faster than any Olympic runner Peter had ever seen.

Peter's eyes widened as Rusht flew past him. "Okay! I'm sure you can out run them, but–."

Threebeard raised his hand and nodded to Quirken. Quirken turned and looked at Peter with his penetrating eyes. Suddenly, a weird sensation came over him. He felt light, like he was being lifted up. Looking around frantically, he realized he was floating in mid air. Panic seized him and he began to flay the air with his arms and legs. Threebeard let out a thunderous laugh and the others joined in. Finally,

265

Quirken relaxed his concentration and Peter fell to the ground.

He got up, brushed himself off and shook his head, "Okay, I'm impressed. So, how do I summon these Seafolken if I need them?"

"Go to the edge of the water, close your eyes, and say silently 'Come Seafolken, soldiers of the Southern Sea, I command you to come and do battle!"

The boat lurched, nearly knocking Peter out of his bunk. He sat up and looked around. Sy was snoring and Red had one leg dangling over the side of his bed. Tam was awake and looking at him.

"You talked to Threebeard?"

Peter nodded. "I guess I did, kind of."

"That's good. We'll need all the help we can get."

"How much longer until we get to Lortec?" Peter asked.

"We're half way there. Go back to sleep. You'll need every morsel of strength you can muster at daybreak."

Peter nodded and laid his head back on his pillow. This time his dreams took him back to Lucinda's bed. She was sleeping peacefully. As he watched her breathe, he longed to be with her and wished somehow he could transport himself back to LB1 to hold her and smell the sweet scent of her body. Suddenly the ground began to rumble and there was a bright flash of light. Peter's heart stopped as he saw the walls implode and Lucinda's body tossed across the room and plummeted with rubble.

"No! Oh, please, no! Lucinda! Lucinda!" he moaned.

Tam put his hand on his shoulder. "It's just a dream. You're okay, Leek. Nothing actually happened. Relax."

Peter sat up sweating profusely. "Are you sure? It seemed so real."

"Dreams often seem real, but they are not."

"But my dreams often come true. What if—?"

"But usually they don't," Tam said. "Don't worry about fate. It will do you no good. You'll just have to trust your God and Sandee."

Peter took a deep breath and said, "I can't sleep. How much longer? I want to get this over with."

"Not long now. We should be seeing the lights of Milvess soon."

"Milvess?"

"Yes, that is the name of the town where we saw the harbor and the fishing boats. Or, I should say, you saw it. I was crammed into the storage hold and saw nothing."

266

"Milvess. Hmm. I wonder what life is like in Milvess."

"It's probably a boring place to live unless you are in love with fishing."

"I do love to fish. It was something my father did with us a lot. It was one of the few times I saw my dad totally relaxed and having fun. Usually he was stressed out over one case or another, but when he went fishing it was like we had entered into another world. There was nothing on our minds except finding the fish and catching them."

"Maybe the General will give you this boat when the war is over. Then you can become a fisherman," Tam said.

Peter laughed. "Nah. Fishing is great for a day or two but then it gets boring. I don't know how these fisherman do it day after day."

Squinting, Peter could see lights in the distance. They indeed were close to Milvess. He figured it would be less than a kyloon now before they'd be docking in the harbor. Peter's stomach felt funny, like it did before it was his turn to debate or when he played baseball, just before his time at bat. He knew it was normal—a combination of fear, excitement, and the effects of too much adrenalin in his system.

"We should get everybody up and start getting our gear ready to go," Peter said. "We don't want to dilly dally in the harbor. The quicker we get off the boat, the better."

"Okay, I'll wake up Sy and Red," Tam said.

Although it was very early, the harbor was bustling with activity. Peter had forgotten that fishermen would be up early to get to the fishing grounds by dawn. This made it a little scary coming into the harbor. They couldn't afford to be stopped and questioned. There would be no way to explain the armaments they had on board. The captain came in slowly, being careful not to create a wake that might attract attention. The ship moved slowly toward slip 32 where they were to dock. Just as the slip came into view Peter noticed a TGA patrol boat approaching from the opposite direction. His heart skipped a beat.

34
Evacuation

Lorin watched Peter's boat disappear in the bank of fog lurking just offshore. She turned and walked back to the PV that had brought her out to the docks. She had to get back to headquarters immediately as she had been given a message that General Zitor wanted to see her. She wondered if it had something to do with the shift in the weather stream. It had been the main topic of conversation all day. There was fear that LB 1's position had been compromised anyway; but even if it hadn't, if the weather stream shifted the sky might clear giving the TGA a birds eye view of the air traffic going in and out of the base. The TGA had a large network of satellites that would be trained on the Beet Islands, but normally the dense pollutants in the air would hide them. As she rode back to headquarters she gazed at all the magnificent buildings the Namomites had built for them. What a waste it would be to blow them up, she thought, but they couldn't leave them for the TGA to use against them.

Back at headquarters she joined General Zitor in the strategy room. He was deep in conversation with several other officers. She stood by the door until he was finished.

"Are they gone?" he asked her when the last officer had left.

"Yes, they're on their way to Lortec."

"Good. I hope Leek's plan works."

"If they get into position without detection, I think it will."

"I pray you are right. It's important we win these first few battles. Our people need a taste of victory if they are going to make it through the long struggle ahead."

"We'll give it to them, Sir. I'm sure of it."

General Zitor smiled. "I'm going to be busy with the attack on Lortec tomorrow, so I'm going to need you to handle the command evacuation."

"Yes, of course. I'll get right on it."

"I know it will be difficult to leave in the midst of battle, but it's important that we're not captured. You should bring Lucinda with us. We must be sure no harm comes to her for Leek's sake."

Lorin was a little angry over the prospect of having to babysit Lucinda. She had so much to do and she knew Lucinda would be an irritating distraction. Why was Peter so obsessed with her? She wasn't extraordinary in any way. She was just a guide, for sake of Sandee. What did he see in her?

Lorin nodded without revealing her distaste for the assignment. "I'll tell her to prepare for immediate departure. Where will we be going?"

"The mutants have secured a good portion of southern Tributon and there's a base there where our forces can stay until we find a new LB 1. I need to meet with Threebeard and the mutant generals. We'll stay there until it's time to go to your father's investiture."

Now that the civil war was underway it had been decided that a new government should be formed under the Supreme Mandate. Councillor Garcia had been the obvious choice for Chancellor since he had spearheaded the Loyalist movement from its inception. In order for the new government to have any credibility there had to be a memorable ceremony to commemorate the historic occasion.

Lorin didn't like the idea of gathering the most important leaders of the Loyalists movement together in one place. Such a meeting was an invitation to Videl to attack them. If he was successful he could end the civil war before it really got started. She had voiced her concern to her father, but he had assured her that the gathering could be protected. He told her that if there was to be any chance of victory he had to show the people that he wasn't afraid of Videl and could protect those who followed him.

"All right," Lorin replied. "There's a Lukon PT22 available, I believe. It should be big enough to take most of the command staff."

"Go then and make it ready."

"Yes, Sir," Lorin said turning to leave. "What about Leek? Will he be coming with the command staff?"

"Not immediately. We definitely need him at the investiture, but it will be too dangerous for him to come back to LB1 after the battle is over. In fact, by the time the battle is finished, LB1 will no longer exist."

"Where will you send him, then?" Lorin asked.

"If he survives the battle tomorrow, we'll send him somewhere far away where he'll be safe until the investiture. It's important that he be there when your father is sworn in."

Lorin left the general's office and set out for the hanger to inspect the Lukon PT22 that would take them to their hideaway in Tributon. Lorin was excited that she'd soon have the opportunity to meet with Threebeard. Next to her father, she considered him the most important asset of the Loyalists movement. His intelligence and wisdom were legendary and she was anxious to find out what his battle strategies would be to drive out the TGA from Lamaine Shane. She also had a few ideas herself she wanted to share with him.

The main hanger was crowded with mechanics, pilots, and crew readying their planes for battle. Lorin hurried past them to where she'd seen the Lukon PT22. Two men were walking around the plane with clipboards. She approached them directly.

"Who's the pilot of this craft?" she asked.

The taller of the two men straightened up. "That's me. Evohn Cystrom."

"I'm Lorin Boskie, military liaison to Councillor Garcia. You came in from Pogo with Leek Lanzia, didn't you?"

"Yes, ma'am," the pilot said. "How can I assist you?"

"General Zitor is going to need this plane for the evacuation tomorrow. I'll need you to get it ready and pilot it for us."

"Yes, ma'am. Where will we be going?"

"It isn't necessary that you know that information now. I'll advise you our destination an hour before we take off, so you'll have time to input our course into the computers."

"But I'll need to know how much fuel to take on and how many passengers to take provisions for."

"You can assume you'll have a full plane and it will be traveling a very long distance. You'll have to refuel along the way. We'll give you instructions once we get airborne."

"Yes, ma'am. What time will be leaving?"

"Midday tomorrow," Lorin replied. "You're the one whose father was killed by Videl, isn't that right?"

"Yes, ma'am."

Lorin nodded. "You sure you can fly this thing? You've only had basic flight training. Have you even flown it yet?"

"Oh, yes, ma'am. I picked up recruits from Lower Azallo just yesterday. It was no problem. I was the top in my simulator class, even better than Leek."

"Very well. You'll have very important passengers, so nothing must go wrong."

"It won't. I'll deliver all of you safely to wherever you want to go."

"Until tomorrow, then," Lorin said and walked off a little uneasy. She had no doubt that Evohn was smart and capable, but he had no experience. What if the computers failed? Would he be able to take over manual flight and get them to their destination? She hoped it wouldn't come to that, but it didn't matter. She knew there were no other pilots available. Every pilot would be committed to the battle at Lortec tomorrow and Evohn would have to do.

With transportation arranged Lorin's next task was to advise Lucinda that she'd be leaving. She didn't relish this task as she'd just dragged her half way across the world to be with Leek, and now Leek was gone and she'd have to journey across the world again with no idea when she'd see him again. She knocked on her compartment door. The door flew open.

"Lorin. Hi. Is everything okay?"

"Yes. Can I come in?"

"Sure," Lucinda said and motioned her to a table with two chairs. Lorin walked in and took a seat.

"Leek got off okay. I watched him leave. They'll be in Lortec before daylight."

"Oh, I hope everything goes well. I'm so worried about him. Do you think he'll be back by evening?"

"No. That's why I'm here. There's been an unusual shift in the weather streams. It seems that tomorrow will actually be a clear day—something extremely rare."

"So, that's good. It will be nice to see the sun."

"Yes, except that with a major military campaign underway, it will make it easy for the TGA to discover where all our planes are coming from. From their satellites and high altitude recognizance drones they will no doubt discover LB1."

Lucinda swallowed hard. "So, what does that mean?"

"It means Leek will not be able to return to base and we must all leave here before the missiles hit and destroy the island."

"Where will you send Leek?"

"I can't say, but he'll be safe. On the other hand, our situation is more desperate. We must leave here by midday tomorrow or face annihilation."

"Oh, Sandee save us! Where will we go?"

"I can't say, but you'll be traveling with me and General Zitor, so you have nothing to worry about."

Except your pilot has less than nine kyloons flight time. Not to mention that the TGA will be desperately searching for our plane since it will be carrying half of the Loyalists high command on board.

Lucinda frowned. "This isn't what I expected. I thought I'd have more time with Leek."

"You will. This weather stream shift is very unfortunate."

"Maybe it's a sign from God that he is not with us?" Lucinda said.

"No," Lorin replied hastily. "God would not be with a man like Videl. Videl is evil. Our God is good."

"But, such an unusual weather pattern. Why has it happened?"

"There is some reason for it, I'm sure. In time, perhaps, we'll understand it."

Lucinda nodded and looked at a stack of boxes and suitcases against the wall. "As you can see, I've barely begun to unpack, so it will be little trouble to be ready tomorrow to leave."

"Good," Lorin said. "I'll send some soldiers by first thing tomorrow to take your things to the plane."

"Thank you," Lucinda said. "You are very kind. I know you have more important things to do than keep track of me."

Lorin looked at Lucinda and sighed. "If I've let any resentment show, I am sorry. This isn't easy for either of us, I know. Hopefully, you'll be with Leek soon and he can look after you. Then, I hope, we can be friends."

Lucinda smiled. "I'd like that."

Lorin's thoughts turned to Jake as she walked back to her compartment. She had her own mate to worry about. He'd be flying into battle before dawn's first light and only God and Sandee knew if she'd ever see him again. This was the first big battle of the war. Up until now all their preparations had been theoretical—almost game-like. Now, however, she knew Jake would really be up there in the sky with hundreds of TGA soldiers and pilots trying to shoot him down. She shuddered at the thought of it. He was waiting there for her when she stepped into their compartment. They embraced.

"Oh, Jake. I prayed this day would never come."

"Why? I'm excited. I think we're going to catch them by surprise. It was so lucky that Leek and his friends stumbled across the base at Lortec."

"I hope you're right, but they must be on high alert after the attack on Muhl."

"Maybe. But they knew those few planes were stolen planes from Pogo. I doubt they realize we have hundreds of fighters just like them ready to strike."

Lorin sighed. "Don't try to be a hero up there. I don't want to be have to register for a new mate."

Jake pulled her to him and they kissed long and passionately. When he let her go he said, "Don't worry. This is God's war. He'll watch over us."

Lorin looked away. She wasn't as religious as Jake, she was a politician who believed in science more than religion. She believed God existed and Sandee saved Tarizon from self destruction, but she knew a lot of good people would perish in the coming civil war despite the fact that they were God fearing people. Not because God was evil, but because their sacrifice was for the greater good. She prayed Jake wouldn't be one of those sacrifices. She needed him. She couldn't imagine life without him. Was this what the Earth children called love? She didn't know, but whatever it was it was powerful and felt wonderful. She thought back to the day of her mating selection.

It was just before her sixteenth birthday that she received her mating notice. She was to report to Central Authority Headquarters in Shisk to be assigned a mate and to meet him for the first time. Central Authority didn't make you live with your mate immediately. After selection you met your mate and had one cycle to get to know each other and plan your life together. Lorin was very nervous and apprehensive about the process. She didn't like the idea of Central Authority telling her she had to mate. She had little interest in men and wanted only to help her father in the struggle against Videl Lai that, even nine cycles earlier, was beginning to take shape.

She had received her envelope and taken a seat along with hundreds of other young girls her age. A large woman with a clipboard stepped to the podium and addressed the group.

"Good morning ladies. Central Authority welcomes you to Mate Selection Day. Today you will learn the identity of the person the computers have found to be most compatible to you. What this means is that after considering countless measures of personality, background, physique, intelligence, and interests, the computers have searched our vast census databases and found the most likely person to make you happy and productive during your adult life.

"I know today's events may seem quite overwhelming to you, but the mating process has been going on for nearly fifty cycles and it's worked very well. Just keep an open mind and follow the instructions and guidelines in your mating manual. We also will have counselors available should you need them tonight or at any time during the mating cycle. Now you may open your envelopes and find the identity of your mate. You will also find the number of the meeting area where you can find the man who will share you destiny."

Lorin tore open the envelope and rifled through the contents for the picture of the man who she'd be spending the rest of her life with, whether she liked it or not. She pulled out the color glossy and froze. She recognized the face. It was Jake, the Chancellor's nephew. She liked Jake. They'd run around together for years. But Jake as her mate? Yes! She could see herself with Jake. He was a smart and a lot of fun. They'd be good together. She looked for the paper telling her where to meet him. She couldn't wait to see what his reaction would be to the match. She found the paper and walked briskly to the meeting area. When she saw Jake she went over to him casually.

"Jake. I can't believe this," she said teasingly. "What are the odds that the computer would mate two people who were already friends?"

Jake smiled and shrugged. "About a million to one."

"Uh huh. So, how do you suppose this happened?"

"Ah. . . . Well, it may be my fault. You know when we were taking all those tests to help the computer make its matches?"

"Yes."

"Well, I answered every question in such a way that the computer could only pick you as my mate."

"Oh, I see. Very clever. Now tell me how you did it."

"Are you unhappy?"

"No, I'm delighted. I'd love to be your mate, but I want to know how it happened. It couldn't have been by computer selection."

"Okay, I'll confess. I told my uncle that if I was mated with anybody but Lorin Garcia, I'd volunteer for an Earth shuttle and he wouldn't see me for fourteen years."

Lorin laughed. "You didn't!"

"I did. So, he made sure the computer picked me the right woman."

Lorin took his hand. She smiled up at him. "I'm so relieved. I was afraid I'd get stuck with some guy that looked like a durkbird or had the personality of a Nanomite."

"It pays to have connections," Jake said pulling her close to him. "I'd kiss you, but someone might get suspicious."

"Hmm. You're right. We better act like we've just met."

She took a deep breath as the memory faded. She'd been fortunate to be mated with Jake. She loved him. Yes, she did love him. Even if love was not sanctioned on Tarizon, it didn't matter. There was no doubt about it. She loved Jake and she'd die if he didn't come back to her.

35
The Battle of Lortec

The crews on most of the ships they'd passed coming into port seemed too busy preparing for the day's work to pay them much heed, but the TGA patrol boat coming at them pulled up close and the two soldiers on deck gave them a hard stare. One the soldiers yelled to the captain. "What's wrong? Why are you coming back into port?"

The captain yelled back, "The engines are sounding a bit rough. I was afraid she'd break down at sea—thought I should check them out."

The soldier nodded. "Did you see anything unusual out there?"

The captain shook his head, "No."

The soldier glanced around the ship one last time and then nodded to the pilot to drive on. When they finally arrived at Slip 32 they were relieved to see the slip empty and the pier quiet. After tying up the boat their first order of business was securing their transportation. It was about two kylods to the track where the pacers were garaged. It took them about ten loons to get there, walking quickly but trying not to attract attention. Along the way many fishermen and merchants saw them but only showed modest curiosity.

They were dressed, not in Loyalist's uniforms, but their old uniforms of the TGA. They thought since there was a big TGA base just a few kylods away seeing a few soldiers around wouldn't be unusual. Of course, impersonating a TGA soldier was a serious crime, but it didn't much matter since they'd be shot anyway if they got caught.

The big sign in front of the park read: "Southern Sea Zodilla Run—Wild Zodilla Racing—Races Daily." Fortunately the place was deserted this time of morning so they went straight for the barns where the Zodilla pacers were located. This time the barns were locked up with double padlocks. Apparently management hadn't been too thrilled about their last visit. Two laser blasts destroyed the locks, without making too much noise, and the doors to the barn swung open.

Inside there were eight black and white pacers. They only needed six as their party consisted of Tam, Red, Sy, Peter and two soldiers, Lotis and Curillo, who had defected from the TGA base at Ock Mezan. It took less than ten loons for them to get back to the ship and five more to load up their gear and get on their way.

Their next obstacle was to get in position without being detected. The plan was to station themselves about a kylod from the end of the runway. Before they left, General Zitor had given them a map of Lortec and some aerial photographs of the base. Their plan had been to drive along the southern perimeter of the Zodilla range and cut across the east end of the range to a position near the base runway. Unfortunately, they discovered that would be way out of their way and throw them off schedule. They had no choice but to cut across the Zodilla range to their position.

When they stopped midway along the perimeter of the range, Red said, "Why are we stopping?"

"I'm afraid we've got to go across," Peter replied.

"What? You've got to be kidding. Don't you remember what those Zodillas did to the TGA soldiers the last time we were here."

"Yes, I remember quite vividly, but we have no choice. Besides, these pacers are designed to outrun the Zodillas."

"Sure they are, but we're not exactly accomplished drivers. We've only driven these things one time, for the sake of Sandee."

"Do you have a better idea?"

Red didn't reply, so Peter turned and blew a hole in the fence with his laser gun. He hoped the Zodillas slept at night and their intrusion wouldn't awaken them. Unfortunately, he was wrong. The pacers, they learned later, were designed to stir the big monsters and get them running before a race. Not five loons after they were on the track the ground began to shake and they saw the first ones racing after them. By the time they were at midfield, the whole herd of Zodillas was on their heals.

"I told you this was a bad idea!" Red screamed through his personal communicator.

"Don't look back. Just keep it at full-throttle. If our engines don't fail, they can't outrun us."

"What about the fence?" Sy asked. "If we stop to blow the fence, we'll get trampled."

Tam replied, "I'll drive ahead and blow a hole in it and then drive through. Just follow me."

That sounded like a great plan except that if the laser didn't cut a big enough hole, Tam could be seriously injured or even decapitated trying to go through it.

"No!" Peter said. "I've got a better idea. After you blow the hole don't go through it. Make a hard right and let one of the Zodillas go through the hole first. The rest will probably follow and cause all kind of hell on the base."

"Great idea," Tam said as he stood up to fire his laser one handed. He looked like a gladiator with one hand on the steering wheel and the laser rifle in his other. The pacer lurched sharply and Tam nearly fell off. He regained control and when he was less that a hundred strides from the fence he fired. The fence lit up like a neon sign as Tam made a hard right. They each followed his lead and took a sharp right before going through the fence. The first Zodilla tried to follow them but his momentum carried him through the fence. The rest of the herd followed his lead, stampeding onto the TGA base.

After the dust had settled, Peter and his squad went through the gaping hole and set up their position at the end of the runway. They heard screams of terror and gunfire as the Zodillas rampaged through the base. Then Lorin broke radio silence.

"R1, come in," Lorin said.

"R1, here. Go ahead," he replied.

"Phase one, complete. Standby for phase two."

"Acknowledged. We're ready."

Phase one was designed to lure away the fighters in the sky above Lortec. The plan was to send a small band of fighters into Lortec airspace and then to run when the patrols came to intercept them. The hope was to draw them away from the island so that the main force of fighters could attack the base without interference from the air.

Phase two was the main assault on the TGA base by over one hundred and fifty fighters and twenty-five bombers. Peter's squad's job was to keep the TGA fighters from taking off and interfering with the attack. Their reconnaissance had determined that there were over 525 fighters on the base. Most were conventional fighters that had to use the runway. Twenty-five, however, were vertical lift fighters that wouldn't need the runway and were kept on another part of the base. Peter and his squad couldn't do anything to stop them from their position, so they would be the first targets of the fighters attacking the base.

Suddenly there was a sonic boom. Peter looked up in the sky, knowing their fighters had arrived. He couldn't see them in the bright sun until they came swooping down on the base like lava from a volcano. Only chaos and ruin were left in their wake as they flew off, only to return moments later to wreck more havoc on their disoriented foe. Close behind the fighters were the bombers with their genius bombs each programmed to hit within a few feet of each's specific target. Peter wondered what those targets would be and how they'd been selected.

The bombers looked like a flock of birds coming out of the sun. The loud shriek of falling bombs gave Peter goose bumps. The time had finally arrived—the first major battle of the Tarizonian Civil War had commenced. Peter motioned for his men to get ready. They nodded and checked their weapons. They all had portable missile launchers called PMLs. They were firing a version of the Muscan missile, but a smaller one with a shorter range. It would be adequate for shooting planes trying to take off just 300 strides away.

The first fighter came screaming down the runway anxious to do battle. Sy lifted his PML and waited for the target to lock. When the green light went on he pulled the trigger. The muscan missile made a gushing sound as it shot up to toward the plane barely off the ground. The plane exploded scattering burning debris all over the runway.

Another plane was right on its tail and climbed rapidly in the sky. A missile from Red's launcher shot up at it and made contact just a few hundred strides in front of them. Debris came falling down and they had to scatter to avoid being hit.

"Don't wait so long," Peter barked. "You almost got us killed. Get them just as they take off."

A rattled Red nodded and started to reload his PML. It was Peter's turn and he didn't want to make the same mistake Red had made so he aimed his missile just as soon as the next fighter came into view. The green light went on and he pulled the trigger. The missile gushed forward and struck the plane dead on just as it left the ground. The plane dropped, skidded, and then burst into flames as it hit the debris left from the previous fighters they'd downed.

By this time the Loyalist fighters and bombers could be seen everywhere, blowing up anything that might be of value to the TGA. The sound of exploding bombs was deafening. Smoke billowed up into the air until it was so dark it was difficult to see. It looked like a massacre, until Peter saw two more fighters coming down the runway side by side with four more right behind them .

It was Tam's turn, then Lotis and Curillo, so they were ready, but Sy, Red and Peter were reloading. That meant that three birds might get in the air if Sy, Red, and Peter were unable to reload and fire in time. Lotis and Curillo got their missiles off right after Tam. All the missiles ran true and blew the planes from the sky. Sy finished loading his launcher and pointed it up toward the fourth plane now almost out of range. He fired and the missile screamed after the T47. The explosion was so close it nearly knocked Peter over. The other planes took off but none of the squad were able to get reloaded in time to fire at them.

"Three birds got by us," Peter said into his communicator. "Sorry, there were too many of them." Peter was tuned into the frequency of their attack squadron. The squadron leader come back at him.

"We're on them. Don't worry. You can't do all the work."

"Confirmed. Good luck."

The runway was quiet for a moment. Peter assumed the TGA command was getting six planes to launch at them all at one time again since that had just worked. Then they heard the sound of planes coming in from behind them. "Shit," Peter said. "The hounds are back from chasing the fox."

Tam looked up and replied, "We're sitting durk birds where we're at. We'd better head back to the boat."

"My thoughts exactly," Peter replied. "Let's pack 'em up and move out."

Just as Peter gave the command a missile exploded not fifty feet from them, knocking them to the ground. Peter got up and said, "Forget the missile launchers. Just get in your pacers. Let's get the hell out of here."

Another missile exploded behind them and Peter saw a plane coming in low to strafe them. He jumped in his pacer, started the engine, and took off to the right. The others followed him but he couldn't see what happened to Sy. Then he heard the steady rattle of machine gun fire. He glanced back and saw Sy trying to evade the plane that was right on his tail. Peter wheeled around trying to attract the pilot's attention, but he didn't stray from his deadly course. The line of bullets from the T47 cut through Sy's stomach. Peter winced in horror.

"No!"

The plane flew by. Peter gunned his engine and was at Sy's side in a tik. He jumped out, knelt beside him, and lifted his arm to take his pulse. There was nothing. Red drove up, skidding to a stop a few feet away. He jumped out and knelt next to Peter.

"Is he okay?" Red asked.

"No," Peter moaned. "He's dead."

"Oh! Sandee."

Red raised his fist to the plane that was circling for another run. Just as it had completed its turn one of the Loyalist fighters got on its tail. The TGA fighter suddenly dived in an evasive maneuver. The Loyalist pilot reacted quickly and stayed close behind. Then there was a puff of smoke from the Loyalist fighter, and the TGA fighter exploded.

"Yes!" Red yelled, his fist raised high.

Peter said, "Let's put Sy on my pacer and get the hell out of here. I don't want to lose anybody else."

As they were loading Sy's body onto Peter's pacer, Tam arrived. He jumped out of his vehicle and grabbed a hold of Sy's mid-section immediately becoming saturated with blood. Peter didn't have to tell Tam what had happened. One look into Peter's eyes and he knew the whole story. After Sy was secured they took off toward the Zodilla range, but when they got to the place where the Zodillas had stampeded through the fence, there was a squadron of TGA soldiers blocking their retreat.

Before the soldiers could see them Peter stopped his pacer. Tam,

Red, Lotis and Curillo came up along side and stopped too. Peter shook his head and said, "We'll have to go around the fence."

They nodded and were off. It was five kylods out of their way but Peter didn't think they had a choice. Five of them were no match for a dozen TGA soldiers. As they rode along the fence line Peter watched the battle in progress. Planes were screaming by, bombs were exploding everywhere, and the smoke in the air was so thick he could hardly breathe. He wondered how the battle was going. They'd obviously caught them by surprise and dealt them a serious blow, but they'd survived the attack and were now counter attacking. Peter feared the worst. What if they attacked LB1?

At the northeast corner of the fence line Peter stopped to call base. He wanted to report in and get instructions from command. "Squadron leader. Come in."

"This is squadron leader. What is your status?"

"We were under heavy assault and had to retreat to safe ground. One man is down."

"Sorry about that, R1. . . . Standby for orders."

"Okay, standing by."

"R1. Return to base. Repeat. Return to base. You've done all you can."

"Confirmed. We're on our way."

Peter looked at his squad and said, "Back to the boat."

They nodded and they all took off in a southerly direction along the southwest perimeter fence line. The sound of the battle raging behind them subsided and the air cleared as they approached Milvess. As they were driving Peter wondered what had become of the Zodillas. Were they all killed by the TGA? He felt a little guilty sending them to be slaughtered, but there was little else he could have done. He vowed then to make it up to them. He'd do all that he could do to end Zodilla confinement and exploitation on Tarizon.

As Peter saw Milvess in the distance he felt greatly relieved—relieved that they'd survived, that he'd soon be on his way back to LB1, and that tonight he'd be in Lucinda's bed. But as they got closer his heart sank. The city was completely surrounded by TGA soldiers and there were check points at every entrance. They stopped and Peter was about to report in for

283

instructions when a sentry spotted them and sent a patrol out to apprehend them.

Peter and his men took off toward the beach as there was no other way to go. To their back was the Zodilla range. If they turned around and went the way they had come, they'd be back in the thick of the battle and soon surrounded by the enemy. But fleeing toward the beach didn't do them much good either, Peter realized. Soon they'd run out of real estate and then what? Their situation seemed hopeless. They sped along toward the Southern Sea with their pursuers close behind hoping for a miracle. Peter heard a shot fired and felt the bullet glance off the body of his pacer. Adrenalin flooded his system. Soon they were at the end of the road. All there was between them and the Southern Sea was a thin strand of beach.

They lined up their pacers and knelt behind them for cover. Peter figured it would be their last stand. They'd go out in glory and kill fifty men before they spent their last breath. Peter looked out at the soldiers coming at them, then back at the sea. Suddenly he felt a presence in his mind. His dream of the previous night flashed through his head. Could it really happen? He got up slowly, walked to the edge of the water, and closed his eyes. "Come Seafolken, soldiers of the Southern Sea," he said silently; "I command you to come and do battle! . . . Come Talhk, Rusht, and Quirken. Gather your soldiers and bring them to me."

Before he had finished his last command there was a great churning in the water. Tam and Red looked back when they heard it. As they all stared out at the water wide-eyed, hundreds of Seafolken began to emerge one by one from the depths of the sea. Soon they were in formation and marching past them toward the approaching TGA soldiers. When the soldiers began firing on them the first column of Seafolken picked up large rocks and began throwing them at the soldiers. Their aim was true and soldiers began falling like needles off a dead Christmas tree.

Many of the Seafolken were hit by rifle fire, but their skin was so thick the bullets couldn't penetrate it with enough velocity to do any serious damage. When the remnants of the first wave of soldiers and the second wave made their assault, hundreds of Seafolken broke ranks and did an end run around them until they had them completely surrounded. The third line of Seafolken then came up to look at their captors.

"Throw down your weapons and surrender!" General Quirken screamed.

There was no response from the bewildered soldiers, so Quirken raised his hand and the third wave of Seaflolken stepped forward. The soldiers opened fire but their bullets did no damage to the Seafolken and before they took a second shot, guns began flying out of the soldier's hands. Some Soldiers were thrown to the ground in the grip of an invisible force, others grabbed their throats like they were being choked, and the rest raised their hands in surrender.

General Quirken looked at Peter and said, "Follow us and we'll see you safely to your ship."

Peter nodded; they got back in their pacers and followed the army of Seafolken toward Milvess. The Seafolken were running fast, forcing Peter and his squad to travel at cruising speed to keep up. They passed many TGA soldiers along the way but none dared challenge them in the company of their fearsome allies from the sea. When they got to their ship, they launched immediately; the Seafolken dove into the water and swam beside them until they were safely out at sea. Then the Seafolken disappeared without a word.

36

Diversion

At dawn LB 1 was teeming with activity. Since 0600 a steady stream of planes had been flowing down the runway and taking off over the orange glow of the volcano. Jake was in one of the first fighters. Lorin was glad because that meant Jake would be part of the first wave of fighters sent to lure away Lortec's air defense squadrons. Hopefully, they'd never engage the enemy and only come back to fight when the battle was well underway. She reasoned that when they finally made it back into battle much of Lortec's air defenses would have been destroyed and their planes shot down. If this indeed happened, Jake would be less likely to perish in battle. She was sure General Zitor had done that on purpose in deference to her and the Councillor.

By 0900 reports on the battle started to come in. The diversion had worked and the first wave of bombers flew over Lortec without resistence. When the remaining fighters tried to get off the ground to intercept the intruders, Peter's squad frustrated every attempt to get them airborne. The bombers hit with devastating effect, destroying almost forty percent of the enemy aircraft within the first kyloon. Eventually the battle evened out as the vertical lift fighters got in the battle and Peter's squad was finally forced to retreat opening up the runway again. But it was too late for the TGA. They'd lost most of their aircraft and thousands of men who'd been caught still sleeping at dawn's first light.

Although command was elated with their victory, they didn't have time to relish it, as the sky above them had cleared. The freak weather pattern had materialized as feared and the satellites orbiting above had begun to train their lenses on the Beet Islands. It was only a matter of kyloons and the bombs and rockets would be descending upon them. The bombers, after finishing their work on Lortec, were refueled in the air and sent to southern

Tributon where the mutants were in control. Some of the fighters joined them, but others were sent all the way to Rigimol to shore up security for the investiture of Chancellor Garcia.

By 1600 the island had been evacuated with the exception of the command staff that was set to leave in the Lukon PT 22. Lorin checked her roster with the passengers who were on board and decided everyone was accounted for. She nodded to the pilot, Evohn Cystrom, who was watching her from the cockpit and then closed the hatch. The plane immediately began taxiing down the runway. Soon they were in the air and circling back over the base. Two fighters were flying with them as escorts. General Zitor pulled a small control device out of his pocket. He looked out the window at LB 1 and shook his head. Then he pushed the red button on his controller and a series of explosions ripped across the island. Beneath them LB1 lay in ruins.

"What about the Nanomites?" Lucinda asked. "Did you evacuate them?"

"Yes. They were relocated immediately after they'd finished building the base. They're already at work in Tributon."

"Good. I'm glad you had the foresight to do that. Peter would be upset if anything happened to them."

"You needn't worry. There are many capable people in Loyalist Command," Lorin said icily.

Lucinda was hurt by her sarcasm, but didn't say anything. She didn't understand the reason for Lorin's occasional show of resentment. She'd detected it before when Lorin and Peter had been together. Lorin didn't exactly like Peter, that was obvious. It was some political game Lorin was playing. Lucinda hadn't thought much about politics in the past. The focus of her life had been her mate, her job, and her desire to be a mother. Now, suddenly everything had changed. By consenting to mate with Peter, she had become a Loyalist and would be killed if she were ever caught by the TGA. Why had she let this happened? Fear crept over her like the morning mist. Why hadn't she said no when Lorin came to see her? She was safe in Shisk. The civil war wouldn't have effected her all that much. She could have had her baby and lived in peace, oblivious to the struggle around her. Now she'd been thrust into a world of uncertainty and fear. What kind of spell had this boy from Earth cast upon her? But, she knew if Lorin came to her now and offered her safe passage back to Shisk, she'd refuse, no matter what sacrifices she'd have to make or inconveniences she'd be forced to endure to be with Peter. Their lives had become inextricably intertwined and neither of them would ever be happy without the other safe and close at hand.

As Lucinda was thinking, she heard the pilot tell Lorin that they were flying between Muhl and Ock Mezan. She knew that had to be a dangerous part of the flight as both Muhl and Ock Mezan were under TGA's control.

"Any sign of the enemy?" Lorin asked.

"No," Evohn replied. "We're traveling at 55,000 feet so it's unlikely they'll see us."

"I hope you're right, but they must suspect we'll be flying this way."

"I'll let you know if I see anything."

Lorin started to leave the cockpit when a light began flashing on the control panel and an alarm buzzer went off. Lorin stopped and looked at Evohn. "What's that?"

"Oh, God have mercy! There's a missile locked on to us. Twenty tiks to impact."

"What! Can't you do something?"

"*I* can't, but maybe somebody else can."

Evohn picked up his mic and said, "E1, we've got a Muscan coming at us. Can you intercept?"

"Will do, Com 1. Break hard right."

Evohn thrust the control stick to the right and the plane made a hard turn. The escort fighter came at them and had it not been for the hard right turn, they would have collided. The escort was now flying directly at the Muscan missile. Suddenly there was a burst of light from the fighters wings. Two tiks later the Muscan missile exploded into oblivion.

"Oh, Sandee!" Evohn said. "That was close."

"Yeah, and now that they know our location we'll be sitting ducks," Lorin complained.

General Zitor stepped up to the cockpit. Lorin moved aside so he could talk to the pilot. She shook her head and went back to her seat.

"Lt. Cystrom, isn't it?" the general asked.

"Yes, sir."

"Well, Lieutenant. That was a close call. What's the maximum altitude this plane can fly?"

"It's certified to 75,000 feet."

"Then why are we flying at 55,000 feet?"

"I didn't think it was necessary to go that high, sir."

"Obviously, it is."

"Yes, sir."

The general backed out of the cockpit, turned, and returned to his seat. Lucinda folded her arms in a vain attempt to stop them from shaking. Lorin noticed her trembling and went to her.

"You all right?"

Lucinda swallowed hard. "Yeah, I'm fine. Don't worry about me."

"What about your baby? Does the turbulence upset him?"

"A little. He's been kicking a lot. I'm sure he senses the danger."

"He's probably more upset with the altitude change," Lorin said. "Flying this high has to be a major shock to his system."

"How much longer until we get to our destination?"

"A few kyloons," Lorin replied. "Try to sleep. It will make time go faster."

Lucinda nodded and Lorin went back to the cockpit.

"How we doing?" she asked Lt. Cystrom.

"No sign of the enemy, but take a look to your left."

Lorin looked out the left window and saw a large island shaped like a clenched fist.

"That's Pogo. If we're going to be attacked before we get to Tributon it's going to come from there."

"Can you give it a wider berth?" Lorin asked.

"No, that will take us off course and we won't have enough fuel to make it to Tributon. We've got to stay on course."

Lorin sighed. "All right. Let me know if you see anything suspicious."

"Yes, ma'am."

Lorin returned to her seat. She thought about Jake and wondered where he was at that moment. She felt fairly certain he was okay. After all, if he'd been shot down she would have heard about it by then. Logic, however, wasn't always all that comforting. Jake could just as easily have crashed somewhere and be dead or seriously injured. She tried to clear her mind. She needed to be thinking about Threebeard and her meeting with the Mutant generals. She couldn't afford to be distracted. She took a deep breath, closed her eyes, and tried to relax. Her fatigue suddenly hit her. She hadn't slept the night before the battle and she was exhausted. Sleep now, she thought, it will be five kyloons before we get to Tributon. Sleep now, it may be the last chance you get for God knows how long.

Lorin wasn't the only one who was exhausted and had succumbed to slumber. In fact, only Lt. Cystrom and Lucinda were awake when the PT22 started its descent over eastern Quori well short of Tributon. Lucinda looked out the window to see if their fighter escorts were still there, but she didn't see them.

A sudden pocket of turbulence shook the plane harshly. Lorin woke up and looked around sleepily. Seeing her awake, Lucinda smiled. "It's a lot smoother at 75,000 feet."

Lorin looked out the window and then at her watch. "We shouldn't be descending yet."

"Yeah, I wondered about that. Where are our escorts?"

Lorin frowned and put a hand on General Zitor who was seated next to her.

The General sat up with a start. "What?"

"Sir. We may have a problem," Lorin whispered.

"What sort of problem?"

"It seems our pilot is taking us off course."

The General looked up to the cockpit. "Well, let's find out what's going on," he said getting up quickly.

"Careful, General. We don't know what we're dealing with here."

The General nodded and proceeded to the cockpit. Before he made it there, however, one of the flight crew pulled a gun from his flight suit and stuck it in the General's face.

"What the hell!" the General protested.

"Get back to your seat."

"Who do you think you're talking to, soldier?" the General protested.

The soldier hit the General hard with the butt of the revolver and pushed him back into his seat. Several of the command staff had now

291

awakened and were up and starting to pull their weapons. From behind them another soldier brandishing a laser pistol said, "Sit back down! Put you weapons on the floor in the aisle!"

The General motioned for them to comply, so they all carefully drew their weapons and placed them on the carpet in the center aisle of the plane. After they'd returned to their places the soldier said, "Now sit down and relax for the duration of the flight. And don't even think about trying anything."

Lorin just looked at the soldier in shock. "What do you want?" she demanded.

"I want you to shut up!" He replied then turned to Lucinda and handed her a large cloth bag. "Gather up the weapons in this bag."

Lucinda took the bag, quickly gathered the variety of weapons the command staff had surrendered, and handed it to the soldier. He refused it pointing instead to an empty seat behind where he was standing. Lucinda took the bag to the seat the dropped it there. When she tried to go back to her seat the soldier grabbed her and wrestled her into the seat next to him.

After she quit resisting and was sitting quietly he said, "If anybody causes any more trouble we'll kill this pretty mate here, and I don't think the Liberator will like that much."

Lorin let out a gasp. "Leave her alone! She's not part of this."

The soldier who'd just struck General Zitor pointed his gun at Lorin. "Sit down and shut up! I doubt the Councillor would like me to put a bullet in his daughter's head."

Lorin's mouth dropped. She realized all this was a carefully orchestrated kidnaping. There was a traitor in their ranks and she knew who it was; Lt. Cystrom. Only he could have done this and these pointing guns at them were his men he'd brought from Pogo. As she was thinking this, the plane made a hard landing throwing the kidnapers off balance. She thought about trying to take one of the soldier's guns, but knew if she did Lucinda might die. Could she live with that? Probably, she thought, but by thinking about it she lost her window of opportunity. It was too late now. The plane was gliding smoothly to a halt.

When Lt. Cystrom stepped out of the cockpit Lorin spat on him. "You traitor! I thought you hated Videl. He didn't kill your father, did he?"

Lt. Cystrom laughed. "No. I never knew my father. He died when I was a child. But I'm not the traitor. You're the ones who have rebelled against the lawful government of Tarizon. You're the ones who have committed treason and you will all die for it."

"You're going to kill us without a trial?" General Zitor said bitterly. "We have a right under the Supreme Mandate to a trial."

"Well, since the rebellion certain rights and liberties have been temporarily suspended, in case you've been out of touch. One of them is the right to a public trial. You'll be tried but it will be by a military tribunal and justice will be swift."

"When will it happen?" Lorin asked.

"Just as soon as my father comes. He wants to see you all die for your crimes."

"Your father?" Lorin repeated.

"Yes. Well, not my natural father. Chancellor Lai raised me as his son. He was very good to me, so when rumors of a conspiracy against him led by this so called Liberator began to circulate I asked my father how I could help stop him. He said I should find this Liberator and join his cause."

"Leek thought you might be a traitor," Lucinda said. "But Sgt. Baig vouched for you."

"Yes, well Sgt. Baig's a fool. He thought we didn't know of his treasonous intentions, but we did, so we told him what we wanted the Liberator to believe."

"What I don't understand," Lorin said. "is why you didn't contact your father and give him our position. Had he known it the TGA could have destroyed us."

"Unfortunately, I had no way to communicate with him, so I did the best I could," Lt. Cystrom noted. "Don't you think he'll be pleased, though, under the circumstances—capturing the Councillor's daughter, a traitorous general, and the Liberator's mate?"

"You won't get away with this,"Lorin said. "Our plane was being tracked. Our soldiers will be here soon to rescue us."

Lt. Cystrom laughed. "Sorry to crush your hopes, but your escorts were destroyed. There's no rescue party on their way here to save you. Nobody knows where you are and there's no one close enough to pick up the signal from your plane's E-box. So, just as soon as Videl gets here you *will* die. You will all die for your treason to the people of Tarizon!"

37

A Hollow Victory

When Lortec was out of sight, Peter reported in to command to find out the outcome of the battle. He learned that early assessments indicated that they'd killed or wounded nearly seventy-eight percent of the TGA forces on Lortec. Most of the munitions stored on the island had been destroyed or spent in the battle. Seventy-five percent of the TGA planes were eliminated by the bombers, the ground team, and in aerial combat. The Loyalists had lost thirty-two fighters and three bombers. Clearly they had been the victor in this battle, but the day wasn't done.

Command reported to Peter that the location of their base had definitely been compromised and several TGA aircraft carriers and battleships were headed toward LB1. He was warned that the submarines were already there lurking about the waters around the island. Accordingly, a full evacuation of the base was in progress and Peter and his unit could not return there. Their instructions were to find a deserted island, anchor, and wait for further instructions.

Peter's heart sank into bitter despair. He wondered what had become of Lucinda? Was she okay? When would he see her again? He'd asked these questions to the communications officer who had taken his call, but he had gotten no answers. He'd have to wait to hear from command in a few days when the evacuation and base relocation was complete. Then they'd get their orders and find out where to report.

They cruised for several more hours until they came to an island that the captain thought was deserted. He pulled them into a small cove and dropped the anchor. Before nightfall they rowed a small boat with Sy's body in it to shore. After finding a suitable location, they dug a grave and buried him. Red made a crude headstone out of scrap wood on the boat. It read: *Here lies Syril Johs who died in the first battle to save the Supreme Mandate. Sandee be with him.* As the sun was setting in the west, everyone on the ship gathered at the grave to pay their last respects. Peter spoke first.

"Sy was the most courageous person I have ever met," he said. "He was always the first to volunteer for any assignment no matter how dangerous it was. He always wanted to be point man—in the thick of battle at all times. . . . He was fiercely loyal to his friends and to the Supreme Mandate. Although I only knew him a short while, I will always consider him one of my closest friends. I will miss him."

When Peter was finished, Red stepped up. "Sy was like a brother to me. As you know, I'm the nervous one in the group—the 'chicken' as they say on Earth. As Leek said, Sy was the complete opposite. He had incredible courage. But Sy was also very patient and compassionate. He never chastised me for my fears, but instead assured me everything would be okay and not to fear the future. May Sandee be with you, my brother. Rest in tranquility."

Red stepped back and Tam came forward. He stood there in silence a moment before he spoke. "What I liked most about Sy was his sense of humor. I guess that's how he handled stress. He'd make a joke of a bad situation and put everyone at ease. And he was a man you could trust. I never worried about him covering my back when times got tough. My biggest regret is that I only knew him for such a short time. He's the kind of friend you want to have for a lifetime."

After the memorial they set up camp on shore. With submarines lurking about they didn't feel safe aboard ship. It was early evening, so the captain made a fire and his crew made supper. It was quiet around the campfire. They had just lost a friend and nobody felt much like talking. It was strange for Peter sitting out in the middle of nowhere with nothing to do. It had been non-stop action since he'd left for Muhl. Now there was too much time to think and worry about what would become of them. Was the Loyalist cause lost? Where would they move the base? Was there a even a ghost of a chance they could defeat Videl with his vastly superior forces? Peter finally decided some conversation might be better than continuing to worry and going slowly insane.

"Those Seafolken were amazing," Peter said.

"Yes, I've heard stories about them," Red replied. "I thought it was all just a myth, but I was wrong. Did you see them pick the bullets out of their skin?"

"Yes. So, if they are so powerful and impossible to kill, why don't they rule Tarizon?" Peter asked.

Tam replied, "They do rule the sea, actually, and it is said they do so with justice and wisdom. But who cares about what goes on beneath the ocean?"

"So, how did they become slaves? How were they conquered?" Peter asked.

"Well," Tam replied, "they've always been a peaceful life form without political ambitions. They only ruled the sea because the lesser life forms asked them to. You see, if they didn't take charge, the ocksharks would rule and they were an evil species who delighted in killing and murdering other beings. Luckily the Seafolken were invincible and even the Ocksharks dared not challenge them. The Ocksharks, I understand, have allied themselves with Videl."

"That figures," Peter said. "So, you didn't answer my question. How did Central Authority enslave the Seafolken if they were invincible?"

"Yes, sorry. It was technology that brought the Seafolken to their knees. You see their abilities are all from nature, bestowed by the will of Sandee. They are happy with the domain that God built for them and had no need for technology. So, initially Central Authority left them alone, until they figured out a way to kill them."

"How do they kill them?"

"Well, you saw that bullets could not pierce the Seafolken's thick skin?"

"Yes."

"Well, the scientists worked on that and came up with a split-finger bulletbomb."

"What's that?" Peter asked.

"It's a bullet that is really a combination bullet and bomb. The front of the bulletbomb is a traditional bullet and fires normally. The bullet lodges in the target and then a tik later the other end of the bullet explodes. That's why you saw the Seafolken picking out the bullets that lodged in the skin and casting them aside. They were afraid they might be bulletbombs. If you're quick you can yank them out before they explode. Of course, you might lose a hand or a finger in the process."

"Hmm."

"Anyway, as I was saying, it was the great volcanic eruptions that drew them out of the sea. The sea became so polluted that the fish they usually fed on couldn't survive. At first Central Authority fed them as a humanitarian gesture, but soon they demanded service from the Seafolken in exchange for food. Eventually it turned to slavery and those who refused were killed.

"That's why the Seafolken love to go to Earth. While they are there they get to feed in the clear rivers and lakes there. The sea around Lortec is almost back to normal so the Seafolken who have been lucky enough to escape bondage have come here to live."

When the fire went out and everyone finally went to bed, Peter couldn't sleep. The ground was just too hard to get comfortable. Every position he tried soon became painful. When he did get into a tolerable position, he'd start to worry about Lucinda, his family back on Earth, or Sy. He wondered where Sy was that night. With God? He prayed that was the case.

It was a long night but the sun did rise the next morning and, as usually was the case, with the new day came new hope. The despair of the previous day was replaced with determination to go on and to ultimately defeat Videl no matter what it took.

38
Glacier Dome

Luckily their new orders came around midday. They were to sail southeast to Glacier Dome. This news surprised Peter because Glacier Dome was a cold and barren place. How could they muster an Army in such an inhospitable location? But who was he to question command? He figured they must know what they were doing so he made no protest. Perhaps the isolation of the location made it the perfect hiding place.

They waited until nightfall before setting off for Glacier Dome. They sailed without running lights and on radio silence. They didn't want to make it easy for any submarines to spot them. Hopefully the subs had moved on and they'd have clear sailing to their new destination. It was a good day's journey to Glacier Dome so they used the extra time to catch up on their sleep. It was likely the moment they reached their new base that command would have them off on another assignment.

Peter wondered if Lucinda would be waiting for him when they arrived. In his heart he doubted he'd be so lucky. It was more likely she had been shipped back to Shisk where she'd be safe—or would she be safe anywhere now that she was the Liberator's mate? Suddenly a great fear overwhelmed Peter. Would Lucinda now be another target for Videl's assassins? He felt like breaking radio silence and demanding to know where she was but, of course, he couldn't do that and jeopardize the crew and his squad. All Peter could do was pray and hope that God or Sandee heard him.

When Peter awoke the next morning and went out on deck, it was very cold. Even with a heavy jacket on he was freezing. The sea was half frozen and they were cruising through some sort of channel where the ice had been cleared. He asked the captain how much longer it would be and he said they'd be there before nightfall. As they continued on he marveled at the beauty of the glaciers and the ice-covered mountains in the distance. As he was taking in the scenery he noticed a flash of light from behind them. He watched it for awhile until he realized it was a submarine periscope. They were being followed!

The captain didn't flinch when Peter told him what he'd seen. He said he'd spotted them several hours earlier. When Peter suggested he may not want to lead them to their new base, he laughed. "There's no base out here. Do you really think command would move us to a place like this?"

Peter shrugged. "Well, I did think it a little odd."

"No," the captain said, "command knew you were being followed so they sent us down here to mislead the TGA."

Peter frowned. "Aren't you worried when they discover your deception that they'll sink us with a torpedo?"

"No, they don't care about this piece of scrap iron. Besides, it will be a long time before they discover the truth. We're going to make them think we are setting up a base down here."

"How are we going to do that?"

"Well, we've got several transport planes and a couple of fighters down here. You and your squad are going to be doing a lot of flying."

"Where to?"

"Ledium is about thirty kylods from here. You'll be flying back and forth from there. Each time you land we'll change the call numbers on your planes so that the observers from the submarine will think a lot of different planes are flying in supplies and personnel. Or course, the planes will be empty."

Peter chuckled at the brilliance of the strategist at Loyalist command. While the TGA was mounting a force to attack a non-existent enemy base, the Loyalists were thousands of kylods away getting ready for their next offensive. He wondered where that would be. If word had gotten out about the Loyalist victory on Lortec by now there were bound to have been a lot more defections to the Loyalists' cause.

Flying a transport between two islands six times a day wasn't Peter idea of excitement, but he understood the need to do it. During their layovers they'd often watch the flocks of leaprohds along the coastline. They were a fascinating breed scurrying along the ice at breakneck speed. He wondered where they were going and why they traveled so fast. He wished he had the time to follow them and find out.

When Peter wasn't watching leaprohds, he was longing to find out what had happened to Lucinda. It was pure torture to have seen her so briefly and then been forced to leave her once again. Their communication with Loyalist command was minimal at best, so they had no idea what was happening in the war with Videl. Peter was overcome with a deep depression as the hours dragged on at Glacier Dome. He prayed for a new assignment that would get him back in the war where we could actually fight and do some good.

Fortunately, that day finally came five days later, although to Peter it had seemed like a fifty. The captain brought orders and handed Peter his. He ripped open the envelope and glanced over them. He was to report to Shini, the capital of Rigimol, in a few days for the investiture of Councillor Robert Garcia as Chancellor of the Loyalist provisional government. He knew this was the first step in creating a new government to rule the territories controlled by the Loyalist military and eventually to replace Videl's government once it was defeated. Red and Tam's orders were identical. Lotis and Curillo were ordered to remain on duty at Glacier Dome.

Peter was glad to be leaving Glacier Dome. It was a beautiful place but far too cold and remote for his taste. Being from Texas he was used to hot weather most of the year and hated the cold. They flew out of Glacier Dome that afternoon in one of their transport planes. Their first stop was Lortec. After the devastating attack on the base there, the TGA had apparently decided they couldn't defend it anymore and had evacuated the Island. They moved what was left of their troops and aircraft to Ock Mezan and Muhl. This left Lortec for the taking and gave the Loyalist command a base of operations in the Southern Sea. Peter also learned that soon after the Battle of Lortec, the TGA had launched all out assaults on the Loyalist bases in Tributon but were unable to destroy them. Because of these two successive TGA defeats there had been massive defections to the Loyalist cause and now two of the biggest countries on the continent of Lamaine Shane, Rigimol and Tributon, were loosely controlled by the Loyalists.

Lortec was in shambles from the previous air assault, forcing Peter and his men to land on a makeshift landing strip. Peter inquired around as to what had happened to the personnel at LB1 but nobody knew or, if they did, they weren't talking. He even got on his GC and tried to raise Lorin at her direct number, but she didn't answer his call. Peter thought that strange because she'd always had her GC with her and had never yet failed to respond to his call.

Peter and his unit were assigned for the night at one of the few barracks still standing after the battle. They were well fed and got a good night's sleep. The next day they were scheduled to fly to Rigimol. It would be a long dangerous flight over enemy territory. Fortunately, there were three T47s for them to transport up there, so they would be able to fly in stealth mode undetected. Just as they were about to go to their planes, they were summoned to the base commander's office. They were greeted by the officer in charge, Colonel Brazzel.

"Lieutenant Lanzia, before you go there is something you should know," Colonel Brazzel said. "Some of our command personnel traveling up to Shini for the investiture are missing. They were last reported near the coast of Allso!"

"Do you have any idea what happened to them, sir?"

"No, we knew something was wrong when they failed to make a scheduled stop in Tributon to meet with General Threebeard and his staff. They should have been there eight days ago. Usually they show up on radar about three hours before landing, but control tower personnel have advised us that they never made contact with them."

"How many in the party?"

"Seventeen. General Zitor, Lorin, a few aides, the flight crew and . . . ah, well . . . I'm sorry to say, but your mate was on board too."

"My mate? Lucinda? My Lucinda was on the plane!"

"Yes, I'm afraid so," Colonel Brazzel replied.

"Oh, Jesus. No!, " Peter winced. "What kind of plane were they in?"

"A Lukon PT22."

"What's that?"

"It's a small troop transport plane. It carries up to twenty-five passengers. Very fast and it can fly at altitudes up to 75,000 feet."

"I can't believe this! What gave them the idea they could fly twenty-five hundred kylods through enemy airspace? That's suicide."

"It's done all the time. At that altitude it's rare that anyone would detect them."

"When there's no war, sure. But now the TGA is keeping a close eye on the sky. I hope they weren't alone."

"No. There were two T47s escorting them."

"Two? Is that all," Peter asked shaking his head. "And you haven't heard from any of them either?"

"No. I'm sorry."

"Oh, God!" he said. He was sick inside. If they were alive he figured they could be anywhere in radius of 500 kylods from Allso. That was a lot of territory to search. Peter paced back and forth trying to think. He was so upset he could hardly breathe. "

Tam said, "We'll have to search for them."

"Yes, that's what we want you to do on your way to Shini," Colonel Brazzel said, "but you only have one day. You must be at the investiture on time."

"One day?" Peter protested. "Give me a break. You're asking us to search an area the size of Texas in one day? Can't they do the investiture without us?"

"Actually no. You're the Liberator, don't forget. You're the hope of the Loyalist movement. You've got to be there."

Peter just stared at the Colonel in disbelief. Loyalist command apparently thought his presence at a ceremonial political event was more important than rescuing three of their top military strategists. Of course they didn't care about Lucinda, but certainly General Zitor, his staff, and Lorin were far more important to the Loyalist cause than he was. Peter took a deep breath. There was no use arguing. Colonel Brazzel was just following orders and there wasn't time to try to get them changed.

"Doesn't the plane have a tracking device for emergencies like this?"

"Yes, an E-box, but it hasn't been generating a signal."

"How is that? Don't they make those things indestructible?"

"Yes and they have a backup system too. The antenna may have been damaged on the primary unit. If so, the backup system should be operational but it only has a range of fifty kylods or so."

"50 kylods. So, we'll have to make a 50 kylod grid and fly each line. If the tracking device is working then we'll eventually pick up the signal."

"What about fuel?" Red asked. "That's a lot of flying."

The base commander replied, "There's a refueling drone on a low orbit between Pogo and Allso. It belongs to the TGA but I've got the access codes."

"It's unmanned?" Tam asked.

"Yes, no one will bother you unless—"

"Unless what?" Peter asked.

"Unless, you just accidentally get there when a TGA aircraft is refueling."

"Great," Red said. "That will be our luck."

"How did you get the access codes?"

"Before Videl seized power the drone was under my command. So that's why I have the codes."

"You don't think they changed the codes when people started defecting?"

"I doubt it. It's mainly used for aircraft that ferry passengers between our two moons. The civil war hasn't got into outer space yet and that's not likely to happen any time soon."

Red didn't seem convinced the codes would still work and Peter felt the same way. They'd be taking a big chance flying all that way and then not be able to refuel. Yet, the commander knew the TGA inside and out and he seemed convinced this was a loose end nobody would have fixed. They had no choice but to trust his gut instinct. Besides, Lorin meant a lot to Peter and he couldn't live without Lucinda. He couldn't just sit around and do nothing.

Peter said, "So, when do we leave?"

39

Rescue

Before they left to search for the downed plane, the base commander advised them that if they found the plane and needed help rescuing the passengers there were some allies in southern Tributon that they could call upon for help. He said to go to a city called Gulh and find a tavern called the Mighty Jolly. The name sounded familiar but Peter couldn't remember why. He said the place was owned by a mutant and he would help them. Then it hit him. Threebeard had a tavern by that name, but it was in Shisk. Peter wondered if he owned this one as well. Peter was glad to hear there was help waiting in the wings, because when they found the plane there was no telling what they'd be up against. They no doubt would need all the help they could muster. At least Peter hoped that was the case. He didn't know what he would do if they found the wreckage and everyone was dead. That was too horrible a thought to even contemplate, so he purged it from his mind.

When they finally got to their planes they fed the grid into the onboard computers and prepared for takeoff. Tam and Peter were flying T47s but they gave Red a PT22 in case they found the missing plane and there were survivors. Red complained that he'd never trained on this plane, but they finally convinced him flying it wasn't much different than the T47s.

The PT22 could only travel at Mach 2, so it would slow them down. At Mach 2 it would take them several hours to get to the search zone. Then they'd start flying the grid lines. He figured he'd have to refuel about midway through their search. That would be interesting and a little scary. A lot of things could go wrong, assuming the access codes even worked.

Soon they were in the air and flying low over the Southern Sea. They decided to stay clear of Ock Mezan as they knew the TGA had a large force there. They thought they could probably fly over it safely but then TGA command would know they were in the air and could try to find them. Their plan was to fly over the water between Muhl and Ock Mezan and then swing northeast across the Coral Sea until they were 600 kylods due east of Pogo. Their search would begin there. Peter just prayed the E-box was functioning properly.

As Peter watched the sea fly by below him, he thought of Lucinda and his baby and prayed they were alive. In his mind's eye he imagined every possible scenario that could explain their disappearance. They might have had mechanical problems and been forced to land. They could have run out of fuel. If either of these things had happened they'd find them alive and all would be well. Conversely, they could have crashed or been captured. Of these possibilities, Peter hoped it was capture. If they were alive there was still hope. They could rescue them.

The horrible feeling in the pit of Peter's stomach that he'd been suffering with ever since he'd heard that Lucinda was missing, was getting worse by the minute. He couldn't wait to get to the search zone. He knew he'd feel better once he was actually doing something to try to find them. Traveling at Mach 2 was very agonizing. They could have already been there had they not been instructed to stay with the PT22.

Looking at their navigation systems Peter saw that they were finally coming up on the grid. The hunt was about to begin. At the edge of the grid Red went straight, following the center line. Tam and Peter split left and right and covered the first two parallel grid lines. They each had their receivers tuned into the frequency of the E-box and listened carefully for the signal.

They had six vertical lines and six horizontal lines to cover. They heard nothing from the receivers while traveling on the horizontal grid lines and were about to start on the vertical lines when Peter noticed he was getting low on fuel. He said through his communicator, "Time to find mother so we can feed the babies."

"Affirmative," Red said. "I'm nearly empty too."

"Follow me," Peter said breaking out of the grid and setting his navigator to the coordinates of the orbital fueling drone. As they were climbing, Peter kept a close eye out for enemy fighters. He knew they could run across one at any time. When he saw the drone in the distance he pulled a piece of paper out of his pocket with the access codes on them. He prayed they'd work because if they didn't they'd have to land in enemy territory.

Just as he was about to move in on the drone, Peter spotted an aircraft above him. "Back off, enemy aircraft at fifteen degrees. Stand down," Peter said into his communicator.

"Copy, R1, standing down," Red said.

"Copy, R1," Tam said.

"I wonder if he's alone," Peter said.

"If he is we can take him out," Tam replied.

"If he spots us, we're in deep trouble," Red warned.

"Yeah, and if a plane goes missing that's almost as bad as being spotted. Let's keep away for awhile and hope he's not paying attention to his radar."

"Acknowledged," Tam said.

They waited at a safe distance until Peter's fuel warning light started blinking. "Shit, I'm going to have to go in now. If he's still around one of you are gonna have to take him out."

"Not me," Tam said. "My light's been flashing for 60 tiks."

"I've got fuel, but I'm not armed," Red said. "You two go in and I'll pray to Sandee."

"Acknowledged," Peter said, and started to make a move on the drone.

There were two lines flowing out from the fueling drone. Red went left and Peter went right. After they'd locked on Peter held his breath and punched in the code. Nothing happened for a moment and his heart nearly stopped. Then a green light came on and Peter heard the rush of fuel coming into the fuel tanks.

"Thank you God and Sandee," Peter said. "That was a close call."

"Oh, durk birds! Our friend is back," Red said. "What should I do?"

"Crap," Peter replied. "Ah . . . try to lure him away from us so we can finish refueling."

"But what if he locks on to me. I have no defenses."

"Wait," Tam said. "No one's had time to change the markings on these planes. He doesn't know if we're friend or foe. Maybe we can bluff him."

307

"I doubt I can," Peter said, "but go ahead and give it a try."

"He'll be on frequency 24. I'll switch over and try to make contact."

"Copy, God be with you," Peter said.

Peter switched over to frequency 24 and waited. After a moment Tam came on the air, "T47 approaching drone, please identify."

"Liberty one here," he replied.

"Haven't you already sucked on mama?" Tam said.

"Affirmative, just checking to see who was feeding," he replied. "Wasn't told anybody was out this way."

"We're on escort duty. On our way to Shisk—got some brass going to a meeting. After the disaster at Lortec everybody is scrambling."

"Heard about that. Okay. Have a good flight."

"Where are you headed?" Tam asked.

"Just my regular patrol. Looking for anybody going north to Rigimol—big Loyalist party starting soon."

"You out to spoil the party?" Tam said.

"That's my orders."

"Good luck."

The radio went dead and Peter switched back to frequency 21. "You think he bought it," Peter asked.

"Don't know," Tam said. "I'll watch him on my radar."

Red said, "He's moving away pretty fast. I think we're okay."

"I'm full," Tam said, "Breaking off."

"Me too," Peter said. "Red, get on the line and then let's get back on the grid."

"Affirmative, approaching line," Red said. "This shouldn't take long."

Moments later they were on their way back to the grid. If the E-box was working, Peter thought, one of them should be picking up the signal soon. It was just a matter of time now, he told himself. As Peter soared along the grid line he wondered if Lucinda and Lorin were still alive. He couldn't fathom the possibility that they would be dead. Lorin had hated him in the beginning, but that had changed. Peter thought she at least respected him now and he'd always had nothing but the greatest admiration for her. She was smart, determined, and fiercely loyal to her beliefs—and she wasn't hard to look at either.

"I've got a signal," Red said excitedly.

"Where are you?" Peter asked.

Red gave them his coordinates and Peter changed his course to intercept him. When they all had met up they followed the signal until they had a ground location. It was near the southeast corner of Allso which was a thick jungle area. Allso was on the equator and very hot and wet most of the time. It wasn't going to be easy even to find a place to land.

As they flew over where they thought the signal had come they were astonished to see a large clearing in the midst of the jungle. As they approached they saw a huge military complex and a runway. Near the runway Peter spotted what he believed to be the plane Lucinda and the others had been on when they left Lortec. His pulse quickened. *They were alive!*

They didn't dare do another run over the base. That would attract too much attention. Peter thought about what he'd seen as they flew by. There were many barracks, several fighters, an armory, headquarters building, and a parade ground. The base also was completely surrounded by a ten foot steel fence. This wouldn't be an easy rescue. They'd need help.

The base commander had told them if they needed help to go to Gulh and find a tavern called the Mighty Jolly. They inputted the location of Gulh on the computer and set on a course northeast. To get to Gulh they had to cross Quori which was TGA territory, so they went to stealth mode until they'd crossed the Tributon border. When they got close to the airport they radioed in for clearance. The air traffic controller welcomed them and gave them clearance to land.

Gulh didn't have many Loyalist troops but the local commander did manage to send them over a couple of local transport vehicles to take them around to where they needed to go and offered bunks in the barracks for them to rest. After eating and getting a little shut-eye, they proceeded to the Mighty Jolly Tavern. Much to Peter's surprise and delight, Threebeard met them at the door. He introduced them to Tam and Red.

"We meet again, Liberator," Threebeard said.

"What are you doing here?" Peter asked. "The last time me met it was in a place like this in Shisk."

"I'm afraid I had to abandon the Mighty Jolly in Shisk. The last I heard, Videl was arresting any mutants he could find and shipping them off to work camps. He'll use the ones that can to help the war effort and exterminate the rest."

Peter winced at the thought. "It's hard to believe anyone could be so evil."

"For you, perhaps, but Tarizon has no shortage of evil men."

"Well, I guess you know why we are here then," Peter said.

Threebeard smiled and replied, "To summon your army I hope."

"Yes, I'll need some men to help rescue General Zitor, Lorin Boskie, and my mate, Lucinda."

"Lucinda. Didn't I meet her?" Threebeard asked.

"Yes. You did."

"So quickly you found love."

"Yes, but we've had just two brief meetings since I left Shisk. I've got to find her."

"And we must rescue the Councillor's daughter and General Zitor before they are tortured and give up critical information about the Loyalist organization," Threebeard said. "They were on their way here to meet with me when their plane went missing."

"Yes, we found their plane. It appears to have been diverted somehow and is sitting on the ground in southwest Allso. I don't know now they managed to intercept it unless they had a spy at LB1."

"When I talked to General Zitor he said he thought there was a spy on the base."

"Yes, that's what he told me, too. I don't know—"

"The spy must have been on the plane and commandeered it."

Peter thought about that idea and it made sense. "Yes, that would explain everything. We've got to hurry. I can't bear to think that they might be torturing them for information."

"They won't be torturing Lucinda. They know she knows nothing. Likely they'll think she's the Liberator's Achilles heel."

"Achilles heel? You read Greek mythology?"

"No. Remember, I download all your American movies. Very good stuff. Don't pay royalties, though. I guess that makes me a pirate, right?"

"I wouldn't worry about it. I don't think they'll be sending the FBI after you."

Threebeard laughed hard. "No, no FBI."

"So, what do you think they'll do to her?" Peter said almost afraid to hear the answer.

"I don't know, perhaps just keep her from you so you will be angry and lose your focus. She'd also make a nice prize for Videl to show off to his friends and allies."

Peter shook his head. "That scumbag! He just wants to torture me."

"Yes," Threebeard said, "and you are right; we must go now before it is too late. . . . Your army is ready."

Peter nodded and replied, "Good. When do I meet them?"

"The ones you need for this mission will meet you at the airport before sunset."

"Good. Will you be there?"

Threebeard shook his head. "No, I've been asked to go up to the investiture. I'm no warrior, anyway. I would just hinder your rescue. The men that will meet you are extraordinary soldiers who will serve you well. When you take off tonight you can inspect your army. They will salute you as you leave so you will know they are with you."

"Before you go, could I ask one favor of you," Peter said.

"Anything. Just name it," Threebeard replied.

"I was told you can talk to the Nanomites and that you have showed others with telepathic abilities how to do it."

"Yes, that is true, but I regret it now since Central Authority used my pupils to exploit them."

"I know, but if I'm going to lead them, I need to be able to talk to them."

"Yes, you are right. I should teach you how to fully exploit your telepathic abilities. Unfortunately, there's so little time." Threebeard thought for a moment. "I guess I could postpone my flight. We'd have all night then, but you'd be exhausted for your mission."

"It's okay. I can sleep later. This is important."

"Indeed it is. Then I'll give you a lesson tonight."

Peter smiled. "That would be great. Thank you."

"I must caution you, though. Not everyone can talk to the Nanomites. I went through hundreds of persons claiming telepathic abilities until I found one strong enough to speak to the Nanomites."

"Rupra Bruda," Peter said.

"Yes. So, you've heard the story?"

"Un huh. From Colonel Tomel. He said Bruda helped Videl enslave the Nanomites."

"Actually, it was the other way around. Bruda was Videl's mentor. He was much older than Videl and was a master of telepathy and telekinesis. Bruda tried to teach Videl those disciplines but he didn't have the natural capacity to learn them. He did manage to fill his mind with evil and hatred, though."

"So, was Bruda the founder of the Purist Party?" Peter asked.

"Yes, he could claim that as much as any man."

"So, why did you teach him how to contact the Nanomites?"

"I was under orders from Central Authority to do it and, regrettably, I followed those orders. Now Rupra Bruda is Videl's bodyguard and closest confidant."

"So, he's telekinetic? You have that ability, right?"

"Yes."

"Do those with telepathic abilities have telekinetic ability too?" Peter asked.

"Not always, but often if you have one gift you'll also have the other. Telekinesis is much more difficult to master, I'm afraid."

Peter nodded. He wondered if he could make objects move. He'd never tried it or even thought about it.

"Well, I hope I don't meet up with Bruda any time soon. He sounds like he's out of my league."

"For now he is, but that may change," Threebeard said. "We'll see how well you do tonight. I'm anxious to see the extent of your abilities."

"Don't expect much," Peter laughed. "It's all been pretty much trial and error, so far."

"Trial and error is a dangerous way to learn, particularly when your adversary is a master at the game. After the briefing tonight we'll get started and perhaps I can show you enough that you, at least, won't make any fatal errors. Go get some sleep now. You'll need your strength tomorrow."

Peter said goodbye and left to go back to the airport. Peter wondered what kind of a fighting force Threebeard had for him. Knowing Threebeard's reputation, it would be quite extraordinary. When they arrived back at the barracks Peter went straight to bed. He was exhausted and if he was lucky he'd get four hours sleep before Threebeard arrived for the briefing.

When he awoke Tam and Red were waiting to go to dinner. When they were finished they went to the airport for the briefing. The fighting force waiting there was impressive; three choppers, each carrying thirty-two tough-looking soldiers loaded down with an assortment of guns and ammunition.

The soldiers were mutants, which didn't mean much to Peter at first. All he knew about mutants was that they were different from an ordinary human. In the case of the soldiers that would be accompanying them in the rescue, he was told each possessed some unique ability that could be useful in combat. Peter couldn't wait to see them in action.

After Peter had explained all they knew about the location where the hostages were being held, Threebeard outlined a suggested plan of attack. He said it was imperative that they catch them by surprise or the hostages might be killed. He told them about two of his men that he used as scouts. Their body color changed with the landscape and the light to make them almost invisible. Additionally, they walked barefoot moving through the jungle without making a sound. He suggested they go in first and look for weaknesses in the TGA security. Then they could fine tune the attack.

There was another mutant Threebeard told them about, who could crack into almost any security system and disable it. Not only was he a computer genius, but he had a sixth sense when it came to codes. Before the war he worked as a code breaker for the TGA. Threebeard said with these three men he was certain they could get them in the compound undetected. Once inside it would be up to Peter and his unit to find the hostages and get them out.

The mission commander was Lt. Leode. Before they took off, he presented them with detailed blueprints for the all the buildings on the enemy base. He said once Peter had told Threebeard where the hostages were being held, Threebeard had hacked into the TGA computers and downloaded the blueprints. They discussed the most likely places to keep hostages and the best way to get in and out quickly.

Threebeard adjourned the briefing and told everyone to report at 0500 the next morning. Tam and Red went back to the barracks to sleep and Peter stayed in the briefing room with Threebeard for his lesson. When they were alone, Threebeard began. "Mental telepathy is all about will and focus. You must have an intense desire to penetrate the targeted mind and the ability to focus your thoughts to that end. If you have willing target it doesn't take a lot of effort. You and I could converse with our minds right now effortlessly if we both willed it. It also doesn't take much effort to penetrate the unprotected mind and I suspect that's all you've done so far.

"It's a different story if the targeted mind doesn't want an intrusion and is guarding against it or if you are trying to converse with another species like the rhutz or Nanomites. Even if your rhutz wanted to converse with you, since your brain patterns are different, it takes much more will and focus to make the connection. It took me a long time to make contact with the Nanomites because they are so small and their brain waves so fragile. I knew they must communicate through a common consciousness because trillions of Nanomites couldn't act in unison unless they had a common link."

"So, how did you do it?" Peter asked.

"I camped in the desert near one of their homes for awhile watching and studying them. I was hopeful they would get curious about my presence and reach out to me. Each night I would clear my mind and think of them, what they were doing, what life would be like as a Nanomite. Many times I'd feel a presence but I could not quite connect with it. What kept me going were the signs that the Nanomites knew I was there and reaching out to them. Once they built a symbol by my head while I slept—a circle with two dots in the middle. I had no idea what it meant, but I did know it was an effort at communication.

"Then one night when I was near exhaustion and ready to give it up for the day, I found them. It was like jumping into a river and being immersed in their thoughts. A wonderful feeling came over me as I began to understand them and their world. Of course, they had the same experience with me and I felt them search my mind, hungry for knowledge and understanding."

"Wow. That's amazing," Peter said.

"You have an advantage over me, though," Threebeard said. "You know that it is possible to talk to the Nanomites and the Rhutz and they are anxious to talk to you. It will not take you nearly as much will and focus to make the connection as it did me."

"That's fantastic. I wish I had Rhin here so I could give it a try."

"You'll be seeing her soon, I'm sure."

"I did have a dream where I saw through the eyes of a rhutz back on

Muhl. Could that have been real?"

"Oh, yes. Connections with others often come in our dreams when our minds are relaxed and wide open, but only if there has been a past connection so that the two minds know the way to each other. This is a vulnerability that leads me to the topic of our first lesson. How to protect your mind from unwanted trespass."

"You mean if I connect with an enemy he can come to me in my dreams and search my mind?" Peter asked.

"Yes, if you don't put up barriers to stop him."

"How do you put up barriers?"

"Again, it is will and focus. In your mind you imagine a wall, an impenetrable fortress that cannot be breached. While you are drifting off to sleep you must focus on the fortress and tell your subconscious mind to guard it and wake you if there is an intruder."

Peter just stared at Threebeard in amazement. "That doesn't sound too hard. Are you sure it will work."

"It will work if your will and focus are strong enough. It is not good enough just to think of these things. You must will that their be no intrusion with all your might, energy and focus. It takes discipline and a passionate desire to protect your mind."

Peter nodded. "Okay. I see."

"This is the same way you protect yourself while you are awake. If someone is trying to touch you directly, to probe your mind, you must build an impenetrable fortress in your thoughts and protect it with all your strength, passion, and might. It's a battle of wills and if your will isn't strong enough your enemy will plunder your mind and learn your most guarded secrets."

Peter felt uneasy and less confident than he'd felt before the session with Threebeard had begun. He realized now how dangerous these battles of the mind could be and almost wished he wasn't telepathic. Suddenly he felt a presence in his mind. It was Threebeard consoling him, telling him not to worry, that his gift was strong and that he could defeat anyone if he just focused. Then he felt a jolt as Threebeard's memories came flooding through his mind. He saw flashes of his life, images of places he had been, people he knew, and bits and pieces of emotions he'd felt—fear, frustration, anger, love, peace, and joy. Peter grabbed his head as he felt his mind was about to explode.

Volcanos erupted in his mind's eye, billows of smoked plumed out of exploding volcanos, people ran in terror, and darkness came over the land. Then a flash, the city exploded into riots and chaos. He saw murder and mayhem, sickness, disease, and death, many deaths—people dying everywhere. Troops marched through the streets, planes streaked across the skies, and missiles fell to earth bringing death and destruction.

Then it stopped and he saw himself immersed in a pale green fluid flowing swiftly, effortlessly through time and space. He felt a thought spring into his head. "Why do you reach out to us? Who are you?"

"I am Threebeard of the human race. Who are you?"

"You can call me Alo."

"Alo of the Nanomites, greetings. I have so long sought to reach you. As you know our planet is in distress and near ruin. All life forms must work together to bring back the balance or face extinction."

"What could we possibly do that would have any impact on these events?" Alo replied.

"You are great builders. You can build magnificent structures to house and protect your people, but your size prevents you from going beyond the borders of your small desert world. We offer you the planet. Help us build the structures we need and we will help you multiply and spread throughout Tarizon."

"Yes, that sounds magnificent, but how do we know we can trust you? We don't you know you and all we see in your world is chaos."

"You must pray to your gods for guidance. We can accomplish great things together, but we have to trust one another. Most of our people are good but I will not lie to you, some are evil. Is your world like ours?"

"What is good and evil?" Alo replied. "All Nanomites think and do as one. Survival is our purpose. We must survive. If you can help us spread and multiply our survival becomes more secure."

"What about happiness and the quality of your lives?"

"If we survive we are happy."

The liquid began to boil, then dried, and turned to dust. The wind carried it away and Peter's mind calmed. He opened his eyes and looked at Threebeard and gasped. "What was that?"

"Since we were short on time and your purpose on Tarizon is so

316

important, I've given you my memories and experiences to help you fulfill the Prophecy. It will be confusing at first until your mind sorts everything out, but eventually you'll be able to draw on these memories to help defeat Videl and the TGA."

Peter, still rubbing his temples, replied. "Thank you. This was a gift I hadn't expected. I'm already feeling the power of it. My God! I didn't know you could transfer so much information so quickly."

"You've been using very little of your mind, Peter. You must learn to use all your powers. Few minds are as powerful as yours, but you must unleash this power with determination and focus. Unless you do this you we won't be able to defeat our enemies and end slavery on Tarizon."

"I know. I'll try harder. I promise," Peter said feeling exhilarated.

"That's all we can do tonight," Threebeard said. "You must go and meet your army."

It was still dark when Peter left the briefing room and went to the staging area where his assault force was waiting. Soon they were in the air and on their way back to Allso. As they gained altitude Lt. Leode told them to look out the window. Peter did and was amazed at what he saw. There was an ocean of lights flickering below. It was a beautiful sight but Peter didn't really know what to make of it.

"That's your army down there—over 1.2 million strong. They're protecting the southern border between Quori and Tributon now and await your orders," Lt. Leode advised, beaming.

"Are you serious? They'd follow my command?"

"Absolutely, they believe you'll one day lead them to victory and freedom."

Peter shook his head in wonder. "Well, I'm not giving orders quite yet, but I'm glad you were able to recruit such a great army. We'll need every last one of them to be victorious."

As Peter settled back to rest before they reached their destination, he felt good about their chances of success. The only thing that worried him was the fact they'd flown over the compound the day before. If the TGA had seen them, they'd be expecting their return visit. He just hoped they hadn't moved the hostages.

As he fell into a shallow slumber he had strange dreams, dreams of places he'd never seen and people he'd never known. They were Threebeard's memories and they seemed as real as if they were his own. He woke up with a start. The plane was descending. They were near the jungle base.

When they arrived at the location, they came in close to the ground, dropped the scouts a kylod from the base fence, and waited for them to do their survey of base security. About twenty loons later the scouts returned and indicated the perimeter of the base was heavily guarded, but that there was one entry point that was unguarded for about one loon out of every ten. This looked like their best bet, so their pilots took them as close to entry point as possible and dropped them off. It was agreed that the pilots would hide the planes in a clearing in the jungle, they'd seen on their way in, until they got a call for pickup.

Their security expert inspected the perimeter fence and said it was not only electrified but came with sensitive motion detectors that would immediately inform command of its breach. He suggested they tunnel under it, but that the tunnel would have to be more than three feet below the surface as there were motion detectors buried two feet below ground.

Peter protested that they didn't have the time or tools to dig a tunnel under the fence, but Lt. Leode just smiled. He motioned and two soldiers came forward. They had strange looking hands that looked more like hoofs than hands. Lt. Leode talked to them in a strange language but surprisingly, Peter understood it perfectly. It was such a strange feeling that he broke out in gooseflesh. Then he realized, Threebeard knew every language on the planet and he'd just transferred that knowledge to Peter. Peter gasped at the reality of this but was quickly brought back to the present situation by the sound of frantic digging.

The soldiers dug at an incredible pace, sending dirt and rocks flying out behind them in a steady stream. Before Peter could express his wonder and amazement at their tunneling abilities, the mutants were halfway under the fence. Five loons later, the last soldier was scrambling under the sensors and heading for the headquarters building, where they were pretty sure the hostages would be located.

Their scouts had warned them that there were patrols circling the building ever six loons. This meant their security expert would have just five loons to deactivate the building security system giving them just two more to get into the building without being seen. They rushed to the building perimeter just after the patrol had left. Their security man immediately went to work, but after four loons hadn't been able to crack the code. Just as the next patrol came by he motioned that he'd done it and they were safe to go inside. They all quickly scrambled in the door and prayed they hadn't been seen.

Once inside, Peter could feel that Lucinda had been there, but it was a faint wisp of a sensation that disturbed him. He feared they had killed her already!. He immediately took off in the direction of the force he was feeling. Everyone followed him, although many were wondering how he knew where to go. They went through a large common area and then down a long hallway. When they got to a door with a sign that read *Interrogation Center*. Peter's pulse quickened and he could feel his heart beating furiously.

"This is it," he whispered.

Three mutants rushed over, blew the lock, and rushed in. Two startled TGA soldiers were at a table playing some sort of game. They went for their weapons but were quickly silenced by two laser blasts. The soldiers blew open another locked door and behind it found cells where many prisoners were being detained. They rushed in behind them searching for the hostages.

"Leek! Over here," Lorin said.

Lorin's voice brought joy to Peter's heart. He rushed over smiling. "Oh, thank God! Where are the others?"

"I don't know. They separated us. Perhaps in the other cell blocks."

One of the soldiers blew away the lock on the cell door and Lorin rushed out. Peter and her embraced. "Come on," she said and started running through the cell block. When they came to the end she pointed to a door. "Through there." The soldier shot the lock with his laser and the mechanism shattered. Lorin rushed through the door into another cell block. She led them through cell after cell full of prisoners yelling and begging to be freed. Finally they saw General Zitor. They rushed over to him.

"Thank Sandee you are safe, General!" Peter exclaimed. He looked at Lorin and then the General. "So, where's Lucinda?"

Lorin sighed. "I'm sorry, Leek. They took her away yesterday without a word. Hopefully she's around here somewhere."

"Where? We've got to find her. We can't leave without her." Tears began to well up in Peter's eyes. He was so scared and frustrated he could hardly think.

Tam took his arm. "Come on, Leek. We'll find her."

Peter took a deep breath and followed Tam as they searched the rest of the cell block, but to no avail. Finally, they entered the last cell block and raced through it, looking left and right searching frantically for Lucinda's pretty face, but only saw more outstretched hands of sick and malnourished prisoners begging to be rescued. At the end of the block Peter sank to his knees in utter despair.

Lt. Leode came up from behind Peter and put his hand on his shoulder "I'm sorry, sir. We've searched everywhere. They must have taken her to another installation."

"No!" Peter screamed. "Isn't there any other place they could be holding her?"

"Perhaps," Lt. Leode said, "but we don't have time to search anymore. If we don't leave now, we might not get out at all."

Peter stood up and clinched his fists so hard he could feel them throb. He felt like screaming but knew that would do no good. Where was his Lucinda! Why would they separate her from the other hostages? Then he remembered Threebeard's words. *She'll make Videl a nice trophy to show off to his friends and allies.*

"We must go, sir. Now!" Lt. Leode insisted.

"Find me a guard. I'll probe his mind."

"We've killed everyone we've seen. We don't have time to find another. We must go!"

Peter took a deep breath and nodded dejectedly. "Very well. Move out. I'm right behind you."

Lt. Leode began to run back down the hall. "Free as many of these prisoners as you can," he ordered. "They'll provide a nice distraction for us."

The mutant soldiers began blowing each cell door as they ran by. Soon prisoners were fleeing from their cells. As Peter watched the melee unfolding in front of him, he said to Tam and Red, who hadn't left his side, "I'll get even with Videl one day. That skutz! He'll regret what he's done!"

Tam nodded and then took Peter's arm, "We'll find Lucinda, Leek. Don't give up. We'll find her, but we've got to go. Come on."

Red took Peter's other arm and between the two of them, got him running after Lt. Leode and the mutant soldiers. It was slow, weaving their way through the disoriented prisoners milling around. He felt sorry for them and wished they could rescue them all, but that was out of the question. When they got out of the cell blocks Peter heard laser fire ahead. At the exit door Lt. Leode advised them that a security patrol had discovered them and opened fire. He told them to wait a minute until they'd been neutralized. A moment later he motioned for them to leave. They ran quickly through a protective corridor provided by the mutant soldiers. Soon they were at the fence and in the chopper. Lorin sat next to Peter and put her hand on his shoulder.

"I'm sorry, Leek. I know you must be devastated."

Peter looked at her but said nothing. It was all he could do to keep his composure in front of the other soldiers. Finally, he said. "Well, at least we saved you and the General."

"Yes, and we are very grateful. I thought our lives were over. I couldn't believe it when I saw you break through the cell block door. We'll always be in your debt."

"It wasn't just me. Thank Lt. Leode and his men. Without them you'd still be rotting in your cell."

"I will thank him, but I know it was you who found us."

Peter looked at her. "Where did they take my mate? Do you think she's alive?"

Lorin swallowed hard. "It was Evohn Cystrom. He's betrayed us. He's not Videl's enemy as he swore to us, but his adopted son. He's taken Lucinda to Videl."

Peter looked at Lorin in horror. She put her arms around Peter's neck and drew him into her bosom. "We'll find her, Peter. Don't worry. You'll get her back. I promise."

40

The Investiture

The next day Peter and his entourage made it to Shini and were put up in the renown Linzcot Hotel named after Rikin Linzcot, the first Chancellor of Tarizon. Much to his delight Rhin, his rhutz, had been flown up and was waiting for him in his hotel room. She looked great and was very happy to see him. Peter wondered why they'd brought her all the way from Shisk. Then he remembered the rhutz was part of the Prophecy and if people were to believe he was the Liberator he'd have to have his rhutz at his side.

Jake was also there to greet Lorin when they arrived. She was so relieved to see him, having imagined the worst. That afternoon they attended a special service for Sy, to award him the medal of valor posthumously. Apparently the Councillor had decided to make him a martyr and had flown his parents and family up to accept the medal for him. This was nice surprise, as Peter had wanted to meet Sy's parents and tell them what a great son they'd had and how honored he'd been to know him.

When they met after the service, his parents were excited to meet Peter, and wanted to know all the details of Sy's time in boot camp and his service to the Loyalist cause up until his death. Peter told them everything he could remember and they seemed to relish every word. If you have to die, Peter thought, going out in a blaze of glory is the way to do it. Syril Johs had certainly done that and soon he would be a household name and a hundred years from now children would be reading about him on their computer terminals.

Lorin and Jake accompanied Rhin and Peter back to his compartment after the service. They talked about the Councillor and the

323

investiture. Lorin said there would be much celebration, and many parties and balls to attend. Peter told them he wasn't looking forward to that, as he found it awkward to talk to strangers and never knew what to say. Jake offered to loan Lorin to Peter for these events as he had military strategy sessions that he urgently needed to attend. Peter happily accepted the help, and then asked Jake if he thought it was very wise to have all the leaders of the Loyalist Movement in the same place at the same time. It seemed to Peter to be an invitation to the TGA to launch an attack during the event.

"It's important that we show that we are not afraid of the TGA and can protect our cities," Jake replied.

"I can understand that, but what if a half dozen T47s show up? In stealth mode you'd never see them coming."

"You forget this is a domed city. A T47 couldn't penetrate the dome. It's been tried a couple of times and the fighters crashed."

"Really? What about bombers? Couldn't they drop bombs down through the dome. I thought the dome was fairly thin."

"Our fighters would intercept any bomber coming anywhere near the city."

"What about missiles?"

"We have an anti-missile defense system that's 99.7 percent effective. Any missile that came close to Shini would be shot down."

"Wow! That's great," Peter said. "That makes me feel a lot better. I had a bad feeling about the ceremony. I don't know why, but I'd hate for anything to happen to the Councillor."

"Nothing is going to happen to him," Jake replied. "We've taken every precaution."

"Good. I'll sleep better tonight."

Despite Jake's assurances that their security could not be breached, Peter still had a bad feeling about Councillor Garcia's appearance at the event. Unfortunately, there was nothing he could do about his feeling other than to be alert for any trouble that might develop.

That night in their compartment Peter opened his mind and began conversing with Rhin. She told him of her mother's fight for survival in the chaos that ensued after the great eruptions, the death of many in her pack from the deadly gases, and the constant pursuit by the Purists, led by Rupra Bruda, who killed the rhutz for sport.

"When Threebeard reached out and told us of the Prophecy that a great Liberator would come to save us from extinction, we were greatly relieved and asked how we could help him," Rhin said in her thoughts. "He told us when the time was right he'd summon us. When you came to Shisk I was the closest of my kind and heard his summons. We don't usually trust humans as many are evil, so it wasn't easy for me to befriend you. I feared Threebeard may be wrong."

"I would never hurt any creature unless it was a matter of survival," Peter thought.

"I sensed that but still had my fears. I knew, though, that I must protect you so that you could fulfill the Prophecy."

Peter smiled. "Thank you for saving my life and tell your brother in Muhl he's one courageous rhutz to take on a Drogal."

"You already thanked her by destroying the TGA base on Muhl."

"How do you feel about the Investiture tomorrow? I'm worried."

"For good reason. I feel a traitor in our midst."

"Then we will have to be alert to discover him and protect the Councillor. I wonder who it is?"

"If I see him, I will know him. Let me wander among the delegates."

"They won't let you go by yourself. You'll have to be with me. Humans are afraid of you."

"We must search until we find the traitor."

"We will. Don't worry. We'll find him."

The next day Rhin and Peter went to the investiture. It was held in the Assembly Hall at Rigimol's capital complex in downtown Shini and there wasn't an empty seat in the house. The media was there in force. The investiture would be seen on VC in all territories controlled by the Loyalists. Security was tight and everyone was searched for weapons and sniffed for dangerous chemicals. They made Peter put a leash on Rhin, which she didn't like much. Peter asked if they could wander around the auditorium before the ceremony began, but were told the rhutz would scare the delegates. Peter protested but was overruled, so they were escorted to a seat on the stage next to General Zitor. There was a band playing in a pit in front of the stage. The music was strange to Peter, but upbeat. General Zitor shook Peter's hand and told him he had some good news.

"What's that?" Peter asked.

"I've decided to give you another battlefield promotion. You and your men's tireless efforts to find and rescue us was extraordinary. Tonight you'll be promoted to captain."

"Thank you, General. I really appreciate that."

"I don't know of any soldier who has made captain in their first year of service, but you've earned it."

"I'm determined now more than ever to rid Tarizon of Videl Lai since he's kidnaped my mate. I won't rest until he's dead and buried."

The general nodded and replied, "Yes, I can see that. Kidnaping Lucinda may have been Videl's first mistake of the war."

"I think it was. Now all I can think about is killing that piece of slime."

"Listen, there is talk that the Seafolken and Mutants have pledged themselves to you."

"So I've been told."

"You know they must report to Loyalist Command?"

"Yes, of course. I've never claimed to be the Liberator as they call me. I wouldn't know what to do with such an army anyway. I've only been a soldier for a few phases and know so little about Tarizon."

"Good. We must all be united if we are to defeat the TGA."

"Of course. . . . I saw Threebeard and he said he would be here today. Have you seen him?"

"Yes, he's at the military strategy sessions. I guess he told you he's going to be appointed Minister of Defense."

"No. He didn't mention that to me. That's great!"

"Yes, he's a brilliant man. If anyone can outsmart Videl he can do it."

The band stopped playing and the presiding officer walked to the podium. He introduced himself and those seated on the stage. Then speaker after speaker went to the podium to denounce Videl Lai and Central Authority. They praised Councillor Garcia and all those who had the courage to join the Loyalist cause. They talked about the victory at Lortec and the rescue of General Zitor and the Councillor's daughter. Sy's name came up repeatedly as one who had given his life for the people of Tarizon. They praised God and Sandee, promised to defeat the TGA, and restore the principals and dictates of the Supreme Mandate. Then Councillor Garcia took the podium to accept his unanimous election to be Chancellor of

Tarizon's provisional government.

"Citizens of Tarizon. I am honored that you have selected me to lead you in this dark hour of our history. I promise you I will work tirelessly to restore freedom and dignity to all the citizens of this great planet. We will not allow a tyrant like Videl Lai to exploit Tarizon for his own personal gain and profit. This planet belongs to the people, not to Videl and his greedy followers."

The audience clapped and yelled their approval. While he continued to speak Peter searched the crowd for any sign of trouble. Everything seemed fine until Rhin got up and started to growl. Peter looked in the direction that Rhin was looking but saw nothing. Then the Councillor began to grab at his throat, turned blue, and gaged like someone was choking him. An aide came over and tried to help him loosen his collar. Someone else slapped him on the back. Finally a doctor arrived and laid the Councillor down. Peter looked again out into the audience to see if he could see if someone was causing the Councillor to choke. Rhin growled again. Peter said, "Rhin get him," and let go of the leash.

Rhin took off into the crowd and lunged for a man in the third row. The man was thrown back in his chair and tumbled into a crowd of startled spectators. The Councillor stopped gagging and his body became still. Rhin seized the man's thigh and it was all Peter could do to get her off him. A contingent of security men rushed over to help. They arrested the man and dragged him away kicking and screaming.

"You're all traitors!" the man screamed. "You're all going to die!"

By this time the Councillor was gone. Security had whisked him away. The room became noisy as stunned spectators tried to make sense out of what had happened. The General came over to Peter and said, "Was that man responsible for the Councillor choking?"

"I think so. He must be telekinetic. A Seafolken did that to me once, but only as a demonstration. Is the Councillor going to be okay?"

"I don't know. They've taken him to the casualty station."

"God. I hope he's okay. I had a bad feeling about today's ceremony."

"Our medical facilities are very advanced. I'm sure he'll be fine."

Peter nodded. The General said, "That's quite an animal you have there."

"Yes, sir. She's saved my life once and now she's hopefully saved the

Chancellor's."

"How'd she know who was trying to kill the Chancellor?"

"She's a bit telepathic herself, I think. Her life form communicates that way. That's how she and I communicate, too."

"So, it's true. You are telepathic?"

Peter nodded. "A little, I guess. I never knew it until I came to Tarizon."

"Well, we're going to have to give your rhutz a medal, I guess."

'There's another rhutz on Muhl who deserves a medal too."

Peter told him about the rhutz who had saved them from the Drogal and then lured the TGA patrol away from them so they could get back to shaft 22. General Zitor said he wanted to talk later to discuss how the rhutz life form could be incorporated into the war effort. Peter agreed that was a good idea and he'd be happy to help with that effort in any way he could.

There was a sudden murmur in the auditorium. A lady shrieked. "Oh, Sandee, No!"

Peter and Rhin rushed toward the casualty station where they'd taken the Councillor. They ran inside and saw a group of people huddled around an open door. He rushed over and muscled his way inside. Lorin was holding her father's head in her lap, tears streaming down her cheeks. "Oh, Father I will kill the coward who did this to you! I won't let Videl Lai get away with this, I promise. He'll pay for his crimes!"

Peter knelt beside her and put his arm around her. "I'm so sorry, Lorin. I'm so sorry. We got to him too late."

Lorin turned, "You have the skutz! Where is he? I want to kill him with my bare hands."

Peter restrained her and held her in his arms. "Don't kill him yet. Let me first probe him for information, then he must stand trial. We must follow the Supreme Mandate or be no better than Videl."

Lorin buried her head in Peter's shoulder and wept. A few moments later Jake came and took her away. Peter left the room and went over to General Zitor who was running his fingers through his hair nervously.

"Peter," he said. "TGA troops are moving toward the Tributon border. They've engaged the mutant forces. There are heavy casualties. Lortec is under siege as well."

"Oh, my God," Peter replied.

"You must go to Tributon. The mutant soldiers expect you to lead them."

"But I'm just a captain with little experience."

"You're also the Liberator. It's the Prophecy. They believe you must be there if they are to defeat the TGA."

Peter exhaled slowly, "But—"

"Don't worry. Threebeard will guide you," the general said.

"Who will be Chancellor now that Robert Garcia is dead?"

"I don't know. The Provisional Assembly will have to select someone else. There's talk that Lorin might be asked to take the position. She's a strong and capable woman with her father's tenacious drive."

As they were speaking, sirens began to blare and they could hear explosions in the distance. "What's happening?" Peter asked nervously.

"We're under attack, but don't worry. They can't cause us serious damage. They're just trying to cause panic and undermine the momentum we've obtained this last week. You must go ready yourself. I'll have a someone pick you up at dawn."

"Yes, sir," Peter said reluctantly. Although he wanted to do all he could to help the Loyalists' cause, he was disappointed he'd have to leave right away. He wanted to search for Lucinda and he couldn't do that very well from the jungles of southern Tributon.

"Sir, before I go would it be possible for me to speak to the assassin? He may know something about Lucinda."

The General frowned and eyed Peter warily. "I suppose, but I doubt he'll tell you anything."

"Probably not, sir, but it's worth a shot."

"Very well, I'll arrange for you to speak with him before you leave in the morning."

"Thank you, sir."

The next morning Peter and Rhin were taken to the detention center where the assassin was being held. The detectives had been trying to interrogate the prisoner all night without success. They advised Peter his name was Rupra Bruda. Peter nearly choked on the name.

"That's one of Videl's closest confidants. How did he get through security?"

"We don't know. He somehow talked his way through."

Peter thought of a number of ways he could have done that using his formidable telepathic abilities. Fear swept over him. He didn't feel ready to face someone as powerful as Rupra Bruda. He almost turned around and left, but somehow forced himself to go inside and face him. The guards made him leave Rhin outside.

Bruda had a turinium hood over his face so he couldn't use his telekinetic powers against his interrogators. Peter sat down and started to introduce himself, but Bruda already knew the identity of his next interrogator."

"So, I sit before the Liberator," he laughed. "I'd kill you like I did the Councillor if you had the guts to take off this hood."

"You've killed your last victim, I assure you."

"So you think," he spat.

"Where did they take my mate?"

"Lucinda? Such a sweet thing. It's a shame you'll never see her again."

"Where have you taken her!" Peter demanded.

Bruda laughed. "Why don't you take off my mask and probe my mind? I hear you're telepathic."

"You'd like that, wouldn't you. I'm not that stupid. I know you're a student of Threebeard and have talked to the Nanomites."

"Indeed I have, but you're the Liberator. Hasn't God sent you here to destroy us? Is the Liberator a coward?"

Peter knew he was being baited. It would be suicide to take off the mask, but he had another idea. "Tell me where they've taken my mate or I'll bring in my Rhutz to have another go at you."

"Hah! Your rhutz is lucky she's still alive. Bring on the ugly beast, but if you do I'll just kill her. And you'll never see your darling Lucinda again anyway. Videl plans to parade her through the streets to show the citizens of Tarizon how impotent you are. The crowds will spit on her, and then they'll hang her in a public place so everyone will know what happens to traitors! But don't worry, the whole thing will be on the VC, so you won't miss a minute of it."

Outraged by Bruda's words, Peter got up and kicked the table hard into Bruda's chest. He shrieked in pain and jumped to his feet struggling to get out of the way in case Peter kicked it again. Peter rushed over to him and started choking him. Bruda's hood was ripped off in the struggle. "I'm going to kill you, you skutz!" Peter screamed.

The door to the interrogation room flew opened but before anyone could come to Peter's aid the door slammed shut and latched itself. There were loud thuds as soldiers tried to force open the door. Peter suddenly felt himself flying through the air. He slammed hard against the wall, fell to his knees and when he looked up saw Bruda standing over him.

Peter grabbed his own throat as he felt an excruciating pain. He couldn't breathe. Bruda was killing him just as he'd killed Councillor Garcia. Peter's life flashed before his eyes but before his last breath he remembered Threebeard's words. "Build a fortress in your mind and will, with all your might, that it not be breached. Peter closed his eyes and saw himself before a massive steel door a hundred feet high. He pushed a button and the door slowly closed. Tremendous bolts latched the door securely and there was silence.

The pain stopped and Peter sucked in a breath. Bruda scowled at this and kicked him in the mouth. Blood came spurting out of Peter's mouth but he managed to grab Bruda's foot and knock him to the ground. Peter pounced on him and began smashing in his face with his fist. Suddenly a chair flew across the room and struck Peter on the back of his head. He recoiled and grabbed his head allowing Bruda to squirm out from underneath him.

The two men scampered to their feet and faced each other eye to eye. Peter winced as he felt Bruda;'s mind attack his. He grabbed his head feeling like it was going to explode. He focused on his wall. In his mind's eye he added layer upon layer of steel and heavy lead. It had to hold! His wall had to hold! He couldn't let Bruda break into his mind no matter what.

Finally the attack let up and furniture began flying at Peter again. He ducked, barely escaping the wrath of the heavy table. Then he thought of Lucinda being paraded through the streets in front of an angry crowd. He had to find out where they were holding her and any other information Bruda might have that would be valuable to the Loyalist cause. Peter peered into Bruda's green eyes and focused on the information he needed. He thought of the Nanomites and the Mutants who Videl had enslaved. He thought of the rhutz and his Loyalist comrades who were sworn to uphold the Supreme Mandate. He thought about Earth and how he must protect his

331

own world at all costs, and about Lucinda, the woman he loved.

Bruda's face contorted in pain. He began to scream in agony as he fought to maintain his defenses. Peter kept his focus but couldn't quite penetrate Bruda's mind. Then Peter felt a boost of energy that let him plunge deep into Bruda's consciousness. It was Rhin. She had made a connection and was infusing power into Peter's mind. Bruda jerked and twitched and then collapsed. Immediately images began to flash before Peter's eyes. All the information he'd wanted, and much more, came into his consciousness like they were from his own memory.

The door finally crashed open and soldiers rushed in, followed by Lorin and General Zitor. Lorin went over to Peter and knelt down.

"Peter, you're alive!"

"Barely."

She inspected his battered face and shook her head. "Oh, God. When they said you'd gone in alone with Bruda I thought we'd lost you too."

"I'm okay, I think."

She glanced at the lifeless body of Rupra Bruda sprawled out on the floor. "Did you kill him?"

Peter shrugged and wiped away the blood trickling down his chin. "I don't know, but I did find out where Lucinda is being held and all that Bruda knew about Videl and the TGA's war strategy."

A smile came across Lorin's face. "That's great news. I can't believe this," Lorin sighed, a look of wonder on her face. "I never thought I'd say this, Peter, but it's true."

"What's true?"

"The Prophecy. The Prophecy is true after all! You are the Liberator!. There is no doubt about it. May Sandee be my witness, Leek Lanzia, you are the Liberator!"

Tears began to well in Peter's eyes. He knew she was right. He could no longer deny it. He *was* the Liberator and he *would* fulfill the Prophecy or die trying.

General Zitor put his hand on Peter's shoulder. "Peter, the delegates are panicked after the death of Chancellor Garcia. The TGA is attacking us everywhere and we have no one to lead us. You must speak to them, give them hope, and keep them focused on the struggle ahead."

Peter looked at General Zitor and then at Lorin. He smiled. "Of course. Are they in session now?"

"Yes," General Zitor replied. "You should go there now."

Peter got Rhin and they all went directly to the auditorium where the delegates were debating how to replace Chancellor Garcia. Lorin went to the stage and whispered to the moderator. He nodded and then announced. "I've got good news. Captain Lanzia has managed to extract important information from Rupra Bruda. Information that will help us immeasurably in our effort to defeat Videl Lai."

The crowd erupted in excited applause. Peter smiled at them.

"Captain Lanzia is about to leave for Tributon to lead the Mutant forces in the battle to repel the TGA forces on our southern front. Before he leaves, he'd like to address all of you and the people of Tarizon."

The delegates came to their feet and gave Peter a rousing ovation. He walked to the podium, thanked them, and waited for quiet. When the applause finally died down he began. "When I came here from Earth I was ignorant of your plight here on Tarizon and resentful that I'd been torn away from my family and friends on Earth. It didn't occur to me that God might have plans for me other than living a quiet life on Earth. I apologize for how long it has taken me to realize this.

"Chancellor Garcia and his daughter Lorin took me in and were very patient in preparing me for my role here on Tarizon. It was hard for me to accept that I could have such a noble destiny and for too long I resisted it. But now I know what I must do. I have made contact with Alo of the Nanomites, Threebeard of the Mutants, the three Seafolken generals, Talhk, Rusht, and Quirken, and, of course, Rhin of the rhutz. All of these great leaders of Tarizon have pledged their support for our Loyalist cause."

The delegates jumped to their feet and screamed their approval. Peter smiled and looked over at Lorin, Jake, and General Zitor. Then Rhin began to howl which delighted the delegates even more. When the auditorium quieted, Peter continued.

"As you know we are under attack on all fronts, but this is not unexpected. What else could the TGA do to save face after we crushed them at Lortec!"

The crowd was up again screaming and yelling. They began to chant Leek . . . Leek . . . Leek. Peter raised his hand and the chanting stopped.

"It's time to summon our armies and lead them to victory. Our cause is a righteous one. God and Sandee will stand beside us because we fight for freedom and the abolition of slavery on Tarizon. We must defend and preserve the Supreme Mandate, for it will be our guiding light in the dark days ahead."

Again the crowd was on its feet screaming, but Peter didn't stop this time. As he continued the crowd grew quiet. "Videl! Are you listening? We will not allow murder and genocide on Tarizon. We will not allow you to suspend our right to gather, to vote, to travel, to speak freely, to have a fair trial and to live our individual lives as we see fit!"

There was a roar of approval from crowd and they began to chant Leek . . . Leek . . . Leek. Peter motioned for Lorin to join him on the podium. When she reached him he took her hand and looked her in the eyes. "Lorin, I'm so sorry about your father. He was a great man and we will all miss him terribly. I wish he were here today to lead us to victory, but I'm thankful, at least that we have you, for you have much of your father's wisdom and cunning."

The delegates erupted in cheers and applause. Lorin bowed slightly.

"Your father's murder was an outrage and I swear to you and Sandee that I will avenge his death! No matter what the future holds for us, I promise I will one day crush Videl Lai and spit on his corpse!"

Tears flowed down Lorin's cheeks, so Peter pulled her to him and they embraced. The crowd went wild.

As General Zitor had hoped, Peter's speech did raise the spirits of all the Loyalists forces around the globe and gave them the courage to continue the war against Videl Lai despite his vastly superior forces. Peter had promised them victory because their cause was righteous and just and because he was sure God and Sandee stood beside them. But the General knew that good didn't always prevail over evil; the future of Tarizon depended on Peter's ability to fulfill the Prophecy.